Dimitri

Immortals of New Orleans, Book 6

Kym Grosso

Copyright © 2014 by Kym Grosso
All rights reserved. No part of this publication may be reproduced, distributed, or transmitted in any form or by any means, including photocopying, recording, or other electronic or mechanical methods, without the prior written permission of the publisher, except in the case of brief quotations embodied in critical reviews and certain other noncommercial uses permitted by copyright law.

MT Carvin Publishing, LLC
West Chester, Pennsylvania

Edited by Julie Roberts
Formatting by Polgarus Studio
Cover design by Cora Graphics

DISCLAIMER
This book is a work of fiction. The names, characters, locations and events portrayed in this book are a work of fiction or are used fictitiously. Any similarity to actual events, locales, or real persons, living or dead, is coincidental and not intended by the author.

NOTICE
This is an adult erotic paranormal romance book with love scenes and mature situations. It is only intended for adult readers over the age of 18.

ACKNOWLEDGMENTS

While the characters speak to me and I tell their stories, my books aren't released without the assistance of so many wonderful people. I'm very grateful to everyone who helped me with my book:

~My husband, Keith, for encouraging me to write and supporting me in everything I do. Thank you for managing my business so that I can concentrate on writing. I love that we can laugh and learn on our journey. I look forward to reading you more naughty passages from my books and getting your feedback. You are the most amazing husband and father, and not a day goes by that I'm not grateful for your support.

~Julie Roberts, editor, who spent hours reading, editing and proofreading Dimitri. You've done so much to help and encourage me over the past two years. As with every book, I could not have done this without you!

~My pre-beta readers, Rochelle and Maria, who help give me such important feedback and insight during the editing process. You both are awesome!

~My dedicated beta readers, Brandy, Denise, Elena, Elle, Gayle, Jerri, Jessica, Julie, Karen, Lacy, Leah, Rose, Sharon, Stephanie, and Tanner, for beta reading. I really appreciate all the valuable feedback you provide.

~Cora Graphics, cover artist, for designing Dimitri's sexy cover.

~Stuart Reardon, cover model, for the amazing image on Dimitri's cover.

~ Love N. Books, for image acquisition.

~Polgarus Studio, Jason, for formatting Dimitri. You do terrific work, presenting my books so they look their best digitally and in print.

~Gayle, my admin, who is one of my biggest supporters and helps to run my street team. I'm so thankful for all of your help!

~My awesome street team, for helping spread the word about the Immortals of New Orleans series. I appreciate your support more than you could know! You guys are the best. You rock!

Chapter One

Dimitri yanked on the restraints, his wrists firmly secured above his head. The sweet scent of a woman danced through his mind and he swore he felt the warmth of a smooth hand on his thigh. A moan alerted him to the fact that he wasn't alone, and his cock hardened in response. If it weren't for the caustic pain tearing through his muscles, he'd have thought he was having a wet dream. But as he attempted to open his eyes, memories of his last thoughts slammed into him.

Teeth. Claws. Blood. Submission. As his chest heaved for breath, his hands curled into the bed and saliva dripped from his mouth as he recalled being attacked on the beach. A pack of feral wolves had torn into him. Helplessly, he'd fought them, unable to shift. At some point the slashing agony of the attack had ceased; the smooth sound of a woman's voice curled around him in comfort as he surrendered to unconsciousness.

"Shh…you're okay. Stay still."

Not his Alpha's command, yet Dimitri's mind quieted. His dried, cracked lips parted. But before he had a chance to utter a word, the seal between where her skin met his began to heat. His eyes flew open and rolled back into his head as tendrils of healing seeped into his skin. Instinctively, he thrashed against the bindings. His hands fisted the leather, and he shook the bed's metal frame until it rattled uncontrollably. As the tingling spread throughout his body, overwhelming relief from the pain swept through him and he gasped. By the time it was over, tears ran down his face. Not only had the crushing misery disappeared; for the first time in weeks, his wolf howled in celebration.

"My wolf," he cried. "You healed me? How? What are you?"

"You should be okay once you shift…for a few days, anyway," the female responded breathlessly, her lips accidentally brushing his chest. "Can't promise you any longer. You need to see a witch. A shaman may be able to help."

"But how did you know? My wolf…" Dimitri's words trailed off as his vision slowly came into focus. He glanced down to the silky raven hair that brushed over his abdomen.

"Your wolf…he recovers."

"Jesus Christ, the pack. They tried to kill me. How did I get here?"

"You've got an awful lot of questions for an almost dead man," she responded.

"What can I say? Near death does that to a guy. Last thing I remember, those dogs were takin' a bite outta my neck. As much as I wish I had nine lives, I ain't no cat, if you noticed."

"Oh I noticed." She laughed, concealing her face. "Seems to me, you should be doing a little more thanking and a little less asking."

"Now don't take it the wrong way, cher. It's not that I don't appreciate ya healin' me with whatever voodoo you do, but you've gotta see this from my perspective." He gave a small chuckle as his wrists tugged the straps taut. He glanced at his makeshift handcuffs, noticing she'd used belts to restrain him. "So ya want to tell me why I'm tied to the bed? Believe me, I'm down with the kink as much as the next wolf. But call me crazy, this doesn't really seem on the up and up."

"Sorry, lover boy, but I did it for my own safety. You were a bit wild when I brought you here. You know what they say when a dog gets hit by a car…it can bite out of fear and pain."

"Hey now, no need for name calling. There's no dog here. You got yourself a wolf, darlin'."

"I know what you are. Doesn't matter. I take my life pretty seriously. I admit I'm not in the business of tying up men, but I can assure you that I trussed you up for self-preservation purposes only."

Dimitri felt the lilt of her smile curl against his skin and silently cursed as his dick twitched in response. He laughed inwardly at his predicament, as he jerked at his bindings. Sure, he was tied up good. On the up side, he'd survived the attack and had woken up with a beautiful woman next to him. Not the optimal situation, but it could be worse. He was alive and damn, if it didn't turn him on to feel the top of her thigh brush against his own. 'Bondage anytime anywhere' just might become his new motto. He knew it was wrong to be thinking about sex, given the seriousness of the situation, but hey, when in Rome…

"You never did explain how a lil' bit of a thing like yourself took out a wolf pack." Dimitri left the statement open, hoping for an explanation. As much as he wanted to demand answers, he was tired and enjoyed the warmth of her next to him. He was horny, no doubt. But moreover, he needed comfort.

"No I didn't," she hedged.

"Seriously, I need to know. Why rescue me? How did we get in this shitty hotel room?"

"I'm a healer." Gillian pushed upward, releasing herself from the warm embrace she'd provided to Dimitri. She sat on the edge of the bed, her face toward the door and looked to her palms. "I usually use just my hands."

Dimitri resisted the urge to beg his savior to come back to bed. As the covers fell away, he caught sight of her white cami, which had ridden up, exposing a small tattoo written in Chinese. Before he had a chance to read it, she tugged down the fabric, concealing the ink. Her black thong trailed down into the cleft of her perfect heart-shaped ass.

He closed his eyes for a split second, knowing full well he shouldn't try to flirt with the sexy stranger who'd rescued him. But his wolf, seeking mischief, howled in amusement. Curiosity got the best of him. He lifted his head, straining to see her face, which was hidden beneath a stream of silky hair. A small growl of frustration escaped his lips. He wished he could touch her, but fuck it all, his hands were bound.

"Listen, cher. I'm feeling better now. Promise I won't bite. How's about you loosen up these belts?" he suggested, eyeing his bindings.

Her pink lips parted in a devious grin as she climbed up him, straddling his torso. It was then that he finally caught sight of the gorgeous female holding him hostage.

"Tell me how you did it. How'd you save my ass from that pack?" he asked, distracted by her scent. One of her hands pressed firmly next to his face, and he instinctively turned his nose toward her skin and sniffed. Underneath the clean cucumber smell of the soap, he detected the presence of shifter blood. "Are you a wolf?"

"No," she responded as she checked to make sure his hands were still well secured to the bed and that the strap wasn't cutting off his circulation. She leaned over and unbuckled his ankles. Still bound, he wasn't going anywhere. "I'm just the person who healed you. Nothing special about me."

"Excuse my French, but I call bullshit. You've got to be something special. No man or woman interferes with a pack attack and walks away unscathed." Dimitri sensed her distrust. Despite the untruth that slipped from her lips, she wasn't successful at looking him in the eye while she said it.

"Let's just say I've got a few tricks in my bag. I got lucky and managed to get you away from those assholes. All you need to know is that I'm a healer and that it worked."

As she attempted to retreat, Dimitri rattled the bedframe, attempting to free himself. "Why? Please. I need to know why you saved me. Why you're half naked in bed with me. Don't get me wrong, what you did...you look..." *Beautiful.* "Nice." *Real smooth D*, he thought to himself.

Gillian focused in on his rugged masculine face. His deep brown eyes met her own. "I use my hands to heal. Your injuries...you almost didn't make it," she sighed. "I don't heal people very often."

"But you did a helluva job here." He glanced to his torso as she moved to peel a large bloodied bandage off his neck. Her fingers trailed over the newly scarred skin.

"Don't take this the wrong way." She gave him a broad smile and lifted herself off him. "As cute as you are, I don't jump into bed with strangers. Well, maybe I did for you, but that doesn't include sex. It was just necessary to heal you. I had to use all of me. Skin to skin."

Skin to skin, huh? Dimitri laughed as he watched her leap off the bed. Oh yeah, he could think of quite a few things he'd like to do with this little minx, skin to skin. He bit his tongue as she continued.

"I've only done it one other time. All you need to know is that on the beach I healed you enough to stop the bleeding. Then, I paid a few guys to help me move you here. You know, a no questions asked kind of thing," she explained, and began to rummage through her canvas backpack.

"So you think I'm cute," Dimitri teased.

Gillian stopped cold, her jaw dropping. She turned her head to him and glared, before returning to her task.

"Doesn't matter what I think of you." She blew out a regretful breath and yanked out a pair of jeans. "You're not the only one who's got trouble. I've gotta go."

"Hold up there, girly. You did notice you didn't untie me all the way. I suppose I could break this freakin' metal if I yanked hard enough…"

"Just cool your jets, wolf. I called your friends. They'll be here soon enough, and they can untie you. You know… so you can shift." She slipped on her pants, zippered up, and turned around to face him. "I healed you, but that doesn't mean you can go ballistic over there trying to get out of the damn bed. You need to shift. But not while I'm here."

Dimitri licked his lips. His gaze fell to her perfect little nipples, which were standing at attention. His eyes darted up to hers, and he laughed, aware she'd seen his actions. He thought it interesting that she pretended not to notice him. Instead, she retrieved a black leather motorcycle boot from under the bed and hastily shoved her foot into it. Even though his Alpha was the shopper in the pack, he recognized the expensive camera equipment she had stowed on the dresser. They may have been holed up in a shithole of a motel, but this girl had assets. He suspected that she might be a photographer and wondered what kind of trouble was chasing her.

"Why don't you explain to me exactly why I can't shift in front of you? Afraid of the big bad wolf? I'm not lookin' to eat you."

"No offense, but you don't scare me. I do recall it was me saving your ass."

"I've got a fine one."

"Yes, yes you do." She laughed, shaking her head. "But did it occur to you that maybe it is you who should be afraid of me?"

"Never crossed my mind, cher. Come on now, let me go. I promise to be a good boy…shift and shift back. I can't imagine they allow pets in this," he looked around the seedy hotel room, "flea shack."

"No, I don't imagine they do. Just please don't…"

"Dimitri…Dimitri LeBlanc. Rolls right off the tongue." He gave her a broad smile, attempting to throw her off her game.

"Dimitri, I just can't be around another wolf. Please, I swear your friends will be here soon," she said nervously. She plucked a black tank top out of her bag and slipped it over her head.

"You're telling me you're not a wolf?" he began.

"Yep." She offered no information.

"But you saved me from a pack of wolves."

"Yeah, I guess you could say that."

"And you're not going to tell me how you did it or what pack you've been hangin' out with?"

"Um…" She turned to him, smiled, and shook her head. "Nope."

"And you think that just because you saved me, you get to call the shots."

"Well, let's see. I'm here. And you," she laughed and yanked on her other boot, "you're indisposed…at least until someone comes for you. Not much you can do about it, huh?"

Dimitri had had enough of her games. The rush of the challenge surged through his body, and his wolf pressed him to take her, to show his majestic presence. He jerked his right arm and tore open the metal clasps of the belts. Quickly releasing his other hand, he leapt off the bed, wearing nothing but his boxers. As quick as lightning, he backed her against the wall, his hands on either side of her head.

His beast unleashed, Dimitri lowered his face, sniffing his prey. The wolf had gone feral, too long kept hidden away in a dungeon of despair. It trusted no one. As he took in the exquisite scent of the female, he drew closer, yet still didn't touch her body.

"What are you doing?" she breathed against Dimitri. Her palms reached up slowly until they were laid flat on his chest. Gillian didn't want to stop him; she secretly wished to feel him one more time, to soak in the power of his wolf.

"Your blood," Dimitri growled. "You're shifter. But how does one woman take on an entire pack? I sense no wolf…you are something…something special."

"I…I…I'm not wolf," she protested breathlessly.

"You smell heavenly," he breathed. Dimitri reined in his wolf, exhilarated that he'd found the animal within. Taking a deep breath, he slowly raised his head, and stared deep into her amber eyes. A small rectangular section of brown bled up into her irises. Captivated, he drew closer still.

"Your eyes," he whispered.

"I know." Flustered, she broke eye contact and looked to the floor.

"No." Dimitri gently caressed her chin until her gaze once again met his. "Don't hide from me. Let me see your eyes."

"Heterochromia, um, that's the technical term. I was born with…"

"They're beautiful. Like a cat." He smiled, pondering her origins.

"Yes," she agreed, unable to stop the burn that grew in her gut.

"Very pretty eyes. Unique. Tell me your name," he asked. Unable to resist, he brushed his cheek against hers.

"Gillian…Gilly. My name's Gilly," she confessed. A shiver ran through her body as his soft beard brushed her lip.

"Thank you, Gilly." He smiled, retreating. "I'm grateful you saved me."

"Well, yes, but you'd better let me go. As I told you, I've gotta get out of here. They're after me," she said nervously.

"Let me help you, repay you for your kindness," he told her. *Now, just what kind of trouble are you in? Tell me why you saved me. How do you know the wolves that attacked me?* Yes, he wanted to help her but this interesting woman was hiding something. His wolf would not rest until he knew everything. It had been his experience that neither humans nor immortals did good deeds with no reward in mind. Whether to relieve their own conscience or get compensation, there was always a reason. "At least let me see you home. If you called someone from my pack, they'll help us."

"No, the people after me are going to track us eventually. They'll know your scent. I'm sorry, but it isn't safe. Your wolf is weakened. What you need to do is find a witch to help you. I don't know where you live, but you need to go home…alone. We can't stay together. You can catch a flight out. The airport's only about twenty minutes from here. I'll divert them…I'm going by land," she rambled.

"Darlin', I'm the beta of Acadian wolves. You don't need to worry about me."

Is she serious? Does she really think I'm going to up and leave her when she has someone chasing her? Dimitri registered the look of disbelief that crossed her face in response to his previous statement, and grinned.

"Let me clarify that statement. Now that you've healed my wolf...I can hold my own."

"Acadian wolves? New Orleans?" she gasped, trying to break free of the cage he'd built with his arms.

"You'd like to test me?" His eyes fell to her mouth, watching her tongue tease over her bottom lip. *Kiss her,* his wolf demanded. *Fuck no,* he replied. Reason won out and he quickly averted his gaze. Unfortunately, it fell from her lips to her bosom.

"No, please," she whispered. Gillian followed his line of vision and parted her lips in expectation. "You have to listen to me. This is no joke."

"Come now, cher. Let me help you. Don't fight this. Besides, from the looks of things," he glanced down to his naked chest, and then met her eyes with a wicked smile, "you've had your sweet hands all over me. Cleaned me up real nice. Warmed me in your arms. It's almost like we're already dating."

"We're not dating. I...I..." Gillian stammered.

"Say yes." Dimitri leaned forward until his breath warmed her lips, and he fought the temptation. Unfortunately weakness took over and he moved to her ear, his tongue darting out to the hollow behind it. His cock hardened, and he pressed a kiss to her skin.

A knock at the door startled them both. Dimitri briefly turned his head toward the noise.

I've lost my mind, Gillian thought. *Goddammit.* The only reason she'd saved the wolf was out of guilt. The pack had been after her that night, not him. They'd chased her down after she'd escaped. When they'd attacked the stranger, she'd shifted, protecting him from certain death. A healer by nature, she couldn't tolerate the deliberate infliction of torture on another being. At the time, she'd thought the man on the beach was a human, but by the time she'd gotten him back to the room, her beast had recognized his.

Gillian had used every ounce of her power to heal his wolf. With her skin against his, her hands had explored every hard ridge of his abdomen as she gave of herself. She'd indulged, letting her fingertips trace his tattoos while he'd slept. The man was undeniably hot, and she suspected he could be the kind of man who'd make her want to give into a mating.

Gillian had known her whole life that mating wasn't in the cards for someone like her. Steadfast in her decision, she refused to sacrifice her own beast for a man. The secrets she kept inside were what had almost gotten her killed when the Alpha of Anzober wolves, Chaz Baldwin, discovered what she could do for him.

She should have known coming to San Diego on a too-good-to-be-true photo shoot was a bad idea. She'd been working in New York City, making a bare bones living as a photographer when she'd been contacted by an agent who was willing to pay her top dollar for a high-end magazine spread. When she'd arrived in the desert to check out the location, she'd been confronted with the cold reality that Chaz had deliberately drawn her into his web.

He'd taken her captive to his beachfront home, all the while promising not to hurt her. Chaz had pressed the issue of a mating, knowing that it was impossible. After three days of living in the Alpha's gilded cage and a brutal assault, she'd summoned the courage to shift and tore apart her guards. But as she took off down the beach, she hadn't considered the collateral damage she'd leave in the wake of her escape. *Dimitri.*

She hadn't known his full name until he'd told her in bed. When she'd taken his cell phone and called the first three numbers, the men on the other line weren't forthcoming about his identity, threatening retribution if their friend wasn't found alive when they arrived. With the knock on the door, she was reminded that not only did she have to fear Chaz; the gorgeous but deadly beta could attack if he shifted. His friends, who'd made it clear to her that he not be harmed, were now on the other side of the paper-thin door. Would they try to kill her? Would they return her to Chaz? What if they'd found out about her background? No, she couldn't let that happen.

Gillian waited until Dimitri took his hand off the wall. As he turned toward the door, she reached into her backpack and picked up the gun she'd stolen from the pack house.

"Who's there?" Dimitri yelled.

"Open the fuck up, D," Jake replied from the hallway. The door flew open and he caught the sight of Dimitri smiling, wearing only his underwear. A woman stood near the dresser, aiming a firearm at him.

"Hey, bro. Thanks for coming." Dimitri gave him a quick hug. As much as he enjoyed getting to know his prickly but lovely female rescuer, the sight of Jake came as a relief.

"Good to see you, too. What the hell happened to you?" Jake grimaced, taking sight of the fresh scars marking Dimitri's chest and throat.

"It's okay, really. I just have to shift." Dimitri downplayed his injuries. "I almost forgot, this is Gilly…"

"You mean the hot chick pointing the gun at us?"

"Gun?" Dimitri's eyes widened. Surprised that she'd pulled a weapon, he held up his hands in a defensive posture and slowly approached her. "What've ya got there, cher? You can put that down. This is Jake. He won't hurt you. He's a good friend of mine. Acadian Wolves."

"Jake." Gillian tilted her head and then nodded at the handsome man who'd come to save his beta. "Nice to meet you. Now that we have all of the pleasantries out of the way, it's time for me to leave."

"But I just got here," Jake protested.

"Sorry, but I've gotta run. As I explained to your beta here, I've got some nasty folks after me. Same ones who attacked him, as a matter of fact. The good news is, that if you get your asses on a plane and out of here, I'm pretty sure that'll be the end of your troubles. The bad news is that they are going to find me soon. They've got my scent and his. My plan is to high-tail it out of here to Vegas. I'll lead them away from you. This is my mess, not yours."

"It may be your mess but I told you that we're not leaving you," Dimitri said, his voice serious.

"That's where we're going to have to agree to disagree. You need to shift and heal. If you go up against the pack, who knows what will happen? The evil you carry is only temporarily suppressed by my magic. It won't last and I won't have your death on my hands...I can't do that to you." Gillian fought the emotion that welled up in her chest. The truth was that she was scared shitless to go it alone, but the beta wouldn't be strong enough in his current condition to survive another wolf attack.

"What the fuck is wrong with your wolf?" Jake exclaimed. He'd been suspicious that something had been off with his friend.

"Goddammit." Dimitri turned and pounded the wall with his fist out of frustration.

"How long, D?"

"A couple of weeks. I don't know. Too fucking long."

"Your girl here says it's evil. Now the only place I know you could've picked up something like that is that hell-infested demon pit you jumped in with Leo."

"I don't want to talk about it." Three weeks before, Dimitri had followed his friend Léopold into a netherworld to help him save his girlfriend and ever since, he'd had difficulty shifting.

"Well, you should've fucking told me."

"I didn't know how bad it was. That night on the beach...I couldn't shift," Dimitri confessed. He raked his fingers through his hair and glanced over to Gilly, who was hoisting her bag onto her shoulders.

Jake blew out a deep breath and his lips formed a tight line. Things were going to be all fucked up to the tenth degree if his beta couldn't shift. It was kind of a requirement that if you were a member of a pack, you actually could shift. He had to know for certain how badly his friend was still affected by whatever the hell had attacked him.

"Shift."

"What?" Dimitri asked, incredulous at the demand.

"Just hold it right there!" Gillian yelled. No fucking way did she want to be in the room when two wolves fought or shifted. Her beast would be called to the surface, and she'd have little control to stop it.

"What's the issue?" Jake began to approach her but quickly stopped as she raised the weapon again.

"No shifting until I'm gone. And lucky for you, I'm outta here."

"Gilly, please. You can't fight an entire wolf pack on your own. I'm not letting you go," Dimitri said.

"See, that's the thing. I'm not asking for permission. Follow me and I'll shoot you in the leg. I know you can shift but are you willing to chance it?" Gillian kept her eyes trained on both men, moving slowly to the entrance. She wrapped her fingers around the doorknob and twisted it open. "Yeah, I didn't think so. Okay, then, well, be safe. Go home to New Orleans. Find a witch and have a

Bloody Mary for me. Just remember that this is my problem, not yours."

Neither wolf moved to stop her as she gave them a wink, slamming the door shut. Jesus Christ almighty, she prayed that she was doing the right thing as she ran toward the rental car. Fear coursed through her, but she continued on, clicking the car locks open on the Audi she'd had delivered.

Gillian swallowed the hard lump in her throat and threw her bag into the car. There was nothing in the world she would have liked more than to go with Dimitri to the airport and hop a plane to the east coast. But her paranoia was stronger than her desire to get to know the handsome beta. Aware that she was putting her own life at risk in order to divert attention away from him, she sucked a breath and told herself it was for his own good. It was her fault he'd been attacked. It was her who Chaz sought. It wasn't fair to Dimitri or his friend to let them help her. At the end of the day, she could die in peace if she got caught. Putting Dimitri in danger again was simply not an option.

Chapter Two

Dimitri insisted on following Gillian. If she thought she'd dismiss him, she had another think coming. *Nice try, cher. You will not escape so easily.* After she'd slammed the door to the hotel room, he'd quickly shifted to heal his remaining injuries. It wasn't long before he and Jake had taken off after her in their car.

Loathe as he was to admit it, whatever had latched onto his soul was still there. Like a dark shadow, it lingered. Part of him knew he needed to get back to New Orleans as soon as possible to see Ilsbeth, the one witch he knew who could help him. But given the brief interaction he'd had with his Florence Nightingale, that'd have to go on the back burner. For once his brain and his dick were in perfect agreement; get the girl.

"Tell me again why we're following some mystery chick? One who I'm pretty sure was responsible for helping get your face torn off," Jake commented, hoping Dimitri would catch his eye roll.

"Her name's Gilly. And because the lady was nice enough to save my ass and now I plan to save hers."

"You wanting her ass is one thing we probably can agree on. Why? Well, that's a whole other question."

"It's nice. That should be reason enough."

"I bet she exercises a lot. Squats would do it."

"She was in the room with you for all of two minutes and you took reconnaissance on her ass?"

"Special ops, bro. I've got eyes in the back of my head," Jake joked.

"Then you must have also noticed that she needs our help."

"Whatever you say. It's just that with your wolf on the fritz, don't ya think we oughtta get back to NOLA? Listen, I know you and the witch had a bit of a fallin' out, but damn; it's your wolf. This is some serious shit. When Logan finds out what happened…"

"Logan doesn't need to know right now." Dimitri knew he should tell his Alpha, but Logan hadn't even noticed that his wolf had gone silent. Both he and his mate had been over the moon, doting over their newly adopted daughter. Dimitri didn't want to worry him any more than necessary. He'd tell them when he got back to New Orleans. As he figured it, he'd catch up to Gillian and convince her to fly back to Louisiana with him. When they got to the city, he'd ask Logan to call the asshole Alpha from California and smooth things over. Since their packs didn't abut boundaries, no territory disputes would arise.

"You must've knocked your head in when you were attacked. You really think our Alpha doesn't know what happened? You do know your girl called every number on your damn cell, right? Said she wasn't going to chance having someone forget she called."

"Fuck," Dimitri swore, blowing out a breath. "Give me your phone."

"Finally, you see reason." Jake dug his cell out of the console and tossed it to Dimitri.

"Yeah, yeah." Dimitri began tapping at the screen.

"You aren't calling Logan, are you?" Jake slammed a palm down on the steering wheel.

"Hell, no. If I tell him what's happenin', he's gonna leave his mate and babe and come runnin' out here. He's been through enough. They've both been through enough."

"What about Léopold?"

"What the hell? How many people did she call?"

"I told ya. She called your contacts."

"All of them?" Dimitri exclaimed, stroking his goatee. It looked more like a full grown beard, since he hadn't shaved in a week.

"How the hell am I supposed to know? I can tell ya that she called Logan, Léopold and me. It's possible she called a few of your *special* friends," Jake drawled, knowing that it would irk Dimitri.

"Fuck me."

"Yeah, well, Logan sent me. You're lucky that he and Leo are up to their eyeballs in love or Logan'd be out here in a pack war. And Leo? Hell, he'd probably be ripping out hearts and sucking wolves dry…including your little shifter girl. Speaking of which…what kind of shifter is she? I couldn't get close enough to tell by her scent…"

"I don't know," Dimitri said flatly, unwilling to share that she'd been nearly naked, skin to skin against him but he still hadn't been able to tell what she was.

"You sure she's not wolf?"

"Nope. Not a wolf. Why do they make these buttons so fucking small?" Dimitri swore, continuing to toy with the cell phone. "I don't get why an Alpha wants to mess with another shifter?"

"Why, indeed?" Jake glanced over to his friend. "And how the hell are we supposed to find her? She's been gone for a while now. As good as I am, and oh, I am good, there's no way in hell we're gonna track her from the wind flyin' by on a highway."

"No, but we will find her using a tracking app." Dimitri smiled and waved the device in the air.

"Clever wolf. I just assumed she trashed your phone afterward."

"She likes me." Dimitri waggled his eyebrows and chuckled. "She's still got my phone. Just couldn't give up a piece of the big D."

"Yeah, yeah. Where's she headed?"

"Sin city. She's on I-15. Looks like she's stopped for gas. It's only about five hours to Vegas from here."

"What's the deal with this woman? Do you think she was in on it? Logan put a call in to the local Alpha. He denies that he approved the attack. Claims they were rogues."

"No. The girl's on the run. As for the Alpha, I'm not buyin' his story. It had to be his wolves."

"I get that you didn't check in with him right away, but the odds of them finding and attacking a non-aggressive stranger are pretty low. It doesn't sync."

"They were after her, not me. I was just a casualty." Dimitri shook his head. He knew that he should get his ass back on a plane to New Orleans, but there was something about Gilly. The need to protect her, to repay her was overwhelming. Like a compulsion; he hadn't given a second thought to chasing her. If she'd been wolf, he might have been worried that she could be his mate. But since she wasn't wolf, there was no way that she was. Maybe she didn't want to reveal her nature, but once he found her, he planned on getting the truth. "She's a shifter. Whatever she is, it must be badass. 'Cause Jake, I'm tellin' ya, bro, I was messed up bad. I called for my wolf…" His words trailed off into silence.

"I've never heard of such a thing happening. Whatever was in that pit…we've gotta get you to Ilsbeth. Maybe we shouldn't worry about Gilly. I know you think she's something special, but for all you know, she shifts into a skunk."

"Fuck you," Dimitri snorted. "There's no way. I've had her sweet little body wrapped around mine. My girl's probably a fox….sly and smooth."

"Or a bear."

"Hey, don't hate on the bear. A bear? Well, she'd probably be wild in bed. Uninhibited."

"Not many people survive bear attacks."

"Oh, I'd survive and love every minute of it. I like it a little rough. Besides, it doesn't matter. Whatever she is, my wolf likes her. She saved him, and he wants to return the favor."

"Yeah, your wolf wants to do something with her, all right. Somehow I don't think it involves just savin' her."

"Yes, he does." Dimitri laughed. "And why not? He deserves a little fun."

"Seriously? She just held a gun on us. Do I need to answer that question?"

"No, and it doesn't matter, cause it's gonna be cool when I do find out what she is. I know I'm gonna like it."

"Maybe you need to take it easy."

"I'm fine now," Dimitri said, not sure if he was trying to convince himself or Jake.

"Just sayin', D. You just recovered from a beat down. We don't know when or if your wolf is going to go on the fritz or whatever else the hell could happen. I know you are, uh…" Jake tried real hard to select his words carefully. Near-death experiences had a way of giving one a new perspective on life, yet Dimitri seemed as courageous and impulsive as ever, "…compromised. Dying has a way of doing that to you. Let's face it; we're used to being immortal. But with your wolf gone, you and I both know that you were nothing more than human."

Dimitri

Dimitri tried to shake off Jake's comments, meeting his observations with a quiet contemplation. He'd known it was serious. He was damn lucky Gillian had done whatever magic she had to heal him.

"It's not like I don't know you're right. I mean, going to the airport and flyin' home would be the rational thing to do. But Gilly, she saved my life. Yeah, I don't know her. I guess I don't owe her a damn thing. But the way she left…she's in danger. She may look tough, but she's not. I'm telling you, I watched her, the way she moved. Did you hear how she talked? She strikes me as more of a city girl. She's scared, hiding something. I don't know why…I just can't walk away and wash my hands of her."

"You wouldn't know if something happened to her or not. You don't even know if that's her real name, for that matter," Jake replied.

"We're friends, right?" Dimitri asked.

"Seriously?"

"Oh yeah, I'm going there."

"Yeah, we're friends," Jake sighed.

"If you don't want to go with me, you don't have to, but this is something I have to do. Once I make sure Gilly gets safely to wherever she calls home, then we'll fly straight to the witch. It's the least I can do. If it weren't for her, I'd be dead."

"If it weren't for her, your biggest worry would be which bikini-clad Cali girl to hit on."

"Can't deny the possibility." Dimitri gave him a broad smile, knowing that was exactly what he'd planned on doing. "But she needs me. And I owe her. So are you in or are you out?"

"Bellagio or Hard Rock?"

"Venetion?" Dimitri countered, relieved that Jake had agreed in his non-conventional way.

"Four Seasons?" Jake suggested.

"The Four Seasons it is. Viva Las Vegas, baby." Dimitri glanced down to his phone. Her car had begun moving. "We'd better speed it up if we're gonna catch our girl."

Gillian felt feverish as her anxiety took hold. She only wished it was the fucking desert heat. No, she knew exactly why she was drenched in sweat, and it had everything to do with the Alpha who had kept her captive. Coming out to California was one of the single biggest mistakes she'd ever made in her life. She should have known that it was too good to be true. When she'd gotten the email from the agent explaining that they'd seen her work and wanted her, a mid-list photographer, to shoot an A-list actor in front of an Anza-Borrego metal sculpture, she should've verified the job.

As the sun melded into the horizon in her rearview mirror, she cursed. She should have driven directly to the airport. But the guilt in her chest bubbled like hot lava. The only reason the beta had been attacked was because they'd been after her.

She suspected that Dimitri would have been able to fend off Chaz's pack had his wolf not been impaired. As she'd lain in bed healing him, allowing her mind to explore his energy, she'd felt the spirit of a warrior wolf, a man whose pure sexuality threatened to shake her resolve to remain single. If he'd only been mortal, she could have remained in control. Yet as soon as he'd awoken to her touch, she'd nearly caved.

It had been so long since she'd been with a man, let alone a wolf. In order to remain true to her species, she'd sworn herself to celibacy when it came to wolves. She simply couldn't risk meeting her mate. If she did, she'd be forced to give up the only beast she'd ever known, with no guarantee that she'd remain immortal. *Weak. Defenseless.* She refused to succumb to the consequences of a mating.

She sighed. It wasn't fair; a girl needed release every now and then. And her current strategy just wasn't cutting it. Although humans were a poor substitute for what she craved, Gillian had implemented a 'mortal men only' dating rule. That was how she'd survived her teenage years, passing as human, dating boys, then later colleagues she'd met at work.

Yet her nature drew the wolves to her like moths to a flame. She'd hidden the secrets of her heritage to the best of her ability, but it hadn't been good enough. The Alpha of Anzober wolves had discovered her secret. How, she wasn't sure. All she knew was that he'd made it clear he intended to force their mating. A forced mating wasn't natural, although it'd been rumored that it could be done by an Alpha.

She rubbed the back of her neck where he'd bitten her. Tears pricked her eyes as the memory of his attack played in her mind. He'd ordered his men to restrain her with silver. They'd tied her face down to his bed and stripped her shirt off in preparation for his mark. He insisted that he'd never take her sexually against her will as he ground his erection into her bottom, pressing her into the bed. Her poisoned restraints kept her from shifting as he dug his claws into her shoulders, sinking his fangs into her neck. As his foul-smelling breath drifted into her nostrils and the pain faded, she shook uncontrollably against the satin sheets, expecting him to mount her.

She'd bitten her lip bloody, refusing the satisfaction of letting them see her cry as he hoisted himself off of her, declaring that he'd marked her. His goons made the mistake of misinterpreting her silence as acquiescence and they'd released her bindings. As soon as they'd left the room, she'd called on her beast, killing all three wolves as she fled.

Gillian had to get back to New York. Her brother was the only one who could get her out of this mess. Her fingers grazed the spot where Chaz had bitten her and she thanked the Goddess that he'd failed to mark her. He was not her mate. And as long as she got her ass back to the Big Apple, she'd be safe from the predator who'd lured her all the way to California.

After a quick stop for fuel, she double checked the address of the Las Vegas airport in her GPS app. Even though she'd bought an extra-large coffee to stay awake, the truth was that her nerves had her lit up like a Christmas tree. There was no way she'd fall asleep; her mind was running races. The hot beverage was for comfort only. Even though it tasted like sludge, the bitter fluid reminded her of home. As she looked out onto the dark highway, it was as if a cold claw clutched her chest, reminding her of the danger she faced. *Fucking desert.* Of all the trips to make in the middle of the night alone, driving to Nevada wasn't up there with the world's safest sightseeing trips.

She considered that she might have been able to make the trek as a shifter had she known where she was going. But since this was her first trip to the golden coast, she had no idea in hell how to get there. Given her limitations, this was a time to rely on technology. She glanced quickly to the red dot on her cell phone that was moving slowly down the green line toward the border.

A light flashed in the distance. What the hell was that? Lightning? A desert storm? *I thought it wasn't supposed to rain in California. Get a grip, girl, there's no way he can find you out here.* Gillian reached over to turn up the radio. *Hotel California* wailed through the speakers, and she quickly flipped it over to *Fuckin' Perfect* by Pink. *Yeah, that about sums things up nicely.*

Gillian took a sip of her lukewarm coffee and grimaced as it coated her tongue. Shoving the paper cup into its holder and glancing into her side mirror, she noticed the rare sight of headlights approaching in the distance. As her eyes flashed back to the road, she caught a glint of metal fifty feet ahead on the highway. Two seconds too late, her foot slammed on the brake. Her car hit the shiny silver spike strip. Gripping the steering wheel, she lost her fight for control. As the car slid across the dry road, she screamed. A cold hiss was all she heard before the car rolled over into the dusty desert.

The airbag inflated, knocking her unconscious for several minutes. The creak of the car door alerted her to their presence. In a haze, she barely felt the blade against her belly as they cut her free and her body tumbled onto the ceiling of the car. Unable to move, she groaned as someone tugged on her legs, her face scraping the jagged broken window as they dragged her limp body out onto the cold ground.

The shock of the scent of her own blood drove her into consciousness. Roused, her head bobbed up as meaty hands jolted her upright. Her feet scraped a trench through the gritty sand as the strangers dragged her into the night. The sight of her headlights became pinpricks as they drew her further into the darkness.

Gillian heard Chaz's voice and her blood turned to ice. *How the hell did he find me?* She'd suspected they would have found the motel room where she'd stayed overnight. But she couldn't piece together how they'd found her on the run. She plotted to shrug off her captors, intending to shift, but when she attempted to yank her arm free, she was swiftly rewarded with a silver chain around her neck. The metal immediately poisoned her blood, stifling any chance of a transformation.

"Get off me," she cried, her voice barely audible.

A cold laugh echoed ahead of her.

"Gilly, Gilly, Gilly. My dangerous but lovely mate. You've been a bad girl," Chaz taunted.

He nodded to the two thugs who'd taken Gillian, instructing them to drop her. He smiled coldly as she grunted in pain, her palms stretched out onto the dirt. She attempted to push up onto her feet but fell back onto her hands and knees. Chaz rounded behind her, leaned over and gripped her hair, yanking her up into a kneeling position.

"Ah, yes. Now this is how I shall like to see my queen. On her knees. Submissive. With my cock in her mouth." He laughed, and dragged his hand along her chin. "But not right now. No, no, no. Penance must be done. You killed my wolves. Pity, but you must receive your punishment."

Gillian spat blood up at him and he shoved her toward the earth, wiping the saliva away with the back of his hand. He reached to her collar and wrapped the chain around her neck once more, ensuring her compliance. As he gripped her leather jacket and peeled it off her arms, Gillian fought the fear that wrapped around her mind. The sound of fabric tearing spiked her anxiety, but she refused to give him the satisfaction of her tears. She watched helplessly as he threw her tattered shirt aside.

Wearing only a bra, her skin was exposed to the cold air, and she shivered in response. Gooseflesh rippled across her skin.

This man is incapable of mating me. No matter what pain he plans to inflict, I will not become his. Her beast would never allow it. Any submission he gained would not satisfy her nature. Rationally, she knew the truth of the situation, yet she also was cognizant that he could easily kill her in her disabled state. His voice jarred her back into the moment.

"My wolves...they will bear witness to my mark." He lifted her hair, inspecting his work. Shocked and aggravated with what he saw, he slapped the back of her head with his palm. "What the fuck, bitch? What did you do?"

"I told you," she coughed. She shook her head, the sting of his slap still fresh on her skull. "You cannot mate with my kind. You cannot force a mating."

"Like hell I can't," he growled, his canines descended. Clothed, Chaz mounted her from behind, slamming her face into the dust. "Guess I'll just have to bite you a little harder this time."

Gillian screamed in terror as his teeth sliced into her shoulder. Even though she knew that his mark would be gone the next time she shifted, disgust and loathing roared to the surface.

"No, no, no," she repeated. Tears began to fall and she cursed the silver that restrained her far more than any creature could. Heaving breaths rocked her lungs and she flailed, trying unsuccessfully to get away from him.

Gillian's blood gushed fresh from her wounds as Chaz retracted his teeth. The Alpha licked his lips, smirking with satisfaction. He pushed to his feet, releasing a frightening howl into the night. The four men who'd helped him abduct her joined in chorus, celebrating.

"Your taste was made for me," he continued, reaching to accept a whip from his colleague. "I could fuck you right now in front of everyone, but unlike you, I'm capable of restraint."

"Fuck you," she cried, once again on her knees. Her defiant eyes met his, refusing to submit in any way, shape or form. The crack of the whip didn't shake her resolve. As far as she was concerned, he could shove his demand for her submission down his throat. The only way she'd submit was if she was cold, dead and six feet under.

"Don't worry." He laughed, cracking the popper, enjoying the thunderous sound it made throughout the valley. "I plan to fuck you nice and hard. But first things first. You must be punished for your indiscretions. I want you to remember your place. You're nothing more than a wild animal, one who must be tamed by the lash of my whip. I plan to teach your beast the discipline she needs. I assure you that your beating will hurt you far more than it will me."

Dimitri had grown worried the second the flashing dot on his GPS had gone still. Viewing the satellite image, he immediately knew that she couldn't have stopped to refuel. As far into the desert as she was, there wasn't a gas station within thirty miles of her location.

"Jesus Christ," Dimitri exclaimed, as the wreckage came into view.

The Audi rested upturned thirty feet from the asphalt. Its interior remained dimly lit, and the driver's door hung wide open. Jake slammed on the brakes, and Dimitri hit the ground running toward her car. His gut told him that she was gone but he still wasn't prepared for the shock of seeing the empty cabin. Her camera lay smashed against the windshield. Reaching inside, he snatched her open backpack off the floor and threw it to Jake, whose lips were pressed tightly together.

"They fucking took her," Dimitri raged.

"We'll find her," Jake said.

"Turn off the car lights," Dimitri ordered, fumbling for the headlight controls inside the wreck.

Jake ran over to his vehicle and hit the switch. Except for the light of the stars, the desert was blanketed in darkness.

"Now we look and listen." Both wolves could see in the dark, but the absence of light accentuated the illumination that danced several miles into the desert. "There, south. They're out there. She's out there."

Jake set his eyes on their target, awaiting his beta's orders. Dimitri took a deep breath, sniffing, and was relieved when he smelled her in the wind.

"She's bleeding." The coppery tang of her scent angered him.

"Goin' wolf?" Jake asked.

"Yeah." Dimitri began to strip.

"Either way, it'll be tough to keep under the radar."

"I love a challenge." He shrugged off his pants, readying to shift.

"Never known you to back down."

"You get Gilly. The fuckers who took her are mine," Dimitri ordered, suspecting that her abductors were the same people who'd attacked him.

"You sure?" The concern about his beta's wolf was left unspoken.

"Mine," Dimitri growled. Shifting, he took off into the brush.

Gillian swore she scented Dimitri and thought she was losing it. No, it must've been a hallucination brought on by the fear. She steeled her mind, preparing to embrace the cut of the whip. She felt the vibrations in the dirt before the crack of the tail reverberated into the night. Chaz was drawing out the torture, forcing her to wait for the punishment.

"I think ten lashes will do nicely," the Alpha declared.

He drew his hand upward. His sight aimed toward Gillian's bare flesh, pleased that she was shaking. With the flick of his wrist, he prepared to implement what he believed was not only justice, but the means to her submission. But as the braided cord flew backwards, not even a hiss was heard.

"Sorry pal, clowns aren't allowed to handle the big boy equipment at the circus." Dimitri smirked as he snatched the braided cord mid-air, thoroughly enjoying the shock and surprise that crossed the Alpha's face.

With a jerk, Dimitri yanked him to the ground. As Chaz fell, the beta pounced. Sitting atop his waist, Dimitri pressed him onto his back. Chaz fought for control and attempted to dislodge his attacker so he could shift. But before he could do so, Dimitri deftly coiled the leather around his neck until only a short length remained on either side. Holding tight to the hilt and the tail, Dimitri tightened the noose, forcing the Alpha to gasp for air. He pushed up onto his feet, dragging Chaz upward, leaving his feet kicking up dust.

"Do you know who I am?" the Alpha spat.

"Don't know. Don't care."

"Chaz Baldwin. Alpha of Anzober wolves."

"Yeah, still don't care. Call off your wolves," Dimitri ordered.

Jake lunged at the wolf who stood watch over Gillian, tearing at his throat. Before he knew it, he was surrounded by two other wolves, and braced himself for the pack's wrath.

"Back off or your Alpha dies tonight," Dimitri commanded, his voice bellowing at the wolves.

Dimitri hid the rage that surfaced as he caught sight of Gillian on her knees, bared in front of the others. He observed the blood streaking down her back, and his heart clenched. The fucker had bitten her. It made no sense. Had she been wolf, he'd suspect the Alpha had tried to force a mating, to mark her. But she wasn't wolf, so that only left torture.

"Get the silver off her. You do it." He nodded to one of the wolves who immediately submitted to his order. He didn't want Jake touching the poison. They were already outnumbered as it was.

"You fucking piece of shit. Look real close...your wolves do my bidding," Dimitri taunted. Chaz revived and struggled to free himself, and Dimitri kneed him in the back, stilling his actions.

You'll be lucky if I let you live when this is all over."

"Need to shift," Gillian whispered as the chain fell to the ground. She raised her head and saw the dominant beta forcing Chaz to submit. Her eyes met his and her beast came to life. *Dimitri.* He'd come for her.

Jake heard her request and gave Dimitri an inquisitive look, as if to ask for permission to take off her clothes. They both knew she had to shift but there was no way in hell, with the way his beta had gone feral, overpowering another Alpha, that Jake would attempt to touch a woman who Dimitri perceived as his.

"Do it." Dimitri's gaze fell to Gillian, whose eyes were glazed with tears.

He watched as his friend peeled off her clothes and even though he was altogether comfortable with nudity, possessiveness stabbed at his chest. He didn't want anyone else looking at her right now but him. He took a deep breath and shook off the disturbing emotion.

Dimitri and Jake had been too focused on Gillian when a wolf attacked Jake from behind. Jake fell to the ground and spotted the silver chain that had been around the female. His finger extended, scooping up the metal. The smell of his burnt flesh wafted into the night but he didn't let it deter him from his task. Within seconds, he'd tied it to the wolf's forearm, rendering him back to his mortal form. Dimitri never once let go of the Alpha as he watched Jake with confidence, knowing he'd subdue the lesser wolf.

A roar cut into the melee, alerting everyone of the new danger that had arrived. Dimitri nearly dropped his prey as his eyes focused on Gillian. *Spectacular.* It was the first word that popped into his mind as he watched the white tiger leap onto a second wolf and tear its throat open. Blood sprayed into the air, and the great feline shook her head in delight.

"What. The. Fuck?" Jake transformed back to his mortal form, slowly backing away from the enormous animal. A smile broke across his face when he realized it was Gillian. "You win, D. She's not a bear."

"Told you she'd be awesome."

Dimitri contemplated what to do with the Alpha, who'd gone still in the presence of Gillian's beast. The ramifications of killing the Alpha weren't worth the price. Dimitri knew that if he ended Chaz's life, he'd have to take over his pack. While he had the strength and heart of an Alpha, his loyalty belonged to Acadian wolves. As he considered his dilemma, he looked to Gillian and decided there was no rule against giving him to her. *I love loopholes.* He smiled, throwing the bound Alpha at her feet.

Dimitri watched with pride as the slender cat eyed her nemesis, stalking toward him, emitting a low menacing growl. Within seconds, Chaz unraveled the whip and transformed into his wolf. He curled his lips upward, and assumed a defensive posture. Gillian's dark eyes fixed on his neck. A thunderous roar exploded from her muzzle as she attempted to pounce on the Alpha. Faltering, she missed her target, grazing his hindquarters with her paws. Chaz yelped in response. He seized the opportunity to escape, sprinting off into the night.

It was clear to Dimitri from the wolves' hasty retreat that Chaz knew he'd never survive a fight with a tiger. The magnificent feline could have easily caught the wolf had the fight been fair. But apparently, she was still reeling from being poisoned. After nearly a one hundred yard chase, she came to a stop, glaring at her prey.

Jake approached Dimitri, the two men still nude. "What's wrong with her?"

"She's sick," the beta observed, rubbing dirt from his eyes. *Shit.* He'd wanted so badly to kill the Alpha but consequences were a bitch. He'd made a calculated decision to let him live. It was the right choice, he knew. But his wolf thirsted for blood.

"The silver," Jake agreed. He looked to Gillian who'd circled around, slowly padding toward them. "You didn't kill him."

"Nope." Dimitri's lips tightened.

"The fucking asshole was about to whip her."

"He's sadistic," he replied, growing annoyed with the topic.

"That must've taken some great restraint...not to end it."

"You know it fucking did, but number one, I have no desire to lead that asshole's wolves. Two, I love my own pack. And three, well, we both know Logan'd have my nuts in a sack if I'd killed him. Things are just getting settled down at home. The last damn thing he needs is to lose his beta and have to deal with the shit people will give him about my mistake, which was thinking I could have two fucking minutes in the sand without declaring my presence to a pack."

Dimitri blew out a breath, realizing that he'd just taken a well-deserved rant. He caught sight of Gillian staring at him in the distance. She'd gone still, her gaze upon him like a thick fog. He'd raised his voice and she'd heard.

Goddammit. She'd been attacked and was traumatized. He knew better than to yell, especially after he'd just gotten finished demonstrating his dominance over the man who'd tortured her. Was she expecting him to do the same?

He needed to try to get her to shift, to get her back to the car. Despite their short-term victory, it was the middle of the night and dangerous to remain in the desert. For all he knew, they could return any second with a high-powered rifle and take out all of them.

Dimitri eyed Jake and gestured to the ground. In order to make himself less imposing, he knelt on one knee. Jake followed and they both faced off with the tiger.

"Gilly, it's okay now. I won't hurt you," he said, his voice soft. The great cat growled in response and he tried again to earn her trust.

"Jake won't hurt you either." He glanced to Jake and gave her a small smile. "Darlin', as much as I love seeing your beautiful kitty cat, we've gotta get moving. You wanna shift? We'll go to the car, drive to the airport. All three of us. I'm goin' to make sure you get home safe. I promise."

The majestic beast took a few steps toward him and bared her teeth. A hiss tore through the air.

"Okay, okay. No shifting." Dimitri held up his palms, letting her know he wasn't going to fight her. Frustrated, he couldn't fully communicate with Gillian, but he was certain she understood him. "Look, Gilly. We've got to go. They could come back any minute now…with weapons."

He didn't want to scare her but it was the stark reality of the situation. She turned her head as if she was looking for the enemy.

"That's right, baby. You don't need to be afraid of me. You know that. I know you saw what I did to the Alpha, but I'd never hurt you…ever."

Gillian stalked toward him a few more steps, and he sighed in relief. He was getting through to her.

"Come to me, Gilly," he gently instructed, extending his hand. "You know my scent. You healed me, touched my skin. You're safe."

Dimitri held his breath as she approached, pressing her head upward into his hand.

"Aw yes, darlin'. You're so soft. So gorgeous. I know," he whispered. "The silver is hurtin' you. It'll be okay in a few hours. If you want to stay how you are for a while, that's fine, just fine."

As he lifted his head, he looked over to Jake whose jaw was wide open in disbelief. Dimitri gave a small chuckle, unashamed of his interaction with his kitten. *Fuck, since when is she my kitten?* He knew it was ridiculous to feel this kind of connection to another shifter, but there was something about her. But in the heat of the moment, he wasn't going to try to overanalyze it. In the past seventy-two hours, both she and he had been attacked. She'd saved him. He'd saved her. Maybe it was a hero complex but he didn't care what the hell Jake thought.

"She's not going to hurt you, man," Dimitri said with a grin.

"Okay, whatever you say. You did just see her tear through that wolf's throat, right? It's not like the fight was even close."

"I saw it, and *you* were awesome," he cooed, rubbing her ears.

"Oooookay. Well, I'm a wolf. And she's, uh, a little scary."

"Did you hear that, Gilly, girl? Badass Jake is actually afraid of something. I want to remember this moment." He stopped to laugh and look at Jake, who huffed, not at all amused. "So, you need to go easy, okay, kitten. Jake and I are going to shift and the three of us are goin' to run back to the car. We won't be able to communicate when I'm wolf, so just follow us back. Your sense of direction might be a little off…it's just the poison."

Dimitri waited on Jake to go first, concerned how Gillian would react to him. As his friend took off toward the car, he let his hand fall from her mane. He recalled how she'd embraced him in her human form, her soft tendrils caressing his skin. Letting the pleasurable memory drift, he focused on their task.

"Time to go, cher," Dimitri said, as he called on his wolf. With the transformation complete, he and Gillian ran together toward safety.

Chapter Three

Gillian contemplated her fate, staring into Dimitri's dark eyes. If she'd let arousal rule her thoughts, she'd have capitulated long ago. From the second she'd laid her bare skin against his, she'd known Dimitri was powerful. But the sight of him nearly killing Chaz confirmed her suspicions about his abilities. The image of the beta almost killing her captor, an Alpha, was seared in her mind. Why he'd let him live, she wasn't sure. Instead, Dimitri had thrown the flailing wolf at her feet, as if he'd bestowed on her a precious treasure. As much as she appreciated the gesture, he'd overestimated her ability to catch prey, her body sickened from the silver.

When he'd called for her, she considered running away. But her beast recognized his actions as one of an Alpha, and she found herself respecting, fearing and desiring him all at once. The way he'd easily restrained and commanded Chaz demonstrated to her that she should be wary of him. It was true that she was lethal in her own right, but it was in that moment she knew that Dimitri could do her far more harm than she could ever inflict on him.

How Chaz had discovered her in the first place, she wasn't sure. Even though her mom had isolated her and had gone as far as to change her name after her father's death, Gillian's birth was well known. Given Chaz's influential status, he would have access to detectives who must have unearthed her identity. The existence of her breed, while rare, was known in the feline community. The secrets surrounding her kind, however, were kept closely guarded. The undesired destiny that could befall her was not one that she advertised. Her mother had warned her of what would happen should she meet a wolf who was her mate, a wolf that would be so devastatingly compelling that her beast would gladly submit to him. This man would destroy her nature, transforming her into a weaker being. No longer would her tiger surface. Generations of women before her had suffered the same fate. If Gillian found her mate, she was destined to lose herself, possibly losing her immortality altogether.

Unfortunately, it wasn't easy for her race. Other than immediate family, the great cats wandered life as loners, never congregating like prides or packs. Even if she was lucky enough to find another tiger, they'd be reluctant to breed with a hybrid, to continue the impurity of her line.

Gillian's mother, hopelessly in love, had relinquished her status, mating with an Alpha. As a result of doing so, she was left mortal, unable to ever shift again. After her mate died in an attack, she'd left his pack, relocating them to Washington. It was there in the open space of the mountains where Gillian had learned how to shift into her cat. Strong and swift, she had grown up secure, knowing that she could protect herself from virtually anything.

Upon graduation, she'd moved to New York City to attend NYU. It was in the rich cultured city where she'd learned photography. From a distance her mom had encouraged her hobby, which soon grew into a profitable business. At twenty-eight years old, she wasn't in the top echelon yet. But her career was advancing and she'd slowly started picking up editorial shoots here and there.

Gillian couldn't risk being around wolves, accidentally finding her mate. There was no such thing as fate, only determination, at least that was what she told herself. She loved being a tiger, and wolves represented her death. If she happened to find a tiger, she'd consider it. But since the odds of that happening were slim to none, dating humans was the only safe option. She'd never met a man who'd broken her resolve, someone who'd light every one of her nerves on fire just by breathing the same air…until Dimitri.

Gillian was drawn out of her reverie as the beta patted the car seat. He talked to her as if he were speaking to a lover, his voice sweet and gentle. She hated it…mostly because it was working. She was scared. But it was his witty repartee that made her want to know him more. When he'd saved her, demonstrating his commanding nature, one that would match hers, the man had been magnificent. He'd been incredibly dominant, yet promised not to hurt her. She told herself not to trust him, because if she did, it would only give her an excuse to be near him, to breathe in his scent like she'd done in bed....his delicious, intoxicating scent.

She looked to his nervous friend. He feigned nonchalance, but nude, he defensively flexed his hands, poised to shift. *Does he seriously think I'm going to eat him?* Well, had she gone truly feral, she might have, she supposed. Sure, she'd killed the wolf, but he'd participated in her torture, allowing his Alpha to attack her again. They'd held her captive, intent on breaking her beast's spirit. But Jake, he, too, was a man of honor, one who'd risked his own life to save hers.

Dimitri smiled at her as if he'd read her thoughts and the battle shield around her heart cracked. Slowly she crept toward him, gingerly taking a place on the seat. The simple act of allowing him to touch her fur had been submission in itself. *What if he has the capability to steal my beast away, to mark me?* She could feel her feline nature rebel at her concern, yearning to take him. No, she couldn't allow that to happen.

Gillian fought a yawn. So tired...if she could just nap for a bit, heal her own body, she'd thank them and say goodbye, thwarting the developing lust that grew in her belly. As a hybrid wolf, there was always a chance that he'd be the one. The one for whom she'd make the ultimate sacrifice. As she fell asleep in his lap, she gave him her trust.

Dimitri took a deep breath and nodded. Fuck it all, he was about to let a two hundred pound cat get into the back seat with him. *I must be an idiot. No, just horny*, his brain answered. Jake gave her a wide berth, not wanting to get too close, but Gillian still hadn't gotten into the car. It occurred to Dimitri that perhaps he wasn't the only one having second thoughts. Summoning up the courage, he decided a few encouraging words were in order.

"Now I know it looks like a tight fit, but you know you want to cuddle up with me. You're a very tired kitty. Come on, now. Let's go. Poor Jake is going to get cold out there. Just look at him." Dimitri cocked his head and smiled at his friend, who'd hesitated to get dressed. He suspected that Jake didn't want his clothes to restrict him, not until he was sure that Gillian wasn't going to attack. As long as he was naked, he could easily shift back to defend himself if necessary.

Unlike Jake, Dimitri had yanked on a pair of pants. There was no way in hell he was about to get into closed quarters with a clawed tiger, leaving his dangly bits swinging in the wind.

"Remember your first time?" Yeah, it all came back to sex for him. Maybe she wouldn't get the analogy but it was the best he could do, given the circumstances. "Is this the first time you've shifted with wolves? I bet it is, cher. Well this is our first time, too. Jake's a little nervous over there. We're all a little nervous. I'm tellin' you that you can trust me, trust us. Come sit with me, come rest. You can stay tiger as long as you need to," he reassured, patting the seat.

"She can't go on a plane like that…" Jake started to say, when Dimitri held up his hand to shush him.

"Gilly just needs a little time. She needs to be with me, don't ya, darlin'?" he coaxed sweetly. His breath caught as she pushed a fat paw onto the leather seat, and he was relieved that she hadn't extended her nails. With the grace of a ballerina, she quietly ascended into the interior and settled down next to him. The crushing weight of her forearms on his thighs was yet another reminder of her power. But as she relaxed her muscled body against his chest, the pressure became more comfortable. Both his hands moved to stroke her fur. "That's a girl. Just rest. I've got ya."

"Your girlfriend is a cat," Jake stated with a blunt tone.

"She's not my girlfriend, but if she was my girlfriend," Dimitri looked to the giant tigress in his lap, who gently snored, "it wouldn't matter what she was. She's brave. And funny. And she smells nice."

"What's, up, Pussycat….ooooooh," Jake broke out in his best Tom Jones impression.

"You're hilarious."

"And I thought Logan was bad enough bringing one home from the pound. You topped him, all right. You slept with one, and not in the cuddle-me-kitty kind of way."

"Hold up. Sure, she was on top of me...I'll give you that. But we didn't have sex. The bottom line is this; no matter how much I'd like to get to know her," he shook his head, wishing they'd met under different circumstances, "she's not pack. Therefore she's not my mate."

"That hasn't stopped you before. You just fucked a vampire, for Christ's sakes."

"Yeah, well, Lacey is a lovely little memory. But she knew the score. One night or two....nothing but play. There's been no play with this one. Oh no, she tied me up. Not that I mind a little bondage, but shit, she just left me there." Dimitri stroked his hand over her fur and sighed. "Gilly, here, is on the run and not just from that Alpha back there. She's got a thing about wolves."

"She's got a thing all right...a bad thing."

"Yep. She's spooked."

"As well she should be. You saw what they did to her."

"He marked her," Dimitri said softly, disgusted at the thought of another wolf piercing her creamy white skin. "It makes no sense."

"Probably just a dominance thing. The guy doesn't strike me as mentally stable, shall we say."

"Ya got that right. Hell, he was gonna fucking whip her. Something's missing, though. He knew she wasn't wolf. The question is, did he know she was a tiger? And if he did, why is he trying to keep her? Why mark her as his own in front of others?"

"Look, you and I were just guessing what she might be. Maybe they guessed right…or knew exactly what she was."

"This doesn't make any sense. I know we've gotta get home, but before we leave, I intend to get answers. Kitty, here, has some explainin' to do." Dimitri gingerly reached into Gillian's backpack, which Jake had thrown onto the car floor. He fumbled inside, finding his phone. "I'm texting Logan. I'll give him the deets when we get back, but for now, I want him to send the jet. It'll take a while but who knows how long she's gonna stay cat."

"Coach sucks anyway."

"No first class on the way out here? Poor baby," Dimitri teased.

"It was brutal."

"My ass doesn't fit in those tiny seats anyway. Even first class feels like a tin can," he laughed. "Truth is that we can't risk goin' commercial. Chaz could have someone try to stop her, or board the flight. I want a pilot I know and trust to get us home safely."

Dimitri tapped at the glass clumsily with one hand and kept his other on Gillian's back. It made it difficult for him to type, his large thumbs tripping the autocorrect. After several minutes of messaging with Logan and a few curse words later, he'd made the arrangements to have the private plane meet them tomorrow.

"Let's hit the hotel tonight. Logan's getting things in motion but it'll take time."

"You think Chaz's reach stretches to Nevada?"

"I don't think so, but a guy like that doesn't strike me as someone who follows the rules. Just to be safe, Logan was calling the Vegas Alpha to let them know we'd be in the territory. We'll get some rest and then get the hell out of there."

"What about her?" Jake asked.

"What about her? She's...I don't know. She's gotta go home." Dimitri glanced out the darkened window. His stomach clenched in what he blamed on hunger, but part of him knew it was his wolf pining for Gillian. He rubbed the scruff on his face, his lips tight with concern. "I wish we could take her home but I don't think that's such a good..."

The weight on his legs lightened considerably, and he lost his words, watching Gillian transform into a beautiful woman. *Shit, now I really am going to have a hard time with this.* Part of him had hoped she'd stay tiger. Then he wouldn't have an excuse to pursue her, but his mind warred against it. He told himself that he needed to talk to her so he could get answers, but in reality, he just needed her. Naked and against him.

"A good, what?" Jake asked. His eyes flashed to the rearview mirror; he could no longer see the white cat. "She shifted? Let me see."

"Eyes on the road, bro," Dimitri said. He glanced to his own hand, which rested on her belly. Her back was pressed flush against his abs, her long mane feathered over her shoulders and breasts. He took note of a dusky pink tip that strained through the dark waterfall and his cock jerked in response. *Not now*, he thought. "Throw me my bag."

Jake laughed and launched the duffle over the seat. Dimitri caught it mid-air with one hand. He bent over, careful not to crush her, and tugged a button-down shirt out of the bag. Gingerly, he draped it over her bare skin, so she was covered. Looping his forefinger through the edge of her hair, he brushed it back, revealing her full lips. She smiled as if she were going to wake up and then mewled, reaching her fingers between his thighs. Dimitri sucked a deep breath as her thumb brushed over his burgeoning erection. As she settled once again, he closed his eyes, praying for self-restraint.

Fucking hell. Why does she have to be so goddamned beautiful? And a tiger? Really? I barely survived being killed and the universe doesn't owe me one? Guess not.

He blew out a breath and caught Jake's gaze in the mirror, who gave him a knowing laugh before setting his sight back to the highway. Dimitri knew right then that he'd better get Gillian back to New York as soon as possible, because if not, he was pretty sure the next time he caught sight of her sweet nipple, it would be nestled between his lips.

Chapter Four

Gillian watched the numbers light up as they ascended in the elevator, and considered her attire. She'd bitten her lip, attempting to pretend it was completely acceptable to stand in bare feet, dressed only in a man's dress shirt in the lobby of the five star hotel. As they'd passed by the concierge, she smiled demurely. *What happens in Vegas stays in Vegas.* She was fairly sure it wasn't the strangest thing he'd ever seen.

She took a deep breath, taking note of the large pair of feet on either side of hers. Afraid to make eye contact, she mentally shrugged and stared ahead, reflecting on how she'd gotten herself into this situation.

When she'd woken up naked in Dimitri's lap, she hadn't said a word. She could hardly believe that she'd fallen asleep for hours with her head snuggled against his warm thighs. The only saving grace had been that she hadn't buried her face in his crotch. Thankfully, she'd slept in the opposite direction, allowing her to hide her reddened face. In the darkness, she'd pushed up, sliding her arms into the shirt and buttoning it. She scooted over to the opposite door, stealing a glimpse at the striking beta. Stealth wasn't her strong suit, she noted, as he pinned his eyes on hers. Her breath caught, feeling as if he could see into her heart, knowing her deepest thoughts. A warm smile bloomed on his face, breaking their heated interaction.

Silence lingered and she knew then that she was on borrowed time. He'd want an explanation. Reason told her to be afraid, very afraid of going up alone into a hotel room with two wolves. But instinct won over. This man would not hurt her. He'd saved her life. She'd give him what he wanted and then some. But in the morning, she'd be back to her life and home in New York.

Dimitri exchanged glances with Jake. Gillian had been unusually quiet in the car. He had to admit that she was well composed, considering her attack and the fact that she was barely dressed. As he glanced down to her toned legs, all he could really think about was touching her again, feeling her skin against his.

The elevator bell sounded and they came to a smooth halt. He reached and took her hand, happily surprised when she laced her fingers through his. Easily finding the room, Jake opened the door and led them into the richly decorated suite.

"Through here." Dimitri guided her into a bedroom.

Quietly, he shut the door behind them for privacy. Releasing Gillian's hand, he went to the bar and grabbed them a couple of bottles of water. He unscrewed the tops and handed one to her. She took it without meeting his eyes, and he suspected she needed time to collect her thoughts. A shame that wasn't going to happen.

"You're a tiger," he began. Dimitri strode to the windows and opened the drapes, exposing the spectacular sea of lights twinkling upon the strip.

"Um, yeah," Gillian replied, tracing her finger along the rim. Tears threatened to fall as her emotions rose to the surface. She'd almost died. She shook her head; shame washed over her. "Thank you. If you hadn't come for me…"

"I don't get it, Gilly. It's like I'm looking at a puzzle but a few of the pieces are missing. Tell me," he walked over to the bed until he stood towering above her, "why does an Alpha, one who is a wolf, want to mark a tiger? Why are you so important to him? I want the truth and I want it now."

She sniffled, and lifted her gaze to meet his. "He wants me to be his. I shouldn't have ever come here. I've gotta get back to New York."

"I can help you. Tomorrow I'll take you wherever you came from as long as I know you'll be safe. But I need the truth if I'm going to be able to do that."

"You don't understand. I'm not what you think I am."

"You're a shifter. I knew that from the second I opened my eyes. A tiger? Well, yeah, I didn't expect that, but you were amazing."

"I don't know how he knew about me…Chaz. Tigers, we're not like you. We're loners."

"I'm sorry, but you're losing me here. He's a wolf. You're a tiger. What am I missing?"

"I'm not all tiger," she coughed. It was the first time she'd ever said the words out loud to anyone in her life. "My father…he was a wolf. An Alpha."

Dimitri's blood pressure spiked as she spoke. A hybrid. A tiger-wolf hybrid. And her father was an Alpha. A million questions spun through his brain. He took a deep breath, attempting to stay calm. The last thing she needed was for him to lose his shit, scaring her further.

"So he was going to mark you?"

"It's the second time he's tried," she admitted softly. Gillian reached her hands back into her hair, twisting it up into a ponytail, revealing the area where she'd been bitten. "But it doesn't work that way. See? The magic. It's a curse really. My mother called it a destiny, but it's not."

Dimitri couldn't help himself. In an instant, he was on the bed beside her, the pads of his fingers smoothing over where the bite mark had been. Nothing but smooth skin remained. He wasn't sure why but relief that she remained unmarked coursed through him and he winced.

"Why does he think he can mark you?"

"He was trying to force me to mate with him," she divulged.

"But a wolf can only mate with another wolf. A human hybrid? Yes. But any other shifter combo; it's a no go."

"True…for most. But not for me."

"Cher, I don't think you know what you're…" Dimitri began, but didn't want to insult her. She'd been through a lot. The trauma must've confused her. Shifters could mate only with those of their own kind. That fact gave him great comfort, considering he wasn't looking for one. He'd already watched Logan's boat sink. No way was he going down that road.

"The only way it could work is for me to submit. I'd die before that happened," Gillian continued, ignoring his comment. She couldn't help the tears that had begun to fall. Her nerves had been like steel throughout the duration of her abduction. Dimitri offered her soul respite from the danger, a safe place to be herself.

"Come here, darlin'. It's okay. He's never gonna get you again." He hoped. Dimitri hadn't heard the entire story yet and suspected part two of whatever nugget she was hiding was not going to be good.

"I'm sorry. I don't even know you." She pressed her palms to his bare chest, and lifted her eyes to meet his.

"We know each other just fine." Dimitri smiled, trying to lighten the mood.

She raised a questioning eyebrow at him.

"Okay, maybe I don't know your favorite color yet."

"You don't know anything about me," she smiled.

"Not true. I know you have a tattoo on your back. And we've already cuddled in bed," he joked. "Hell, you've even tied me up. I'll admit that I've never been with a woman who's tied me up on a first date but I'm not knockin' it."

"It wasn't a date," she laughed.

"I do feel somewhat slighted. You tied me up and I didn't even get kissed."

Gillian's gaze fell to his lips and her stomach did a nervous flip. She fluttered her lids, and forced herself to look away. Her heart began to race as he wiped a remnant tear from her cheek with the pad of his thumb.

"Our second date wasn't too much fun either. I got in a fight and ended up in the backseat with a stray cat," he teased, his fingers playing with her hair.

"You weren't afraid of me."

"No, but let's say I had a healthy respect for you. My mamma didn't raise a fool. I've seen a lot of things, cher. But seeing a full grown Bengal tiger up close and personal is pretty impressive."

"So you like my kitty?" she asked.

"Oh I like her all right, but I like who's in front of me more." Dimitri smiled, enjoying her flirtatious banter. His hand fell to her bare thigh, and he consciously warred to keep it from sliding up under her shirt.

"I guess I owe you that kiss, then. I mean, it is our second date, after all," she said.

Dimitri gave her a broad smile, briefly contemplating the temptation. *Naked girl. Hotel room. Don't do it.* But the devil on his other shoulder disagreed. After all, he just saved the girl. *What harm could one little kiss do?*

Slowly, he leaned in. His gaze fell to her lips and quickly darted upward, connecting with her soul. Just one small kiss to let her know he liked her was all he needed; one to make sure she wouldn't doubt that he wanted to see her again after they sorted out all their issues. He smiled slightly as he caught her eyes, inwardly nervous that his action would change his life.

As his lips took hers, he groaned in delight. The little minx who'd saved him tasted more delicious than he could have imagined. As he pulled her against him, he stiffened in arousal. She climbed atop, straddling him with her knees. His hands speared upward into the back of her hair. Sliding his fingers through her silken mane, he fisted her locks, drawing her closer to him still. The sweep of Gillian's tongue against his, her soft lips against his own, drove him out of control with desire. When she placed her hands on his chest, and drew her finger over his nipple, his cock hardened to rock. As she began to grind her bared center onto his denim-covered hardness, he ripped his lips from hers, panting.

Dimitri rested his forehead against hers, his thoughts racing. He was going to fucking lose it. This woman was aggressive and sweet like honey. The craziest part about the situation was that she was right; he didn't really know her. They'd both nearly died in the past few days. It had to be the stress of the situation that was causing his reaction to her. The chemistry was undeniably explosive. If he kissed her a second time, he'd be balls deep in sixty seconds. *Deep breath. Deep breath.*

"Cher," he breathed. "Before we do something we'll both regret, I'm going to put you down. Okay?"

"Okay," she nodded, still trying to catch her breath. She removed her hands from his chest and carefully slid off his lap, back onto the bed.

"Okay," he repeated. The sexual fog lingered in his brain. He groaned loudly as he righted himself and stood. Despite the granite bulge in his jeans, he managed to hobble over to the door. "So, yeah, thanks for the kiss. Great date."

"The best. Um, well, thank you." She giggled, wrapping her arms around her waist. She crossed her legs, remembering they were open and that she wasn't wearing panties.

Dimitri looked away as one leg went over the next. *Fuck, she's going to kill me*, he thought. He curled his fingers around the doorknob, and turned it.

"I'm goin' to let you use the shower in here. I'll, uh, go use Jake's…that way we won't….you know, get in anymore trouble. I'm goin' to order us up some room service. Come on out when you're done."

"Okay," she managed, her face red with embarrassment.

"Guess I'll go get ready for date number three. You in?" Dimitri brushed his fingers over the sensitive nipple that she'd fingered only seconds earlier, and winked.

He didn't bother staying to watch her reaction to his invitation. As soon as he shut the door behind him, he blew out a breath as if he'd been holding it all night. *Fuckin'-A.* If he didn't get back to New Orleans in the next twenty-four hours, he'd be dating a tiger *for real*.

With his wolf impaired, he risked losing the ability to shift. No, he'd get Ilsbeth to do whatever magick she had to do to fix this mess. He swore to stay stronger than the little feline in the room next door who already had him purring.

Holy Fuck. Gillian pressed her face into her palms as the door clicked shut. *What the hell am I doing?* She'd just climbed Dimitri like she was scaling Mount Everest. Her tiger paced, encouraging her to go after him. Gillian had never spent this much time around wolves. Being around Dimitri and Jake rocked her equilibrium. Her beast didn't see them as a threat, leaving her mind open to the possibilities. She'd spent so much time avoiding pack members, hating what they represented - the loss of her tiger - that she'd never given much thought to what it would feel like if she liked them, or worse, desired one.

She closed her eyes, imagining her tongue tracing Dimitri's tattoos from the curves of his shoulder to his neck. Still damp between her legs from their kiss, the thought of licking him took her breath away. Gillian knew she had to get back to her brother, beg for his help. But Dimitri was a pleasant unforeseen wrinkle in her plans.

As she pushed off the bed and trod into the bathroom, she sighed. *What am I thinking? I want to date a wolf? Just no.* The trip to California must've done something to her brain, because that was a rule she'd never break. It was a choice. Preserving her tiger took priority over looking for love in the eyes of a wolf.

As Gillian stepped under the hot spray, she considered what she'd do once she reached New York. Several months ago, she'd been approached by a sophisticated gentleman at a photo shoot for a new coffee club in Manhattan. He'd introduced himself as the New York Alpha, Jax Chandler, owner of the chic magazine, ZANE, who'd paid for the images. Jax and his beta, Nick Sterling, had expressed interest in seeing her portfolio with the intent of hiring her. Gillian had been thrilled with the prospect of being offered a staff position. When she called her mother and mentioned his name, she'd confessed to Gillian that she had a half-brother, who also lived in the city. An Alpha…Jax Chandler.

Gillian, concerned that he'd force her into his pack, cut off contact with Jax, giving him no explanation. If he found out that they were family, he wouldn't relent. He'd want her to mate with one of his wolves, let her tiger die. It had crushed her to alienate her only brother. Growing up with just her mother had been a lonely existence. She'd spent many days dreaming she had a sibling, someone close who'd be family. Giving up her nature in order to gain family, however, was simply not an option.

Thanks to Chaz, Jax now represented survival. Chaz had told her repeatedly that he'd never give up on finding her, stealing her gift. Jax was the only one she could trust to protect her.

Dimitri had his own battles to fight. He didn't need to fight hers. While he'd surprised her in the desert with his insurmountable strength, it wasn't fair to ask him to help her. They both knew that at any moment, his wolf could falter. And what if he died because of her? She couldn't allow him to sacrifice himself for her. She'd never let that happen.

She stepped out of the shower, catching sight of her swollen lips in the mirror. His kiss. *The* kiss. She'd felt her tiger calm in his arms, and it terrified her. The more she talked to him, the more she felt herself entangled in his web. He was charming with a flair for humor that brought a smile to her face. Dominating and sexy, his powerful presence told her that he'd take her in ways she'd never known. The thought of him driving deep inside her core made her ache with need.

She cursed, rolling her eyes. Here she was in a hotel room with two shifters, knowing full well they'd scent her arousal the second she opened the door. She had to get her shit together, or at least try not to throw herself at Dimitri...again. *For the love of the Goddess, stop thinking about sex.* Her libido was in overdrive, making her feel as if she was a hot-air balloon about to take off into the wild blue yonder.

Gillian toweled her hair dry and pulled on a white cotton spa robe. She tightened the belt around her waist and pulled the collar tight, as if it would keep her grounded. Slipping on the matching terry slippers, she shuffled over to the door. Closing her eyes, she took a deep breath. Wrapping her hand around the knob, she opened it, praying she could resist the delicious beta in the next room.

Nothing had prepared Gillian for the heavenly scent of steak teasing her nose. Her stomach grumbled and she laughed, catching Dimitri's hungry gaze, one that she suspected had nothing to do with the food. She noticed how Jake tensed his grip on his fork as if he was expecting a wild animal to leap at him. She laughed, finding it comical that such a strong wolf would be afraid of her.

"Hey, darlin'. Why don't ya come sit down here?" Dimitri pulled out a chair for her and eyed Jake. "Relax, man. She's just this itty bitty thing of a woman. She's not going to hurt you."

"Shut it," Jake grumbled, not fond of being on the end of the ribbing. "Maybe I'm just allergic to cats."

"It's okay, really. I know that some people aren't used to seeing me," Gillian said softly, placing a soft hand on his forearm.

"You were really cool looking, I'll give you that. It was a clean kill if I've ever seen one." He gave her a sideways grin, beginning to feel more at ease.

"She's one badass kitty cat, that's for damn sure," Dimitri added proudly.

"I'll take that as a compliment." She paused and picked up her fork. "I just want to thank you both again. I know I kind of asked you not to follow me, but I'm really glad you did. I'd be dead if you hadn't."

"Well, to be technically correct about it, you held a gun on us, but okay, we'll go with asked," Dimitri laughed.

"Threatened to shoot us," Jake interjected.

"I know and I'm sorry." She cut up her steak while continuing to speak. "It's just that you saw Chaz. They're crazy. I knew they'd follow me and I didn't want you to get hurt. It was already my fault that…"

"Bygones, cher," Dimitri assured her. "Tomorrow's a new day."

"Speaking of tomorrow, the plane should be here around twelve. We'll fly to New York and then we'll be back home, hopefully later tomorrow night." Jake picked up his glass of wine and took a deep sip.

"I've gotta call Ilsbeth," Dimitri said, his voice growing serious.

"I'm sure she's got some spell that'll help you," Jake offered.

"What's wrong with you?" Gillian asked quietly, almost regretting her choice of words. She'd felt a touch of the evil on his wolf. She'd healed him but knew it was only temporary.

"Nothing's wrong with me…nothin' date number three won't fix, anyway," Dimitri joked.

"No, there's something. Your wolf…there's something in you…"

"I don't know," Dimitri said, cutting her off. "I helped a friend with a bit of otherworldly business. Seems I've picked up some kind of traveler, for lack of a better term. I couldn't shift that night on the beach. I'd had trouble before that, though. I thought that by getting away on vacay…maybe I'd get my mojo back. Didn't work out so well…except for you."

"Whatever it is, the witch better send it the fuck back because this not shifting bullshit isn't going to go over too well in a pack. I hate to break it to you, D, but it's not like you can go on being beta if you can't shift."

Silence fell as Jake laid the cards on the table.

"Now's not the time or place to discuss this," Dimitri growled.

"Just sayin'….maybe we should go to New Orleans first."

"We've gotta get Gilly home and then we can go home."

"I can get a ticket at the airport and fly by myself," she suggested. Gillian didn't want to see the two friends fight. She could get back to New York just as easily on a commercial flight. She had to see Jax as soon as possible. As painful and awkward as she expected it to be, she had to talk to him in person.

"No," both wolves said at the same time.

"Why not? Nothing's going to happen to me on a plane." She bit down on another piece of the rare meat.

"We have no idea who's going to be on that plane or who's going to be waiting for you when you get off. Not happening," Dimitri said flatly.

"After what I just saw back in that desert…just no," Jake agreed.

"Jake's right. I've been around a long time, and I'm tellin' ya that what that Alpha did...he was going to beat you...with a bull whip. And it wasn't some kink fest out there...no, he meant to torture you."

"So you'd submit?" Jake asked, attempting to conceal the utter disgust on his face.

"Yeah, that and he wanted to punish me for killing his wolves. But it was self-defense. When he'd captured me..." Her voice faltered and she lowered her eyes.

"I'm not sure what's so important about you. Sorry, don't take that the wrong way. It's just that it doesn't make much sense...a pack of wolves goin' after a tiger." Jake paused. "Hell, I guess it doesn't matter. You traveling alone back to New York isn't an option. But D can't travel alone either. No way am I leaving him after what just happened."

"Okay," she said calmly and took another bite of her meal.

Gillian sat quietly listening to the two wolves plan, all the while plotting how she could catch a flight. She reasoned she could use her cell phone to call the airline. In the morning, she'd skip out of the hotel, catch a cab to the airport and be in New York by the afternoon.

As much as Gillian wanted to go with them to New Orleans, she didn't want Dimitri sacrificing any more time helping her. She hated lying to him, but if he didn't seek a witch soon, his wolf would falter to the evil within. Gillian finished eating and looked up, to see both wolves staring at her. They'd stopped talking.

"What?" she asked innocently. Gillian pushed away from the table and stood up, smoothing down her robe. "I'm tired."

"Go ahead, I'll be there in a minute," Dimitri urged.

"What do you mean?" she replied in surprise. *Does he think he's sleeping with me?* A grin crossed his face, and she knew that was exactly what he meant. A date.

"I'll be there in a minute," he repeated, his gaze smoldering.

Gillian took a deep breath, heat rippling over her skin. Whatever they'd started earlier with the kiss was far from over, and damn, if she didn't want to take it further. After everything she'd been through, the thought of being within Dimitri's arms comforted her. She caught a glint of amusement in Jake's eyes and knew that no matter how much he wanted Dimitri home, he also found their emerging relationship entertaining.

"Gilly," Dimitri called as she reached the door.

"Yeah?" She swallowed. Her tiger paced, aware of the sexual anticipation that edged her mind.

"Don't fall asleep without me. I'm bringing you dessert," Dimitri commented with a grin.

"Dessert," she stammered. What was he trying to do to her?

"You know, something sweet before bed. Mama always told me a little sugar washes out the bitter taste of a bad day. I thought you could use some."

"Yeah, okay," she answered, caught off-kilter by his provocative comment. *Oh my God, this man is making me lose every last brain cell. Kinda hard to think when all that's in your head is sex.* He was teasing her, enjoying making her blush in front of Jake. Before she could stop the words, she heard herself flirting in return. "Well, I guess I shouldn't argue with your mama. Hope whatever you bring me has some whipped cream on top."

Gillian held her breath as she entered the bedroom. The door closed, and she rested the back of her head against it, taking a deep cleansing breath. *Holy shit.* This was exactly why she shouldn't be around wolves. Dimitri excited her, but the thought of being with a wolf, making love to him, was beyond her comprehension. She had to fight off her desire to touch him. *I should make him sleep on the couch.* Yes, that would save her from the temptation of entertaining the carnal fantasies that danced in her mind.

Better yet, I should tell him to sleep in Jake's room. Immediately, she pictured the two hot men together in bed and sucked a breath. The image of her wedged between them flashed in her mind. Her pussy tightened and she swore, admonishing herself for indulging the idea for even one second. How long had it been since she'd had sex? Too damn long. Her lack of male contact had to be what was driving her wild thoughts. *Get with the program, girl. No wolves. No Dimitri. No sex.*

Gillian spied her bag that was sitting on the floor. She needed to get home and work things out with Jax. As she picked up her cell phone and looked up the airline, she knew Dimitri would be pissed. But she'd rather him be angry as a healthy wolf, than risk his very being just for her.

Chapter Five

Dimitri cracked open the door, cupping chocolate mousse in one hand as he entered the bedroom. He spotted Gillian's robe, which was lying across the guest chair, and wondered if she'd gone to take another shower. But as he glanced to the bed, Gillian pushed upward to sit, bunching the covers over what he believed to be her naked body.

"What do you have?" Her eyes went wide, spying the decadent confection.

"Ah, cher, if there's one thing you can count on with me, it's that I'm true to my word. Dessert in bed is something we all should experience," he said, climbing onto the comforter. The mattress dipped as he walked across the surface on his knees until he was at her side. He laughed, attempting to balance himself and the delicacy he'd brought.

"You're funny, you know that?" she grinned.

"I'm determined." With surprising grace, he settled next to her. He crossed his legs and gave her a sexy smile.

"I thought you were a beta, not an Alpha," she observed. Despite his status, everything about him screamed dominance. She wondered if he was even capable of submitting.

"I'm beta of Acadian wolves, but then again, you already know that." Dimitri dipped the spoon into the creamy mixture and held it up to her lips. "Eat."

She parted her lips at his demand. Her eyes met his as he slid the mousse into her mouth. She moaned in delight as the rich cocoa coated her tongue. Closing her eyes, she savored the taste and then quickly opened them, realizing the way she must have looked. He'd practically just given her a food orgasm in under ten seconds. *Clever, clever wolf.*

"You distract me," she admitted.

"You like?"

"What's not to like?" Her eyes fell to his mouth and she swiftly looked away. She nervously plowed her fingers through her hair. "You could have killed Chaz…but you didn't."

"And?" He took a bite and licked his lips.

"You could have been Alpha," she stated, accepting another spoonful.

"I'm good right where I'm at in New Orleans. Cali is nice, but it isn't home."

"Don't all wolves want to be Alpha?"

"No. Sometimes being Alpha chooses us, but it's not something we always choose. My Alpha, Logan, didn't want to be Alpha…but that's a story for another day."

"But out there in the desert tonight, it was clear to me that you were the smartest, the strongest…"

"You're goin' to make me blush," he teased, shaking his head. It wasn't that he didn't know what he was capable of; he knew all right. So did every wolf in Acadian wolves. "Let's just leave it at this, shall we? I wasn't about to kill Chaz so I could run his pack. I don't want to leave home. I've got my own Alpha and pack."

"Do you submit?" she asked softly. The question seemed innocent enough when she'd thought it yet the air was laced with sexual tension. Her lips curled in amusement.

"The question is, 'do you?'" he replied in turn. "Open."

"Never," she promptly answered, yet her lips widened at his demand.

Dimitri laughed, watching her obey his command. He supposed tigers didn't submit, but things were not always as they seemed.

"What?" she asked. The tip of her tongue traced over her bottom lip. "What's so funny? Do I have chocolate on my face?"

"So you never submit?"

"Of course not. I mean, it's not like I don't take directions when I'm working but I'm not a doormat."

"What about in other ways?"

"What other ways? Wait…are we talking about, you know?" Gillian blushed.

"What do you think we're talking about? Last bite…here you go. Open." Dimitri smiled as she listened to him once again. Perhaps she was incapable of seeing what she was doing. "To answer your original question, I will submit, but only to my Alpha. I do it for the pack. It benefits all of us. We are more powerful collectively than we could ever be on our own."

"Well, I guess that makes sense, but I'm not in a pack. Tigers don't do packs."

"But wolves do."

"Yeah, but I'm not…"

"You're hybrid. Somewhere inside you, your wolf lies in wait."

"No. No, she doesn't," she said flatly. Gillian felt her pulse race at the thought of turning wolf. "I'm a tiger."

Dimitri considered Gillian's denial of her wolf. Maybe she was right. He'd never met a tiger hybrid. It was rare. He'd seen her shift, and she was one hundred percent feline, yet his gut told him there was more. Something about the way she'd already submitted without intending to do so.

"Well, my little kitten, you know what you are. But the lesson for you is that often the strongest submit for reward. Within a pack and in other areas of life as well." *I'd like you to submit to me*, he thought. *Hell, yes…on your hands and knees, with me driving into you from behind.* The fleeting thought was all it took to stiffen his dick.

Noticing a smudge, he reached out, cupping her chin. He dragged his thumb across her bottom lip, catching the chocolate. When she wrapped her fingers around his wrist, Dimitri hesitated, wondering if she would stop him. Instead of resisting, she pressed her cheek into his hand and closed her eyes. Her lips took his thumb into her mouth, licking its tip.

The temptation was too great, Dimitri knew. He'd be taking advantage if he made love to her. His stomach churned, aware that with any other female, he'd bed her and leave her without a second thought. Wolves were sexual creatures, yet Gillian wasn't truly lupine. It wasn't fair to her to let her think that they could have some kind of a long-distance relationship. Exercising what he didn't know existed in control, Dimitri gently pulled his hand away.

Gillian's heavy lids opened, her chest heaving slightly from the exchange. The delicious taste of his skin lingered in her mouth. *Where is he going?* She clung to the sheet as he pushed off the bed. She opened her mouth to speak but held back the words that faltered on her tongue. Never before had she felt so drawn to a man. And for the first time in her life, she didn't care what kind of shifter he was, nor did she care if all she felt was pure lust and nothing more. All that mattered was that this beta called to her heart, causing her breath to catch. The nervous butterflies in her stomach weren't just dancing; these babies were moving full tilt into a heated Paso Doble.

"Where're you going?" Gillian breathed. She blinked her eyes, disbelieving that he'd left her alone.

"I'm just gonna sleep over here for a while, let you get some rest. You've had a tough day," Dimitri mumbled, gesturing to the couch. He set the bowl on the night table.

"Okay," she said softly, disappointed that he hadn't continued.

She settled back down into the mattress, bringing the fluffy white cotton down comforter up to her chin. The weight of the blanket did little to ameliorate the tingling that singed her skin. But she felt as if it somehow hid her true feelings, the desire to make love to the wolf. A deep breath centered her thoughts. It was short lived as she took sight of Dimitri stripping off his pants.

His curved glutes flexed in the dim light. Even though she'd seen him nearly nude when she'd dragged him into bed after he'd been injured, sex had been the furthest thing on her mind. But now? Lust was paramount, coursing through her veins. It was so wrong…so very, very wrong.

She knew she'd be breaking her rules. But it was only one teensy weensy night, she reasoned. Her tiger couldn't possibly have time to decide if she wished to submit, to give herself over to a wolf. In the morning, she'd be off on a plane, never seeing him again. Jax would provide her with protection, and she'd go back to her safe but otherwise uneventful life.

By the time her eyes switched over to night vision, Dimitri had yanked a spare blanket off the shelf, shielding his yummy man-bits, and she threw her head back onto the pillow in a huff. *Seriously?* It was as if someone had just laid him out on a platter and handcuffed her wrists. Even then, she supposed she'd happily use her tongue. Her fists pounded the bed in frustration.

"Can you throw me a…" He was about to say, 'pillow' when a large white mass launched across the room at him. Catching it with one hand, he smirked. *My little kitten has her own case of blue balls?* Satisfaction that he wasn't the only suffering party made his painful erection slightly more tolerable.

Dimitri curled his legs, attempting to jam his six-foot-five body onto the cramped sofa. *How the hell am I supposed to sleep like this all night?* He caught the glint of amusement in her eyes as he struggled to make himself fit into the small space. *Just punishment*, he supposed.

"Comfortable?" she asked through the darkness.

"Yeah. All good," he lied.

"Wow, you do look so relaxed." She grinned.

Dimitri tugged at the blanket, which looked like it belonged in a toddler crib. He blew out a breath and closed his eyes, willing his dick into submission. *Shit, shit, shit.*

"Something wrong?" she asked, the smile evident in the lilt of her question.

"Tell me a bedtime story." Dimitri stared up at the ceiling. *Do not look at her. Resist.*

"A bedtime story?"

"Yeah, come on."

"Once upon a time there was a very lonely girl. She wanted so badly to find love, but she was afraid."

"What was she afraid of?"

"Shh…my story."

"Okay, okay."

"She was afraid of losing herself, her independence. You see she was convinced that if she met the wrong person, she'd never be the same." Gillian stared at Dimitri, who appeared to be avoiding eye contact. "So she built herself a safe world. A bubble."

"Bubbles aren't very sturdy structures. I guess she wasn't an engineer."

"No." Gillian laughed. "No, she wasn't. But the bubble worked for her. It was very comfortable."

"Doesn't sound too exciting."

"It wasn't."

Dimitri listened intently as she spoke. Why would she live a cloistered existence? Why was she so afraid of wolves when she was part wolf?

"But one day, she met someone who made her question what she was doing, even though she'd just met him."

"Did she start living?"

"I'm afraid the story doesn't have an ending. As it stands now, the girl leaves the boy. She's deciding what she should do."

"Wait a second," he said gruffly. "I wanted you to tell me a story."

"I told you one," she said.

"I like happily-ever-afters. Change the ending." He wasn't talking about make believe.

"Yeah, I like happy endings too, but that doesn't mean we always get one," she teased, referring to how he'd ended their romantic interlude.

"Touché. But for the record, I would've been glad to oblige. Being a gentleman isn't easy. I'm hanging by a thread here, darlin'," he replied. Little kitten was still upset that he'd removed himself, he thought. For all the talk about avoiding wolves, it appeared she was interested after all.

"Dimitri?" Gillian wasn't sure why, but she wondered if he was dating anyone. Of course he was dating someone…probably lots of someones, she reasoned.

"Yeah."

"You promise to go see a witch?" She changed the subject, trying to distract herself from the fact that in the course of twenty-four hours she was wavering on her rule not to date wolves.

"Why do you ask?"

"No reason. I just want to see you well."

"Are you saying you care about me?"

"Maybe." She paused. "I felt him, your wolf. I haven't healed many shifters."

"I don't think I want to hear about you being with other shifters if you healed them the way you healed me," Dimitri said seriously. It bothered him to think that she'd been intimate with anyone else yet he knew that she had to have been with other men.

"I've only done it a few times growing up as a teen…easy things like cuts. The truth is that it's really not a super useful skill. Shifters can heal on their own, but hybrids have more difficulty."

"And what you did to me?"

"You were my first. What I meant to say was that you're my first wolf." She bit her lip, recalling how he was attacked. The bleeding wouldn't stop. "I've never gone full contact before. I usually use just my hands. But with you, it wouldn't work. That's why I needed to get you into bed."

"So it wasn't my handsome face that made you take my clothes off? You wound me," he teased.

"No. And if I was going to pick a reason to get you naked, it'd be something else," she laughed.

"Ah…you do like the wolf."

"Maybe," she hedged, shifting in bed.

"You ever been to the Big Easy?" he asked innocently.

"No." Was he inviting her? She shouldn't encourage him no matter how much she yearned to get to know him better. If he were a tiger, hell, any other kind of shifter, he'd be safe.

"Hmm? Is that a 'no', but I'd love to come visit you? Or a 'no' as in hell, no?"

"It's complicated."

"Because I'm a wolf?" Dimitri rolled his eyes, hoping she couldn't see him. Someone had daddy issues. Her father was an Alpha. He didn't understand what her problem was with being around wolves.

"I told you, it's…"

"I heard ya. Just trying to figure this out…Your father's a wolf."

"My father's not alive."

"I'm sorry to hear about your dad. But still, he was a wolf. It's your heritage. Yet you don't want to be around wolves."

"My tiger…it's important she stays away from wolves. That's all I'm gonna say."

"Date number four," Dimitri drawled, noting her evasive answer. If she thought this was the end of the conversation, she was sorely mistaken.

"What?"

"I said, date number four, that's how long I'll give you to come clean about your wolf hang up."

"I don't have a hang up."

"If we're gonna date, you can't lie to me, cher. You've got a free pass for tonight. After that, all bets are off."

"But there's not going to be a date number four," she said, shaking her head.

"See now, that's where you're wrong. There will be another date. And it'll be a proper date. Dinner. Dancing."

"Are you sure you're not an Alpha? Because you're awful bossy."

"You say bossy, I say persuasive."

"You're relentless."

"Ah, perhaps, but I always get what I want." *And I want you.*

"I'm not sure that we should see each other again. My tiger..."

"Date number four. I expect answers before we make love."

"So we've gone straight from a date to sex?"

"Not yet...but I will have you, darlin'," he promised. His cock thickened as he said the words.

Dimitri hoped they'd continue their flirtatious banter, but she'd gone quiet at his statement. He'd purposefully riled her, sensing that she was reconsidering her decision not to be with him. It was only a matter of time before they made love, and the thought made his blood thick with desire.

Sleeping on the sofa might just kill him before the night was through. How stupid could he have been to suggest it? He was regretting his chivalrous gesture. Shifting once again, he pounded the pillow, attempting to get comfortable. Taking his painful erection into his hand, he slowly stroked it in an attempt to assuage the pulsing need.

Gillian squeezed her eyes shut, tucking the covers against her chest. Did Dimitri seriously tell her that they were going to make love? He simply had no idea how impossible that would be. *Consequences*, her mother's voice played in her mind. Her tiger purred, refusing the logical argument. She wanted to cuddle against the delicious beta. Gillian bit her lip and stared up at the ceiling as she wavered. It would be impossible for her to sleep, knowing that Dimitri lay sleeping two feet away from her.

Rationalizing her next move, she told herself that it would be best for both of them, a temporary comfort to get them through the night.

"Dimitri," she whispered.

"Hmm?"

"Come to bed with me."

"I'm not sure that's such a good idea," he growled, his wolf urging him to go.

"You're never going to get any sleep on that tiny sofa," she warned. Scooting over a few inches, she threw open the cover, revealing not only the inviting sheets but her bare thigh.

Dimitri caught sight of her silky skin and groaned.

"I promise to behave," she told him, unsure if she could really keep her hands to herself.

No longer able to keep away from her, Dimitri shoved off the cushions and slipped into the bed. He curled onto his side to face her, their foreheads touching. He deliberately bent at his waist so that his hardened shaft wouldn't accidentally poke her. If he made any kind of contact, it'd be even more difficult not to take her right then.

"Ah, thank you. I can actually feel my legs," he groaned.

"Better?" she asked.

"Better," he confirmed.

Locked in a gaze, Dimitri smiled at Gillian.

"When I get done with the witch, I'm coming to see you," he told her.

Gillian closed her eyes and took a deep breath, but didn't respond.

"Tell me yes."

"To what?" she breathed.

"Date number four. Telling me your secrets."

"I can't..."

"You can," Dimitri countered.

"I...I..." Gillian stammered, mesmerized by his eyes, his voice.

"One date. A real date." Dimitri slid his hand out from under his pillow and cupped her cheek.

"But I live in New York...it's not like we can date," she protested. With her mouth mere inches from his, her heart thumped a hard beat in her chest.

"Say yes," he whispered.

Dimitri knew he shouldn't kiss her, but he was too far gone. Capturing her lips, he gave in to his wolf's inner desire. His tongue swirled against hers and before he knew it, he'd pulled her flush against him. The tip of his cock brushed her stomach and he contemplated how easy it'd be to slide home into her tight heat. The kiss deepened, and he tore his mouth away. Quickly stopping, he flipped her around so that her back was against his abdomen.

One hand reached around her waist, grazing up over her breasts until it was around her neck. He licked her shoulder, biting as he moved toward her ear. His right hand rested on her abdomen, slowly teasing its way downward. Like a predator, he held his prey tightly within his arms, effectively immobilizing her.

"Dimitri," she breathed, brushing her backside against him, seeking his rock-hard shaft.

"Say yes," Dimitri spoke softly into her ear; his hand slid to her mound. As she wiggled her hips in an effort to get him to touch her, he gently bit down onto her lobe as if to warn her. "Say it."

"You weaken me."

"Tell me, kitten. Say it." His fingers flitted lightly between her legs.

"Yes," Gillian cried.

"Yes," Dimitri repeated, gliding his forefinger though her wet lips. He lingered for only a second, pressing a thick digit into her pussy. His hips rocked into her ass as he did so. "Our date is going to be spectacular. How 'bout a little preview?"

"Dimitri…my tiger…"

"Your tiger wants this. And so does my wolf." Dimitri yearned to make love to her, but for tonight, he'd only give her pleasure. Soon enough, he'd have her with no boundaries or secrets.

He plunged two fingers inside of her channel, pumping her slowly. As she began to move her hips in rhythm to his thrusts, he noted the hum of energy over his own skin as if she were magically infusing him with her power. His cock slipped between her legs, and he groaned. Loosening his hold about her neck, he slipped his thumb into her mouth. She sucked and swirled her tongue around it.

"Ah," she managed. "Please."

"Oh darlin', you don't even know how hard I'm gonna fuck you one day. But tonight…" He withdrew from her core, taking her clitoris between his fingers, pinching slightly. She gyrated her hips into his hand, and he applied pressure to her nub, circling it. "You're gonna come so hard you'll see stars."

"Oh Goddess, yes. Harder," she demanded, biting the thumb she'd been sucking.

Increasing the pressure, he circled her taut pearl. His cock pumped between her thighs. He grunted as the urge to come mounted.

"Fuck me, yes, like that. Oh…please. I'm coming." Reaching behind her, Gillian clutched his neck, bringing him closer to her throat. *Mark me*, her tiger roared. Her eyes flew open at the demand. Had it not been for the magic of Dimitri flowing through her veins, she'd have stopped the pleasure right then and there.

"Fuck," he cursed. His orgasm was too far gone to hold back. Plunging three fingers inside her, he sought to drive her over the edge.

Gillian splintered as her climax rolled through her. Breathlessly, she repeated Dimitri's name as she felt the hot spurt of his seed between her legs. He'd come on her skin and she fought the urge to reach for it, to taste and touch it. Like an animal, she'd gone feral in her own lust.

The knowledge that she'd physically solidified her connection with a wolf rocked her. In her soul, she knew things would never be the same. She'd never get enough of Dimitri. She'd let him make love to her, mark her. What they'd done wasn't merely fooling around. This man would make her submit, and she feared she'd gladly do it. Sucking a breath, it was of no use to stifle the tears that began to flow.

Goddess, how she wanted to hide all the conflicting emotions that churned inside her. Never had she let a man restrain her, touch her until she came so hard she thought she'd need resuscitation. Her beast wanted this man to claim her. It terrified and thrilled her, yet reason would win out, she knew. In the morning, she'd leave him, go to New York. Maybe if she put distance between them, the craving for his touch would subside. He'd be better off without her, able to travel directly to the witch to heal himself. By the time he'd rolled her on her side to face him, she'd recommitted to the heart-wrenching decision to leave first thing in the morning.

"Hey, cher. Did I hurt you?" Dimitri asked. He thumbed away a tear from her cheek.

"No, baby," she whispered, cuddling up to lay her head on his chest. Her thigh draped across his. "What you did…we just did…it felt so good. I wish we could stay like this forever." And she meant it, even though she knew they could never be.

"Shhh…get some sleep. We'll talk in the morning," he said, with a kiss to her head.

"In the morning," she repeated. *I'll be gone.*

Chapter Six

"Where the hell is she?" Dimitri asked, flinging open the door of his bedroom. He took sight of Jake, who was busy making out with a pair of long legs that ended in fuck-me shoes.

Dimitri huffed, ignoring the hand that silenced him. Tearing into Jake's room, he found no sign of Gillian and returned to the living area. He coughed in an effort to get Jake to remove his tongue from the blonde's mouth long enough that he could get an answer. When Jake finally released the girl, he shot him a glare.

"What the fuck, Jake?"

"What? Oh, sorry. Jenny, meet Dimitri," he offered with a slick smile.

"Hi-ya," his perky date greeted Dimitri. She gave him the once over from his wet hair down to his toes, settling her eyes on the small towel wrapped around his waist. "Didn't know you had a friend? If I didn't have to get to work, a threesome might've been fun."

"Yeah, not happening," Dimitri barked, irritated that Gillian was missing.

"He's a grumpy one, huh?" she asked with a giggle as Jake kissed her neck.

"Somethin' like that. He's got a tiger in his panties. Sorry, babe, but I gotta help my friend out."

She raised an eyebrow at him.

"No, not like that. He's, uh, looking for a girl."

"Well, I got a friend if you wanna meet at six."

"Sorry, we're outta here today. Maybe next time I'm in Vegas."

"Or I'm in NOLA?"

"You bet," Jake promised, opening the door.

"Thanks for last night, sweetie. See ya round. And you too, big guy," she added with a wave, stopping to whisper in Jake's ear. "Maybe next time. I love tattoos."

"Yeah, maybe," he lied, knowing that Dimitri was out of sorts.

Dimitri paced while Jake said his goodbyes. Where the hell had she gone? When he'd left to go take a shower, she'd been sleeping soundly in bed. She'd given no warning that she was getting ready to fly the coop. Rubbing his scruffy beard, he blew out a breath.

The familiar cadence of his cell phone sounded. Running back into his bedroom, he picked it up off the bed stand and read the message: *Thanks for last night. Sorry to kiss & run. Gotta get back home. Go see the witch.*

Dimitri threw the phone down on the bed and tore off his towel. *Fuck. Fuck. Fuck. She did not just leave me without saying goodbye. Yeah, that's exactly what just happened.* Rummaging through a dresser drawer, he pulled out the same pants and shirt he'd worn the day before, and sniffed. They smelled like blood and wolf…Chaz. He shook his head in disgust.

"Here," Jake said, tossing him a new pair of jeans.

"Where the hell were you?" Dimitri growled, snatching them. He shrugged into the stiff denim, wincing as the rough material nicked his dick.

"Thank you so much, Jake, for getting me new clothes. I feel so much better not stinking like the Alpha pig that I almost killed last night," Jake taunted.

"Fuck you," Dimitri said as a t-shirt hit him in the head. He shot his friend a nasty grimace before slipping the garment over his head. Dimitri glanced down to the slogan printed boldly across his chest in bright gold letters. He shook his head.

"For real?"

"Elvis has Left the Building!" Jake joked, reading it aloud. "The king's the bomb, bro."

"Where the fuck were you? How did you not hear Gilly leave?"

"Uh, for the same reason you didn't."

"I was in the shower."

"Yeah, my guess is that you were strokin' off a case of blue balls in there. I, on the other hand, was making love to my sweet lil' Jenny."

"Showgirl?"

"Too cliché. Travel agent. We met at home. We were busy, making up for lost time and all that."

"I am a goddamned idiot. I should've known she would take off. Come on, if we hurry we can catch up to her." Dimitri grabbed his cell off the bed and pecked at the phone number from where she'd sent the text.

"What are you doing?"

"What does it look like I'm doing? I'm calling her. It's not safe out here. Who the hell knows if New York is safe?" The call went to voicemail and he ended the connection. Sending her a quick text back, he told her to wait at the airport for him.

"Listen, D," Jake began, plowing his fingers over his cropped hair. "I know you're sweet on the tiger but you've got to let her go."

"We're going. Now," Dimitri ordered, sliding his feet into the pair of Vans that Jake had provided. He strode out toward the exit.

"I'm just saying that we can try to catch up with her, but if we don't find her," he paused, trying to keep up with Dimitri as he opened the door and started toward the elevator, "I think she's right. You need to go see Ilsbeth. You're vulnerable."

Dimitri grabbed Jake, shoving him up against the wall. Quickly, he realized his transgression and released him.

"I'm not vulnerable," he denied. *I'm compromised. I'm a liability.* Dimitri's jaw ticked in anger as he mulled over the situation.

Dimitri

"I know this can't be easy, but ya know, Gilly left because she wants you to go home. She healed you and knows that whatever piece of shit evil took your wolf from you the first time could happen again. And then what good are you to her?"

"Let's just see if we can catch up with her." A ding resonated, alerting them the lift had arrived. They entered and Dimitri stabbed at the lobby button with his finger.

"She'll be okay. You saw what she did last night."

"Yeah, I saw, all right. I saw her tied up like an animal for a whipping. If we hadn't gotten there in time, they would have..." *Raped her. Killed her...she'd never submit.* "...hurt her."

"But we did get there, and now she's skipping town to where she'll be safe. She's lived in New York for a while. New Yorkers are tough."

"Badass," Dimitri added, hoping their speculation was true.

"Yeah, that's right. She's tough. Nothing happened to her while she lived there. The danger's here. Chaz would have to have a death wish to go to New York City. You and I both know that Jax wouldn't take kindly to strangers in his town, causin' a ruckus."

"Maybe." Jax Chandler, the New York Alpha, was an arrogant prick who wouldn't have allowed a rogue wolf anywhere near his territory, let alone another Alpha who was looking to attack a shifter.

Still, it rubbed Dimitri the wrong way that Gillian was on her own. He was angrier at himself that he couldn't guarantee that he wouldn't end up mortal, unable to protect his woman. He quickly corrected his runaway thought. *His woman?* Yeah, right. Dimitri didn't keep women like belongings. It was more like he entertained the ladies, no ties, no promises.

His rule may have gotten him in trouble a few times. A certain witch in New Orleans came to mind. But for the most part, women respected his honesty and he respected them. One hundred and twenty years of dating, and he hadn't tired of the revolving door of beautiful ladies who'd warmed his bed. So why did it bother him so much that one gorgeous kitty cat went stray?

They reached the car and his phone buzzed. Another text: *Don't try to come to the gate, baby. Won't pass security w/out a tix. Go see the witch.*

Dimitri huffed, irritated that she'd called him a term of endearment while telling him what to do. *Baby? Baby, my ass.* The girl had a lot of freakin' nerve. Not only did she just leave him holding his dick in his hands, but she'd bossed him no less than twice in the course of the day. Clever little kitty knew how to sneak out and then found bravery behind her texts. If she thought this was the end of things, she was dead wrong. When he saw her next, he planned to spank her ass pink. For the first time in the day, a smile broke across his face.

No matter how cheery she'd tried to sound in her texts to Dimitri, Gillian was scared shitless. She was certain that Chaz would be hot on her trail. On the way home from the airport, she'd considered calling her mom, but knew if she spoke to her that she'd spill every detail about what had happened in California. Instead, she'd sent her a short text, letting her know that she was okay and that she'd returned to New York. Gillian hated lying to her mom, but didn't have the heart to worry her.

Carbon dioxide gushed out of a passing pickup truck, and Gillian choked on the fumes. Her taxi swerved to the curb, and she tossed the driver a twenty. She yanked her hoodie down over her head, and ducked out of the cab, then slid into the shadows of an alley and waited. She wiped the city grit from her eyes, observing the steady flow of pedestrians. Her gut told her to be cautious. Her salary didn't afford her a doorman. She knew that just about any good-looking guy could talk her neighbor, Mrs. Beasley, into letting him into the building. A nice smile and a smooth story was the key to the kingdom.

Deciding a disguise was in order, she lowered her head and hoofed it two blocks to the corner store. As loathe as she was to do it, she needed to change her looks. She sighed, vacillating between her choices. Blonde or redhead? Blondes may have more fun, but something about red hair appealed to her. She pondered her options for only a second, taking care to be cognizant of her surroundings.

Gillian grabbed a box of the strawberry hue, praying she'd chosen wisely. The only other time she'd dyed her dark brunette hair was in high school, and she ended up looking like Ronald McDonald. Instead of fretting, she'd proudly worn it until the roots had grown out. Her mother had fits over the two-toned tresses that graced her graduation pictures. The memory caused her to chuckle in spite of the danger that could be lurking back on the streets.

In haste, Gillian swiped her credit card, and made quick work of getting back to her building. Trekking toward her apartment, she got the distinct feeling someone was watching her. Her stomach clenched, and she glanced over her shoulder and back again to the passing crowd. A young mother hurriedly bustled her children down the sidewalk. An older woman fussed over her toy poodle, who apparently was having trouble doing his business. Gillian jumped as a teenager bumped into her, obviously not looking where he was going as he tapped at his phone. The strangers appeared innocuous, but her instincts remained on high alert. Crossing past the threshold of the entrance, she panted a small breath, relieved that the lobby appeared empty. Tapping in the security code, she prayed she'd make it safely to her home.

Gillian could have won a medal for the world's fastest dresser, because she'd gotten in and out of her apartment in less than thirty minutes. In the time it took to go from brunette to red, she was on her way to see the Alpha. Unsure of how to best approach Jax, she hadn't called him, deciding it would be best to go see him in person. Within seconds of entering the building and asking for her brother, she'd been ushered into the elevator. Glancing up into the small orb on the ceiling, she got the distinct feeling she was being watched. Her eyes fell to the bellman, whose fake snobbish accent told her he thought she was some kind of bottom feeder, who didn't belong in his lobby, let alone in the penthouse. She twirled a strand of her newly dyed hair, and glanced down to her royal-blue toenail polish. She supposed that in her rush to pack, she hadn't taken great care tending to her appearance, but she was merely grateful to have made it safely across town.

Gillian tried not to think about the melancholy that had washed over her when she'd opened her apartment door. She was relieved that there hadn't been a thug waiting for her inside, but the sight of her portfolio on her kitchen table brought tears to her eyes. Although she'd been lucky enough not to lose her wallet and cell phone during her ordeal in the desert, her new camera was lost and that was going to cost her money she didn't have. Replacing it would have to wait, though. Right now, her first priority was securing protection. Security from a family member who didn't even know she existed.

Gillian's heart raced in tandem with the overhead flashing numbers that ticked away. Her stomach lurched as the lift came to a stop. Within seconds, she'd face the Alpha who had the potential to save her. This was either going to go really well, or she'd be out on her ass. Would Jax help her? Would he accept her as his sister? If he did, would he force her to live with him…as wolf? She took a deep breath and tried to halt the tornado of questions that whirled in her mind. A gruff demand brought her out of her contemplation.

"You're here," he grumbled, nodding toward the opening doors.

"What?" she asked, taking a second to steel her nerves.

"I said, 'you're here'. Mr. Chandler is waiting," the bellman announced, extending his arm to usher her forward.

Putting a foot over the grate, she stepped onto the shiny Spanish marble. The enormous modern glass chandelier that hung from the cathedral ceiling captivated her, and she nearly tripped as her shoe slid over the smooth floor.

"Easy, Gilly," she heard Jax say. The rumble of his voice caused her to startle.

"J…Jax." Surprised to hear his voice, she turned her head toward the large sunken living area. The commanding Alpha stood tall behind his beta, Nick, who was sitting on the sofa, stroking a small white wolf who lay in his lap.

Although she knew that wolves thought little of clothing, the sight of them only wearing jeans took her off guard. Both men, with their tan sculptured bodies, looked as if they belonged in the magazine they ran. Gillian's eyes met Jax's and she studied his face, recalling how their eyes were the same shade of gold. Even though she'd rehearsed her speech well, no words left her lips and tears pricked at her eyes.

"Here, kitty, kitty," he taunted, giving her a wry smile.

He knows. "Jax…I…need your help," she managed.

"Come sit. We need to have a chat," he told her, walking around the large red leather sofa. Looking toward Nick, he nodded. "In private."

Gillian slowly moved toward her brother but abruptly stopped as the animal on the couch shifted into a naked woman. Intrigued by the transformation, she watched as Nick kissed her before letting her off his lap. She gave Gillian a sideways glare before traipsing down the hallway.

Stunned at the display, Gillian forgot what she was doing. Being a tiger, she wasn't used to the open sexuality that wolves exhibited. She, too, stripped bare before shifting into her beast, but unlike the wolves, she ran alone. Taking a quick breath, she composed herself and returned her gaze to Jax, who gestured for her to take a seat. Her heavy backpack remained on her shoulders as she sat in the far corner of the couch.

Nick scooted across the sofa until his thigh brushed hers. He sniffed and smiled, and she flinched in response. Yet when he reached over to help remove the straps of her bag from her shoulders, she relaxed enough to allow him to take it. The close proximity of the other wolf brought forth an odd familiarity, making her think once again of Dimitri. She closed her eyes, forcing herself to concentrate. Now was not the time for lust or pipedreams.

"She smells of a wolf," Nick noted, brushing his fingers through her red locks. "And chemicals."

"Well, she is a wolf, isn't that right, sister?" Jax asked, his expression impassive.

"I'm…I'm a tiger. But you know that, don't you, brother?" Sweat beaded on her brow as her anxiety rose, but she refused to show fear.

"A sister?" Nick clapped his hands and laughed. "Now this is an interesting development."

"Indeed, it is," Jax replied.

"How did you know? I didn't say anything…" Gillian stopped speaking and shook her head, feeling both inexperienced and vulnerable. Dammit, she'd been foolish to think she could hide from an Alpha.

"This morning, I got a call from Logan Reynaud."

Gillian stared back at Jax, putting the pieces together. *Logan Reynaud?* She recalled her conversations with Dimitri. He'd mentioned the first name of his Alpha: Logan. Dimitri must have called his Alpha. He'd gone back to New Orleans, all right, but not before making sure she was protected by Jax.

"Dimitri," she whispered. "But how did you know about me…my tiger…about us?"

"Ah well, after you blew me off a few months ago, it got me to thinking. Why would a starving photographer refuse to speak to someone who was offering her the job of a lifetime? So I did a more in-depth background check. Your mother, Mirabel, I knew her many years ago. When my father died…"

"She was devastated…couldn't live here anymore. I don't have any memories of my father…our father…or you."

"It isn't surprising you don't remember. When Alpha died, Father, you were a toddler. I knew you existed, but when Mirabel asked me to leave her alone, I did. I understood that you were a tiger and the dangers that would be presented to you should you grow up around pack. What I didn't expect was that Mirabel would change your name to one I didn't easily recognize. I knew you as Kaitlen. But here you are…Gillian Michel."

"Gillian…it's my middle name. My last is a family name on my mother's side. She wanted to protect me. I didn't even know you existed until we met a few months ago. You have to understand, I've gone to great lengths not to be around wolves. When I told Mom about you, the opportunity, that's when she told me…that I had a half-brother in New York."

"You stopped calling. Wouldn't return my calls. You do know that doesn't go over too well with an Alpha, don't you? Did you really think you could get away with that?"

She gave him a small grin, sensing he was teasing her. She'd thought it difficult, but not impossible.

"It's part of the reason I went to California. It seemed like such a great job, but..." She sighed. "I guess if you talked to, um, Dimitri's Alpha, then you know why I'm here."

"We'll get to that in a minute. Let's be frank, shall we? I know why you don't want to be around wolves. Mirabel, she couldn't shift. She gave up everything for my father. Yet in the end, the gifts she gave him were wasted. He died fighting for all of us during that attack."

"I'm sorry." She'd never known her father but sympathized with his loss.

"I killed his murderer," Jax stated without emotion. "I lost everything. My father. My stepmother. I know what it feels like to mourn. I would never have done anything to compromise your ability to shift."

"I'm relieved that you understand why I can't be around your pack. I do. But I need your protection. If you could just talk to Chaz or do whatever Alphas do...please," she pleaded.

"Jax, I don't mean to interrupt, but when I said she smelled like a wolf, I wasn't referring to her," Nick explained further.

"Well, that's not at all possible. I'm a tiger and you both know that, not that I let people go around sniffing me like a dog. No offense," she added, upset that she could have been so careless as to compare a wolf to a domestic animal. *Shit. This is so not going well.* "I'm sorry.

It's just that I'm afraid. Dimitri almost killed Chaz. I should have done it…I wanted to do it, but the silver…it made me sick."

"Did you just say that Dimitri almost killed the Alpha?" Jax exclaimed.

"Yeah, he could have easily killed him but he released him."

"Isn't that interesting?"

"I don't think he wants to be Alpha. I don't know Dimitri that well, but he seems loyal to his pack."

"Well, I wouldn't say that," Nick laughed. He got up and crossed the room. Slipping behind the wet bar, he rummaged underneath it. "Something to drink? Soda? Water?"

"Beta, be clear with your thoughts. Do you think our sister lies about her relationship with the Acadian wolf?"

"His scent is all over her," Nick confirmed. He pulled out three tumblers and set them on the counter. "Maybe we need something stronger. Wine or whiskey?"

Jax's eyes flew to Gillian, who wished she could cower behind the furniture. Her face grew hot, as she wondered how they could smell him on her. She'd taken a shower, but apparently that wasn't nearly enough to hide the intimacy of their night together.

"It's five o'clock somewhere," Jax quipped, rubbing his chin. "Wine. Bring the bottle."

"I'm not sure what you think went on between Dimitri and me but I'm telling you that nothing happened. Not that I need to report who I sleep with to you." Gillian looked over to Nick. "Wine. Best idea of the day."

"I'm your big brother, kitty cat." Jax smiled and raised an eyebrow at her.

"Very funny. Thank you," Gillian said. She gladly accepted the filled glass that Nick handed her. Taking a sip, she thanked the Goddess for grapes.

"You do know what happens if you mate with a wolf?"

"Mate," Gillian choked, spitting out her drink. "Who said anything about mating?"

"You carry his scent. That means you've been intimate," Jax noted.

"Oh my God, do you wolves have no secrets?"

"This is our nature. Besides, a simple review of the facts would tell me you care about him. You saved him from certain death. He reciprocated. You left without him. Now that I don't quite understand, but and this is a big but, he specifically had Logan call me to tell me everything and to request protection on his behalf. It's a very unusual circumstance for an Alpha, one in a state hundreds of miles away, to call another Alpha to ask for protection for an individual who is not even in his pack. He is now indebted to me, you realize? Of course, I owed him one, but nonetheless, this is a sacrifice on his part."

Gillian sat silent. She hadn't needed him to summarize the past seventy-two hours for her to tell him that she cared about Dimitri. But as she sat quietly, her beast purred at the thought of seeing him again, yearning to have him inside her, his mouth and hands taking whatever he wanted. One night would never be enough.

"Are you listening?" Jax asked.

"Yes, sorry, I just was thinking."

"Good, I want you to think, because Mirabel lost her ability to shift when she mated with my father. I'll admit, I don't know the details. Perhaps she denied her wolf and that is why. But nevertheless, there was a sacrifice. Her tiger died."

"Don't you think I know that?" Gillian responded, frustrated with her predicament. She missed Dimitri, and despite her otherwise good judgment, she knew she'd end up in his arms again.

"This thing with Chaz…you're in deep, lil' sis. What exactly made you think you could travel to Cali, into another wolf's territory, without notifying him?" He changed the subject.

"It was supposed to be a job. Technically, I'm wolf, I know that. But Jax, I'm a tiger. You haven't seen me yet…but believe me, Chaz sure as hell did."

"What did he do to you?" Jax asked softly, knowing that she'd been attacked.

"You don't want to know," she said, unconsciously rubbing her shoulder where he'd bitten her.

"We're family, Gilly. We may have been alone before, but no longer. What did he do?" he continued.

"He wants to mate with me. He tried to mark me," Gillian admitted. She glanced up to Nick, who left the room, and she swore she heard him growl. "It didn't take, though. If you know how it works, then you know I've got to choose who I mate with. He knew I was tiger but he underestimated my abilities. I shifted, killed his wolves and escaped. But he tracked me down...that's how he found Dimitri."

"Ah yes, that part of this story is quite interesting. One minute he can't shift, the next he overpowers an Alpha."

"That night on the beach...I healed him."

"Yes, I do recall Mirabel had that ability as well."

"It's not a big deal really. As I told Dimitri, not many shifters actually need help recovering from an injury. But he did...and it worked," she recalled.

"And the desert? What did they do to you?" Jax pressed.

"Stripped me." Gillian lowered her eyes. It wasn't her fault, she knew. Yet she was embarrassed that she'd been caught, tortured. "He was going to beat me...make me submit."

"Sister, I'm very sorry for your ordeal. Good and evil exists in all beings. I swear to you from now on, you'll be protected. As always, I have a plan. But first things first....Nick," Jax called into the open foyer.

The hairs on Gillian's arms stood up, waiting on the beta. A painful grunt tore into the air, and she sprung to her feet to view the source. Two large men, shackled in the arms of guards, stumbled into the foyer. She recognized them as two of the wolves who'd attacked her in the desert. Her chest pounded, adrenaline flooding her veins. *What are they doing here?*

A caustic mixture of fear and hate seized her. The assailant who'd dragged her from her car was tall, with the musculature of a body builder. His eyes locked on hers as he exuded venomous hostility. She could tell he wanted nothing more than to kill her, but despite his huge size, Jax's wolves easily held him in place. His partner, who was of smaller stature, was badly beaten; a red welt formed around his eye and blood dripped from his lower lip. Tears pricked at her eyes as she realized he was the same person who'd stripped off her clothes.

"You're safe, Gilly. Breathe," she heard Jax tell her. He placed his hand on her shoulder.

"Jax...what's happening?" Gillian asked, looking at her abductors and back to her brother. "Where did they come from?"

"I picked them up a block from my place. They knew you'd come to me for protection. Probably hoped they could nab you again before you got here."

"But how would they know I'd come to you? Oh my God, I knew I felt like I was being watched. I think they may have been at my apartment," she rambled. Unable to control her anger, Gillian's tiger roared to attack, smelling blood in the air. The desire for vengeance grew strong. Certain she could kill them, Gillian kicked off her shoes, readying to shift.

"No need, sister," Jax cajoled, stroking her arm gently. "You're under my protection now."

"But Jax...they won't stop. Let me kill them," she protested.

"The need for revenge is sweet only in the moment. One must consider the big picture. These mongrels are but insignificant links in the pack chain of command. Nick," Jax called to his beta, nodding for him to come take his place by his sister.

Gillian rooted her bare feet onto the cool tiles. She fisted her hands tightly, fingernails digging into her palms. *Stay calm. Stay calm. Stay calm.*

Nick obeyed, flanking Gillian. He gave her an understanding smile and reached for her hand. He loosened her balled fist until she allowed him to put his fingers in hers.

"What we must do is address the source…the cause of your difficulties. The root of the problem, if you will." Jax strode over to the tall, muscular wolf and pinned him with a cold stare. "This man, he attacked you? Was going to allow the Alpha to beat you?"

"Yes. He took me." She nervously licked her lips, itching to shift. She'd never asked for permission to do so, but it was as if her tiger knew her brother was Alpha, acquiescing to his request to stay human. "He dragged me from the car…by my hands and hair. Held me down."

"You attacked my sister?" Jax growled at the wolf.

"Fuck, yeah. She killed our wolves…she deserves to die. If my Alpha didn't want to mate the bitch, I'd kill her now," he challenged, glaring at him eye to eye.

"Now that is rude," Jax said, glancing at the other prisoner, who lowered his eyes in submission. "You see, there's an order in a pack. And guests, I'm afraid they're not excused from rules."

Gillian jumped as the large wolf ripped his arms away from his guards and lunged at Jax's throat. Nick put his arm around her shoulders, keeping her from going toward her brother. She screamed, watching as Jax punched his entire fist into the chest of the wolf. As he retracted his bloodied arm, a beating heart pumped in his grip. A loud thump reverberated throughout the home as the dead man hit the marble.

Even though Gillian had killed as tiger, she'd never seen such a violent act. She closed her eyes, willing the vomit rising in her throat to retreat. Within seconds, she'd composed herself, nausea replaced with relief. She wasn't normally an aggressive person, but she was glad that her attacker could no longer harm anyone.

Jax approached the smaller wolf, who'd urinated at the sight of his friend's death. Opening his palm, Jax rolled his wrist and the crimson organ fell to the floor with a splat.

"Don't worry, friend," Jax assured him, tilting his head. As if he'd tacked a fly to an insect board, the Alpha observed his work. "You'll live. And you're going to go back to California with a message for your Alpha. Are you listening?"

"Yyyyyesssss," he stuttered.

"My sister, Gillian Michel, is off limits. Tell your Alpha that not only does he not have my permission to pursue a mating," Jax paused, well aware that the bomb he was about to drop would shock his sister. He wished he didn't have to take such extreme measures, but considering what they'd done to her in the desert, the California Alpha wouldn't be deterred easily. He blew out a breath and continued, "My sister is going to be mated. To the beta. I will be announcing it tomorrow night but now you can save me the trouble."

"What?" Gillian gasped. *Did he just say I'm going to mate his beta?* She glanced at Nick who wore a huge grin as if he'd won a giant stuffed panda at the fair.

"Gillian is to be mated. She has chosen. So you see, she is no longer available. Do you understand?"

The wolf turned his head away, refusing to answer.

"You will tell your Alpha! Do you understand?" Jax yelled, shoving him up against the wall.

"Yes," he cried.

"Get him outta here," Jax ordered. "And clean up this mess. You two...my office, now."

"What just happened?" she asked. Jax silenced her with a hand and pointed down the hallway.

Gillian shook her head, trying to wrap her mind around what her brother had said. Did he seriously think she would choose to get mated just to keep an Alpha from kidnapping her? *He's out of his damn wolf mind if he thinks that's happening*, she thought.

As Nick pulled her into Jax's office, she wished she had stayed with Dimitri. She'd never really needed anyone besides her mom before, but her feelings toward her beta hadn't faded like she'd expected. She knew it was irrational, but she had to see him again. When this was all over, she swore to herself that she was getting on the next plane to New Orleans.

"I apologize for killing that wolf," Jax began, but Gillian interrupted him.

"I would have killed him myself, but still…the way you killed him." She stopped herself from chastising him. He was an Alpha. He could do whatever he wanted, she knew. She held her palms up in the air, surrendering, and then raked her fingers through her hair, forgetting that she'd shortened her locks. "No judging. I will not judge you, okay. But Jax, I'm not mating with Nick."

"Tomorrow, I'm going to announce that you're to be mated to the beta. We'll do it at one of the magazine events. The press will be there," he replied, unfazed by her reaction. Snatching a decanter off his desk, he poured himself a shot of whiskey and downed it. Refilling his own, and two other glasses, he fell back into his leather chair and slid the tumblers toward her and Nick. "Sit."

Gillian was too tired to argue and did as he asked. Reaching for the liquor, she gladly took a healthy swig as if she were a pirate.

"No," she coughed, the amber liquid burning her esophagus. While she was unable to speak, Jax was quick to contradict her.

"Yes. Even the announcement probably won't keep this asshole from coming for you. I'm thinking that the best we can hope for is that he'll come to New York, and I'll kill him here. Worst case, he kidnaps you back. This is serious shit, Gilly. He wants your gift."

"But I can't mate…"

"Of course, I know you can't mate with Nick. We're just going to lead him to think you're with him," Jax explained.

"If we're lucky, he might give up," Nick offered.

"You think so?" Gillian asked.

"I don't know Chaz very well, so it's hard to say. It won't hurt that I killed his wolf. He'll know he's in danger if he comes here or sends anyone to get you," Jax speculated. "But for now, this is the best plan I've got to keep you safe. I know you're not going to like this but you'll need to stay here with me. I'll keep the pack members out of the house."

"But my work…"

"Congratulations. You're officially employed at ZANE. Staff photographer. I was getting ready to offer you a job before you stopped calling anyway. When you go on shoots, I'll send protection. If you don't want wolves, I'll get other security."

"Jax, I can never repay you for your help," she whispered, staring into the bottom of her glass.

"Repay me? Why would you ever even think that? You're my sister. We're family, G."

"G?" she laughed.

"Hey, I owe you a few silly nicknames. Lost time and all that." Jax shoved himself up from his seat, and approached Gillian. He took the glass from her hands and pulled her up into an embrace. "When and if you decide you want to mate for real, I'll be there for you. But until then, I'll keep you safe, okay? You're family…the only family I have."

"Family," she agreed, grateful for her big brother.

Gillian hugged Jax, still apprehensive about their plan. With her budding feelings for Dimitri, she wasn't sure she could pull off a lie. Her beta would never understand that she was just pretending. She was sure that she'd have to at least touch Nick tomorrow night and there was a good possibility he'd kiss her. Her tiger paced, distressed by the idea of another man's hands on her skin. Gillian yearned for Dimitri, the only wolf she desired. The craving burning in her chest reminded her that she was growing precariously close to breaking every rule she'd ever known.

Chapter Seven

Dimitri lay nude on the cold slab of concrete, staring up at the stars. Two dozen chanting witches circled him, and he pondered why the sight of the naked women hadn't even caused so much as a twitch of his dick. He should be focusing on healing his wolf, he knew, but it bothered him that he wasn't feeling the slightest bit aroused during the skyclad ceremony. He was a red-blooded wolf, after all. Suspecting the tigress was the cause of his erectile dysfunction, he planned on calling her as soon as Ilsbeth set him loose.

With Gillian's scent ingrained in his mind, he couldn't shake off the attraction he felt for her. He'd been so pissed off that she had slipped out of the hotel room and hopped a plane to New York City, that he'd called Logan on their flight home. Caring less whether she wanted to be around wolves or not, Dimitri knew that Jax Chandler would see to her safety. Dimitri had asked his Alpha to call in the favor for him directly, so there'd be no misinterpretation of the request. He'd come clean with Logan, telling him every detail of the trip, including their romantic tryst the night before. Like brothers, they kept no secrets.

After he'd hung up, he'd nodded to Jake, pretending as if he'd washed his hands of Gillian and the west coast danger they'd faced. Lying to himself wasn't his usual style. Dimitri was honest and straightforward in all aspects of his life. But at no time had a woman gotten under his skin the way Gillian had. Still, it made no sense to him, as he really didn't know her.

True, they'd saved each other's lives. He knew well enough that tough battles had a tendency to forge deep friendships within pack. But this was something more, something causing his wolf to howl in distress, knowing she was on her own without him. At no time had his wolf cared one way or another who he'd bedded. The scary part was that he hadn't even made love to her yet. Oh, but he planned to one day, hard and all night long. Maybe that was his problem, he mused. If he could just have sex with her, then he'd get it out of his system, move on and come back and ask for another 'healing ceremony' from the witches.

A smile crossed his face as he heard the words of Marvin Gaye run through his mind. *Sexual healing?* He was pretty sure Ilsbeth, the sexy head witch, would be happy to give it to him. Sure they'd had somewhat of a disagreement when he'd refused to see her exclusively, but she'd still agreed to try to heal him. When they'd had their falling out, he'd given her a tuft of his wolf hair, hoping to mend their friendship. In return, she'd given him the cold shoulder a few weeks ago. Today, however, when he'd shown up on her doorstep, begging for help, she'd welcomed him with open arms.

As he glanced to his right, she gave him a small smile, wearing nothing but her birthday suit. He sucked a breath as she approached, wishing that for one second he could put Gillian out of his mind. *Naked women everywhere but not a drop to drink. What was the saying? Not women, it's water*, he laughed to himself. Regardless, he should have been hard as a rock by now. Several witches approached him and began to brush anointing oil over his skin. Ilsbeth, at his head, reached forward, her taut nipples grazing his face as she leaned to smear the earthy-scented mixture from his temples to his abdomen, clear down to the crease of his groin, where his torso met his legs.

Her fleshy nubs rubbed across his open lips. Panic seized him as the realization hit that he hadn't even needed to resist the temptation to suck the pink tips he'd once coveted. His limp cock hung heavy on his leg, despite the fingers that massaged tincture into his inner thighs. *Holy hell. No fucking way.* Like lightning striking down a tree, he knew instantly his promiscuous bachelor days had been decimated.

Something was terribly wrong. Dimitri screwed his eyes tight, attempting to concentrate on finding a solution to the quagmire. *Could Gillian be my mate? How could this happen? Tiger wolf hybrids don't mate wolves, do they?* Goddess almighty, this was exactly why Gillian didn't want to be around wolves. She'd been afraid something like this could happen to her. He wasn't sure why she wanted to avoid being mated but he sure as hell knew why he did. Dimitri had never tired of his endless nights with blondes, redheads and brunettes. His lovely rainbow of ladies had all just come to a screeching halt, the epiphany hitting him as a bevy of beauties pranced around him in their glory. Some might call it poetic justice while others might call it fucking bad luck.

Maybe he was wrong about Gillian being his mate. Maybe he was just experiencing some sort of performance anxiety. Stage fright. He wished he could laugh this one off, but his stress wasn't eased at all by the sound of Ilsbeth's voice calling him.

"Dimitri," Ilsbeth said softly, running her fingers through his hair.

"What?" he asked, blinking his eyes open.

"You okay?"

Dimitri wiped his hand across his mouth and noticed everyone was gone. Only Ilsbeth remained. The empty garden courtyard smelled of the fragrant sweet bay magnolias and wisteria. The white and purple petals reflected the moonlight like a mirror. Crickets serenaded them as silence fell. Warm spring nights often led to romance on the bayou, and Dimitri hoped that whatever conclusions he had about having a mate weren't true.

"Where is everyone?" he asked.

"We're done. They're going home. How do you feel? Can you stand up?" Ilsbeth stroked his cheek. "Let me help you."

Was she seriously talking to him like he was an injured animal? Didn't she realize he was the kind of wolf who others feared, one who could be Alpha any damn day of the week if he wished? Bristling with angst from his revelation, he knew he was redirecting his anger at her, when the real problem was his mate. *Mate?* He shook his head and shoved up off the table.

"I'm good."

"You sure?"

"Yeah, thanks."

"We need to talk, Dimitri." Ilsbeth gracefully glided around the altar. She reached for his knees. When he didn't flinch, she pushed his legs open further, sliding her body between his thighs.

"Hey there, cher," Dimitri laughed.

He wasn't sure if he was uncomfortable or not that she'd pressed her belly against his softened cock. As her arms laced around his neck, he settled his hands on her hips. The look in her eyes was recognizable as the lust they'd once shared and he found himself unable to hold her gaze. He wrapped a finger around a lock of her platinum blonde hair and tugged, lifting his eyes with a small smile.

"Whatcha want to talk about. How bad is it?" he asked.

"I shouldn't have let you leave for San Diego," she admitted. "I feel like this is my fault."

"You knew?"

"Something just felt wrong when you came out of that hell hole, but you know, I couldn't be sure. I was so mad at you...I just, I didn't take time to find out."

"It's not your fault, darlin'. You didn't do this. Now stop beating around the bush. What's the prognosis?" Dimitri knew that whatever Gillian had done to heal him had only been temporary. By the time he'd landed in New Orleans, he could feel his ability to shift starting to slip again.

"It's not gone, Dimitri. What we did tonight, it'll only keep the evil at bay for so long. Maybe a week. Maybe less."

"What the hell is it?"

"It's not possession, if that's what you're worried about. It's more like a parasite, eating away at you...your wolf. I need a stronger spell to get rid of it entirely, but I don't..."

"You don't know if you can do it?"

Ilsbeth nodded. Surprising Dimitri, she pressed herself into his arms and laid her head on his shoulder.

"You can do this. You're the most powerful witch I know."

"I have something you can take...a tonic of sorts. I made it earlier today, using your own hair, the sample you gave me before this happened to you."

"Okay, so I'll drink it or rub it, whatever you want me to do with it until you find a spell that works."

"It may take a while. Maybe you should stay here with me," she suggested. Lifting her head, she pressed her cheek against his. "I can be there in case the tonic stops working…to help you."

"Now you know that's not a good idea. I've got to be with Logan," he hedged. Dimitri considered that he could make love to Ilsbeth if he wanted to have her. Even though she was bare in his arms, he felt no hint of desire.

"I want to help you," Ilsbeth breathed, moving her lips to touch his. Desperation laced her voice as her eyes met his. "I may not be able to cure you tonight but I can keep this from killing your wolf…I promise."

"I need to find a way to end this…permanently," he said. There was a time when he couldn't get enough of Ilsbeth, but she wanted too much. And now with her in his arms again, all he could think about was the woman he'd only known for two days, *Gillian*.

"Please Dimitri. Just think about this…us…we could be good together."

Before he could stop her, Ilsbeth pressed her lips against his. He thought that he should force himself to kiss her, to prove his theory wrong. But as he tasted her, both his mind and wolf revolted, solidifying what he'd suspected. He'd always known that Ilsbeth wasn't his mate. She'd been a friend and lover but nothing more. And what they'd shared, once upon a time, was truly over. He pushed her away, shaking his head.

"What? Why are you stopping?" she asked, breathlessly. As she attempted to fall into his embrace, he held her at bay.

"I can't do this…you and I, it's over. I'm sorry. I'm so damn sorry. I shouldn't have let you…I've gotta go. Just give me whatever mojo juice you've concocted and I'll be on my way. Where are my clothes?" Dimitri pushed up to stand on the grass, and gently pried her fingers off his arm. *Goddess, how I've fucked this up.* He felt terrible for letting her kiss him, for leading her on, unsure whether he even had or not.

"Where are you going?" she said, her voice laden with anger.

"Look, Ilsbeth. Whatever we had a few months ago was great while we had it, but it's over. You and I both know it's not going to work out. You know that despite your snarky remarks a few weeks ago, I still care about you. I just can't," he gestured back and forth with his hand, to her and to his chest, "I can't do this…have a relationship. There are things going on with me. Things you don't know." *Like that I've got a mate.* "I need your help, but I'm not going to sleep with you and go and make things worse between us."

Dimitri crossed the courtyard, locating his clothes on a hammock. He picked up his jeans and shoved his legs into them.

"Fine. Have it your way. But when you can't shift again, and you need help immediately, don't be surprised when I can't get to you right away. I do have a life, you do know that? I'm not going to come running, just because you snap your fingers. If you stay with me, then I'd be around you more, maybe could work with you to fix this thing that's eating you from the inside out."

"I can't live with you." Dimitri slung his head through the t-shirt and continued dressing.

"Who is she?" Ilsbeth said, grabbing her robe off a nearby chair.

"What?" Dimitri pretended not to hear her as he slid his shoes onto his feet.

"Who is she? The shifter who healed you? You never did tell me. It's an unusual ability to heal others," she commented with a flip of her hair.

"Okay, well, number one, I never told you the shifter was a woman, but yes she is. And number two, you don't need to know who she is because she's not from around here."

"Really? Nothing special?" she asked.

"Ilsbeth, how about we not do this, okay? You and I...we're friends. Some day when you need something, and you know you will, you have in the past, and you will in the future. When it happens, I'll help you. But right now, I need your help, okay? I need you to find the spell."

"You're lying." Ilsbeth stomped out of the garden and returned just as quickly. Holding out her hand, she opened her palm, revealing a small flask.

"What do I do with it?" Dimitri took it from her.

"Well, if you'd stay, we'd have time to discuss this further..."

"Done talkin', cher. Let's have it."

"A couple of teaspoons a day. If you feel like you're losing touch with your wolf, call me. In the meantime, I'll put some calls in to a few people who owe me favors. That should last you a few days, but you'll have to come back."

"Ilsbeth…" He wanted to hug her goodbye. She'd helped him and he appreciated it but touching her again would send the wrong message. He shoved the flask in his pocket. "Thanks for what you did tonight. I wish things were different, but you wouldn't be happy dating me."

"Don't tell me what makes me happy or what doesn't. This isn't over," she warned.

"Thanks again," he said, making no move toward her. She crossed her arms and grimaced, and he took his cue to leave.

Dimitri followed the long outdoor path around the garden to get to his car, not wanting to go through her home. He figured that he'd best get out of dodge before she either hexed him or attempted to seduce him again. Ilsbeth, one of the most powerful witches on the east coast, was not one to be trifled with.

Dimitri had known Ilsbeth for over sixty years, and they'd weathered many a storm together, but he never trusted a jealous woman, let alone a jealous witch. Green with envy could get you turned into green mold if you rubbed her the wrong way. The only reason he was getting off without harm was because she cared for him. He'd pissed her off well and good tonight, and he knew she suspected that he fancied another woman. No matter what she thought, he wasn't going to tell her anything about

Gillian, not until he knew the truth about whether or not she was his mate.

In the face of not knowing for sure, he wasn't going to admit his suspicion to anyone yet. Logan would know instantly if he had a mate, as would most of his friends. It would be hard to conceal. He needed to go to her tomorrow, confirm what he suspected to be true.

Unlike how Logan had hidden the knowledge from his mate, Gillian would be the very first person he told. Dimitri wasn't even sure she'd accept it. She'd already run once. He wouldn't be surprised if the little hell cat tried to go on the lam again. *Fool me once, shame on you. Fool me twice, shame on me*, he thought. He planned on teaching his feisty tigress a lesson or two on submission. He smiled inwardly, knowing he'd fully enjoy the challenge.

As he reached his car, his phone buzzed in his pocket. Reading the text from Jax, he gave a small chuckle. *Ready or not, Kitty, here I come.*

Chapter Eight

Gillian's feet hurt. She shifted again in the painful heels she'd chosen to wear and cursed the personal shopper that Jax had assigned to dress her for the evening. She smoothed down the black strapless couture gown, thankful for the thigh-high slit, which allowed movement in the otherwise skin-tight material. Given her impaired mobility, she felt unusually vulnerable.

She wrapped her hands around the brass handrail, and glanced down to the theater patrons who were busily taking their seats. Even though felines weren't typically afraid of heights, she tightened her grip, revealing that the human side of her feared the very thing her beast craved. But she knew it wasn't just the distance from the floor causing her stomach to tie in knots.

Gillian had thought of a million different ways to tell Dimitri that Jax would be announcing her mating to his beta. Jax had explained that this evening's event was for the magazine, which employed both humans and supernaturals. Although mortals and wolves were well integrated in society, mating was a term used only by the shifter realm. Marriage, on the other hand, would be seen as more socially acceptable to the humans in attendance. Jax had warned her that their engagement would be presented as well, so that all understood his intention.

She'd attempted to reach Dimitri, but he hadn't returned her calls or texts. Waiting alone for Nick to join her, her heart ached. Gillian wiped a small tear from her eye, the disappointment more than she expected. Goddess, she felt so stupid. She'd only known Dimitri for a couple of days, and she'd allowed herself to form an attachment. What had she expected? That he'd come for her like he'd said? That he'd decide to date her after she'd insisted that she wouldn't be with a wolf?

Maybe he'd already found out from his Alpha about her supposed mating with Nick. She shook her head at the thought. It wasn't even a real mating for Christ's sakes, but still, it was being publicly declared. Nick told her he planned to kiss her, insisting that it would be best to make it more believable, and foolishly she'd agreed. ZANE was planning on doing a feature on them, and they needed to make it look real. She could just imagine Dimitri seeing a picture of her kissing someone else, a wolf no less. If she needed a nail driven into the coffin of her fantasy of seeing Dimitri again, an image of her locking lips with Nick would be the hammer.

She heard footsteps behind her, and assumed Nick had finally come up to join them. Earlier, he'd accompanied Gillian to her seat. He'd left momentarily to check with the guards, explaining that although none of Chaz's wolves had been spotted, they expected he'd send in humans to report back to him. Lilac scented perfume alerted her that she'd been wrong about who'd entered, and she turned to the source.

"What are you doing here?" Gillian asked. The woman who she'd seen curled on Nick's lap sidled up next to her. She wasn't sure of the relationship between her, Jax and his beta, but sensed hostility from the second the woman had shifted, back in his apartment.

"I'm Star," she announced, affording herself the view below. Never making eye contact, she presented herself with an air of entitlement.

"I'm Gillian."

"I know who you are. Jax's half-breed sister."

"Excuse me?" Gillian's eyes flared in anger.

"Listen, I don't know what's going on with you and Nick, but he's mine, do you hear me? And your brother shares my bed as well. So whatever you've done to get me kicked out of their place, you better fix it or let's just say you might become uncomfortable with your new home." Star flicked her candy-red fingernails, admiring her manicure.

"Are you threatening me?"

"What do you think?"

"I think you're dumb as shit if you think you can threaten a tiger. And must have a death wish doing it where my brother can hear you." Gillian released a small growl but tamped down her cat's urge to shift. *A tasty wolf would be very satisfying right now.* She took a deep calming breath, and her eyes flew to Nick who stood in the doorway.

"Nick darling," Star sang, her demeanor sweet as taffy. She sashayed over to him, her see-through dress tugging at its seams.

Gillian turned her head away from both of them, willing her feral eyes back to their golden hue. She didn't want Nick seeing her lose control, but she knew he'd heard every word she said. Grateful he'd come along, she used the opportunity to compose herself. Patience was a commodity she was running short of, and Jax would be less than pleased if she ate one of his wolves at his elegant event.

She heard Nick dismiss Star, and went to ask him when Jax was supposed to speak. All the attendees had been seated and the lights began to dim, signaling the performance was about to begin. But when she turned around, he was gone. The curtains to the entrance of the booth had been drawn. As she was about to leave to find him, the theater darkened and a single spotlight shone on Jax who stood smiling on stage.

With his typical charismatic and voguish style, he adjusted his tie and waved to several ladies in the front row, who swooned in response. For the first time in her life, Gillian felt sentimental, wishing she'd known her father. Had he been like Jax? Larger than life, lethal with a casual flash of his smile?

He began to speak and she quickly sat in her red velvet chair. Her heart started to beat faster, and she opened her purse to check her cell phone for the twentieth time today. No calls. No text. With no time to wallow in her disappointment, she heard Jax call her name.

"I'd like to welcome everyone to ZANE's celebration of the arts. As you know, ZANE is dedicated to many charitable causes, and all proceeds from tonight's performance and silent auction will go directly to our local chapter of Community Hospice and Service Pets International. This organization primarily helps to house and train animals for local hospices and has recently started to train service animals to work with autistic children and adults. I appreciate your support tonight and also the generous time and donations by the Lyceum Philharmonic who plan a Broadway-themed performance. Please give them a hand for their dedication."

Jax gestured to the director, who came out from behind the curtain only briefly to acknowledge his contribution.

"Before we get started, I'd like to take a minute to indulge in a personal announcement. Many of you in the audience work for or with ZANE, so this will directly affect you. Recently, I've connected with my sister, who happens to be a terrific photographer. She's going to be joining the ZANE team, and promises to bring a fresh eye to future spreads. Please say hello to Gillian Michel. Stand, Gilly," he told her.

Gillian's legs shook as she pushed out of the chair. A light blinded her as she waved, plastering a smile on her face. She thought she'd be sick, embarrassed that she was deliberately about to lie to hundreds of people, that the lie would sever any chance she'd be able to see Dimitri again. She steadied herself by holding onto the railing, and waited for Jax to continue. Nervously, she stole a peek over her shoulder. *Where is Nick?*

"There's my baby sis. And I have wonderful news that I'd like to share, as it appears I'm going to be expanding my family further." The faces of a few of the females in the audience went pale and Jax laughed. "This news directly affects my sister, ladies. No worries…our date is still on for later," he joked.

Gillian waited for him to drop the bomb, and forced herself to open her eyes that she hadn't realized she'd closed. Like watching a scary movie, she couldn't take the suspense and had looked away. Everything about the moment felt incredibly wrong. She contemplated sneaking off to the airport, hopping a plane to some remote island where no one would ever find her. But running wasn't really her style. Even though she'd left Dimitri in Vegas, she'd done it to protect him. Hearing Jax's laughter reminded her that any minute now, her mating to Nick would be announced…that was if Nick actually showed up.

"So as I was saying, my family's about to grow. I'm thrilled to announce her intended mating to someone I'd be proud to call my brother." His declaration was met with several whistles from shifters in the audience. "In other words, she's getting engaged."

The patrons broke out in loud applause and Gillian thought the smile frozen on her face would get stuck. Her dry teeth glued to her lips, the muscles in her cheeks began to hurt.

"Before we get started, I'd like to introduce her mate, her fiancé, Dimitri LeBlanc. Everyone please put your hands together, and wish them a long life together," he told them with a broad smile, and gestured upward to her opera box.

Gillian's knees buckled as she heard Jax tell everyone in attendance that Dimitri was her mate. *Dimitri?* No, she must have heard him wrong. Where was Nick? Bewilderment rushed through her as a large familiar hand wrapped around her waist.

"Congratulations, darlin'," Dimitri whispered in her ear. His hard arousal left no room for interpretation. She gasped at his greeting, and he continued. "What do you say? Shall we put on a show?"

Gillian's heart stopped, hearing his voice. How could it be? What was he doing here? Shocked, her eyes widened as she turned her head to see Dimitri standing next to her. Towering over her small frame, he gave her a dashing smile, turning her legs into jello. Her gorgeous beta, dressed in a tux, casually slid a hand down her back. The well-fitted suit did little to hide his extraordinarily well-built physique, and the sight of him took her breath away. Her mouth gaped open; she was at a loss for words.

"I'll take that as a yes. I do enjoy an audience."

Gillian melted into Dimitri's arms as his mouth captured hers. Her tongue swept against his and she purred in pure joy. She moaned as Dimitri broke his kiss, yet she remained happily within his embrace. Overjoyed to see him, she slid her hands underneath his jacket, relishing his hard muscular body against hers. The taste of him remained on her lips, and she clung to him tightly, remorseful that she'd left him in Vegas. She heard him give a small chuckle and opened her eyes. Remembering that there were a couple of hundred people watching them, Gillian cleared her throat and caught sight of Jax, his eyes pinned on their display. All the while, she never let go of her beta.

"Well, folks, uh, now that we've had our first performance of the night, let the real show begin. I give you the Lyceum Philharmonic," Jax introduced and walked off the stage.

Chapter Nine

Dimitri didn't need more than one kiss to confirm that Gillian was his mate. Goddess, the woman looked stunning in her gown, but all he could think about was peeling it off of her. When Jax had called him with his plan, he hadn't been convinced it was the best course of action. He wanted to see Gillian again and had planned on coming to see her already, but to tell the world he'd found a mate? That pushed him straight out of his comfort zone, not to mention he wasn't sure how Gillian would react to the news.

Just the scent of her had turned his shaft harder than concrete. By the time he'd touched her, it took every ounce of restraint not to make love to her with the lights on. The touch of her hands burned through the thin fabric of his dress shirt and as the lights dimmed, he knew self-control was a lost cause.

The music roared to life and Dimitri guided them to their chairs in the private booth. His hand found her thigh and he gently squeezed.

"Did you just purr?" he whispered.

"Maybe," Gillian laughed.

"You missed me, didn't you?"

"I plead the fifth."

"Something tells me I'm going to enjoy being your mate." He waggled his eyebrows at her.

"I, um, did Jax tell you about…"

"Ah, yes, our great hoax. I'm here, aren't I?" *And it's no hoax, cher. You're my mate.*

Dimitri knew it'd only be a matter of days before the urge to mark her would surface. Fortunately for them both, she'd have to make a conscious choice to accept him, otherwise their mating would never happen. He was torn about this dilemma. On the one hand, he wasn't terribly thrilled about giving up his fun-loving bachelor days. On the other, Gillian drew him like no other woman; the attraction was unbearable. The fact that he'd flown up to New York City to engage in a public fake mating was proof of that.

"I'm surprised Jax called you. My brother…"

"Whoa, step back a second…you have a brother?"

"Jax."

"What about Jax? He's the Alpha of the New York pack. I had Logan call him, to protect you. Then Jax texted me last night."

"Yes, Jax." She looked out into the theater for Jax. He caught her gaze, nodded and gave her a knowing smile. She leaned back into her seat, realizing that Dimitri hadn't known about her family ties. "Dimitri...you do know that Jax is my brother?"

"Now that is an interesting development," he quipped.

When Jax had contacted Dimitri directly, asking him to assist with Gillian's protection, he'd suspected that the Alpha knew she'd met her mate. Even if she'd taken a shower, it was likely his scent was all over her skin. He'd have known they'd been intimate, that their relationship involved more than saving each other's lives. But Jax was her brother? That was a surprise. Nonetheless, it wouldn't deter him in the least from pursuing her.

"I take it you didn't know," she said softly.

"You guessed correctly, but it doesn't matter. Jax asked me to be here, and I already had the flight plan in before he called."

"You were coming...to see me?"

"Hell, yeah. Date number four. Although I'm afraid I won't be able to find out your secrets while we're here."

"No? Why not?" She smiled.

"Because making love to you is the only thing on my mind, cher."

"Here?" she whispered, her eyes widened.

"Here and now," he confirmed.

"But there're people down there...shifters...Jax. He'll know."

"And the problem is?" His fingers began to bunch up the fabric of her dress.

"Someone could hear us...scent us."

"You know what I love about these booths? They're nice and private. The folks across from us can barely see us...and so what if they do? This wall here in front of us, it's very handy." He tapped his palm on the rail.

Dimitri stood and lifted her chair, sliding it into the shadows. A deafening crescendo filled the air as the orchestra finished their first piece. As it ended, the theater went dark and Dimitri knelt before her. He gripped the hem of her dress and slid it upward, exposing her legs. Pressing his forehead against her knees, he heard himself groan in delight.

"Open," he ordered, his fingers pressing between her legs.

Dimitri caught the look of surprise in her eyes, but she obeyed, her thighs falling outward. His hands drifted over her smooth skin until he reached the edge of her lace panties. With his forefingers, he traced the rim down to her core, finding her drenched with arousal. Slipping under the fabric, he glided his fingertips over her mound until he was at her hips. Slowly, he dragged her thong down, until it hooked over her heels and he shoved it into his suit pocket.

"You're beautiful," he said, pressing his nose into her sex. "And mine."

Using only his tongue, he licked open her pussy, dragging the tip over her clit. With his thumbs, he separated her folds so that he could have better access to his prize. He laved around her swollen nub, never directly making contact. As her hips began to undulate in response, he hummed against her flesh.

Removing a hand, he sucked two of his fingers, and swiftly plunged them deep into her hot channel. In tandem with the music, he licked at her clitoris, curling his fingers against the thin strip of nerves inside of her. Her fingernails dug into his shoulders. He glanced up to her face, and caught her staring at him, lost in ecstasy. There was no one in the room as far as either of them was concerned.

Taking her swollen bead into his lips, he gently sucked and tugged. Gillian moaned as her pussy tightened around his fingers. Adding a third finger, he plunged in and out of her, until he felt her shake in release. Her juices flooded into his mouth as she clutched the back of his head, pressing his face to her clit.

Wrenching himself away from her, he stood, took her hand and led her to the back corner of the darkened room. In a theater full of shifters, they'd be heard, but in the recesses of the alcove, they wouldn't be seen. Roughly spinning her around, he unbuckled his pants and took out his rock-hard arousal. Gillian braced her hands against the wall, panting with desire. Dimitri stroked his dick, seed leaking from its tip.

"I'm going to fuck you, Gilly. You want this?" Dimitri prayed she'd say yes, but he wouldn't go forward if she didn't agree.

"Yes, please....don't stop," Gillian found herself begging. Her head spinning with lust, she needed him inside her.

Dimitri wrapped his hand around her waist, bending her ass toward him. Finding her wet opening, he guided his cock to her entrance and plunged into her in one smooth stroke. Her hot lubricated core immediately tightened around him almost making him come.

"Jesus, darlin'. You feel so good. Don't move...just hold it a sec." Dimitri felt as if he was a virgin, afraid he'd explode inside of her right away. He took a deep breath, regaining control, and began to slowly move, gradually increasing his pace.

"Dimitri...yes," Gillian breathed.

"You've been a very bad kitty, leaving me in Las Vegas." Dimitri pounded into her, sweat forming on his brow. "I'm looking forward to punishing you for taking off on me."

"Oh God, Dimitri. What? I'm sorry," she said, gasping.

"Goddess, you're incredible. So tight. And your pussy..." He reached to cup her mound, sliding his middle finger through her lips. Using the tip, he flicked at her clitoris.

"Ah yes, there. Don't stop...yes...yes."

Dimitri bent his knees, pumping up into her, harder and harder. His left hand pulled down the front of her dress, exposing her breasts. Gentle wasn't on the menu as he cupped her soft flesh, pinching her hardened nipple.

She cried out, and reached to cover his hand, encouraging him to continue.

"Shhh, baby. You want everyone to hear?"

"You started this," she bit back at him, pressing her bottom into his thrusts.

"That I did, my little wild cat. How about we finish it together?" With his thumb, he applied pressure to her hooded pearl, circling and caressing.

"Dimitri…Dimitri…yes," she began to scream, despite his warning to quiet her moans.

He laughed, moving his hand from her breast to cover her mouth. But as he got near her lips, she bit him, sucking his fingers into her mouth and swirling her tongue around them as if she was giving him head. Between her pussy and mouth, he lost it, thrusting, heaving up into her. She contracted around his cock and his orgasm slammed into him.

Gillian wasn't sure whether it was the taste of him or his touch to her clit, but her senses crashed into overdrive. Her climax spread from her toes to the top of her head. She shook with ecstasy, incognizant of space and time. All that mattered was Dimitri. Her tiger begged her to submit, to let this man make her his. Only a thread of sanity remained, allowing her to refuse the beast.

As the last of the tremors left her body, Dimitri withdrew himself from her. Strong arms turned her around, taking her lips once again. This time, however, his searing kiss was gentle and all too intimate. As their lips lost contact and he carefully guided them to the floor, she rested her head on his chest.

Gillian couldn't believe she'd just made love with Dimitri. It was all supposed to be a great deception, one to lead her to safety. Yet within his loving embrace, she knew this was much more than just a passing one night stand. She craved him, mesmerized by his charming personality and dominant demeanor.

"You okay?" he asked, still catching his breath.

"More than okay. You?" she replied, not at all convinced that what she was saying was true. Sexually, she was spectacular. Emotionally, not so much. Stunned with the knowledge that she was officially addicted to a southern beta, she attempted to hide her obsession, praying it was just a chemical reaction.

Dimitri kept her comfortably wrapped in his arms, but released her hand to look at his own. Finding a perfect set of teeth marks indented into his skin, he laughed. And he'd thought he'd been too rough with her?

"Damn girl, you bit me!"

"Let me see." She took his palm and examined the damage. Kissing it, she spoke softly into his hand. "I'm so sorry I left marks on you. Are you bleeding?"

As soon as the words left her lips, she went still. *Marks. I marked him.* Not in the true sense of the word that a shifter would consider for mating, but she'd taken a step toward it.

"It's nothin'," Dimitri lied. His tiger had bitten him. In her defense, he'd put his fingers in her mouth, but the implications were that she'd considered claiming him. Despite the innocent nip, he suspected she had no idea she was his mate.

They lay quiet for several minutes, allowing the lull of contemplation to set into their minds. Rodgers and Hammerstein floated through the air and Dimitri closed his eyes, enjoying the feel of his mate against his chest. As *Some Enchanted Evening* came to a close, he sighed, deciding it was time to find out the truth.

"Why don't you want to be around wolves?"

"I can't."

"You just did."

"You're the first shifter I've ever been with," she admitted quietly.

"No other wolf? Not even a tiger?"

"Nope." She shook her head, still keeping her cheek close to his shirt.

"We're goin' to be spendin' a lot of time together."

"I suppose we are. This plan of Jax's. I'm not sure it's going to work."

"We've gotta smoke em' out. Chaz is a bad guy. If he hadn't sent those thugs here to find you, this would be a different conversation. I've been around a long time, and it's rare that someone's got the balls to send his pack onto another Alpha's territory. This guy, there's something not right with him. You're not safe."

"I'm glad you came."

"I told you we were going on another date. And as I recall, you said yes."

"I was under duress."

"Since when is coming considered duress?" he asked, his hand stroking over her stomach. Shit, he'd just made love to her and his cock was stirring once again.

"That was amazing."

"Now or then?"

"Both," she laughed. "I've never been able to just let go. I really am sorry that I bit you."

"We're just getting started, cher. I assure you. We're goin' to be doin' all kinds of things."

"I wish I could say I wasn't looking forward to it, but I am." She kissed his chest.

"That's the spirit," he cheered. Dimitri reached up and untied his bow tie, unbuttoning the first few buttons of his shirt. "You're avoiding my question."

"I know. Too many ears here in the theater."

"Fair enough, but you owe me, understood?"

"Yes." She smiled, aware that she wanted to tell him, not because he was asking, but because she wanted a solution to her problem. The beta had been relentless, and now, she feared she couldn't go back to the lonely life she'd once led. In the course of a week, her entire perspective on life had shifted.

It was no use to lie. They'd be pretending to be mates. Gillian had no idea what that really meant. But the warning of her mother's words rang in her ears. *Mate a wolf, your tiger will die.*

Chapter Ten

Gillian raised her head, gazing into Dimitri's eyes. When the music stopped, the curtains to their booth flew open. Jax, the devastatingly handsome Nordic wolf, leered down on the lovers, who smiled up at him in amusement.

"I said pretend to be her mate. At any point, did you hear me say, 'Come up to New York and fuck my sister in public…during one of my company events?' Did I say that? I really don't recall saying that." Jax scrubbed his fingers over his tightly cropped hair. He moved to the balcony, overlooking the patrons who were shuffling into the lobby for the intermission.

"Sorry." Dimitri laughed. He knew that they should have been slightly less conspicuous but the draw of his mate had been too much to resist.

"Sorry? Really? That's all you've got?" He turned to Gillian, who scrambled up to her feet, adjusting her dress. "And you? What's your excuse, little sister? Seriously, every shifter in the room could hear you."

"Um, well, yeah, sorry about that. But technically this is your fault. I mean, what did you expect? You asked Dimitri to come here…to pretend to be my mate." Gillian reasoned that her comeback sounded solid, inexperienced in dealing with her Alpha brother.

"This isn't funny, Gilly," he growled.

Dimitri put himself between Jax and his sister, hiding his grin.

"It's cool, man. Look, the only ones who could have possibly heard us were shifters. You just announced us as mates. You know full well that any shifters wouldn't think twice about us puttin' a little rhythm into a musical number. No harm, no foul."

"You don't know what harm you can do to my sister…"

"Jax." Gillian shot her brother a glare in warning. It was her place to tell Dimitri her secret, not his.

Jax sighed, reconsidering his words. "I asked you up here because it was obvious to me that you already had a relationship with my sister. That, and that you can protect her. Don't make me regret it."

"I swear it on my life, but I'd like to remind you that even though I saved her, she saved me. She's badass when she goes cat."

"I'm sorry, it's just that some of the folks in my pack aren't too crazy about having a tiger stay with the Alpha. They don't trust her. I haven't seen hide nor hair of Chaz's pack and…" Jax paused. Retrieving his cell phone from his inner jacket pocket, he swiped at it with the pad of his finger. "Goddammit."

"What's up?" Dimitri asked. The hard crease in the Alpha's forehead told him something bad was going down. He'd seen that look too many times from Logan, and he knew the shit was about to hit the fan.

"Drive-by shooting in front of my building."

"Not good."

"But this is the city...I know you live uptown, but still..." Gillian argued.

"Something's off. I can't explain this to you, sis, but I just know. It's part of the reason I asked Dimitri to come for you."

"But you killed that wolf yesterday."

"Yes, but the fact that they were able to get in the city unnoticed...it's not safe for you here. I need to stay and sort things out as best I can, and then I'll come for you."

"It could be internal," Dimitri theorized. Someone within Jax's own pack may have known about Chaz's wolves, allowed them to get close to his home.

"I'd like to think it's too early to speculate. As much as I trust you to take care of Gilly, you're not from our pack. So this discussion's done."

"No worries. I hear ya." Dimitri knew that Jax would keep his cards close to the vest. No matter how cordial he'd been so far, Jax was an Alpha for a reason. Dimitri had almost killed one Alpha on the west coast, the last thing he needed was to challenge Jax.

"What are you trying to say?" Dimitri heard Gillian ask. He felt a tinge of sympathy for her. She hadn't grown up around pack, and was clearly having trouble seeing the picture that Jax was drawing.

"You're leaving. Now," Jax said, putting his phone away.

"What do you mean I'm leaving? I just got here. You said I had a job with ZANE. I've gotta work. You can't just cart me around." Her voice grew louder.

"Gilly, it's going to be okay," Dimitri began. He got that she felt out of control. The past week had been hell for her and she sought some peace in the storm. But Dimitri knew that yelling at an Alpha was a bad idea even if she wasn't a wolf. "We're mates. It'd be expected that you'd travel with me, and I with you. You ever been to Mardi Gras?" Dimitri gave Jax a knowing look, hoping he'd throw him a bone.

"That's right, Gilly. We can do a spread for the magazine on Mardi Gras. Maybe a 'past meets future' feature. Talk to locals, get some photos. Help readers who don't live there get a feel for what it's like."

"That's a great idea. There's so much history. We can check out the parades. I know you'll enjoy it."

"Chaz is going to come for me there, you know."

"Yes, he is. And we'll be ready. Believe me, he won't be able to hide in the shadows like he's doin' here. We can always go straight to the bayou if we think the city's not an option. We'll call Logan from the plane, set up a plan of action."

"Nick and I will be down as soon as we clean things up here. I swear it."

Gillian silently resigned herself to the fact that she'd be leaving New York. Wrapping her arms around herself, she nodded in agreement.

Dimitri took off his jacket and draped it over her shoulders. He locked eyes with Jax as he put his arm around her. Understanding passed between them; the Alpha knew she was his mate. Logan would know, too. Dimitri, himself, wasn't comfortable with the idea, but it didn't matter. Gillian could easily choose to reject his wolf, his mark and their mating. Chaz had attempted to mark her, and not even a scar remained. Why would he be any different? They'd made love, but he didn't trust that she wouldn't leave him. She'd been upfront, telling him that she didn't want to be with a wolf. It still hadn't made sense to him, because he'd never heard of a wolf mating with a tiger, not even a hybrid.

Everything about her was different. Too different. She was a loner, never relying on others for hunting, friendship. Even if every issue resolved itself, there was the huge elephant in the room; his pack. Would his pack accept another shifter into their lives?

***

Gillian tensed as they pulled onto the tarmac and the deafening engine of the Learjet roared to life. She carefully navigated the steps up into the cabin, the warmth of Dimitri on her back reminding her that she wasn't alone. Trying to appear nonchalant, she slid into a cream-colored leather chair. Gillian wasn't used to this kind of luxury. Flying coach, jammed in the middle seat, last row was more her style.

Dimitri gave her a warm smile, and it was as if someone had wrapped her in a protective cocoon. From the second she'd met him, it felt as if she'd fallen down the rabbit hole. Surreal, it had gone against everything she'd ever known. But as she watched him take off his coat and roll up the sleeves of his white dress shirt, she couldn't help but think about being in his arms again. For the first time in her life, she considered what her life would be like without her feline spirit. Could she wake up in the morning with the knowledge that she couldn't shift? Even if she managed to transition to wolf, how would she feel being forced to submit within pack? Would Dimitri only want to mate her so he'd receive the gift she'd sacrifice to be with him?

She gazed out the tiny oval window at the flickering runway lights trailing off into the distance and shoved the thoughts to the back of her mind. She needed to focus, to attempt to shake the lust from her mind and think clearly. Chaz had somehow learned of her gifts. What if Dimitri had found out too? What wolf wouldn't want to have both the power of a tiger and wolf? Dimitri'd told her that he didn't want to be Alpha, but she didn't know him well enough to trust that he really meant it. All she knew for certain was that he didn't want to leave New Orleans, his Acadian wolf pack. Observing him interact with his own Alpha would provide further insight to his intentions.

A familiar voice captured her attention and her eyes caught Jake's. Casually dressed, in jeans and button down shirt, he was as handsome as she'd remembered. *Are all wolves this freakin' hot? No wonder my mom told me to stay away from packs.* She tried to hide the smile that crossed her face, and he laughed. Her stomach rolled, and she prayed he didn't read minds.

"Hey, Gil," he greeted. "Ya ready for a little fun in the Big Easy?"

"Fun? Yeah, if that's what you'd call being on the run from a maniacal jackass." She grinned and nodded. "Something tells me you're a glass half full kind of a guy."

"You bet. Besides, you two seem no worse for wear. Dimitri's in a good mood, that's for sure."

"He either wants to go on another date with me or he really likes cats," she laughed, knowing he scented Dimitri on her once again.

"I suspect it's a bit of both."

"I was just joking. It's more like he and Jax decided I was going on a trip."

"I wasn't. Logan's got a cat. Mojo. Dimitri is constantly talking to it like a baby. Kissing it. Embarrassing really. You'd think the damn thing was the Alpha, the way it does whatever it wants."

"Ah…that's the thing about us cats, we don't take orders very well."

"Is that so?" he chuckled. "I can't wait to see how that works out for the both of you."

Dimitri came out from the cockpit, and caught the tail end of their conversation.

"Don't you worry about Gilly, bro. She'll do just fine. Although I do owe her for leaving me in Vegas," he commented, casting Gillian a devious glance.

"You wouldn't have gone to see the witch if I had let you come with me to New York," she began.

"And that's your first mistake, kitten. It was all good in Vegas." Even though he felt like shit by the time he'd gotten to Ilsbeth, he wouldn't admit it to her. "I know you like your independence, but there's no foolin' around at home with my pack. I give the orders and you listen."

Gillian resisted the urge to roll her eyes…exactly why she didn't want to be with wolves.

"Cat got your tongue?" Jake teased. "I don't think she's gonna submit easily, my friend."

"Submit? Who said anything about me submitting? I'm going on a plane ride to take pictures of Mardi Gras. Technically, I'm working. While you all are begging for doggie treats, I'll be happily on my own, snapping pics of the city," she taunted. Unsure of why she goaded the two men, Gillian cautiously chose her words, aware there was a line she should not cross.

"You've got your hands full, beta," Jake responded. He laughed out loud, holding his hand to his abdomen.

"It'll be my pleasure when you do submit," Dimitri promised, coming up behind her chair. He knelt behind her, wrapping a strong arm around her chest. His fingers lingered on her collarbone as he whispered into her ear loud enough for Jake to hear. "And when you do, I'll make sure Jake's there to watch. After all, you seemed to take quite nicely to it earlier tonight. I'm thinking you liked having a little audience."

Gillian's eyes met Jake's and her nipples hardened at Dimitri's statement. *Damn it all.* Blood rushed to her cheeks, and she fought the urge to moan as his lips pressed to her neck. Her head lolled back onto his shoulder. Closing her eyes, she reveled in the sensation of his tongue behind her ear, causing her to break out in gooseflesh. She sighed, her pussy aching in arousal. Surprised, cold abandonment washed over her when Dimitri stood and walked away.

"What?" she said, blinking her eyes in disbelief. *Wait. Where is he going?*

"Sorry, cher. Gotta sit down. We're taking off. Better buckle up," Dimitri said with a wink. He enjoyed playing with Gillian, gauging her willingness to submit.

"Things were taking off, all right. Just came to a screeching halt." She caught the sly grin on his face, and realized he was teasing her.

"You're evil," she said, feigning anger with him. Jake shook his head and laughed. She'd completely forgotten that he'd been there, watching them. "Both of you."

Gillian crossed her legs and squeezed them tightly together. Her tiger roared, letting her know that she yearned for the beta. Gillian's lips tightened in a fine line.

No, no, no. No submission. No mating. No giving up my nature. She could feel Dimitri's eyes burning through the back of her head as she stared out the window. The plane lifted off and soon there was nothing but blackness.

Dimitri's dick was as hard as a lead pipe. Hours ago, they'd been intimate, and he couldn't wait to be inside his mate again. Glancing at Jake, it wasn't lost on Dimitri how his friend looked at Gillian. He resisted telling Jake to put his eyes back into his head, as they roamed her body. Her fiery spirit and quick wit would be enough for any man to find her attractive, but tonight, she looked incredibly sexy, her toned thigh peeking through the slit. Dimitri wasn't the jealous type, having shared women with both Logan and Jake. Yet the wolf in him wouldn't allow it until she'd allowed him to mark her as his, to begin the mating process.

Needing to talk with her alone, Dimitri gestured with his hand, in an effort to get Jake to leave. His friend shrugged in response and made his way out of the main cabin. Dimitri knew that Jake was probably thinking he just wanted to join the mile high club. While that option was fully on the table, he and Gillian first needed to clear the air about why she was so resistant to dating him. The knowledge that she was his mate was a secret that he couldn't keep for much longer.

DIMITRI

"Gilly," he called to her with a smile. His kitten had been aroused by his words, suggesting the terms of her submission. He suspected that she was intrigued by it, the idea of Jake watching. Interesting that she'd conceal her desires, yet he looked forward to testing her limits.

"Yes," she responded, her face still flushed.

"Let's go lay down. The seatbelt sign is off and Jake's gone up to talk with the pilot," he said, pushing out of his chair.

Dimitri held out his hand, smiling as she put hers in his. He led them to a sofa that had a long chaise. He released her briefly, so he could reach up to retrieve a pillow from out of the overhead compartment. Throwing it onto the couch, he sat down, bringing her with him.

"Lie back," he directed. Pleased that she did what he asked, he took her feet into his hands and slipped off her shoes.

"Not sure how you women walk around in these," he commented, massaging her instep. Gillian moaned, and he laughed.

"Oh my God, that feels so good," she sighed, laying her head back.

"So tell me, what's the deal with not wanting to be around wolves? I know you didn't want to tell me before at the theater, but now, it's just you and me."

"You want the truth?" Gillian's eyes flashed open.

"No, I want you to lie to me. Of course I want the truth. No more coy excuses. The plan ole truth will suffice," Dimitri told her.

153

"Seeing that we made love, I suppose I owe you as much. But for the record, I wasn't trying to lie to you. It's more like I was protecting myself." She tried to pull her foot away from him, but Dimitri held her tight.

"No running. Spill."

"I told you before that a wolf can't mark me," she explained. Even though his touch calmed her animal spirit, she'd never told anyone else and her voice began to tremble. "If I choose a mate, and I must be the one to make the decision, then it will happen. I'm a rare breed of tiger. Maljavan. That's why I can mate a wolf. Most shifters can't mate outside their breed. Even hybrids can't, not unless they're human."

"No doubt, you're strong enough to take on most wolves, individually anyhow, but I still don't get why you don't want to date a wolf."

"Because…if I mate…" her voice faltered.

"Hey, it's okay. You can tell me," he cajoled. Dimitri released her foot, slid next to her and adjusted her body so that she lay on his chest.

"My tiger…she'll die," Gillian managed. It was the first time she'd said the words out loud.

"I'll admit, I've never heard of a tiger, or any other shifter for that matter, mating with a wolf, but shifters don't just die."

"Mine will." Gillian lifted her head and turned to look in his eyes. "She'll die. My mother mated with my dad. The Alpha. Afterwards, she never shifted again."

"She's mortal? I thought you said your mom was alive?"

"She's alive. She hasn't aged but she doesn't shift. Not ever. Jax said he thinks she may have turned wolf when she mated, but denied her beast."

"What do you think?"

"Remember when I healed you?"

"Yeah?" Dimitri pulled her closer.

"Your wolf. It was weak." Gillian slid her fingers underneath his unbuttoned shirt, touching his abdomen. "I can sense him. I haven't done it very often but I knew. My mom, I've hugged her, touched her hand. I feel nothing. It's as if she's human."

"But how do you know what you're saying is true? Is there anyone else you can ask in your family?"

"I told you, we're a solitary species. I don't even know my grandparents. From the small amount of research I've done, it seems that if I mate with a wolf, it's unlikely my tiger would survive. There's a small chance that my wolf, which I highly doubt even exists, would show herself."

"So you avoid wolves because you don't want to meet your mate?"

"I can't risk it."

Dimitri sighed, disappointed that she couldn't feel what he felt. He knew she was his mate. She hadn't a clue. Worse, if she chose him, she might not be able to ever shift again. Yet he suspected there was more to the story.

"It still doesn't make sense why Chaz is after you. What does he get out of it if you're no longer a tiger?"

"I don't know what he knows," she lied. She didn't want to tell him that whoever she mated with would receive the gifts of her tiger. He'd run faster, have the claws of a feline, would possibly even be able to shift into a cat.

"You're sure about that?" Dimitri pressed, sensing she was hiding the truth.

"I don't really know. Maybe he just wants to say he killed a tiger. It doesn't matter because the only way I'll mate is if I choose it. I'm very much like a human that way."

"So if you met a wolf, your mate…you wouldn't consider it?"

"Do you remember what it felt like not to be able to shift?"

"Hell yeah, it was terrible…" Could he ask her to give up her cat just so he could be with his mate?

"What if I couldn't shift? Would you choose a mate who'd never be able to run with you? Someone who was practically human?"

"I'd choose the person I'm supposed to be with. Sorry, darlin' but I believe in fate. I also believe in mates. You can call it chemistry, if it makes you feel better. But with wolves, we know when we find a mate…it's meant to be. The more ya fight it, the worse it gets. The desire to mark, to mate her will become intolerable. The wolf must be satisfied. There are some things in life you can control and some you can't."

"What if you couldn't shift? You felt what it was like on the beach that night, not to be able to shift. What if you were like that, vulnerable, forever?"

Dimitri grew quiet as she spoke his worst fear. Ilsbeth still hadn't found a cure. The tonic in his duffle bag was only temporary. He hadn't told a soul about his prognosis, not even Logan.

"You saw the witch?" When Dimitri shrugged in response, Gillian withdrew her hand from his shirt and pushed up to see his expression. "What? You saw her, right? I can feel your wolf now. What aren't you telling me?"

"I saw her," Dimitri said with a small grin.

"So? What happened? Did she do a spell?"

"Yeah." Guilt churned in his belly as the memory of the naked witches played in his mind. He shouldn't have let Ilsbeth so close. When she'd kissed him, he'd gone cold. Now that he'd made love with Gillian, the knowledge that he'd touched the witch made him sick.

"It worked?" Gillian brushed her fingers over his jaw.

"Yes." Dimitri justified his answer by telling himself that his wolf was alive…for now. He questioned what to do with his mate. Not only could he lose his ability to shift, asking her to mate with him could cause her to lose hers as well.

"Is there something wrong?" she asked.

"No, cher. Just thinkin' is all," he answered. Dimitri yearned to tell her that she was his mate, but now that he knew why she'd avoided wolves, he doubted his original plan. His avoidance couldn't continue forever, he knew. The more he was around her, the greater the attraction would grow. His wolf would demand that he mark her, mate her.

"If you're worried about me being around your pack, finding a mate, I'll just stay away from the other wolves. Jax will come for me soon." She hoped. "We could always just stay in bed for the next five days. I'm sure that'll keep me safe."

"Now what makes you think that? How do you know that I'm not your mate?" he laughed.

"Well, I don't know. I mean, I'm not a wolf, but wouldn't I know something like that? I always just figured that some kind of wolf ESP would kick in if I were around wolves…that I'd just know."

"And then?" *Goddess, she really doesn't know.*

"Well, I'd have to stay as far away as possible. That's always been my plan." She slid her hand lower, past his belly button and wrapped her leg over his.

"Someday, you may find that doesn't work so well," he advised. Soon, he'd be forced to tell her. The closer he allowed himself to get to her, the worse it would be when they had to part ways. As much as his wolf wanted this woman, he couldn't be the one to kill her tiger.

"I never thought I'd date a wolf," she reflected, her fingers grazing his beltline.

"You admit we're dating?" Dimitri's cock thickened as her fingers played with the trail of hair below his abdomen.

"I don't know what's really going on. I just know that tonight when you showed up, I was so relieved."

"Not a fan of Nick?"

"Nick's fine. He's nice," she said and took a deep breath. "But there's something about you. I just…I don't know what it is. Tonight…what you did to me, what we did. I've never felt that way before."

"There's something about you, too, cher."

"I've never done anything like that in public…never even thought about it. It was crazy."

"I'm looking forward to teaching you all kinds of things."

"But Dimitri…we can't keep doing this. It's dangerous."

"How so?"

"I don't want to get hurt."

"I'd never hurt you…ever." His voice grew serious.

"But what if you find your mate?"

"What about it?" *You are my mate, little one*, he thought to himself.

"I'm not the kind of girl who plays around a lot. Between the wolves and not finding a tiger, I've only been with humans. They've never been enough," she admitted.

"Too tame?" he guessed.

"Yeah, it's just, like tonight…when we made love…God, I felt wild. I've never felt like that before."

"So what's the problem?"

"You could find your mate. I've heard that wolves don't commit to anyone else. Don't get me wrong, I mean, we just met, but I'm not a 'friends with benefits' kind of girl."

"What makes you think I wouldn't commit to a woman?"

"Because that's how wolves are."

"That's how a lot of people are, not just wolves," he countered.

"True, but humans are different. Hybrids are different. They aren't sitting around waiting to find a mate. Seriously, have you ever dated someone for a long time, committed to them, knowing they weren't your mate?" she asked.

"Well, no, but that doesn't apply here."

"What would happen if you committed to a girl and then your mate came along?" Gillian pinned him on the spot, getting to the crux of her argument.

"The attraction to one's mate cannot be denied. There've been many women I've cared about. I'm not a callous man. But with my mate, it's chemistry. Nature, fate at its finest. No matter who I'm seeing…who I've seen in the past, they will all pale in comparison to her." Dimitri dug his fingers into her hair, loosening the pins. "I won't be able to resist her. I may have been a single man, but she'll change my life."

"And that's why we can't continue. What if you find her? Even if you weren't looking…"

"I haven't been looking…it'll be destiny."

"Exactly. You won't mean to hurt my feelings, but you will. You won't have a choice."

"I told you once…I'll tell you a million times, darlin', I'll never hurt you. It's not meant to be." Dimitri wished he could tell her she was his mate, but now that he knew the truth about what their mating would do to her, he needed to think about what to do. As he twirled his finger into her hair, he wondered if maybe Ilsbeth could help them. She'd be pissed as hell, but even the witch couldn't deny his preordained future.

"Why do I want to believe you? I really do, you know. But we both know that if you meet your mate, I'll be but a distant memory."

"You need to trust me."

"I'm learning to trust you. But even you can't control what the universe has in store for you. So this is why we can't keep doing what we just did…it's only going to make it harder."

"Do you know how beautiful you are?"

"No. Are you changing the subject?" she giggled.

"I can't seem to keep my hands off you," he admitted, rubbing her neck.

"Staying away from you…it won't be easy," she breathed.

"Impossible," he agreed. Letting his fingers drift down her chest, he lightly stroked her skin. "We'll be careful…we shouldn't stop."

"What you said to me earlier…about submitting. Why'd you say that?"

"Your submission?" He'd meant it at the time, telling her he'd do it in front of Jake. Now, however, that he knew what he could do to her beast, he had second thoughts about moving forward.

"I've never submitted to anyone."

"Maybe you haven't found the right person."

"You mean, the right wolf?"

"No, I mean person. Someone you trust. Someone who you feel so comfortable with that you will allow your true nature to surface. That person…you'd want to be wild and uninhibited without judgment."

"I don't know. Giving myself to someone, unconditionally trusting them?"

"Yes, exactly that…like tonight in the booth. It's not something you have to plan, it can just happen."

"I lost myself…I was so happy to see you."

"What do you want?" he breathed as her hand skimmed under his waistband. "Gilly, do you know what you're doing to me?"

"I want you…now," Gillian found herself saying, unsure of why she couldn't control her own feelings for Dimitri. Her hips began to undulate against his leg and her fingers traveled through the springy hair above his shaft. "Just one more time."

"One more time," he repeated. As she turned her head to look in his eyes, he kissed her gently, licking and nipping.

"Dimitri," she moaned, her tongue sweeping against his. Gillian's hand reached down past his dick, teasing the crease where his groin met his thigh.

"Aw, fuck. Take my cock," he growled. She ran the tip of her fingers over his skin, toying with him, and he ordered her again. "Now, Gilly."

Gillian did as he told her, fisting him, and he hissed. Fuck if it didn't turn him on even more to watch her obey his demand. He could tell she was inexperienced and the fact she'd opened to him the way she'd done told him it was in her nature to experiment. Thankful that destiny had given him a curious mate, he swore he had to find a way to keep her.

"That's it…just like that…ah, yeah," he encouraged as she gently pumped him.

"You're so hard," she whispered, sliding the tip of her forefinger over his wet slit. Using the moisture, she gripped him, stroking his length.

He slid his hand down her chest, tugging the fabric down until she was exposed. Cupping her soft breast, he pressed his lips into her hair. The hard length of him throbbed, needing release. Considering his words, he decided to push her limits.

"Unbuckle my pants," he told her. "Get up on your knees."

"But Jake could…"

"Yes," he responded, knowing that Jake might return. She'd grown aroused earlier when he'd suggested she liked being watched. She lifted her head and her eyes met his. "Do as I say, Gilly."

Gillian's gaze locked on his as she pushed upward, straddling his legs. Her hands reached for the front of her dress to cover herself.

"Leave it. I want to see you," he said, the back of his knuckles brushing over her nipples. They stood at attention in response. "Look how hot you are."

"I...I...what if someone sees me?" she replied, her head turning to the cockpit and back to Dimitri.

"Doesn't matter. Leave it down. You're beautiful."

Gillian's pussy dampened at his demand. On a visceral level she hadn't known existed, she wanted this, to please him, to explore her sexuality with Dimitri. Despite her desire, her face turned red as she acquiesced. The fabric of her dress bunched up around her hips as she leaned forward and began to unbuckle his belt. Slowly she freed his cock from his pants, taking it back into her hands.

"Now suck me," he told her.

With her eyes on his, Gillian bent over, her lips parted as she guided him into her mouth. The salty taste of his essence hit her tongue and her tiger came to life with hunger. She licked his broad head, enjoying the power she felt, knowing she could bring him pleasure. Cold air hit her core as her bottom lifted into the air, reminding her that Dimitri had taken her panties earlier. The ache between her legs grew painful and she tilted her hips, attempting to relieve the pressure.

A sound behind her alerted her that they were no longer alone, and she saw Jake out of the corner of her eye. He looked as if he'd eat her alive. Gillian knew that wolves were a sexually open breed, but she'd never been exposed to their ways. For but a second, she considered her dark fantasy of what it would be like to have both men at once. Even though she found Jake attractive, it was Dimitri she craved. Her eyes fell back to her wolf and his eyes locked on hers. He gave her a wicked smile as if he knew what she'd been thinking. Their connection drove her desire, and her attention went to his thick flesh. Lost in her own lust, she took him into her mouth again.

Gillian had never had sex in front of another man, let alone a wolf. It should have felt wrong but it only made her pussy throb in excitement. She glanced to see where Jake had gone but he was nowhere in sight. Confused by her slight disappointment that he wasn't watching, she shook off the guilt that she'd even had the thought. If she stayed with Dimitri, he'd push her boundaries further than anyone she'd ever dated. This had to be the last time they made love. She had to cut her addiction to him before she needed an intervention to leave. Tonight she'd have him, though. Like eating a gallon of ice cream the day before a diet, she indulged, bingeing on all that was Dimitri.

Releasing his shaft, she climbed up his torso. Positioning her entrance above his cock, she flattened her hands beside his head. She reached between her legs and swiped his hard sex through her wet folds, stimulating her clitoris. Throwing her head back, she hissed, flicking his plump head against her tight opening.

"Ah yes, fuck me. Now," Dimitri demanded. He tilted his hips upward, his erection probing at her wetness.

Gillian grunted as she impaled herself on him. His broad cock stretched her channel, and she lowered herself all the way down until her clit brushed against his bristly hair. Slowly, she began to grind her pelvis against his, her taut nub engorged in arousal. Leaning forward, she darted her tongue against his chest, tracing the lines of his tattoos, until she reached his nipple. Taking the hard tip between her teeth, she tugged until Dimitri released a groan.

She lifted her hips, so that he slid out of her, then with a hard drop, she descended, pressing him deep inside. Her orgasm built as Dimitri increased the pace. His fingers dug into her hips and she moaned against his chest. Her pussy quivered as her climax rolled through her.

Dimitri took her soft breast into his hand as Gillian contracted around his cock. Plunging himself into her over and over, he bent his head forward, guiding her rosy nipple into his mouth. The pulsations around his cock caused him to buck uncontrollably. With a primal cry, he stiffened in release, his seed erupting deep inside her.

Gillian collapsed in ecstasy atop him and they both panted, attempting to catch their breath. Dimitri reached to flip the back of her dress over her bare bottom. But before he did so, he slapped her ass. She squeaked, but didn't move an inch. Seconds passed, and he wondered why she'd gone still. Dimitri pushed the hair away from her face, and tilted his head to observe a small grin on her face. Her eyes closed, she'd fallen asleep. He lay his head back onto the sofa and dreamed of a long life with his mate. The only way he'd be able to have her was if he could find a way to save her, to ease her transition through the mating. But before he did that, he'd have to find a way to save himself.

Chapter Eleven

Dimitri stared at the spread of pain perdu, grits, and creole cream cheese with berries and sugar. Wearing only an apron around his hips, he took a quick swig of his freshly squeezed Satsuma juice before cracking an egg. The timer buzzed and he nearly burned his fingers, forgetting to don an oven mitt.

"Goddammit," he swore.

For the past two days, Gillian had stayed in his home, and he was crawling the walls. True to her word, she'd insisted that making love on the plane had to be their final tryst. As such, he'd situated her in his guest room. Like a teenager with his first girly magazine, he'd spent a good portion of the time since then holed up in the bathroom, jerking off in a cold shower. And she'd been just as guilty, secluding herself in her bedroom. It wasn't as if he couldn't hear her soft moans as she touched herself. The scent of her arousal filtered throughout the house, driving him insane with desire.

Dimitri

The morning after they'd arrived, a delivery containing a camera and computer equipment arrived, courtesy of Jax. Gillian had used it as an excuse to ignore him, but today, he'd told her they'd go to see one of his favorite Krewes' parades.

If he didn't get out of the house soon, he was going to fuck her senseless or lose his mind. His sanity was stretched far. Not hearing from Ilsbeth only added stress to the situation. He'd texted her a dozen times, but she hadn't called him back. He needed a damn cure for his wolf. When he'd made love to Gillian, something about their lovemaking had energized his spirit. But two days later, without his skin on hers, he could feel his ability to shift waning. Earlier he'd taken a double dose of the tonic, and he still wasn't feeling well.

Out of desperation, he'd begun cooking. While he usually found the culinary arts a calming hobby, he was far gone. He'd already cooked enough breakfast to feed the entire pack and he'd just started on the grillades. Hearing a rap on his door, Dimitri called out to Jake.

"Come in," he said, rummaging in the drawers for a meat mallet.

"Holy fuck, bro. What in the hell?" Jake's eyes widened at the sight of all the food and his friend wearing next to nothing.

"Help yourself," Dimitri said. He turned away, postponing the inevitable conversation that he'd delayed since the flight.

"Listen, D. I don't know what the fuck is going on with you but I haven't seen you cook this much food since Marcel died. Not that I don't appreciate a good meal, but damn." Jake sat at the kitchen counter, took a plate and snatched a biscuit off of the tray Dimitri held in his hands. "Ah...so good. You make the best muffins. God rest my mamma's soul, these are the best I've ever had. Butter?"

"Honey?"

"Yeah, now stop with the shit. When are ya gonna spill it? Don't think I didn't notice you weren't sharin' on the plane." Jake raised his eyebrows at Dimitri and smiled. "That's right, beta. You wanna tell me or should I say it? No, I take that back. I'm not making it that easy for you."

"It's complicated." Dimitri lifted the last pastry off the pan and dropped it into the bread basket.

"It always is, friend." He picked up the honey bear and squeezed it onto his plate. "The question is...is it your wolf or your tiger?"

Dimitri picked up a dishtowel and wiped his hands. "Try both."

"What's the good news?"

"What the fuck do you mean, what's the good news? I'm not sure there is any right now. Keep your voice down," he shushed, glancing behind him. "She's in the shower, but she's goin' to be out soon, and I don't want her to hear us."

"You do know I'm a wolf and not a psychic, right?" Jake smeared the sticky sweet mixture onto the flaky bread and took another bite.

"Let's start with my wolf."

Jake chewed. His mouth stuffed with food, he gestured with his hand for Dimitri to continue.

"Ilsbeth didn't cure me. Whatever the hell hooked itself onto me is eatin' at my wolf like a fifty-foot tapeworm."

"Hey," Jake protested. "Easy there…I'm eating."

"She said it's like a parasite. Not like a possession or anything like that. But it's bad. She's lookin' for a spell, but she hasn't returned my calls."

Dimitri took a stool and pulled it to the other side of the kitchen bar. He sat down and reached for a plate.

"But Gillian did something to you in San Diego? She healed you. Can't she keep doing that?"

"Well, yeah. But again, it's complicated."

"Logan's going to know. You're his beta, for Christ's sake."

"Know what?"

"D, you may not mind lying to yourself, but come on."

"Not lying…just hungry." Dimitri took a big scoop of grits and shoveled it into his mouth, with a smile.

"The plane. I saw Gilly with your cock…"

Dimitri held his fingers to his lips and then pointed down to the hallway, which led to the bedrooms.

Jake shook his head and continued. "I saw her. She saw me. You saw me. And neither of you minded. But and this is a big but for you, because I'll give her the benefit of the doubt, you didn't even so much as ask me to watch, let alone join you. Now, I may not know Gillian that well but

I know you. You, me and a hot chick on a long plane ride, and you ignore me? Well, that speaks volumes. And do you know what that says?"

"What?"

"Really? You're going to make me say it?"

Dimitri grinned.

"Okay, fine. Have it your way." Jake snatched another biscuit. "My point is that you like her. A lot. Too much. And you were possessive, a trait that's not necessarily a bad thing but highly unusual for you."

"She's my mate," Dimitri whispered. "Don't make me say it again, 'cause I told you it's complicated."

"Not possible. She's a tiger," Jake replied. "Hybrids can't mate either. You must be confused. Maybe what you feel has to do with what's got your wolf. No way she's your mate."

"Keep it down, will ya?"

"Hey, mum's the word. But I'm still not buying it."

"I know. It makes no sense. She said that something about her breed gives her the ability to mate with a wolf. But the mating isn't a given. She can deny any mate she finds. It's why Chaz's mark doesn't stay on her."

"That's a neat trick," Jake quipped.

"Yeah, I could almost deal with that one. When I'm with her, it's just like we're combustible…she's so hot," he reflected. "The other thing is that my wolf seems to shake off this thing that's killin' him, or at least, I can't feel it when I'm with her, skin to skin."

"So why aren't you with her?"

"Catch number two. Long story short, if she takes a mate, she says it'll kill her tiger."

Jake gave him a look of confusion.

"Apparently, when her mom mated a wolf, she lost her ability to shift."

"Having a wolf for a mate is a death sentence? No wonder she avoids wolves."

"Thanks so much for puttin' it out there like that, but yeah, if we mate, she makes it sound like she'll never shift into a cat again. She's hybrid. Maybe she'd shift into a wolf? Who the hell knows? Like I said, complicated." Dimitri sighed. "And to top it all off, she doesn't recognize me as her mate. Not a clue. Nor does she know that my wolf isn't healed."

"Still waiting on good news," Jake joked.

"It gets better…wait for it…and then there's Ilsbeth," Dimitri continued, pushing up out of his chair. He reached for a bowl of eggs and began to whisk. "She wants me to move in with her."

"You gotta be shittin' me."

"I wish. The ceremony she did involved a bunch of naked witches and one very horny Ilsbeth telling me her spell didn't work and that I should be with her at all times in case something happened."

"Hell, no."

"She kissed me."

"The witch still has the hots for you?" Jake laughed.

"I told her it wasn't going to work," Dimitri continued. "And now that I've found my mate…well, you know that's not going to go over well. Ilsbeth's already a tad cranky."

"Goddess, that woman is beautiful," Jake began, "but so is a samurai sword. Both can kill you or slice your dick off. Knowing Ilsbeth, she'd go straight for your big head."

"And this thing with Gilly...shit, she's so fucking amazing. I want her so bad...fightin' the chemistry is like trying to paddle up the Mississippi with a toothpick."

"I can see that's goin' real well for ya." Jake glanced to the dishes spread all over the kitchen.

"We aren't even sleepin' in the same room, let alone in the same bed. Not only does she not want to be around pack, because she's afraid she'll meet her mate, she doesn't want to date me because she's afraid I'm gonna meet my mate, and leave her. It's all sorts of fucked up."

"Isn't that a kick in the nuts?"

"Worse. My balls are bluer than the sky on a spring day."

"You have to tell her."

"What am I'm goin' to tell her? That I'm her mate and that I want to mark her? That I want to take away her ability to shift? Kill her tiger? No fucking way, man. I can't do that to her," Dimitri insisted.

"Are you sure that she'll die? I mean, maybe something else happened to her mom," Jake suggested.

"I don't know. Honestly, I never heard of a hybrid shifter that wasn't part human mating with a wolf. It's impossible. So this thing about her spirit dying...I just don't know."

"Logan's mate went wolf."

"She was human. And besides, and don't take this the wrong way, I love my wolf, but she's a tiger. You saw her. She was magnificent."

"Badass."

"Yeah, she was," Dimitri said, recalling the way she'd gracefully run over to the car. "I can't do that to my mate…kill her beast. I've got to either let her go or find a way to save her."

"Ilsbeth."

"Maybe. I'm not going to be able to go on for much longer. I've got to be with her. This roommate shit isn't cuttin' it."

"What was your first clue?" Jake asked, a smartass grin crossing his face.

"What? Cooking soothes me."

"Don't take this the wrong way, but it's kind of funny to see you inked and muscled out, wearing pretty much nothin' but an oven mitt. It's a new look for you."

"It is what it is." Dimitri heard Gillian turn the doorknob and again held his fingers to his lips, shushing Jake. "Not a fucking word."

"You have to tell her."

"Just please. Not now."

"Logan's going to freak out the second he sees you. This thing with your wolf…you're the beta."

"I think I know my role in this pack. My wolf is…"

"What's wrong with your wolf?" Gillian asked. Surprised, her eyes went as large as saucers as she saw all the food. "You made this?"

"I like to cook," he said without explanation. "Have a seat."

"Expecting company?" She smiled. A rosy tinge spread across her cheeks as her gaze traveled from his ripped abdomen up to his eyes. Desire ran hot through her body, and she glanced away. Reaching for a glass of juice, she held it to her forehead before taking a drink.

"No, I just, uh…it's a hobby." Dimitri fought the erection that threatened to give his 'Kiss the Cook' apron new meaning.

"We're going to see a parade, right?" Gillian had heard their muffled voices and suspected something was off, but seeing Dimitri half-naked distracted her thoughts. Resisting him was turning into an impossible feat.

Locking herself in a bedroom had been the only way she'd been able to keep her hands to herself. Confused by her out of control libido, she'd immersed herself in the company information that Jax had sent with her camera equipment. Nick had emailed her first assignment, and she was actually looking forward to shooting today.

"Yeah, it'll be fun," Dimitri said.

"Okay," she responded.

"It's Saturday, so that means everyone's going to be out…humans and supes. I've got a few pack members who will travel with us, keeping an eye out for trouble. So far, there's been no sign of Chaz in the city, but we can't be too careful." It wasn't that wolves couldn't handle the issues, but shifting out in the open wasn't accepted. They needed to blend…go get the pictures and come home. The only reason Dimitri was even considering taking her out was because he couldn't take another second of being locked in the house, caged with no hope of release.

"Don't forget. Tonight's the Loups and Sorcières Ball." Jake stood and took his plate over to the sink.

"Ilsbeth better damn well be there," Dimitri blurted out, then quickly regretted he'd mentioned her in front of Gillian. He blew out a breath. Sooner or later she'd find out about the witch.

"What's Loups and Sorcières? Who's Ilsbeth?" Gillian asked. Intuition warned her that her wolf hadn't told her everything, but she kept her own secret held close.

"It's a Mardi Gras event we hold every year with the witches," Jake explained. "Mostly wolves and witches, but he invited a vamp."

"Leo's a friend," Dimitri said, pouring the scrambled yolks into a hot pan.

"He got you into this mess," Jake noted.

"Sorry, I don't follow." Gillian looked to Jake and then Dimitri.

"Léopold Devereoux. Vampire. His woman got herself involved with a demon, and my beta, here, jumped into a hell pit to save her and Logan's kid."

"Your wolf got injured," she commented.

"Yeah, my wolf." Dimitri kept his back to them, not wanting to share his pained expression. Fuck, he needed to get this situation fixed yesterday. Between not being able to make love to his mate, walking around with a hard-on twenty-four-seven and his wolf fading fast, he had to find resolution. But instead of going over to the coven to break down the damn door, he was going to a freakin' parade.

"But who's Ils…"

"Ilsbeth's the witch I saw. She was helping me."

"Why do you need to see her? I thought everything was okay."

"I need to ask her about something else." It wasn't entirely a lie, he reasoned. Aside from asking Logan and Léopold for help, Ilsbeth was the only other person he could think of who would know anything about mating tigers, how to save her ability to shift. He cringed, afraid that once she found out he was lying, she'd throw his ass to the curb. Unlike his wolf, who'd already rolled over in submission to the idea of mating, she had to choose him.

"Gilly's already the talk of the pack," Jake noted with a grin.

"What do you mean?" Gillian's stomach dropped.

"He means that you're my mate. Or did you forget?" Dimitri flipped the omelet, added a sprinkle of cheese and onions. He turned off the gas and set it aside.

"I, um, I didn't forget." Gillian's eyes widened. When he'd said mate, it had taken her off guard; she'd forgotten that they were supposed to be pretending to be mated.

"You should see your face," Jake laughed. "D, I think she forgot."

Dimitri came up behind Gillian, who sat on the bar stool. It had been the perfect excuse to touch her again. His arms coiled around her waist, resting underneath her breasts. Nuzzling her hair aside, he pressed his lips to her neck. The fragrance of her coconut-scented shampoo drifted into his nose, but it was her natural essence that registered with his wolf. His cock jerked to attention, grazing against her back.

"Mate," he growled. "We must be convincing. No more hiding in bedrooms."

"I…I…" Gillian lost her speech with Dimitri so close. Her tiger had gone wild, lusting after the wolf who she had been working carefully to avoid.

"That's right, cher. You feel it too, don't ya? Don't deny it," he told her. Dimitri darted his tongue against her skin, yearning for a taste of his mate. Barely cognizant of Jake walking out the door, he ran a hand down the top of her thigh.

"Dimitri…I…what's happening?" she breathed. Excited and bewildered with her reaction to him, Gillian rested the back of her head against his chest. It should have felt wrong to be with a wolf, to desire someone so badly that she'd give anything to be with him. Rebuking her own feelings for the past two days had done nothing to quell the emotion blossoming in her chest. She was changing, transforming just by being in his presence and she wasn't sure if she could go back.

"Today, you're my mate. Tonight, you're my mate. That's what's happening, darlin'," Dimitri said. Forever she'd be his mate…if he could find a way to keep her.

"Okay," she found herself saying. *Okay? Did I just agree to be his mate?* No, this was role playing, a farce to keep her safe…wasn't it?

"See, that's right. You know me…can feel me…your mate."

"Dimitri, please. We can't…"

"Oh we can and we will, cher, but first we gotta go take some pictures."

"What?"

"Laissez les bons temps rouler!" Dimitri released her, untying his apron.

"Where're you going?" Gillian asked, stunned by the surging electricity running through her veins. As he walked away, her mouth gaped open at the sight of his spectacular bare ass.

"To get dressed. Work before play. And believe me, we've got lots of play to do. So we'd better get busy." It wasn't lost on Dimitri that Gillian had just about chosen him, and she didn't even know that they were mates. Damn if he was giving up the woman who fate had bestowed upon him.

Even though she had a press pass, the enormous crowd kept shifting, rhythmically jostling the spectators like shells being tossed about in the sand by breaking waves. Bracing her arms, she steadied her camera and focused the lens. A series of clicks fired as she captured the brightly colored float. Beads flew through the air like streams of plastic rain. Snap. Snap. Snap.

Gillian felt Dimitri's hands on her waist, his chest at her back. Lowering her arms, a broad smile crossed her face. Even though she was working, it felt like a date. They'd toured the French Quarter so she could take shots of the elaborate purple and gold Mardi Gras decorations that adorned the buildings. Despite the enormous breakfast he'd cooked, he insisted on taking her out to his favorite open-air café. They'd sat at a window table, talking for hours. She'd told him about growing up in Seattle, her life in New York. He'd told her stories of life on the bayou, how he'd come into being a beta within the pack, about his close relationship with Logan and Jake. They'd laughed and people-watched, drinking Bloody Marys and eating oysters and crawfish.

During their adventure, she'd felt woefully underdressed for the celebration in the streets. They'd ducked into a gift shop and she came out wearing a frilly red tutu and a matching mini-hat that clipped into her hair. On the way to the parade route, they'd stopped to listen to street performers, dancing in the streets. Infected by the spirit, Dimitri had taken her in his arms, twirling her as if they were in a ballroom. With a dip, he'd kissed her in front of an applauding crowd.

As another parade commenced, a teddy bear flew by her head, reminding her that she was supposed to be paying attention. Dimitri reached a long arm up into the air, easily catching it. Bright blue beads flew toward her and she extended a hand. With a snap, she caught the slippery chain and screamed in excitement. Laughing like a child opening a gift, she turned to Dimitri, whose warm eyes locked on hers.

Gillian's smile waned as the moment turned to heat. She lifted the beads as high as her hands would go until Dimitri bent over to receive them. At the same time, he turned over the stuffed toy, and gave it to her. She smiled, their lips inches apart, and she prayed he'd kiss her. When he leaned in, only brushing his cheek against hers in a hug, she exhaled, her heart pounding hard in her chest.

Music blared as the marching bands passed for what seemed like several minutes, but she'd gone limp, uncaring of everything and everyone around her. For the moment, the world had stopped. Gillian had lost count of the dates, and knew for certain that she didn't want just one more date. No, she wanted a lifetime.

The gut-wrenching knowledge of their dilemma tore at her heart. In her entire life, she'd never considered abandoning her great cat. Being with Dimitri was confusing everything she thought she knew. His warm lips pressed softly to her hair and she squeezed her eyes tight, hoping she wouldn't cry. From sadness or happiness, she couldn't tell. With the emotion brimming over, she breathed deeply. Clearing her head of all negative thoughts, she simply allowed herself to become immersed in the joy of being with her wolf.

Chapter Twelve

After taking a long shower, Gillian unsuccessfully attempted to put thoughts of Dimitri out of her mind. Fixing her hair, which was beginning to sprout dark brown roots, she imagined dating him for real. Going to the movies. Listening to music in the park. Debating whether they'd be having Chinese or Italian for dinner, knowing all the while she'd choose Cajun delicacies any day of the week.

As they rode in the limo on their way over to the party, she glanced up to Dimitri, who watched her with amusement. He was so easygoing, yet dominant in every single thing he did. Today had been one of the best days in her life. After spending so much time with him, her tiger was ready to roll over like a submissive lap dog waiting for her next treat. When he'd talked about running in the bayou, she envied him, wishing she could have just a taste of what he'd felt. Being free and open. Having others to rely on. All things that had eluded her.

While she'd never admit it, Gillian was beginning to suspect her own wolf existed. Although she'd never felt her, it had to be the reason why she'd fallen so easily under his spell. The call to date a wolf, her wolf, Dimitri, had taken hold.

"You can do this," she heard Dimitri say, as a gentle squeeze on her knee drew her out of her contemplation.

"I don't know. I've never been around so many wolves before…Chaz…well, even he didn't introduce me to his entire pack. How many people are going to be there again?" Gillian asked, fidgeting with the hem of her skirt.

"A hundred, give or take. But there's only one wolf you need to be concerned with." Dimitri eyed the private driver who'd picked them up to take them to the ball. With a flick of a button, he raised the privacy partition.

"Oh God. A hundred?"

"Are you all right?" he asked.

"I'll be okay," she lied.

"It's just a little party."

"Jake said the pack knew about us. Did you tell everyone? That I'm your mate?" She made air quotes with her fingers.

"Yes and no," he replied with a chuckle.

"This isn't going to be good, is it?" she smiled.

"It's kinda like this. Sometimes news is better going through the grapevine. No need to announce it on the PA system."

"A rumor?" she asked.

"Somethin' like that." He smiled.

"What did you do?"

"Miss Edmee. I kind of mentioned it to her. That's as good as tellin' everyone."

"Okay, but we agreed? No big proclamations, right? Just a party."

"Just a party." He brought the back of her hand to his lips and kissed it. "But you're going to meet Logan."

"The Alpha?" Gillian's voiced boomed throughout the cabin of the car.

"Now don't you tell me you're even a little bit afraid of an Alpha. Your brother's an Alpha."

"But he's not…I don't know…he's not scary. Chaz…now that's scary," she said. Her hand began to shake as she remembered her ordeal.

"He's not here," he reassured.

"He will be," she countered.

"Logan's a good man. He knows about us. I didn't have a lot of time to talk to him on the phone but he knows about our plan."

"Our lie."

"That we're tellin' people that we're going to mate. He knows exactly what Jax told everyone. And when I see him tonight, he'll know everything." Dimitri despised pretending. When he saw Logan, he planned on coming clean with all the details, including his wolf and his mate.

"Do you tell him everything you do?"

"Yeah, he's my Alpha. No secrets. We share everything," he disclosed.

"Everything?" she laughed.

"Everything," he confirmed, recalling the night of passion he'd shared with Logan and his mate.

Gillian opened her mouth and promptly shut it, contemplating whether or not to delve further into his statement. She'd heard that wolves sometimes would share sexual partners among themselves. Her understanding of it, however, was limited to stories told by humans, who only knew secondhand.

"It was once," Dimitri said, filling in the pieces of the puzzle. He'd just about had his fill of lies. He refused to pretend that he was anything but what he was. There was no shame in what he'd done with Logan and Wynter. She'd suffered terribly during her transition. Sexually heightened, they'd asked for his help and he'd been glad to oblige. "Logan and Wynter."

"You were with your Alpha's mate? Had sex with her?" Gillian attempted to hide her shock.

"Yes, but I wasn't alone. I was there to help Logan and Wynter get through her transition. She was hybrid and had just learned to become a wolf. Wynter almost died soon after. A vampire…he'd nearly drained her."

"Léopold?"

"No, no, no. I mean, don't get me wrong. Leo's a lethal son-of-a bitch, but he's my boy."

"You're close?"

"Yeah, we're tight. He'll be at the party, too."

"Does he know…about us?"

"No, but he will in about an hour or so."

"Are you sure we're doing the right thing? Lying about our relationship? Maybe Chaz would have come anyway."

"It would have taken too long. We need him to come to us. He's going to want to stop our mating."

"We should have killed him in California." It felt strange to openly acknowledge that they were luring him to his death. But Chaz gave her no option. Kill or be killed.

"Perhaps, but my place is here with my wolves. Had you been well, you would have done it yourself. Chaz had a chance to let this all go but when he sent his guys to New York, he signed his own death warrant. Aside from me wanting to kill him, Jax and Logan will mete out justice."

Gillian knew what he said to be true. Jax had already killed in front of her. The brutality had been shocking, yet there was no other acceptable solution. Pack law dictated the outcome.

Dimitri took her hand in his, and his burning touch reminded her of the spectacular day they'd spent together. She brought her fingers to her lips, recalling the feel, the taste of him. A shiver rolled over her as she thought of how they'd made love on the plane, the incredible ecstasy he'd brought to her world. Restraint was a skill she had practiced ever since she'd first learned to shift. Yet staying away from Dimitri had been nothing short of exhausting.

She'd been willing to dismiss the sex as nothing more than a physical attraction. However, hours of talking and laughing had led to a deep burning need, one that she'd have difficulty denying tonight.

She glanced down to her dress that fit like a glove. Dimitri had taken care of every last detail, down to her strappy heels. At one time in her life a hot pair of shoes would have been enough to make her day, but now, the only thing that mattered was the wolf consuming her thoughts.

"Thank you." She smiled.

"For what?"

"Today. The parade. Everything."

"Ah, darlin'. No need to thank me, and for the record, I haven't nearly finished showing you everything." He winked. "You just wait."

Gillian laughed softly, but was certain that he meant what he said. Like a knife, his words sliced through her reservations. Would she sacrifice her tiger in order to experience love? It terrified her. It thrilled her. Gillian had no idea what it felt like to know that someone was her mate, but if she could choose anyone, it'd be the wolf holding her hand.

Gillian took a deep breath, counting to ten. Like an actress, she plastered a smile on her face, attempting to regulate her breathing so that no one would detect her consternation. Never in her life had she been around so many wolves. She scanned the ballroom, observing the crowd engaged in lively conversation, dancing and drinking as if they hadn't a care in the world. Both males and females wore masks, dressed up for the lavish affair.

Allowing Dimitri to lead her through the mass of celebrating partygoers, she glided across the floor. She nodded to Jake, who was already dancing with a pretty blonde. People passed and greeted her as if they'd known her all her life. It was as if she'd stepped into an alternate universe. They all looked human in their dresses, suits and ties. But it was an illusion. The hum of magic and nature buzzed in the air along with the zydeco waltz.

Gillian held tight to Dimitri's hand as an imposing gentleman approached. Though he was not as tall as Dimitri, Gillian immediately registered the power emanating from him. *Wolf. Alpha.* Instinctively, she lowered her eyes. The shock of her submission startled her as it was the first time she'd felt compelled to honor an Alpha.

"Hey man, how are you?" Dimitri greeted him, intrigued by Gillian's gaze.

"D, I'm glad you're back. Introduce me," Logan told him.

"Gilly, this is Logan, our fearless leader. Alpha, meet Gilly."

"Nice to meet you, Gilly. Can I get you a drink?" he asked, signaling to a server. Flutes of champagne were swiftly brought over on a silver tray. Handing her a glass, he gave Dimitri a knowing grin.

"Thank you. Nice to meet you," Gillian managed. She tried to remember how nervous she'd been meeting some of the most famous subjects that she'd photographed. Holding tight to a thread of calm, she smiled up at him.

"It's I who should be thanking you. I hear you saved my beta."

"He saved me right back. We're even." She glanced at Dimitri and back to Logan. "Thanks for helping me. I'm sorry I've brought danger to your pack."

"Don't give it another thought. I'm looking forward to some payback for what they did to D."

Gillian was about to tell him how incredible Dimitri had been when he saved her, but was interrupted by a pretty woman who'd wrapped her arms around the Alpha's waist. He laughed, bringing his lips to hers. Dimitri smiled at Gillian in understanding; this was Logan's mate. Logan laughed, and broke the kiss with her, and Gillian swore she saw him blush.

"Dimitri," Wynter squealed. Breaking free of her Alpha's arms, she gave Dimitri a quick hug and kiss. Within seconds, she was back in Logan's embrace.

"Hi there. I'm Wynter," Wynter said, reaching for Gillian's hand. "Nice to meet you."

"Hello," Gillian replied, returning her greeting with caution. This was the woman who'd made love to Dimitri. Intellectually, Gillian knew Wynter was mated, yet the idea of Dimitri deep inside another turned her stomach.

"Sorry I'm late. I was busy with our baby girl. This is the first time we've left her with a sitter."

"A baby?" Gillian asked.

"Ava. We just adopted her. I'm afraid we won't be staying all night."

"How old is she?"

"Four months," Logan answered. "Sweetheart, do you mind if I get a minute with D? Just need to catch up on a few things."

"Sure thing, baby," Wynter agreed, giving him a kiss. She smiled at Gillian. "Gilly, would you mind going to the ladies' room with me? I was in such a rush to get out of the house that I didn't have a chance to check my dress. I think I might have a spot of formula on it."

"Sure," Gillian agreed. She gave Dimitri a nod, leery of wandering off on her own in a room full of shifters.

"Don't worry. I'll keep her safe," Wynter told Dimitri with a wink. "Promise not to steal her for too long."

Wynter launched into a story about her daughter, and Gillian forced herself to let go of her jealousy, deciding that whatever had happened was truly in the past. As their conversation progressed, she wondered if the Alpha had told his mate the truth about the sham they were perpetrating. Or like everyone else at the party, was Wynter under the impression that she really was Dimitri's mate? Gillian knew it would only be a matter of time before they all found out she was a fake. If they got close enough, they'd know she wasn't a wolf. She couldn't imagine the animosity they'd feel knowing they had been lied to, and guilt gnawed at her.

With talk of babies, Gillian unconsciously held her hand to her belly and thought of how she'd like to have children of her own someday. Most days, she put it to the back of her mind. Her career had allowed her to do so. Mating itself seemed like wishful thinking. To be pregnant with a child of the man she loved seemed like an impossibility of extraordinary proportions.

"I know that you're pretending to be mates to draw out Chaz, but you're telling me that she's your mate, as in for real?" the Alpha asked, amused with his friend's misery. It wasn't that he didn't love him like a brother, but karma was a bitch. Dimitri had made fun of him, enjoying every last drip of angst Logan went through when he'd found his mate, so turnabout was fair play.

"You betcha," Dimitri said, taking a sip of his whisky. He watched Gillian across the room. Dressed in a slinky red number, she threw her head back, giggling at something Wynter had said. Her amber eyes flickered behind her delicate black metal mask. "Look at her."

"She's sexy, isn't she?" Logan answered.

"My mate, not yours."

"Ah yes, she's beautiful as well. But what are you going to do with a cat? I think it's ironic you had a laugh riot over me adopting a kitten and now you're gonna mate with one." Logan laughed and slapped Dimitri on his shoulder.

Dimitri waved to his friend, Léopold Devereoux, who crossed the room.

"Here comes trouble," Logan commented.

"Bonne soirée, mes amis," Léopold greeted them.

"How's it going? Where's your better half?" Dimitri asked.

"Mon amour is on her way over from Kade's house," he said, referring to Kade Issacson, who led the New Orleans vampires. Léopold was his sire, and unfortunately, Kade's fiancée, Sydney, had been turned vampire, in a tragic accident involving a demon. "Sydney isn't doing so well, I'm afraid. Laryssa feels responsible. The girls have been taking turns, visiting."

"Sydney's seeing visitors? That's progress," Dimitri noted.

"Perhaps. But she's not speaking to anyone. Laryssa goes anyway. Sits with her. Reads to her. I'm not sure she's going to survive the transition. Of course, I haven't mentioned it to Kade. There's no stronger medicine than hope."

"Sorry to hear that, Leo."

"Not to change the subject, but did you tell him?" Logan asked.

"No, I did not." Dimitri glared at his Alpha, who was delighting in his predicament entirely too much.

"Our beta here's got himself a problem."

"He does?" Léopold mused, trying to read Dimitri's face.

"Part of being an Alpha is knowin' when to ask an expert. Leo's older than both of us tenfold. Perhaps he's got a solution for your problem," Logan suggested.

Léopold studied his friend, noting how Dimitri kept his eyes on an attractive redhead at the bar. Listening to his pulse race when she stole a glance at him, he smiled.

"Now this is interesting…a mate for our beta."

"How do you do that? It's creepy, ya know," Dimitri remarked to Léopold. "My Alpha's been 'round me since I've been a babe. But you…what's your secret?"

"And look at her eyes…well, now, that is surprising. A lion? Leopard, maybe?" he asked.

"Tiger," Logan corrected.

"Yep," Dimitri sighed. "She's my mate. But we've got issues."

"Does she even know?" Léopold asked.

"What do you think?"

"I've heard of this happening before. A hybrid, I assume. Her tiger's a rare breed. Maljavan would be my guess."

"Are you making this shit up?" Logan asked with a chuckle.

"Her eyes. Like a cat's. It's a trait of her species. She can mate with a wolf, but she could lose her ability to shift. Like Sydney's transition to vampire, her cat may not survive. May I ask, she's hybrid, but her mother, was she full tiger or hybrid as well?"

"I'm pretty sure that her mother was hybrid. Her father was an Alpha," Dimitri replied.

"Here comes the punch line," Logan warned, waiting on Léopold's reaction to the next tidbit of information.

"Her brother is Jax Chandler." Dimitri took a deep draw of the amber liquid in his glass and exhaled. "Gilly said her mom lost the ability to shift after she mated. But Jax thinks she denied her wolf and that's why she can't shift. I haven't met her, so I'm not sure."

"Jax's father's been dead for a while. Jax and I became friends when he took over several years ago. But he never mentioned a sister," Léopold commented.

"Family secrets run deep, I guess. After what went down in San Diego, she went to him for help."

"Any news on Chaz Baldwin?" Léopold inquired.

"He's not in NOLA," Logan replied.

"Yet. It's just a matter of time," Dimitri said.

"If you mate with her, he can't have her," Léopold told him.

"If is the optimal word in that sentence. And even if I manage that, he's still comin' for her. What I don't get is why he wants her so badly. Why would an Alpha force a mating on someone who wasn't all wolf?"

"It's rumored that she'll give a gift to the one who mates her," Léopold speculated.

"What?"

"A gift," he repeated. "Not sure what it is, but it appears it's worth killing for. Jax's father probably knew.

Therefore Jax knows. And your pretty little pussy cat, mais oui, she definitely knows."

"She didn't say anything," Dimitri grumbled.

"Secrets, secrets…we all have them. Do not judge her harshly, my friend. She's vulnerable," Léopold said, touching his shoulder. A shiver ran through him, and he grimaced.

"There's got to be a way to mate without killing her cat…I can't do that to her."

"Perhaps. Jax is a wise leader. It's very likely that if she's half wolf, her wolf will emerge. If she can go to wolf, then maybe she can also call on her cat. I imagine the transition is similar to Sydney's in that you have to want it to happen. The mind is a powerful influence. You both know this."

"I guess that gives me something to work with." Dimitri's lips tightened as he caught sight of a man watching Gillian.

"Now that we have that settled, let's discuss what in the hell's wrong with you. Does he know?" Léopold pinned his eyes on Dimitri, his tone growing serious.

Perpetrating deceit bored a hole in Dimitri's chest. It was time to share the truth.

"I won't ask how you knew…it's only been a few days since I saw the witch." Dimitri took a deep breath and blew it out. "My wolf. Something's still got a hold of me. Ilsbeth gave me this tonic. But it's not enough. Strange part is that when I've been with Gilly, I felt a little better. You know she healed me."

"She does have gifts," Léopold observed.

"For real. I was near death on that beach. My wolf wouldn't surface," he recalled. "But the witch. She wants me to move in with her."

"What the fuck?" Logan blurted out.

"Yeah, that's about it. I told her no, of course, but she kissed me. And ya know, she was already pissed that I wouldn't date her anymore. She's still holding a grudge. Not sure how the news of my mating's goin' to fly."

"I imagine she'll continue to be put out, but she won't hurt you," Léopold assured him.

"I'm not so sure about that. You and I both know she's one scary bitch. Gorgeous, but scary."

"That she is, mon ami, but she will find a way to fix you."

"Leo's right, D. Ilsbeth knows full well she's not your mate. She may be bitter but she's not stupid. If she wants the symbiotic relationship between the vamps, wolves and witches to continue, she's gotta get over it. It's the only way. In the meantime, I suggest you talk with your woman about you know…your mating status," Logan suggested with a wicked grin.

"Really? Hello, Logan. Pot meet kettle. I recall you marking your mate without even telling her. How soon we forget," Dimitri snorted.

"Oh, I don't forget. It was a little difficult." Logan smiled. "But hey, it all worked out just fine."

"Okay, must be nice rewriting history."

"Ah, I do enjoy a spirited debate," Léopold chuckled. "But in the interest of time, because my sweet Laryssa's going to be here soon, let's just all agree that you'll tell her. I understand you don't want to kill her tiger, but I'm going to side with Jax on this one. If she wants to shift after the mating, she'll do it as a wolf. It's hard to tell from this distance but she seems made of strong stock. You must engage in preparation to make it happen."

"Jesus, Leo, you make it sound so clinical. Holy shit, this sucks," Dimitri huffed.

"Life has not promised us easy, only love."

"I love it when he goes all philosophical on us," Logan commented.

"He's almost as old as Socrates," Dimitri joked.

"Hardly. You're off by a thousand years," Léopold sniffed, grabbing a flute off a passing waiter's tray. "Speaking of ancient, I do believe the witch has arrived."

All eyes turned to the petite woman whose customarily blonde hair had been dyed turquoise. Her stunning appearance captured the attention of everyone in the room, her emerald-green velvet dress trailing several feet behind her. Smiling as if she were the queen of New Orleans, her face drew tight as she caught sight of Dimitri.

Gillian found the Alpha's mate, Wynter, welcoming, introducing her to members of the pack. But she felt disingenuous pretending that she belonged to Dimitri. Sooner or later, they'd suspect the truth. Animals were not easily deceived. Yet as she met one wolf after the other, she grew certain about her feelings for the beta. She might not be his true mate, but she wanted to be.

She blinked over to Dimitri who smiled at her. He talked with his friends, while he protectively watched her from a distance. She smoothed down the fabric of her dress, taking in the sight of her stylish wolf. He wore black dress pants, his white dress shirt unbuttoned so that she could see a hint of the tattoos on his chest. His black leather mask did little to hide the fire in his eyes.

Wynter left Gillian's side to address another pack member when a stranger sidled up to her at the bar. She hardly noticed him as all eyes fell to an attractive woman entering the ballroom, who appeared to glide across the floor, her hair tied up in intricate braids. Her silver mask sparkled underneath the black light, illuminating her iceblue eyes.

Amazement turned to jealousy as Gillian watched Dimitri turn his focus to the beautiful woman. Her tiger hissed as he embraced the blue-haired beauty. Dimitri took her by the hand, leading her to a secluded corner of the room. Gillian's eyes flared in anger, her heart pounding blood through her veins. Did he have a mate? Was everything he'd told her, the way he'd made her feel, all a lie? Was it all part of their hoax? Rage coursed through her. She went to cross the room to confront him, when the stranger spoke to her.

"You're new here," he commented. "Can I get you a drink?"

"Yeah," she responded mindlessly, unable to take her eyes off of Dimitri.

"My name's Alex. I'm visiting my friend, Seth, for Mardi Gras. I live in Chicago," he explained, extending his hand.

Gillian smiled, attempting to be polite.

"You wanna dance?" he asked.

"You're human?" she asked, her thoughts distracted.

"Yeah, pretty crazy, right? The Alpha said it was okay, since I was in town on business. Seth and I go way back. You a wolf, too?"

"Yes." Who Seth was she had no idea and wasn't about to ask. Gillian found it difficult to concentrate on his questions.

"You wanna dance?" he asked again.

What Gillian really wanted was to forget, to run away. The woman stroked her hand over Dimitri's forearm, and Gillian thought she'd be sick. She'd never been a jealous person before, but she could hardly contain the green-eyed monster that threatened to throttle the woman touching her man.

"Um, what did you say?" she asked.

"Let's dance," he said, taking her hand.

Gillian glared at Dimitri, but he didn't even notice as Alex led her out onto the dance floor. He was preoccupied, infatuated with another woman, someone who was possibly his mate. She glanced at the human, reasoning that he couldn't hurt her. Dimitri didn't seem to even care. It was just one dance.

But as the stranger wrapped his hand around her waist to lead her in a waltz, she felt nauseous and attempted to pull away. Alex held tight, yanking her flush against his arousal and her head grew dizzy at his touch. Before she knew what was happening, he'd spun her around, making her lose sight of her wolf. The stranger's hand fell to her bottom and her tiger roared, warning the stranger to free her. She lost control, and her claws emerged.

"You're looking well," Ilsbeth noted, the corners of her lips curled upward.

"Ilsbeth, cut the crap. Have you found a cure?" Dimitri said, taking her by the hand, leading her into a corner. He restrained the anger that had bubbled to the surface soon after she'd purposefully hugged him as if they were still dating.

"Did you finally realize that you need to come stay with me?" Ilsbeth tilted her head. She darted her tongue out of her mouth, seductively dragging its tip along the rim of her martini glass, and smiled.

"Jesus Christ, witch. Not tonight, okay? Did you find it or not?"

"Something's different about you," she observed. Ilsbeth reached for his arm, gliding her thin fingers over his inner wrist until she reached the crook of his elbow.

"Ilsbeth. Please." Dimitri cringed as the words came out as if he was begging.

"What is it? You feel different, too. Your energy is running hot," she noted.

"No, don't," he snapped at her. Across the room, Gillian glared at him, her rage emanating like a laser at having another woman touch her mate. "I'm here with someone."

"Who?" Ilsbeth asked. She retreated somewhat but still kept her hand on his skin. As a server passed, she set her glass on the tray. Taking his hands, she closed her eyes, concentrating on his aura.

"Ilsbeth, I'm sorry. I told you this would happen. This is why I couldn't commit to you," Dimitri answered.

Ilsbeth slowly opened her eyes. Her lips compressed into a fine line as awareness of the situation took hold.

"I've found her."

"No," she whispered, withdrawing her hands.

"You knew this was my fate," Dimitri stated, shaking his head. He hadn't meant to hurt her, but he'd grown tired of asking for forgiveness for something that was beyond his control. It had been months since they'd stopped seeing each other, and he was done apologizing.

"Yes, I did." Ilsbeth took a deep breath. "But that didn't mean I wanted it to happen."

Dimitri smiled but then his face dropped as he saw Gillian talking to a stranger at the bar. Jerking his attention back to the witch, he sought to speak his piece.

"I need your help. This thing with my wolf. Do you have any news?"

"A sorcerer from Miami is arriving tomorrow. He's quite powerful and has promised to engage convocation with our coven. It is at that time I expect an answer. I apologize that it has taken even this long. My offer to stay at my house remains."

"I appreciate that but I can't..." Dimitri's words trailed off as he watched his mate take the hand of another man. He growled as she was swept up into an embrace not his own.

Ilsbeth followed Dimitri's line of vision until she saw the woman who had stolen his heart.

"This is the female who commands your soul?"

"Yes," he spat out.

"She goes with another...interesting."

"She's hybrid...she doesn't know."

"How do you expect this to work?" Ilsbeth honed in on Gillian's eyes, which met hers. "A tiger?"

"Yes."

"The mating is uncertain."

"You're wrong," he vowed. "I've never been more certain of anything in my entire life."

Dimitri's canines dropped as he sensed Gillian's fear and in response, he tore across the dance floor. The scent of human blood permeated the room. The sound of Gillian slapping the man's face rang in his ears.

"What the hell? This fuckin' bitch just scratched me!" the stranger screamed.

Dimitri roared, shoving him across the room into the wall. Gillian, stunned and embarrassed, retracted her claws and fisted her hands. Logan ran over to Dimitri, prying his hands off the man's neck. He held his beta around the chest, while Jake and Léopold dragged the bleeding man out the door.

"It was just a matter of time," Logan quipped, patting his friend on the back. "Take a break, D. Let's get back to the party. Leo will take care of him. Can I let you go now?"

Dimitri nodded, panting as his Alpha released him. Feral, he turned to Gillian, who'd begun to retreat from the dance floor. The room went quiet as his eyes pinned on hers. Stalking his prey, he advanced on Gillian, who shook her head, wiping the blood on her dress.

"It's a lie," she said under her breath, recalling how she'd seen him with another woman. Her voice shook in anger. "I'm not your…"

"You're my mate," he asserted, loud enough so that everyone in the room could hear him.

"But you…you…and her." Gillian's eyes darted to the nearest exit.

"Acadian wolves," Dimitri called to his pack. It'd never be enough for the rumor to spread on its own. No, his wolf demanded a public claiming of his mate. He'd lay it on the line. She may ultimately reject him, but he'd be damned if he'd go one more second lying to her. "This female, she's mine. We'll be mated soon."

Gillian stared at Dimitri as if he'd lost his mind. She'd expected they'd stick to their original plan of letting the news of their mating slowly permeate the pack through the grapevine. A public announcement was over the top. Neither one of them would ever recover from the lie.

"What are you saying?" she croaked as Dimitri took her in his arms.

"You. Are. My. Mate. And as proud as I am that you just tore into that asshole with your claws, no other male puts his hands on you until we're mated," he warned. "Understood?"

"This can't be," she whispered into his ear. The scent of him calmed her, despite the fact that she'd been angry. Every last man and woman watched them intently as if they were on a stage, putting on a play.

"Oh, it be, cher. Choose me or not, you're mine."

Shocked, Gillian blinked. Her heart raced at his declaration. The animal inside of her rejoiced in quiet celebration. Oh Goddess, how had she missed the fact that Dimitri was hers? She hadn't wanted to acknowledge that the desire she'd been feeling could be true. *Choose me or not.* Gillian didn't want to admit it to Dimitri but she'd already made the choice. Her great cat would sacrifice anything to have the wolf who laid claim to her.

Panic set in and she began to hyperventilate. She sucked air, unable to breathe. Her eyes teared, gasping for air.

"Gilly." She heard him call her name, but the circle of black began to close in on her.

"Gilly," he growled, his tone firmer, commanding her.

"I...I can't breathe," she mouthed.

"Feel me, breathe with me...now." Dimitri unbuttoned his shirt and slid her hands underneath the fabric.

"Dimitri..."

"Breathe, Gilly. In and out. Do it with me. You're going to be just fine, kitten," he told her, his voice calm and steady.

"No, I can't..."

"Yes you can. In and out...concentrate on my voice, the feel of my skin on yours." He plowed his fingers into her hair and locked his eyes on hers. "See? You're okay now. This is real and happening. We're mates. You'll be okay. That's it."

Gillian focused on Dimitri, obeying his command. So wrong to submit, yet it felt natural. As her breathing returned to normal, the heat between them combusted.

Dimitri is my mate. Her eyes fell to his lips and within seconds, he'd captured her mouth, drawing her into his embrace. Digging her fingers into his skin, she moaned into his mouth, wild with desire. With the realization that they were still on the dance floor, she nodded as he tore his lips away from hers and followed him blindly as he led her outside.

By the time they'd reached the open courtyard, she was on fire with lust for her mate. She moaned as he took her again, his tongue plunging into her mouth. Returning his savage kiss, she clutched at him, giving in to the passion she'd held back for the past two days. Stumbling back against the trellis, she gasped as he hiked up her thigh and wrapped it around his waist.

"I'm sorry," she breathed. "I shouldn't have gone with him…"

"Stop talking," he ordered, pressing his lips to her collarbone.

"But we're at…ah," she moaned as he tugged at the front of her dress, exposing her breast. Her ripe peak hit the cool night air, puckering in arousal.

"I'm claiming you tonight. I will have you…now," he stated. His mouth latched onto her firm nipple, and he twirled his tongue over it, sucking and nipping at her flesh.

"Oh God, yes…" Gillian couldn't believe she was agreeing to making love, without regard to over a hundred people who partied inside the hall.

As Dimitri shuffled backwards toward the brick wall, he swore. *Goddamn it, I should have done this earlier where there was a bed.* They didn't seem to have a good track record when it came to actually making love in one. No, public displays of affection were more their style.

Laving at her breast, he cupped her ass, driving his rock-hard erection up into her belly. Dimitri bunched the fabric of her skirt and hooked a claw under her panties. The shredded panty fell to the ground and he reached between them, unbuckling his pants. Gillian tore open his shirt, scratching and biting at his chest. His pants dropped around his ankles, and she threw her hands around his neck. Hoisting herself upward, she wrapped both her legs around his waist. Dimitri stroked his hard arousal once, before driving himself up into her hot core.

His canines descended, and he dragged his teeth from the hollow behind her ear down to her chest. Using the only semblance of control he could summon, he turned his head so that he didn't risk nicking her with his teeth. Resolved, he'd already decided that when he marked her as his, she'd submit to him, welcoming his bite. Tonight, claiming her within the shroud of honesty, his mind and animal would be satisfied with the knowledge she was his.

Gillian screamed with each pump of his hips. She breathed into his kiss, biting at his lips. She was barely aware that her own fangs had dropped, her tiger celebrating in a ravenous frenzy. She tilted her pelvis, building a pulsing rhythm against her clitoris.

"Harder, yes, fuck me," she groaned into his mouth.

"You're mine. Do you hear me, Gilly?" Dimitri plunged his cock into her, accentuating every word he said.

"Yes, yes…please. Oh God, yes," she cried.

"Mate. Say it," he commanded, thrusting. His orgasm threatened, but he held back. He needed to hear her *own* their relationship.

"Please." Gillian bit her own lip as her tight channel quivered around him. "I'm coming."

"Not yet. Say it, cher. I swear to God, I'll stop right now," he warned. "You know it to be true."

"I don't know how…"

"Mate."

"Yes, oh my God. You're my mate," she cried out, her forehead falling against his chest. At her admission, a spasm of ecstasy rippled through her.

"Yes, Gilly, yes," he grunted, his fiery release pulsing deep inside his mate. Holding her tightly, he nuzzled into her shoulder. A small chuckle broke from his lips.

"What's so funny?" she asked, slipping gently down off his softening erection.

"Easy, darlin'. You're going to break something if you move too fast," he warned with a smile.

"Come on, what's so funny?"

"I've got a feeling I'm going to need to see a doctor tomorrow on account of my ass being pressed against these bricks."

"I feel like a teenager." She laughed.

"You did *this* as a teenager?"

"Um, no…but the feeling…like I can't get enough of you. God, I can't believe we just had sex out here."

"No worries. Besides, no one saw us," he assured her. *They all probably heard us.*

Dimitri was unconcerned about public sex. That was commonplace in some of the clubs he'd frequented. Even in the wild, on a full moon, wolves were known to make love outdoors, with little regard for others. But Dimitri was worried at how feral he'd become. Never in his life had he lost control like he'd just done. It was the way he'd taken her on the dance floor, forcing her to admit the feelings she had for him, that gave him pause.

"We've got to talk, Dimitri," she began.

Dimitri sighed, knowing this discussion would need to be held. He settled her onto her feet, and yanked up his pants. After zippering up, he took her back into his arms, uncomfortable with the loss of her warmth, and spoke into her hair.

"Listen, Gil. I'm not sure how this is going to work out, and you're right, we need to talk. But tonight, seeing you with that jerk, and shit, even before that…I'm not the kind of guy who lies to anyone, let alone his mate. I'm sorry I even waited this long to tell you."

"Yesterday and last night were the hardest hours of my life. I was just worried…that my feelings for you were getting too strong. I don't want to get hurt. That woman…"

"Ilsbeth. We'll talk about her tomorrow," he promised. Dimitri had been with many women over the past century, but explaining his complicated relationship with the witch to his mate wasn't a conversation he was looking to have tonight.

As Gillian lay her head against his chest, his heart grew heavy with awareness of the consequences of mating. Even though he'd just publicly announced her as his, she remained unmarked. No choice had been made yet, but it would be soon. If Gillian chose him as her mate, her tiger would die.

Chapter Thirteen

Dimitri ushered Gillian into the limo, thankful that Logan and Jake had kept their mouths shut about what had happened at the ball. Despite the missing buttons on his shirt and the tear in the backside of his pants, they'd walked back into the party as if they hadn't just had hot animal sex during the fancy event. Not that a soul in attendance had expected a quiet night anyhow. With Mardi Gras in full swing, everyone tended to be a little more rambunctious. Making love in the courtyard had added a pleasurable amount of crazy to the evening, Dimitri thought. Even Léopold had simply laughed, aware that his friend had taken his mate right there against the wall. Dimitri supposed had he cared what people thought, he'd be apologetic, perhaps embarrassed. But as Gillian gave him a sexy smile on their way out, nothing but desire for her played in his mind. Even the reality of their problems wasn't enough to deter him from enjoying her.

As he settled her against his chest, he considered his trip to the west coast had been one of the worst and best vacations he'd ever taken. Almost getting killed was a snag he hadn't expected. But finding his mate was turning out to be one of his most exciting adventures to date. He knew soon enough, he'd have to settle back down, working for Logan in security in his investment firm and assisting with pack matters.

The only regret he supposed he had was losing one of his favorite bikes. He'd reconditioned the thirty-year-old Harley, and wished it hadn't been trashed on some California beach. But like every other material possession he'd acquired over the years, he'd never gotten too attached. Things could be replaced. Although wolves rarely died, he'd watched as human friends had submitted to the aging process. On their deathbeds, they never wished for more trinkets.

Gillian's caress to his arm brought him out of his reverie. He noticed that she'd gone quiet and grew concerned.

"You okay?" Dimitri asked her.

"Yeah, I'm just thinking about things."

"Things, huh? Like what?"

"Like where we're going? Wondering why you still need to talk to the witch?"

"We're taking a trip outside the city…to my home. Jake's goin' to round up your things and bring them to us, so don't worry about your pictures," Dimitri answered, purposefully avoiding her second question.

"Okay, thanks. I'm not worried, though. I already reviewed some of them…shot Jax an email with a few I thought we might be able to use for the spread."

"Whatever's going to happen with Chaz is going to happen soon. I just prefer to be on the bayou for a few days. Get some fresh air. The full moon's in two nights."

"And the witch?" she pressed.

Responding with silence, Dimitri kissed the top of her head, hoping she'd relent.

"What aren't you telling me? I don't know what it is, but you're starting to worry me. I'm not asking you to explain what's going on between you and her, I'm asking about you." Gillian pushed out of his arms and placed her palms on his shoulder. When he didn't answer her, she slid both her hands under the collar of his shirt, touching his skin. Concentrating on finding his wolf, her eyes flashed open. "Something's off."

Dimitri reached for her hands, taking them in his own. He took a deep breath and glanced out the window.

"Your wolf." Her voice trembled as fear replaced her calm demeanor.

"I didn't want to say anything. It's just that whatever latched onto me, it's not gone. Ilsbeth…she gave me something…but it's temporary."

"A demon?"

"No, some kind of parasite. My take is that it's energy…evil energy. Ilsbeth isn't sayin'."

"What do you mean, it's temporary? Like it's going to go away?"

"No…more like I could lose my ability to shift again. And if that happens…well, you can see how that might be a problem for me. You think Logan would mind if I followed them around in an ATV when the pack goes for a run?" Dimitri tried to play down the serious nature of the issue. If he could no longer shift, he couldn't be beta. He wondered if they'd even let him stay in Acadian wolves.

"I'm so sorry."

"Hey now, this is my problem, not yours. You weren't the fool who jumped in the hell pit."

"You did it to save the baby. For your friend. That makes you a hero." Gillian briefly placed her lips on his, and continued. "We're going to fix this. Together. If that witch can't help you, we'll find another one. I'll ask Jax. I promise you…this is not the end."

"We're a fine pair, aren't we? I'm losin' my wolf. And by mating, your tiger…" Dimitri shook his head, disgusted. Usually optimistic, talking about the situation drove home the reality of their perplexing conundrum. "The witch is bringin' in a sorcerer from Miami tomorrow. As for you, kitty cat, no one says you gotta mate with me."

Gillian paused at his words. *Doesn't he want to mate with me?*

"That's true, wolf. But maybe you're changing my mind about things. And it's my decision to make."

"Don't get me wrong, Gilly. Tonight in that courtyard…I couldn't get enough of you. If this feelin' is half of what happens when we mate, it's goin' to be incredible. My wolf may be distant at times, but he...I...the desire to mark you...I'm not going to be able to hold off much longer."

Gillian gave a silly smile at his declaration. It wasn't rational, she knew. But after being with him all day, getting to know him, she wanted more of a commitment. Seeing him with Ilsbeth drove her to stake her claim on him. Her beast sought to brand him as her own, and despite it being the death of her, the hunger grew with each passing minute.

"What's funny?" Dimitri asked, unable to discern how she felt.

"Nothing...It's just that I've spent my entire life avoiding wolves. And now..."

"Now?" he asked, sweeping his fingers into her hair. Her pink lips parted in anticipation of his kiss.

"Now," she breathed. So close, she could feel the heat of him at her mouth. "All I can think about is staying around wolves."

"Wolves?" he challenged, gently tilting her head, exposing her neck.

"One wolf," she corrected with a sigh.

"Hmm?"

"My wolf," she cried as he nipped at her neck.

"Are you ready to belong to this wolf?" Dimitri traced the tip of his tongue along her bottom lip.

"Ahhh...Dimitri," she moaned. She tried to kiss him, but he held her firmly by her hair, controlling her every movement. Her pussy flooded in arousal with his command. In another place and time, submission wasn't a word in her vocabulary. But in his arms, she'd give him whatever he wanted and then some.

"What's that, kitten? I'm afraid I can't hear you?"

"Please…"

"I do enjoy hearing you beg, darlin' but I want an answer." Dimitri licked at the corner of her mouth, amused when she tried to kiss him. His wolf wouldn't tolerate any more games.

"Yes," she breathed. Her eyelids fluttered open, her eyes locked on his. Fate was stronger than fear. She yearned to belong to him, and his mark on her skin would begin the journey.

"Yes." He smiled, pleased with her response.

His lips crushed against hers, drinking in her essence. Her breasts pressed against his chest, and she clawed at his back. The electricity seared the air, their connection exploding into fireworks. Desperately, they kissed and caressed, lost in each other. It was as if nothing but the two of them existed. Nothing mattered but the realization that they'd chosen each other.

Gillian barely noticed when the car came to a stop. She'd reached to unbutton his shirt, but firm hands prevented her from doing so. Dimitri reluctantly tore his lips away from hers. Panting, he reached for the door handle and exited, helping her out of the car.

"In the house," he told her.

Dimitri

As she went to exit the car, Dimitri effortlessly lifted her into his arms. Gillian giggled, amazed at his strength. She had no idea where she was and didn't care. Tearing at his shirt, she exposed his chest, pressing her lips to his skin.

Barely cognizant of her surroundings, she caught sight of the illuminated herringbone stone walkway. Fireflies lit up the foggy night sky against a backdrop of draping Spanish moss. The scent of the bayou permeated the air while an orchestra of insects played in the distance.

By the time they'd reached the front door, she'd only slightly composed herself, impatiently waiting for Dimitri to unlock it. A few seconds seemed like a lifetime as he punched in the security code. The heavy cedar wood door creaked open, and she wiggled in his arms.

"No time for a tour," Dimitri managed as he carried her up the staircase. His mouth found hers and he fell back against the entryway, kicking off his shoes. He laughed as she reached for his pants.

"Faster," she demanded. The heat between her legs grew unbearable. Yearning to touch him, she attempted to unbuckle his belt with one hand.

"Now that's not very submissive of you, mate. You know I'm lookin' forward to it," Dimitri teased. Oh she'd submit, all right. And he hadn't forgotten about his promise to have Jake watch. But tonight, it'd only be him and her, together.

"I need you," she cried, grazing his nipple with her teeth. Unable to loosen his pants, she slid her hand underneath the waistband and wrapped her fingers around his rigid shaft.

"Damn, girl, now that's gonna leave marks. You're asking for a spanking," Dimitri grunted as she stroked him.

By the time he made it to his bedroom, he was sweating in anticipation. Her lips on his skin. Her hands on his dick. It was too much and not enough all at once.

Gently, he helped her steady on her feet. As the realization hit them that they were about to go forward with their relationship, committing in a way that could not be undone, they paused, gazing in each other's eyes. Dimitri stood statuesque above her, his dark eyes trained on hers. His white dress shirt hung wide open, his bronze chest reflecting the light from the moon and stars. The sexual tension escalated as they stood inches from each other, no longer touching.

Dimitri reached for her waist and found the zipper to her dress. He tugged, until he reached her hip. Hooking his thumbs over her spaghetti straps, he pulled downward until the fabric lay pooled at her feet. Gillian stood smiling in only her black lace bra and matching heels. She wore no panties, thanks to their earlier antics in the courtyard. With care, Gillian glided her palms over his ripped abdomen. When she reached his broad shoulders, she dragged his sleeves off his arms, undressing him. As the shirt hit the floor, she gave him a seductive smile, reaching behind her and unsnapping her bra.

Not giving him a chance to touch her, Gillian braced her hands on his hips. Carefully she descended, softly kissing his belly as she lowered herself onto her knees. Dimitri sucked an audible breath as Gillian unbuttoned his pants, freeing his hardened arousal. She slid her fingers over his muscular buttocks, jostling his trousers until they fell down, joining her dress at his feet. Pressing her cheek against his tight corded thigh, she moaned, her hot breath causing his shaft to jerk in response.

Gillian teased his skin, lightly skimming her fingertips over the backs of his calves, never losing contact until she'd cupped his firm buttocks. Eyeing his straining erection, she darted her tongue outward and laved its broad crown. She licked at its slit, moaning in satisfaction as his salty taste amped her desire. Parting her lips, she took him all the way into her warm mouth and sucked hard. Gillian twirled her tongue against his silken steel, plunging up and down, from his tip to the root of him. She gently dug her fingernails into his ass, pulling him closer toward her so that she could swallow him more deeply.

Dimitri bit his lip as the sweet torture continued. Unable to take her lips around him for another second, he growled. There was no way he was coming in her mouth. She'd had her fun and now he'd have his.

"Cher, up," he commanded. Raking his fingers through her hair with one hand, he fisted it and tilted her head backwards, lifting her chin. Her mouth released him with a soft pop.

Gillian smiled and licked her lips as he slowly guided her upward and onto the bed. She tried to hoist herself further back onto the mattress, when she heard him tell her to lie back.

"Put your hands above your head...that's it...flat against the headboard. Soon enough I'll have you tied to my bed, but tonight, I want to test your self-control." Dimitri smiled as she complied, doing what he'd asked.

He knelt on the bed, his hands opening her thighs so he could get a better view. "Goddess, look at how beautiful you are." Leaning forward, he blew softly on her mound, intending to pay her back for what she'd just done to him. Tracing his thumbs over her swollen labia, he gently spread her.

"You're so soft. Your pussy smells of my scent and yours," Dimitri whispered. He flattened his tongue over her swollen clit, smiling as he felt her shiver underneath his touch. He pressed his lips to her folds, her juices flowing into his mouth. The delicious taste of her made his wolf howl, reminding him of his ultimate goal.

"Dimitri, oh my God, please," she pleaded, her body on fire with need.

Gillian sighed in pleasure as his fingers stroked deep inside her core, teasing her sensitive band of flesh. Dimitri flicked the tip of his tongue over her clitoris, and her body arched off the bed. She screamed, his mouth at her sex setting a thousand synapses firing. Her climax slammed into her. She thrashed and clawed her nails against the bed frame, losing control.

As she fought for breath, Dimitri hoisted her legs over his shoulders. With her eyes locked on his, she gasped as he gripped her thighs, sheathing himself completely. She thought he'd rip her in half, her pussy quivering around his enormous cock. He paused only for a second for her to adjust to the size of him, grunting as he began to move.

"Yes…ah, God," Gillian said mindlessly, lost in the feel of him within her. She fought the desire to reach for him, her palms flattened against the wood.

"Fuck, yes…you feel so goddamned good," he growled.

Her breasts, heavy with arousal, jostled in tandem with each of his thrusts. She contracted around him, her breath coming in punctuated grunts.

"I've got to come…please," she begged, so close to her release.

"That's right, cher. Say it," he encouraged. Dropping his hand between her legs, his thumb found her hooded flesh.

"More…Dimitri, I can't…please right there…" Gillian whimpered as Dimitri flicked over her clitoris, putting pressure on the sensitive nub. Uncontrollable spasms ripped through her once again. With no time to recover, she felt him pull out, flipping her onto her stomach.

"Hands and knees," he ordered, nudging her thighs apart with his knee.

"Don't stop. I need you in me."

"Now," he demanded.

Gillian scrambled into position, her own canines dropping in response and she hissed. It wasn't exactly submission, but for tonight, it would have to suffice.

"Ah, my sweet kitten. You've a lot to learn." He laughed, slapping her ass. She squealed and then moaned as he rubbed his palm over the heated skin. "You like that, don't you, darlin'?"

"Stop playing with me." She avoided answering. He responded by spanking her other cheek. "Ah, yes, I like it…fucking yes…now please, I can't wait."

"No matter what you want…" he glided his open palm down her back. When he reached her bottom, he trailed his thumb down her crevice, stopping to circle her tight puckered flesh, "no matter how dark you imagine the desire, you will tell me the truth."

"Yes," she acquiesced, unable to deny the urge to press back into his hand. She'd never explored anal play, but her body ablaze, she craved to experience everything.

"Don't you worry…we're gonna do everything…I'm gonna take you every way possible…including here," he promised, probing her with his thumb. Dimitri took his throbbing dick in his hand, sliding it over her entrance, moistening it with her juices. She heaved a breath, impatiently pushing back into him. But he held her still, slowly pressing into her anus. "We're gonna make love soon enough, cher. Feel me in you."

"Ah…it's so tight," she whispered, her head lolling forward.

"Relax now…here we go," he warned. Guiding his hot flesh into hers, he slowly entered until he was fully seated, his digit all the way into her ass. "That's it…give in to me, Gilly."

"Yes…please," Gillian breathed. The overwhelming sensation rippled through her body.

Dimitri began a slow pace, in and out, making love to her, but soon the craving to mark his mate overrode everything else. He withdrew his finger, cupping both sides of her bottom. Using her for leverage, he increased the pace, moving deep within her. In rhythmic fashion, he pounded in and out of her. Gillian rocked back into his thrusts, the sounds of flesh meeting flesh sounding throughout the night.

In a frenzy, Dimitri leaned over, his weight forcing them both onto their stomachs. She tightly gripped the sheets as he surged into her from behind. Wrapping her hair around his hand, he guided her head to the side, exposing the tendons of her neck.

"Do it," she cried. In the midst of their fervor, clarity struck and she willingly sought his bite. She was tired of being afraid of what she'd lose, and focused on everything that she could gain. *A partner. A life. A family. Perhaps even love.* The stakes were high. A risk to be certain, yet she refused to cower from fate.

Dimitri's wolf went wild at her call. His fangs descended. Pumping hard into her heat, he struck, clamping down on her creamy flesh. She cried out, and he held her still, careful not to puncture or tear Gillian's skin.

With a final thrust, he came hard, flooding into her. Shuddering, he let the remaining tremors claim him.

Releasing his jaw, Dimitri licked over where he'd bitten. She moaned and he lifted off her torso. He lay on his back, bringing her with him, resting her onto his chest. Embracing her, he kissed the top of her head and sighed.

While he'd initially been consumed by the lust and urge to mark his mate, he now reflected on what was in his heart, which felt tight with emotion. It wasn't just that he mourned the eventual loss of her tiger, although the thought weighed heavily upon him. For the first time in one hundred and twenty years, he'd developed strong feelings for a woman, one he wouldn't give up without a fight to the death.

Chapter Fourteen

Gillian awoke, the sun shining through the window panes. She moved to reach for Dimitri, her hand fondling the sheets. She realized he was gone, but in surprise, her fingertips touched a fragrant object that lay on his pillow. Her vision came into focus and she gazed upon the beautiful bouquet of irises. Each flower was unique with its silky purple and gold petals. She brought them to her nose, taking a deep sniff, and a broad smile broke across her face.

Holding them to her chest, she looked up at the cathedral ceiling, remembering how they'd made love the night before…twice. But it was recalling his bite that generated her deep sigh. Without even looking, she knew it was there. In the limo and then again in the house, she'd given him approval, given herself permission to accept his mark.

Her stomach growled and she marveled that she was more concerned about eating than the fact that she may soon not be able to shift. It wouldn't be decided until they'd mated, but what they'd done last night was the first step. She tried to conjure up a thread of regret. After all, she'd spent so much time trying to avoid the very thing she'd just thoroughly enjoyed. Yet nothing came to her. The excitement of seeing him again was the only thought spinning through her mind.

The sound of a piano startled her, and she jumped to her feet. Altogether nude, she found her way into the bathroom and spied a note on the mirror: *Robe is on the door and toothbrush is in the drawer. Come downstairs when you're ready, my lovely mate.* And he'd drawn a heart...a big ass freakin' heart. No one had ever written her a note. She laughed, thinking that her dominant wolf was a romantic; the more she knew about him, the more fate was convincing her that it knew what it was doing.

Gillian turned her back toward the mirror, and lifted her hair. As she'd suspected, a light pink pattern had appeared on her shoulder where he'd bitten her. Like a fine tattoo, its intricate design colored her skin. Exhilaration mixed with trepidation filled her heart. She could hardly believe she'd chosen Dimitri, that he was hers.

She considered that after it was all said and done, neither of them might be able to shift. Despite it all, the happiness in her chest refused to be thwarted. Though she'd detected his injured wolf when they'd made love, she hadn't thought about the consequences of her actions or the taint on his beast. Her only focus had been on the strong man holding her in his arms. She knew that today serious conversations needed to be had. As she traced the contours of the lines on her skin, pride in his mark superseded every other emotion.

After freshening up, using the bathroom, she tied the robe around her waist. Making her way to Dimitri, she heard classical music. It grew louder and more intense, and she found it interesting that he liked the genre. She'd expected him to listen to zydeco or rock n' roll, with his bad boy good looks, but this was a surprise, reminding her that she still didn't know him very well.

Quietly, she padded down the hallway, taking note of the colorful modern paintings on the wall. Holding tight to the banister, she descended into a bright, airy great room. She smiled at the sight of Dimitri sitting at a grand piano. Shirtless, the corded muscles of his back curved down into his shorts. Even though she was certain he'd heard her enter the room, he continued to play. His body rocked in rhythm, his fingers moving up and down the keys with the fluidity and ease of a concert pianist.

She came up behind him, placing her palms on his shoulders. His muscles tensed as he continued, lost in the piece. Energy flowed through him to her hands, and it was as if he were creating power via his connection to his instrument. As his fingers came to a rest, she pressed her lips to his back.

"That was beautiful," she said.

Dimitri quickly reached around to his mate. Before she knew what had happened, he'd lifted her off her feet and had her cradled in his lap.

"Good morning...or good afternoon, should I say?" Dimitri kissed her shoulder with small pecks until he reached the sensitive area behind her ear.

"You play the piano?" She giggled from the sensation.

"Hmm...yes but I'm more interested in playing with you," he replied. Tugging on her loosely tied belt, he slipped his hand over her skin, laying it on her belly.

"You were amazing." She smiled.

"Why thank you, cher. You were quite the little minx yourself. You ready to go for round two or is that round three? The courtyard counts, right?"

"Stop it." She slapped him softly on the chest.

"What? Is my count off?" Smiling ear to ear, he cupped her breast.

"Is sex all you think of?" she asked.

"That's a loaded question that I refuse to answer. Besides, your nipples don't lie." He gently pinched her pebbled peak. "I'm not the only one thinking of sex."

"Maybe, but that's only because of you. Now come on. Tell me about this." She gestured to the keys.

"This," he leaned forward and took her rosy tip into his mouth, sucking until she moaned, "this is soft and delicious."

She rolled her eyes and laughed. Crossing her legs together, she tried to thwart the ache that throbbed between them.

"I smell you, darlin' and it ain't the bacon that has my mouth waterin'." Dimitri pressed his face into the hollow between her breasts and kissed her skin.

"The....the piano," she stuttered, attempting to focus.

"You are tenacious."

"I am. Please, tell me."

"Mama insisted I learn how to play. 'The classics', she'd say. So the classics I'd play. Bach. Chopin. Beethoven. Once I shifted, well, I took up the squeezebox. Mama wasn't crazy 'bout it but she got used to it. Bought my first les tit noirs after the turn of the century…1910, it was. I've got a small band I play with sometimes. But at the end of the day, I always return to the eighty-eight."

"It's beautiful," she remarked, stroking her fingers over the ivories.

"Oui, ma chérie."

"French?"

"Ah, we're a bit French here, all right, but I'm afraid I've been hangin' out with Leo too much."

"And your parents?"

"Are in Philadelphia. Mama and Papa joined Tristan after he became Alpha up there. They come down from time to time."

"And how do you think they're going to respond to having their son mate with a tiger?"

"After a century, cher, they're happy to see me mate with anyone who makes me happy. Ya'll don't know how fast a rumor spreads 'round here. I'm sure the entire city of brotherly love was ablaze with the news after my announcement last night. I already got a call from my mama this mornin' wanting to know everything about you. I promised we'd come up there next month."

Gillian laughed. "I can't wait to meet them."

"How do you think your mama's gonna react to you matin' with a wolf?" Dimitri asked.

"Not fair. She can't shift. Not to mention that my father was an Alpha who's no longer alive." She averted her gaze and sighed. Raising her eyes to meet his, she continued. "Truth?"

"Truth."

"She's not going to be too happy. She didn't exactly encourage me to get to know Jax, and he was my own brother. I love my mom dearly, but I'm thinking it may be best we break it to her after we mate. You know the saying about asking for forgiveness? Let's go with that plan."

"Are you upset with your mom? About Jax?"

"I don't blame my mom for not wanting me to see my brother. At the time, I was the one who made the decision to cut off contact. She had me so scared about what could happen. She's worried I won't be able to shift. But at the same time, I want to be with you. No one's going to stop me from doing what I need to do."

"All that Alpha in ya…oh my." He laughed.

"What?" she asked with a grin.

"Submitting's not gonna be easy." He shook his head.

"Are we back talking about sex again?"

"Let's just put it this way." Dimitri paused, considering how she'd get along with everyone. She'd have to fall into the natural cadence of life within a pack. "When we mate, I think you're gonna still shift, but you may be wolf. Even if you're not wolf, you're gonna have to learn how to integrate into the pack. In the end, all wolves must learn to submit, to have discipline. We do it to ensure order. Order keeps peace. Peace keeps us safe, well organized."

"Last night with you was great and all. But I'm not that experienced with submission in any part of my life. I'm feline. I don't think I can do it," she confessed.

"Last night was beautiful." He winked and took her hands in his. "You need to look at it this way, cher. Submission is about trust. In bed. In life. Take Logan for example. I trust him to do what's best for us. Now that doesn't mean I don't advise him or disagree at times. But when push comes to shove, his word goes. I support him in the same way the rest of the pack submits to me."

"I guess it's hard for me to understand. It's not like I don't know that my DNA has wolf in it. Technically, I was born into a pack. But my life with my mom…we were isolated. It's not just about having anyone to submit to. It's so much more. I've never had anyone, period. No one to trust. No one to rely on. Sure I have friends, but the kind of thing you're talking about…it's not the same."

"Which is why we'll go slow with the pack. You felt it with Logan, though…the power. I saw it on your face when you met him. Humans can't feel it, they just have a sense that he's dominant. Leo, on the other hand, he acknowledges Logan's power but damn if that old ass vamp isn't putting out some serious high volt wattage of his own. What you felt with Logan is the natural order calling you."

"I felt it…he was strong, but I wasn't afraid."

"It isn't about being afraid. It's about trust, respect and knowing without a doubt that he's in charge. That he'll keep you safe."

"And you?"

"Look, Gilly, I'm not going to sit here and tell you that you not submitting is an option. I think you know that being in the pack…it's a team…a family. My family. And I hope someday yours, too," he said, brushing her hair from her eyes.

"And what if we can't shift? What if we mate and I lose my ability? What if we can't get rid of this thing…whatever it is inside you?"

"We'll face it together, that's what. But I'm a fighter. You don't get to be in my position without battlin' it out every now and then."

Gillian didn't want to know what he meant by that. She wasn't sure she could handle watching him in a challenge.

"We'll get through this," he reassured her. "Besides, I have a feelin' you're going to come through stronger than ever."

"Why hasn't the witch healed you? Last night…when we were together, I could feel it…that evil. But when I concentrate, letting my energy out, I know I can heal you. Why can't we just do that? I'll be there for you…every single day if that's what it takes."

"I wish." Dimitri kissed her forehead and took a deep breath. He hadn't wanted to admit that his wolf had grown weaker. Their recent interludes had done little to help. "Ilsbeth needs to purge this. It can't be done without magic."

"But maybe I can…" Gillian knew of her gifts. She wasn't certain that like her father, he'd be given them when they mated. Her mother had told her stories about how her father had shifted into a tiger. Like a childhood fairytale, she found it difficult to believe. She'd never seen it with her own eyes and didn't want to raise his hopes. But in the back of her mind, it remained a last resort.

"Ilsbeth is bringing in a sorcerer. We'll have to go to them…see what he recommends. She thought he'd have to meet me in person for it to work."

"What's the deal with you and her?" Gillian hated asking but she'd seen how close they'd been, the beautiful woman's hands on her wolf.

"She's a friend."

"No…she's more," she challenged.

"It's not what you think."

"I saw it in her eyes last night. Are you dating?" Gillian held her breath, waiting on his answer.

"She's a friend," he sighed. "Was she more than a friend at one time? Yes. But I'd always told her that we couldn't be more. I'm not goin' to lie to you. I've lived a long time, and I'm not exactly celibate."

"Okay," she said, pensively balling up her hands. The admission punched her in the gut. She knew she shouldn't be jealous. Of course he'd dated, but hearing him say the words pained her.

"Every wolf knows that he or she is going to meet their mate. And when it happens, the chemistry...the call of it...it can't be ignored. It's not fair to lead another person to think that they can be your partner, your spouse or whatever, when you know at any moment you could be walking down the street and bam, it's over. I told her..." Dimitri went quiet, scrubbing his hand over his brow, uncomfortable with the conversation. He didn't want to hurt Gillian but if she was going to meet Ilsbeth, there was no knowing what the witch would tell her. "I told her that we couldn't date. She's been around a long time, too. It's not as if she didn't know. She, uh, isn't my biggest fan right now."

"That's not what it looked like last night," Gillian responded.

"She doesn't know what she wants. Believe me, Ilsbeth is all about Ilsbeth," he mused.

"Are you sure she's the right witch? Maybe she's not helping you on purpose."

"I don't think so. Don't get me wrong, she was pissed at me big time, but she didn't even know about you until last night."

"She didn't know when she did the spell?"

"No...she didn't." *But she asked me to move in with her and tried to kiss me.* Guilt tore at him but disclosing those facts didn't seem in either of their best interests. Ilsbeth knew he had a mate and that was all that mattered.

"We're meeting her tonight?"

"Yeah. So, uh, what about you? No boyfriends?" He smiled, changing the focus.

"Me? Not really. I dated humans. I've only met a few tigers, none were my mates. Avoided wolves."

"Not anymore."

"And look where that got me." She shook her head, lifting her eyes to his. Her lips couldn't help but curl upward despite the unpleasant conversation they'd just had about the witch.

"On my lap, that's where." He laughed. "And the problem is?"

"Are you always so…I don't know…funny? Optimistic?" she asked.

"Is there any way else to be? I may be immortal but I'm not wastin' this life in misery or fear."

"Hence driving your motorcycle cross-country? Single-handedly almost killing an Alpha? Jumping into hell pits with dangerous vampires? What else do you do for fun?"

"Tiger taming…it may be the scariest gig I've taken on."

"Tiger taming, huh?" She laughed, rolling her eyes. "I didn't realize you worked for a circus."

"Oh, no, no. I don't believe in caging animals, darlin'. Wild animals should be free," he proposed, spreading open her robe.

"No ringmaster?"

"I may be a master but only in the bedroom. No circus here."

"I'm impressed with your bravery," she said, tracing a small circle on his chest, "but if you're in the tiger taming business, what makes you think you'll come out unscathed? Tigers are deadly, you know…ferocious."

"Indeed."

"You may get scratched…we like it rough."

"Aw cher, I plan on earnin' a few scratch marks along the way, but my cat, she's going to be purrin' like a kitten when I'm done with her."

"You may get bitten, then what?"

"A few bites never hurt anybody." He glided his hand down her forearm, teasing her inner wrist. "I can take care of myself."

"So you plan on using a whip?"

"Only if she likes it. But you've gotta be gentle when taming tigers…coercing them only makes them more aggressive." Without warning Dimitri lifted her up onto the piano, her bottom hitting the keys. The ping of the notes sang into the air. "Careful, calculated attention…now that's what trains a tiger. You must get close to her…earn her trust."

"Sounds dangerous," she gasped as his palms glided up her inner thighs. Off balance, she held onto the rim of the fall board.

"Lethal," he agreed. Locking his eyes on hers, he skimmed his hands over her knees until they fell wide, exposing her sex.

"You're very confident." The heat grew between them as Dimitri's sensuous mouth approached her abdomen.

"I can be commanding when I need to…my tiger knows she can trust me to take care of her," he said. Pressing his lips to the soft skin below her breasts, Dimitri smiled.

"Yes," she breathed. Her pussy ached as it brushed against his chest. She began to pant as he placed small kisses on her skin, dipping underneath her belly button but never going any further.

Dimitri lay his cheek flat against her stomach, letting her cradle his head with her hands. His fingers glided beneath her robe, caressing the small of her back

"Have I successfully demonstrated my technique?" he asked softly.

"You scare me," Gillian admitted, her lips brushing the top of his head. Dimitri's erotic touch seared her senses, eliciting arousal through every cell of her body. But it was his flirtatious banter, laced with a hint of truth, that had touched her heart. The more she got to know him, the man behind the wolf, the more she realized she'd never be the same. It wasn't just about her not shifting; it was about caring for someone so much that she could barely breathe. She was falling for him.

"You terrify me," he replied, hiding his expression from her.

"This thing between us…it feels so…"

"Yes it does."

"How do you know what I was going to say?" She laughed.

"I care about you, Gilly," he said, not quite answering her question. "I'm not a fool. I know there's this physical thing that draws us together. Whatever that magic is that give us our mates."

"Chemistry."

"I never thought I'd find someone...it's been a long time."

"I haven't lived as long as you, but I know what it feels like to be alone." Gillian rubbed her cheek into his hair.

"No more." Dimitri lifted his head to look deep within her eyes.

"No more." Gillian's heart raced. It wasn't as if they'd declared their love for each other, but the intimacy around their fears and optimism allowed them to share the vulnerable nature of their feelings. A new beginning for them both.

As Dimitri leaned forward, Gillian took his face into her hands, cupping his cheeks. His eyes fell to her lips and then caught her gaze again. Slowly, he leaned into her embrace until his mouth claimed hers. Gently his tongue slipped between her trembling lips. Gillian's fingers tunneled up into his wavy brown hair. Fisting his locks, she hungrily kissed him back.

Gillian's hands fell to Dimitri's waistband, tugging down his shorts, freeing his erection. Her smooth pussy grazed his belly, and she struggled to get leverage, to alleviate the ache. Dimitri sensed her need and bent his knees so that his hardness pressed against her entrance. Using a hand to guide himself, he eased himself into her, inch by inch, gingerly joining their bodies as one. Never breaking contact, Dimitri built a slow rhythm.

Gillian absorbed the way he moved inside her and moaned in pleasure. It was only a matter of time before her beast submitted completely, marking him in return. By doing so, she'd fully accept her fate. Like an all-consuming force of nature, Dimitri destroyed every last preconception she'd held about wolves mating. His intoxicating presence in her life had become a delicious necessity.

"Always," she spoke into his lips as he surged within her, unsure of whether she was talking to him or herself.

"Goddess, yes. You're everything," he breathed. The physical attraction was banging hard, he knew. But the more time they spent together, the more he emotionally committed to Gillian and he started to believe that it'd be possible for him to find love.

The piano keys chimed as he delved deeper into her core, rocking into her body. Her staccato breath told him she was close, and he could no longer hold back the release they both sought. With slow, forceful thrusts, he stimulated her clitoris with his pelvis, throwing them both over the edge of ecstasy.

Gillian screamed against his lips as Dimitri heaved against her, matching his intensity. Merged together, she contracted, shaking as the rush of her orgasm tore through her body. Holding on for dear life, she wrapped her legs around Dimitri's waist, encouraging him to go deeper.

Dimitri felt her inner muscles fist around him, and he no longer fought his impending climax. With a grunt, he came, pouring himself into her. He kissed her again, wishing he could say all the words that lay hidden in his heart. She'd slay him, he knew. Yet the taste of her was like lifeblood, pulsating into him with explosive passion.

Desperate to own their feelings...for each other...for their future, they succumbed to the delicate intimacy that had begun to weave itself into their hearts. As their kiss slowed, they continued to seek each other, not wanting the moment to end. Eventually, their lips stilled, their breath softening. Gillian and Dimitri drew closer, cheek to cheek, eyes closed, lost in the surreal sensation. An intense state of intimacy existed, one neither of them had ever experienced. Danger would come. It lurked outside like an evil cloak waiting to suffocate them. But for the moment they relaxed into their newfound relationship; never again would they be alone.

Chapter Fifteen

Gillian sat at the black metal table, tracing her fingers over the small diamond grate. Her face was frozen with anger, glaring at the witch sitting across from her. After making love and eating breakfast, she'd had a leisurely shower and then taken some photos of the bayou abutting Dimitri's home. The slow-moving stream teemed with wildlife and she'd snapped some amazing shots of an egret in flight. A snake swam across the surface of the water and she squealed but still managed to capture its image.

Her relaxation came to crash when Dimitri told her that it was time to go see Ilsbeth. No matter how many times she told herself that the witch was going to help Dimitri, her intuition told her otherwise. As soon as they entered the tiny bricked courtyard of the private café, her stomach knotted in consternation.

There was something about Ilsbeth that bothered her. While she'd been cordial, shaking Gillian's hand, introducing her to the handsome sorcerer she'd brought to help Dimitri, the petite angelic-looking woman gave her the chills. It wasn't lost on her how the witch had kissed Dimitri's cheeks, lingering seconds longer than necessary. Gillian tried to shake off the feeling that something was wrong. She tried to blame it on their impending mating; her cat would resent any female touching her mate. It was natural to distrust others, especially a woman who'd been in Dimitri's bed. Despite the nagging concerns, Gillian sucked a breath, resolving that she'd give her the benefit of the doubt. Her first priority was Dimitri and she didn't want to do anything to jeopardize their chances of finding a spell, a cure for his affliction.

The waitress set their drinks on the table and Gillian nodded, giving thanks. She immediately picked up her diet cola, wishing she'd ordered rum to go in it. Having restraint she hadn't known she possessed, she forced herself to calmly listen to the discussion as if the woman sitting across from her hadn't fucked her mate a half dozen times. She glanced to Dimitri, who had his eyes pinned on Ilsbeth and the sorcerer. Jake sat on her left side and when she turned to him, he gave her a sympathetic smile. Logan, the Alpha, sat next to Dimitri, but she could tell he planned on letting his beta handle the situation. The tension was so thick she thought it'd wilt the ferns hanging from the balconies.

"Marcus has told me of a spell that can reverse the taint on your soul," Ilsbeth began.

"Reverse? Don't you mean remove?" Dimitri asked.

Gillian resisted the urge to reach for him. The tone of his voice, low and dominant, called both to her need to comfort and the desire to submit. She coiled her fingers around her tall glass, ensuring she'd keep her hands to herself. There was no room for mistakes. She refused to allow her impulsivity to distract him.

"Remove, reverse. Whatever," Ilsbeth repeated. "It's not as if this happens every day. I've lived almost as long as you have and I've never met one shifter who's lost his wolf. Marcus, on the other hand, has experienced it."

"In the 1960s, I worked a case," Marcus said.

"He offers his services to hire for humans," Ilsbeth interrupted with a note of disdain.

"Yes, Ilsbeth is correct," he agreed, visibly annoyed with her assessment. "Supernaturals aren't the only ones worthy to receive our gifts. But I digress…in the case I'd worked, the shifter had become involved with a human, one who'd suffered from possession. As you can imagine, the Church was involved. After the cleansing, the man, let's call him John for the sake of our discussion. Within weeks of the exorcism, John was unable to shift."

"Were you able to use a spell to resolve the issue?" Dimitri asked.

"Yes, we were, but it was a nasty demon who'd metaphysically leapt from one soul to another. I understand from Ilsbeth that your entity is more parasitic in nature. Given that it's non-intelligent, technically, it should be easier to oust."

"Surely it has an instinct to survive?" Dimitri challenged.

"Like any parasite, it's deriving benefit without a true symbiotic relationship. Unlike the demon, which seeks to kill its host, it seeks only to exist without motivation. If it kills its host, that would result in its own demise."

"But it is killing my wolf. I mean, the stuff Ilsbeth's given me has helped. Between that and Gillian…" Dimitri looked to her, as if to ask for her permission to tell them what she'd done to help him. Her ability to heal was a gift, one she hadn't shared with many people.

"No, it's okay," Gillian said. She saw no harm in divulging this information. In contrast to Ilsbeth's secretive disposition, Marcus seemed open and willing to share his experiences. Gillian steeled her nerves, looking to both Dimitri and Logan. "I, um, I can heal people sometimes. Only shifters…at least that's how it's worked so far. It's not like I really get to test it all that often. It's not super-powerful or anything, but I was able to pull back his wolf. You know, in California when Dimitri couldn't shift. When we're together…"

Dimitri reached for her hand, taking it in his and kissed it. "When we are together, skin to skin, I can feel her positive vibes. But it's not working as much. Whatever this is, it's getting stronger."

"Interesting…your abilities." Marcus paused. "It makes perfect sense, though. Even just a week ago, the parasite, it was newer, a larva if you will. But now that it's grown, it's larger, stronger, not as easily subdued by your efforts."

"If it kills my wolf, then it will die?"

"Well, yes. It feeds off your magic…the inherent energy that feeds your wolf, causing you to shift. But I'm afraid if it comes to that, you cannot go back."

"But you can fix it?" Logan interjected.

"The spell we used…for John, it was successful. Ilsbeth and I have discussed the necessary arrangements, and it can be done. But you'll need to acquire the blood. It must be given to you freely, of course."

"Of course," Dimitri said sarcastically. He'd already given Ilsbeth hair from his wolf, gifting it to her in an attempt to make amends for their argument. Clearly that hadn't worked.

"Blood?" Gillian couldn't help but gasp at the suggestion.

"Vampire blood," Ilsbeth stated coolly.

"That's easy enough…I'll ask Leo," Dimitri told her.

"It must be a female," Ilsbeth added. "Tell me, do you know any lady vamps willing to give you their blood?"

Dimitri returned her icy stare. Her comment made him suspect she'd been stalking him.

"Leo's introduced me to some vamps. I'll ask him to help me."

"I'm sure he has," Ilsbeth retorted.

"Is there something you want to say, witch? 'Cause if there is, out with it. I don't have time for games."

"Nothing…just saying that Léopold gets around. I'm sure the two of you have had your adventures."

"In which case, it would be no business of yours," Dimitri replied.

"I'm not sure what you're getting at but I can assure you that all I care about is the spell. Even though we no longer are seeing each other," Ilsbeth looked to Gillian, "that doesn't mean I don't care. We shall do the spell when you get the blood."

"Is there anything else I need to know? Any other freaky-ass ingredients you need?"

"Dimitri, I don't know you that well," Marcus began. He took a deep breath and sighed. "I'm going to be straight with you."

"Please do."

"With these kinds of things…"

"The leech on my wolf?"

"Yes, well, that's one way of putting it. You don't have much time. If this thing is successful, it'll kill your wolf within the week," Marcus surmised.

"The end game?" Dimitri asked.

"You won't be able to shift. Ever again." Marcus spoke with an eerie calmness.

"I'd be mortal," Dimitri stated. He breathed deeply, letting his anger settle like volcanic ash smothering a mountain. It was important his Alpha realize the severity of the situation. He'd no longer be pack. Like other humans, he'd age, die. His life as a wolf would end.

It wasn't as if Gillian hadn't considered what could happen to Dimitri. It was no different than what she was facing by agreeing to mate him. But it was the exchange between Dimitri and Ilsbeth that captured her attention, noting that his cool demeanor had been replaced with controlled irritation. While he may have dated the witch, her words had drawn his ire. Provoking Dimitri, she supposed, took a lot of effort, yet Ilsbeth deliberately had pressed him. Gillian wasn't sure why her question had the effect that it did, but her intuition told her it all had to do with their previous relationship. As she quietly mulled over what Ilsbeth had said, Gillian imagined it might have to do with another woman.

Dimitri tugged at her hand, alerting her that it was time to leave. She pushed out of her chair, wondering about where they were going to find a vampire. Gillian supposed she should have been afraid, but after being captured by wolves, twice, all she cared about was getting the blood. Too bad it had to be given willingly, she thought. Otherwise, she'd happily hold someone down to get a tiny sample.

When she thought about not being able to shift again, she knew she'd be crushed. But Dimitri had so much more to lose…his beast, his place within the pack, his family.

As they left the restaurant, Gillian turned her head to catch one more glimpse of the witch. Her eyes locked on Ilsbeth's, and it felt as if the witch was reaching into her chest. A chill blew over her arms, causing gooseflesh to rise. Gillian recoiled from her gaze, bringing Dimitri's arm around her shoulders. In her gut, she knew that the witch sought her harm. Maybe she had everyone else in the room fooled, but Gillian knew otherwise. Witches kept hocus pocus in their bag of tricks, but tigers took no prisoners. If Ilsbeth wanted to start something, she could bring it, because Dimitri was hers.

Chapter Sixteen

I'm not afraid of vampires. Gillian repeated the phrase as she walked into the dangerous club, Mordez. She dug deep, searching for the courage that she knew existed in her inner kitty. Yet as she took in her surroundings, she reasoned that she was close to being more like the cowardly lion. As she ran through the excuses in her mind for her lack of courage, her reaction seemed perfectly reasonable. In order for her to shift, she'd have to waste precious seconds stripping off her dress. Vamps on the other hand, had the advantage of speed and were always ready to go, their fangs protruding like nails from their gums.

Dimitri had warned her on the way over to the bar to stay close. From the way he spoke, he wasn't exceptionally fond of the establishment, even if Léopold was a close friend. They had entered via a back entrance, a tunnel through a labyrinth of underground hallways. Gillian held onto the back of Dimitri's shirt as he and Léopold parted their way through the crowd. Blinding strobe lights flashed as the band raged toward the back of the room. The low bass pounded loudly, the vibrations filtering throughout the arena. Hard driving heavy metal music blasted them as they reached their final destination.

Some patrons wore gothic clothing and some dressed as if they'd gone to a New York City night club. Many had a dazed, sexual look in their eyes, dancing, drinking, feeding and fucking. It was a chaotic contained free-for-all.

A pale human female writhed on the copper bar. Her breasts exposed and skirt hiked up to her hips, she moaned in ecstasy as two males fed from her. One was latched on at her neck, pinching her nipples; the other suckled from her inner thigh. The threesome appeared oblivious to the crowd that had gathered to watch. Uninterested parties hailed the bartender as if the spectacle was nothing more than a common occurrence.

Gillian contemplated Dimitri's demeanor. On the way back from meeting with Ilsbeth, he'd been uncharacteristically quiet. No jokes or sexual innuendos. He'd been all business, calling Léopold and discussing whether or not they'd bring her with them. Gillian had insisted she come to help get the vampire blood. With Dimitri's wolf weakened, she couldn't bear to leave her mate alone, unprotected.

Although she hadn't told them, she had every intention of shifting if danger presented itself. A wolf or vampire, she was not. But her tiger would battle to the death to protect Dimitri. Regardless of her fear, fight or flight response invoked, she'd fight to the death.

Through the din, Gillian heard Dimitri say something to Léopold, pointing to a raised section of tables. Flowing sheets of white satin hung from the ceiling, bunching onto the floor, effectively separating the area into individual alcoves. Black lights shone onto the white leather sofas and chairs, creating the illusion of privacy within VIP seating.

Jake extended his hand, ushering her onto a loveseat. Dimitri sat next to her while Léopold and Jake took captain chairs across from them. A waitress dressed in a black leather corset and matching panties approached, setting down drinks they hadn't ordered. Léopold laughed and picked up the glass, nodding to her with a cool, knowing smile.

Confused, Gillian glanced to Dimitri, who had already brought the amber liquid to his lips. Although she'd never seen him so serious and determined, she found this new side to him captivating. Exuding sex appeal and power, Dimitri appeared to be unaware of all the females taking note of his arrival. Casually dressed, he wore loose jeans and an untucked white shirt with rolled up sleeves. A smile crossed her face as he caught her ogling, and she laughed. The respite from the dark mood was welcome, yet short lived.

Two women approached and Gillian noted that Dimitri's expression had turned to stone. A striking woman glided toward them, her presence bringing a new level of electricity to the air. Refined, she looked as if she belonged in the eighteen hundreds, her gothic velvet gown trailing behind her. Her blood-red lips accentuated her creamy-white skin and her dark brown hair was coiffed into an updo. Looking as if she'd stepped off the cover page of a romance novel, she smiled and nodded at each person in their party. A second woman, wearing a hot-pink spandex bodysuit, followed.

Nervous, Gillian took a sip of her drink and coughed as it burned her throat. She looked down to her floral mini-sundress and thought she should have worn a different outfit. On second thought, her platform shoes showed off the lean contours of her legs and were easy to shuck in case she needed to shift. She owned a corset and as much as she enjoyed the way it looked, it took considerable time to get it laced up correctly. When she'd worn it, she'd been locked in tight, making shifting difficult.

"Why hello, boys," the beautiful woman greeted them.

"Lady Charlotte. Bonsoir," Léopold replied, standing. "Thank you for meeting with us,"

"How's your lovely nymph?" she asked.

"Naiad. She's doing very well," he answered.

"Dimitri, so good to see you." She extended her delicate fingers toward him.

"Lady Char. Thanks for having us. You look, um," he paused, reaching to shake her hand. "Mysterious, very chic. That dress is one of a kind."

"Why thank you. I take it your Alpha is well."

"Logan's doing great, thanks."

"Jake, long time no see," she remarked.

"Hello," he replied.

"Ah, Dimitri, you've brought a friend." Lady Charlotte set her vision on Gillian. "So pretty. And young."

Gillian concentrated, forcing herself to breathe slowly, controlling her heartbeat that threatened to race, revealing her trepidation. As the vampiress leaned forward, Gillian took her hand. She'd expected a simple exchange but Lady Charlotte held tight, taking the opportunity to hug her, sniffing her hair.

"Fascinating," she laughed, releasing Gillian. She placed her palm on Dimitri's arm. "Where did you find her?"

"We found each other." Glancing at Gillian, who appeared exceedingly calm, he sought to make it clear that she belonged to him. The excitement on Lady Charlotte's face indicated that Gillian had piqued her interest. "Gilly, this is Lady Charlotte. She owns this fine establishment. A good friend of Leo's. Lady Charlotte, this is Gilly. She's my mate."

"Your mate. Now how can that be? What you propose is unheard of. She's a shifter, but not a wolf." Lady Charlotte sniffed again in Gillian's direction. "And she smells so good. Do tell, my lovely, what are you?"

"I'm a tiger, but I'm also part wolf." Gillian looked to Dimitri, whose face registered surprise. Publicly acknowledging her lupine heritage hadn't been planned, but as the words left her lips, she felt relief.

"Hybrid tigers don't breed with wolves, so what is this magic?"

"It's my breed."

Lady Charlotte rounded behind Gillian, lifting her ponytail. Gillian restrained her protest yet her claws extended at the intrusion. She took a deep breath and played it cool, waiting to act. She was in a room full of vampires and it would be risky attacking the owner.

"Easy, pet." Lady Charlotte dropped her locks and eyed Dimitri with curiosity. "You've marked her. I don't think in all my years I've seen such a thing."

"We're here about me, not her," Dimitri said, taking Gillian's hand. "Let's sit."

"My friend needs a favor, one that I'd gladly give him but I need you to do this for both him and me," Léopold told her.

"Out with it," Lady Charlotte said, her voice terse. She smoothed her dress and sat down.

"I need vampire blood," Dimitri replied. "From a woman."

Lady Charlotte gave an insincere laugh, shaking her head. "Léopold, darling, why on earth do you think I'd ever give my blood to a wolf?"

"Because I'm asking nicely. One hand rubs the other." Léopold's icy smile was but a warning. His fingers curled into the arms of the seat.

"It seems as if I'm the one who's been doing all the work lately," Lady Charlotte complained. She glanced at Dimitri and blew out a loud breath, displaying her annoyance.

"I'm not asking you twice. You will assist us," Léopold challenged.

"What is he to you anyway? He's handsome, I'll give you that. Lacey raved about his sexual prowess. But to you? What difference does it make if he dies tonight?"

Léopold sprung from his seat. Before Lady Charlotte had a chance to respond, he stood behind her; his hand delicately squeezed her throat, not quite choking her.

"This beta is my brother; that is all you need to know. Now will you help him? It must be given freely," he told her, his finger stroking the hollow of her neck.

"No need to explain," she said sweetly. Placing her hand over Léopold's, she attempted to pry his fingers loose, but his grip held firm. "Yes, okay, yes."

Léopold released Lady Charlotte and nodded at Dimitri, who smiled, admiring his friend. The ancient vampire emanated power, and had displayed his lethal nature on more than one occasion. Both humans and supernaturals were foolish to cross him.

"Oui, I'm pleased that we understand each other," Léopold commented blithely.

"Oh fine, already. But it won't be me....Lacey, there." She pointed to the female in the cotton-candy-colored outfit. "She'll do it."

Léopold raised a questioning eyebrow at Lady Charlotte.

"What? You can't possibly expect me to give *my* blood to a wolf. You do what you want," she began. A look of disgust crossed her face. "That's right, I know about you saving the Alpha's mate. And now with this 'brother' nonsense. Your prerogative, I suppose, but I for one am not in the business of donating my body to dogs. This isn't an animal shelter I'm running."

"Lacey is acceptable, no?" Léopold looked to Dimitri, who nodded in response.

"The witch said as long as it's given freely, it'll work."

"Now wait a damn minute," Lacey interrupted. The pink stretchy fabric strained to cover her breasts as she rose to meet Léopold's gaze. "If Charlotte needs me to do this, I'll do it. But I think it's only fair that I get something in return."

"If it's money you want, no problem," Dimitri said. A silent understanding passed between him and Léopold.

"I want a dance...maybe even a taste of that hot wolf blood you have pumping through those muscles of yours."

"No," both Dimitri and Gillian said at the same time. Gillian stared at Lacey, challenging her to lay one undead finger on him.

"What? Is it wrong to want something for my trouble?"

"Lacey, I don't think that's a good idea. Gillian's my mate."

"So what? She's already marked up like a chalkboard. Have you marked him back?" she challenged.

"No," Gillian bit out, hostility in her voice.

"Well, that's your own fault. You snooze you lose, pussy."

"No. Just no." Gillian stood up, looking to Jake, Léopold and Dimitri.

"Well then, I just may not feel in a giving mood tonight. Charlotte said I had to give you my blood, but she didn't say when."

Furious, Gillian's canines descended and out of embarrassment, she covered her mouth with her hands. Emotion swirled inside her like a hurricane, and she tried to compose herself. She'd never shifted in front of strangers; it seemed bad form to do so out of jealousy. Turning her head, she took a deep breath, her teeth returning to normal. Dimitri rose to look at her but she held up a hand, indicating she was okay.

"Jesus Christ, Charlotte. Are you really going to let her get away with this?" Dimitri yelled.

"I'm hardly responsible for Lacey's small demand. Seems quite reasonable given your history. You didn't mind letting her taste you the last time you were here. In fact, I recall you did all sorts of things. Perhaps you'll be more careful where you decide to wag your tail in the future."

Gillian's head swung toward Dimitri, her eyes wide. He'd slept with Lacey too? She told herself it shouldn't matter. He had been single and dating; he'd lived a long time. He'd been with many women. But still, the knowledge of his indiscretions cut deep.

"Léopold?" Dimitri looked to his friend for assistance.

"Sorry, mon ami. You know that our blood is a gift. It would be no effort to force her, but that defeats your need."

"It must be given freely," Gillian repeated. Thoughts of Dimitri with Ilsbeth and Lacey forced her to bite her lip, hoping the pain would distract her from her anger. Her eyes narrowed on the blonde vampire who fluffed her hair with a snide smile.

"Gillian, no," Dimitri started to say.

"It's all right. Desperation comes in all forms. Apparently, she hasn't gotten over you either," Gillian noted. "She's right. You aren't marked. Although, judging by the women I've met today, I clearly misjudged things."

"You know it was before you…we hadn't met." Dimitri sought to assuage her anguish over the situation but it was of no use.

The air thickened as reticence set in, Lacey's demand bringing them to a crossroads. Jake shrugged at Dimitri and began silently counting the tin tiles on the ceiling. Léopold laughed, aware that his friend had his dick caught in a trap. For all the chaff Dimitri had given him over the past weeks, he found it slightly amusing.

"We're all grownups," Gillian stated, breaking the silence. Her lungs felt as if they were collapsing as she spoke. She fingered the pleats of her dress, her brow knitted in anger. Gillian took a deep breath, telling herself that it was time to put on her big girl panties and suck it up. Regardless of what happened between her and Dimitri, she wasn't about to put his wolf further in danger.

"Please, Gilly. Let's go talk in private," Dimitri pleaded. He reached for her but she drew back her hands, wrapping her arms around her waist.

"No. We don't have time to waste. Let's get to it." Gillian's lips pursed. Her fury bubbled at the surface but she contained it. "One dance."

"See there, that wasn't terribly difficult," Lacey drawled. She held out her palm to Dimitri; her other hand rested on her cocked hip.

Dimitri turned to Gillian, taking her in his arms. She feigned resistance, but soon gave into him as he cupped her cheek.

"This means nothing, okay?" He brought her close and whispered in her ear. "Remember today at the piano…I meant every word I said. Forever."

Gillian's heart melted as she lifted her gaze to meet his. She nodded, tears brimming in her eyes. Unable to respond, her words choked in her throat. He leaned in to capture her lips, and she accepted his searing kiss, running her hands up his back. Barely aware of their audience, she sought to possess him, reminding him that he belonged to her. As they reluctantly parted, Gillian and Dimitri rested their foreheads against each other's, their eyes locked in understanding.

"Jake," Dimitri called, still focused on Gillian. "Take Gilly. Do not let her out of your sight. I'll be gone two minutes." He turned to Lacey. "I'll get the blood and we're out of here. Leo, keep watch, would ya?"

"Oui," Léopold said. He glanced at Lady Charlotte. "We have business to discuss. I'm not going anywhere."

"Let's go," Dimitri commanded, reaching for Lacey's hand. She laughed and gave Gillian a triumphant smile as they headed to the dance floor.

"You wanna dance? I promise not to step on your toes," Jake joked.

"Okay," Gillian replied, her voice shaky. She gave him a small grin, but never took her eyes off her mate. As Dimitri took Lacey into his arms, Gillian thought she'd be sick.

"Hey, you know he's only doing this for the blood, right? She's nothing." Jake took Gillian's hand.

"I gave him permission, didn't I? I'm not as fragile as I look," Gillian commented.

Jake laughed and placed his hand around her waist, taking her palm with the other. "Oh believe me, sugar, I've seen you in action. Fragile isn't exactly the word I'd use to describe you."

"Thanks...I think." She relaxed into the sway of the music, stealing glances at Dimitri, who wore a pained expression.

"It's a compliment. I like a woman who can take care of herself." He spun her around as a sultry song began to play. "You're good for Dimitri."

"How so?"

"He's been lonely. I think after Logan and Leo, he realized he's been by himself a long time. Take that trip to

California, for example. Sometimes we all need to take a little walkabout…get our thoughts together."

"Didn't exactly turn out how he planned."

"No, it turned out better." Jake smiled and drew her closer.

"How so? He almost died."

"Yeah, there's that. But there's times when…well, death is always there, even when you're immortal. Life's a calculated risk. You weigh the danger. When possible, avoid things that might kill you. It's rare but even wolves die…vamps too. Bottom line is that Dimitri didn't die out in San Diego. He found you."

"And you?"

"And me what?"

"Do you feel alone?" Gillian looked up at Jake. Muscular and clean cut, he looked as if he belonged on a professional baseball team.

"I'm content," he whispered in her ear.

"I've always been alone," she confessed. "But Dimitri…he makes me feel…"

"He's your mate. He'll make you feel things you never thought possible."

"Yes. But more than that, he makes me want to be with others…to find my wolf. Being tiger is everything to me…was everything."

"And now?"

"I don't know. None of it seems to matter. I just want to be free of Chaz. I want Dimitri to be well…so we can be together."

"And if you lose your tiger? Become wolf?"

"I'd mourn her, but I'm in a different head space than I was a week ago. I can't go on fighting Alphas who want me for my gift. It's futile, especially when I've found Dimitri." Gillian bit her tongue. She'd said too much. She hadn't even told Dimitri about how the mating would affect him and here she was blabbing her secret to Jake.

"Your gift?"

"It's nothing," she lied.

"Nothing, huh?" he questioned, not believing a word she said.

Gillian leaned her head against Jake's chest. Regretting her words, she said nothing more as she glared at the woman who touched her mate. Sharp fangs descended from the vampire's ruby-red lips, poising to strike Dimitri's shoulder. As the vampire tore open Dimitri's shirt, Gillian's tiger attempted to shift.

This is the most fucked up shit I've gotten myself in in a while, Dimitri thought to himself. Sure, he'd had sex with Lacey. *One goddamned fucking time.* He didn't have a mate when he'd done it. As a matter of fact, he'd been going through a dry spell and had only been at Mordez to help Léopold. It was that night he'd met Lacey. One drink led to a dance and one dance led to a hot quickie on the corner of the dance floor. It had meant nothing to him or her.

Women, he mused. His entire life he'd been clear with every single woman he'd ever been with that he couldn't commit. He'd refused to date them exclusively, because inevitably it led to feelings. Feelings led to bruised hearts and worse, damaged egos. He'd never been in love, not even once in over a hundred years. He'd been careful to mostly have sex with only wolves, because at least they knew the score. Each and every wolf knew that the universe had selected a special person just for them. Most females from his pack understood and reciprocated his philosophy on dating. They knew that it was just a matter of time, give or take a century or two, before they met their mate. Committing to someone else led to disaster.

He'd told the witch. He'd told the vampire. Decades of having sex and it was never an issue…until now. Why fate had to go and kick him in the balls, he didn't know. He was true-blue honest, easygoing, would give a stranger the shirt off his back. But today had been one of the worst days ever. Sure it'd started off well enough. Making love to Gillian had been a dream. But the day had taken a nosedive, first with Ilsbeth, and now with Lacey.

Seeing the crushing look of disappointment in Gillian's eyes had nearly killed him. He'd never meant to hurt her. But nor would he lie. The past was the past. Gillian was his future; one that would be built on trust, not deceit. If Lacey wanted a dance to inflict some kind of sick punishment on him, he'd let her have one dance, but she wouldn't have his blood.

When he got home, he planned on explaining everything to Gillian. If the cards hadn't been stacked against him with the whole 'tiger hybrid' snafu, they sure as hell were now that she knew he'd slept with both the witch and vampire. He was acutely aware that no matter his desire to mate, Gillian had to choose him...choose their mating. He'd grovel if he had to, but he'd damn well get things straightened out.

The sickening sweet scent of vanilla drifted into his nostrils, causing him to cough. Disgusted, he continued to move to the music, Lacey's fingernails digging into his pecs. He glanced to Gillian whose blank expression told him she'd had enough. It made him sick that he was the cause of her pain. Although he'd imagined the pleasure of sharing his mate with another, watching Jake take Gillian in his arms in order to calm her crushed his heart.

He heard Lacey say something to him, and in his peripheral vision, the gleam of white pointy fangs flashed. Snatching her arm out of thin air, he held her still.

"What the hell do you think you're doing?" he yelled, astonished that she'd try to bite him.

"I told you that I wanted a taste. You didn't say anything, ergo, you said yes. Seriously, Dimitri. Are you so stuck on that hybrid that you don't want to have sex? I can't even get a little bite? It's fucking ridiculous," Lacey ranted. 'Even if you managed to mark her, that kind of mating is unheard of...a wolf and a tiger. How long have you even known her?"

"Are you crazy? She's my mate. I get you're a vamp, but don't play dumb. You see she's marked, and you asked to touch me. I told you flat out when we first met that I couldn't commit. I'm a wolf. Not a human. Not a witch. Not a vampire. I'm a goddamned wolf. You know what that means. But you still play games?" Dimitri saw Jake holding Gillian back; she'd tried to come for him, no doubt. Her eyes were a fierce shade of gold, her claws extended. Screaming, she attempted to yank free of Jake's restraint.

"I was just having fun is all. You wolves are so sensitive. What is it? Maybe you haven't gotten your kibbles tonight. Hungry?" she taunted.

"We're done. You hear me?" he told her, his voice booming over the music. "Go get the blood now. I expect it in a container. No funny business either. Make it clean. Make it quick. If not, you'll have to answer to Leo. As much as I'd love to discipline your ass, I expect leaving it to your kind would be the best punishment I could think of. Yeah, I think Leo would have a lot of fun with you. Wanna try me?" Dimitri jerked free of her hands, enjoying the spasm of terror that twisted her face. "That's right, noob. Leo loves dishin' out a little killin' every now and then. You saw how he grabbed Lady Char around her chicken neck. Imagine what he'd do to you."

"You are making a mistake," she warned.

"Yeah, yeah. The only fucking mistake was being with you. Now scamper off. A little more blood, a little less talkin'," he demanded.

"Fine. You can freely have my blood but trust me, I'm the least of your problems."

Lacey turned on her heel and headed for the back of the club. Immediately, he went to Gillian who growled as he approached.

"Gilly, I'm so sorry, cher," he began, just as she cut him off from speaking.

"Don't cher, me. No." Gillian pried Jake's fingers off her arms and rubbed her wrists.

"I told her that she couldn't…" Dimitri attempted to explain.

"Did you get it? Did you get the blood?"

"She's gettin' it now. Please, I can explain. She's a vampire…this is how they are."

"Just no. I don't want to hear it now. I've got to get out of here. The bathroom. Where's the bathroom?" she asked, scanning the room.

"I'll come with you," he offered.

"No. Just get the damn blood," she told him, confused, hurt. "Jake. He can go with me."

Dimitri's jaw tightened at the slight. He understood her anger. It tasted bitter but was justified. Swearing he'd fix this, he nodded at Jake to go ahead.

Dimitri, disgusted with the evening's events, shook his head. He watched as Jake ushered her off the dance floor through the crowd. Gillian, who was of a smaller stature, was swallowed up into the horde of people. He glanced up to Léopold who caught his gaze, but was soon distracted by Lacey, who impatiently tapped on his shoulder.

"What?" he growled. "Where is it?"

"Here," she said, slamming a vial of blood into his hand.

"Thanks." He took a deep breath. His mama had taught him manners, but he was finding it difficult to appear grateful after the antics she'd pulled. "Listen, I'm sorry, but you knew the deal. I'd never try to hurt you on purpose."

"Yeah, yeah. I'm a vampire. I don't have feelings." Lacey flipped her hair and crossed her arms across her chest.

"Tell yourself whatever you need to, but that's bullshit in my book. Look at Leo. You just haven't found that special person yet. It's just not me."

"Tigers don't mate with wolves."

"I already explained it. It's rare but she's my mate. You've gotta let it go."

"I'm not the one who has to let it go. I feel sorry for you," she said cryptically. Cupping her breasts, she adjusted them, making her cleavage more visible.

"Okay, well, thanks again." He turned to leave, giving a small wave with the vial in his hand.

"Just remember, I'm always here, wolf," she laughed. "If you ever wanna go vamp, look me up."

Dimitri shook his head, stroking his beard. His instincts told him that Lacey had more to tell him, but he'd had enough of her antics and wanted to get Gillian home. Eyeing the crimson gift, he slid the glass tube into his back pocket. He nodded to Léopold, who appeared deep in conversation with Lady Charlotte. He pointed in the direction of the restrooms, and set off to find Gillian.

By the time he'd made his way across the dance floor, he spotted Jake leaning against the wall, looking at his cell phone. Dimitri's eyes caught his as he approached.

"How bad is it?" Dimitri inquired, knowing full well that Gillian was beyond pissed about his past sexual transgressions.

"She's been crying," Jake responded.

"I'd better go in there," Dimitri told him, waiting for him to move out of the way.

"It's died down. She'll be okay. She just needs time."

"You clear the bathroom?"

"What? You think I'm an amateur? Give me some credit, bro," Jake said, patting his jacket, indicating he'd brought a concealed weapon with him.

"Noticed you enjoying your dance," Dimitri commented with a smile. He'd hoped that Gillian would get along with his closest friends. Eventually she'd get to know everyone in the pack a little better. All they knew so far was that she was his mate and that they'd gone at it hard in the courtyard. The thought brought a smile to his face.

"What's not to enjoy? She's a sweet little thing. I give her credit hanging in there. This place...it's not for the faint of heart."

"True dat. This place is hard core. I can remember my first time, coming here with Logan, watching Leo do his thing right out there in the bar."

"No one can ever accuse Léopold of being understated. Although considering you just fucked your mate at the ball, well, glass houses and all that. Just sayin'," he joked.

"Yeah, what happened…it's not like a full moon where everyone's just gettin' their freak on whenever and wherever. This mate thing…it's driving my wolf, making me a little crazy. Now that she's accepted my mark, it's taken the edge off a little. You notice I didn't go berserk when you had your hands all over her?"

"I noticed," Jake smiled. "I do like her, by the way."

"I like her, too," Dimitri responded. *I like her way too much. Falling for her is more like it.*

"I'm sure you've been 'liking' her a lot lately." Jake waggled his eyebrows at Dimitri.

"All night and all day long, my friend. Say, I get she was mad at me but what do you suppose is taking her so long?" The hair on Dimitri's neck stood up as soon as he asked. A high-pitched scream, belonging to his mate, tore through his gut.

Gillian sat on the closed toilet seat, her face in her palms. *I can't do this. I just want to go back to New York.* She regretted the way she'd lost her cool. Yet her emotions felt out of control. One minute she was a lust-filled vixen, the next, she was ready to stake a vampire. She closed her eyes, trying to get in touch with her beast. A flicker of recognition registered, but her connection was weakened.

Unable to take the stress of losing her tiger, and wondering if her mate was capable of being faithful, the tears began to fall. Dimitri had given her no reason to doubt his fidelity but she couldn't help but wonder why the witch and vampire were so attached. They treated their impending mating with as much respect as a bag of soggy diapers.

She wiped her eyes with the back of her hands, taking a deep breath. Trying to put things in perspective, she told herself that she was just over reacting. She'd never seen a vampire try to bite someone before. Perhaps the shock of seeing fangs was the factor that had thrown her into a fit of rage. But that wasn't enough to explain the sheer jealousy that had coursed through her. Her tiger needed to mark her mate, she knew.

As she concentrated on breathing, deeply inhaling and exhaling, she heard a distant noise...a howl. Gillian jumped to her feet, her heart racing. Again it sounded, and she realized the noise was coming from inside her. *What the hell? No freakin' way. Do I have a wolf inside me?*

Gillian grabbed a wad of tissue off the roll, blowing her nose. Panicked, she fumbled with the lock. She had to tell Dimitri what she'd heard. Before she had a chance to open the stall door, a creaking sound caught her attention. Confused, she wondered if Jake was coming into the ladies' room. He'd insisted on not letting anyone in with her while she was in there, telling her that she wasn't safe. She hadn't argued and waited until he'd cleared the area.

"Jake? Dimitri?" she called, slowly sneaking a peek through a crack.

"Sorry, doll. No boys, only girls."

"How did you get in here?" Shocked, Gillian flung the stall open, and stared at Lacey, who admired her own reflection in the mirror, carefully checking her hair.

"Ah…it's a secret. But that's what girls do…we tell secrets." She reached into a sparkly heart-shaped purse and took out a small tube. Popping off the top and twisting it upward, she applied the lipstick to her already heavily made-up lips. "I've got a couple of secrets for you. You'll keep it just between us, right?"

"Are you crazy?" Gillian carefully navigated to the sink furthest away from the vampire and turned on the spigot, washing her hands. "If you're referring to the fact that you dated Dimitri, I got that."

"Fucked, sweetie. We fucked. He let me bite him, too. And we did it all out in public. He's a wild one, all right. But then again, most people who come here are."

"Why are you telling me this?" Gillian thought she'd be sick as Lacey told her details about her relationship with her mate. She couldn't erase his past but she sure as hell didn't need to relive Dimitri's greatest hits.

"Because your mating may not take, you know?"

"Not that it's any of your business, but it's already taking. Hence, his mark." Gillian dried her hands and sighed. "You know, I haven't been around very many vampires, but I always imagined they'd be a bit brighter than you."

"No need to be nasty." Lacey used a fingernail to wipe a stray smudge of red from her mouth. "Personally, I enjoy a fine wolf. He's wrong, though. It's not as though I'm expecting any sort of commitment. I've been recently turned and am very much enjoying the height of my sexual prowess. But the witch…well, she wasn't quite as happy. Wolves mate. No matter what you do, there's no way around that…unless you find a way to make someone a wolf no longer. Tricky business I suppose, but who says it can't be done? Dimitri is in a bit of a pinch, isn't he?"

Gillian closed her eyes briefly and blew out a breath, taking in Lacey's enigmatic rant. *Is she seriously telling me what I think she's telling me? Is Ilsbeth responsible for Dimitri losing his wolf?*

"What are you trying to say?" Gillian asked.

"It's rumored that they'd broken up months before the incident with the demon, that she demanded more of a relationship. Just saying that it's awfully convenient that the witch was in the vicinity right around the same time Dimitri starting having trouble shifting. If he'd lost his wolf completely, even sooner, he wouldn't have been able to detect you as his mate, now would he?"

"Why do you care anyway? I still don't get why you're telling me this." Gillian moved toward the door. Pity for the pathetic vampire rolled in her belly. Despite Lacey's words to the contrary, she must have crushed hard over her one night with Dimitri.

"My other secret is even better. Are you ready for it?" Lacey asked, taking a small key from her purse. She located a raised fleur-de-lis on the wall, and slid it open, revealing a keyhole.

"You've really lost it, haven't you? I'm done here. If you have anything else to say, sorry, I'm not interested. Go tell Léopold. I'm sure he can help you with whatever your issue is. Insecurity? Jealousy?"

"You're wrong. I could care less what bitch that mutt chooses to mate with. I do take pleasure in watching him squirm, however. But money? That I could use. Lady Charlotte hardly pays me enough to stay in this damn job but every now and then I run into someone who makes it worth my while."

Gillian set her hand on the locked door, reaching for the small chain that Jake had told her to lock. As if she'd submerged her fingers in ice water, they clumsily picked at the small metal hook. Gillian swore, watching Lacey turn the key, aware that whatever she was about to reveal was dangerous. A secret panel along the side wall of the restroom slowly slid open as Gillian yanked at the chain. Her heart seized in her chest as she caught sight of a man and a wolf. Chaz's wolves had come for her.

"No hard feelings, doll. Money's money," Lacey sang as she slipped into the clandestine compartment, leaving Gillian alone with her attackers.

"You," Gillian gasped, recognizing one of the men who'd been at Chaz's home. The upside down cross tattoo on his forearm led to a hunting knife clutched in his left hand. In the other, his gloved fist held silver cuffs. A bulky fellow, he walked with a slight limp. But if she remembered correctly, it hadn't kept him from holding her down for Chaz when he'd bitten deep into her flesh.

"Alpha's gonna be happy we caught you," the menacing grey wolf who flanked him replied with a growl. "We got lucky. Stopped in here to ask around and lookie, lookie. Who knew vamps were so easy to bribe? You'd think you'd want to lay low, but no, here ya are, out partying."

"You'll never get away with this," Gillian began. She kicked off her shoes and tore off her dress as fast as she could.

"Should be an easy grab. Whadya think, Rex?" The animal offered no response as he plodded toward her. "You go ahead and strip down, bitch. Once we silver ya, you ain't gonna shift again. Maybe we'll give you a go in the car."

The wolf snarled.

"I didn't say we'd fuck her. No, the Alpha wants that pussy all to himself. But ya still got a mouth. I'll teach you how to open wide on the way over to the airport," he taunted. Flicking open the cuffs, he approached. "Look at those lips on ya. Bet you like a big dick. You're gonna have one real soon."

Gillian didn't stop to remark on his crude comments. Hoping that Jake had his ear pressed to the door, she screamed at the top of her lungs, right as she shifted into her tiger. The transformation was rough, painful like she'd never known. A hot slice tore through every cell. It'd never been such agony to shift, but she kept telling herself that she was changing, her great cat dying, her wolf emerging. If she didn't concentrate, she'd die. She'd cry later. *It's normal*, she told herself. *I'll get through this.*

Transformed, she lunged at the thug, her powerful jaws ripping at the man's arm. His whiskey-soaked blood gushed into her mouth as her head thrashed from side to side. If it weren't for the adrenaline pumping, she'd have noticed the razor-sharp wolf canines carving into her hide. It didn't deter her. Anger at Chaz and his pack fueled her attack. She registered the horrified cry of the man as she crushed through his bones, ripping his forearm from its socket.

As she spat out the appendage, she turned to the wolf, that had lodged its teeth deep into the back of her neck. Her own blood spurted from her wounds, distracting her from her initial attacker. She whimpered as he slapped a silver cuff around her right paw; the excruciating burn flashed through her body. Her naked human form slammed into the floor with a thud, her head splitting open on the red-stained tiles. The wolf continued to shred her throat, growling and scratching as he did so. The last thing she heard was gunshots, before darkness claimed her.

Dimitri shoved at the door, breaking the metal chain off its hinges. The stench of sweat and blood smacked at his senses as he plowed forward into the bathroom. He cried out as he caught sight of the armless man, pinning Gillian to the floor. As she lay face down naked, a feral wolf locked his jaws deep into her flesh and had begun shaking his head furiously.

Enraged, Dimitri stripped off his shirt, calling his wolf, yet only a whimper registered in his mind. He cursed, realizing that once again, he was losing the ability to shift.

"Gun," he called to Jake, who'd begun taking off his jacket.

Jake tossed the weapon to Dimitri, and commenced shifting.

"Get the fuck off of her," Dimitri ordered, taking care to aim so that he wouldn't hit Gillian.

"Piss off, buddy," the stranger replied with a grunt. Ignoring Dimitri, he began to try to undress so he could shift and heal. He pushed up so that he sat on Gillian's legs.

Dimitri had had enough. He fired off a pop and the bullet traveled straight through the asshole's head. Dimitri winced as blood sprayed against the walls. Eyes wide open, the man fell dead against the pedestal sink.

Jake had leapt upon the grey wolf, but it refused to release Gillian from its bite. Without hesitation, Dimitri advanced toward it. Pressing the muzzle into its fur, he pulled the trigger. With a whimper, the wolf stumbled backwards, a breathy rattle coming from its throat. As it shifted, a blonde male, who looked to be in his mid-twenties, came into sight.

"Get him," Dimitri called to Jake as he knelt down next to Gillian. She lay motionless, despite no longer being mauled about by the wolf. The smell of burnt flesh drew him to the cuff on her ankle. Dimitri tugged at the locked silver, singeing his fingers. "Fuck."

Figuring that one of them had brought the keys, Dimitri crawled to the large man, who still wore clothes. He dug through his jeans, locating the metal chain that was jammed deep into his pocket. Dimitri pinched it with his fingers, quickly yanking it free of the fabric. Wasting no time, he unlocked the shackle from her leg.

"Gilly, can you hear me?" he cried to her.

When she didn't respond, Dimitri gently rolled her over onto her back, supporting her head in his lap. Although she was breathing, he immediately noticed the two-inch gash on her forehead as well as her bloodied swollen eyes. He curled her up against his chest, hoping she'd regain consciousness. The wounds on her neck had already begun to heal, but he knew the poisonous metal had injured her tiger, making it more difficult to shift.

Dimitri took a deep breath and fought back the rage that threatened to overtake reason. He glanced across the room, at the detached arm that lay in a puddle of blood. She'd defended herself. What he couldn't figure out was how they'd gotten into the room. However, as he lifted

Gillian into his arms, he took note of the open secret panel.

"Gilly. Please, Goddess," he said, brushing the hair from her eyes. "Jake, leave that fucker. Give me your shirt."

"Here you go." Jake threw it to him and then leaned over to scoop up the weapon that his beta had tossed aside. He toed at the guy who was laid out cold. "I gotta make sure this douchebag isn't going anywhere. He's going to be out for a while. Lucky he's not dead with the plug you pumped into him. Looks like it went straight through. How the hell did they get in here?"

"There." Dimitri nodded to the open door. "They didn't just get in here on their own. Someone did this on purpose."

"Jesus, is she okay? Why isn't she shifting?" Jake asked. Using his jacket, he snatched the handcuffs up off the floor. "Goddamned silver."

Dimitri only heard half of what Jake was telling him as he held his mate. Gillian coughed; her mouth twitched but no words came. Her eyelids slowly opened, and he breathed in relief.

"Darlin', say something," he pleaded. His lips mere inches from hers, he cradled her head, stroking her hair.

"Dimitri," she whispered.

"You're safe now. I'm sorry. I'm so damned sorry." Dimitri looked to Jake. "Grab my phone. Text Leo. I want him here now."

"I think the whole bar probably knows," Jake commented, looking up to the crowd that had gathered around the door. Léopold pushed through with Lady Charlotte following close behind.

"What the hell happened here?" Lady Charlotte began but Léopold unceremoniously cut her off.

"Tais toi." Léopold held up his hand, shushing her. She crossed her arms and rolled her eyes in response, but didn't make a move to disobey his command. "Wolves, no? But how did they get in?"

"I'd cleared the restroom. But apparently vamp lady has secret doors…doors that I'm sure only she knows about," Jake stated, his eyes pinned on Lady Charlotte.

"You did this? You attacked Dimitri's mate?" Léopold accused, gripping her arm.

"Of course not. Why would I do anything like this? I keep these exits…passages for emergencies. Look at me, you know I'm not lying."

"Shut the fuck up," Dimitri yelled.

"I'm sorry," Gillian managed, her voice barely audible.

"Gilly, you're gonna be okay. Do you want to shift?"

"Can't…I feel so weak."

"It's the silver."

"The wolves…where are they?"

"Don't worry about them. I'll tell you when we get home." Gillian attempted to push out of his arms but he held her tight. "Wait a second, cher. Leo, find out what happened…how these wolves got in here without us knowing. If that bitch over there doesn't know about it, go down the chain, starting with Lacey. As much as I'd like to personally kill whoever did this, I've gotta get Gilly home. Can you get these assholes out of here? Give us some privacy?"

"Oui." Léopold gave Lady Charlotte a hard stare and released her, gesturing for her to go. "You heard him. Get rid of your customers. Now!"

Lady Charlotte scurried into the hallway and began ordering everyone out of the area, funneling them onto the dance floor.

"Call Logan. We've got to secure that fucker over there. Keep him for his Alpha. I'll ask Leo to clean up the rest. Can you shut that door?" Dimitri ordered.

"Ya'll broke it off the frame. I'll just," Jake picked up the heavy wooden door and leaned it against the doorjamb, "there you go. No one can see in. Let's get her to shift so we can get her the hell out of here."

"Thanks, man. And thanks for back there...I couldn't...aw, fuck. You know." Dimitri shook his head, reliving how it felt to call on his wolf. The deafening silence was like a knife to his chest.

"We'll fix this," Jake said. He put his hand on Dimitri's shoulder and then turned away to the sink and began to wash the blood off his hands.

"Hey, Gilly. You ready?" Gillian had fallen back asleep. He gently kissed her forehead and her lashes fluttered.

"Yes," she whispered.

"That's a girl. You go ahead and shift right here. I've got ya. Just remember not to claw me up. Go easy, okay?" he joked.

Dimitri smiled as she transformed. Elated that his injured mate had gone to her great cat, he stroked her fur. She roared and licked his face, letting him know she was healed. The magic of shifting never ceased to amaze him, even after having done it himself all these years. The spectacular sight of her tiger caused him to experience both pride and regret, concerned that she'd never be able to shift after their mating. No matter how many times he told himself that she'd be just as happy as wolf, his conscience warned him not to do it.

Chapter Seventeen

The smell of lavender bubble bath filled the air, and Dimitri took a deep breath into his lungs, praying it would calm the tension. He sighed, his heart heavy, as he massaged the shampoo into Gillian's hair. As he sat behind her on the stool, he noticed that her thick dark hair was finally starting to shine through, the cheap dye fading away. Contemplating the night's events, he knew they needed to have a serious conversation about their future.

During the car ride home, Gillian had been quiet. Except for a squeeze of his hand, she'd been essentially despondent. In the bathroom at Mordez, she'd eventually shifted back to her human form. While physically she'd been healed, he immediately knew her emotional wounds had not.

Dimitri had wrapped her in Jake's coat and carried her out to his car where they'd met Logan. After filling him in on what had happened, the Alpha went to help Jake with the lone wolf who was still alive. By the time he and Gillian had arrived back to his house, Dimitri had received a text from Léopold about who'd led the wolves to Gillian. It came as no surprise that Léopold had needed very little interrogation time to affirm the identity of the individual. Apparently the wolves had paid Lacey a considerable amount of money to get access to Gillian. Léopold mentioned that she'd accused Ilsbeth of wrongdoing but that he hadn't given her a chance to explain. Dimitri hadn't asked what he'd done with her, the punishment he'd given. He knew the vampire wouldn't think twice about killing a traitor. Incredulous, Dimitri didn't feel an ounce of pity for her as she had to have known the wolves were planning on torturing his mate.

Dimitri glanced at the gun Jake had given him. It sat on the sink counter, a cold reminder of his affliction. With his wolf unable to respond, he didn't trust himself to be able to protect Gillian. Dimitri had asked Jake to stay overnight and expected him to return as soon as he was finished at the club.

The only saving grace, he thought, was that they'd safely arrived at his home without incident. His sanctuary, it was large and contemporary. The enormous bathroom and shower area, consisting entirely of glass walls, could be viewed through the master bedroom. An oversized tub sat centerpiece. While he rarely used it, he'd personally helped design the layout. The open area reflected his soul, no walls, no pretenses. What you saw was what you got.

"Dimitri." Gillian's soft voice broke his rumination.

"Lift your head up a sec," he told her, turning on the water. He removed the hand-held faucet and sprayed away the lather. "All done, relax back."

"About tonight," she began, pressing the heels of her hands to her forehead.

"You defended yourself." Dimitri wrung the water out of her hair, rolled up a towel and set it behind her head.

"They're not going to stop."

"That's the idea. They'll come to us and we'll take care of Chaz."

"You mean we're going to kill him," she said flatly.

"Yes. I'm not gonna lie about how things are. He'll either give up and go home, which I doubt. Or he'll come here and die on our land."

"Lacey. She told me they paid her."

"So I heard. You know, I'm friends with Leo, but vampires in general...I don't trust them."

"You slept with her."

"Yeah, I did." Her words burned deep, but he knew she had to get this off her chest.

"The thing is, in that bathroom, I talked to her. Lacey doesn't want you or care about you. She reminded me a little of my mom's cat. She'd find a mouse and she'd just kind of bat it around. She wouldn't kill them. She just played with them for entertainment. Lacey is the same way. Tonight, she took perverse pleasure in causing you pain...for fun. What she did to me...that was about money."

"It doesn't matter why she did it. Sometime before she was turned, she learned right and wrong."

"She wasn't attached to you. She understood that you'd find a mate."

"It was just a fling. It meant nothing. I thought that she got that. Vampires usually get it and so do wolves. Single wolves don't make it a habit to fall for someone they've had sex with because they know there's always a chance of finding their mate. There's something innate that tells us it's okay to fool around and we don't get attached. It's just how it is."

"Ilsbeth didn't get the memo," Gillian said quietly. She submerged deeper into the soapy water.

"She's a witch. She knew the deal from the very beginning. I tried to make it up to her, but she's pissed." Dimitri sunk his hands onto Gillian's shoulders, massaging them. "I'm just sorry that you have to be privy to all this nonsense. You know you can feel the difference?"

"What do you mean?"

"I'm not the first person you've dated. Had sex with. This is different. And it's not just the mating, Gil." He paused, pressing his lips to her wet hair. "The heat, the passion we have is off the charts. But it's not just sex, cher. It's everything about us. The way I feel about you." Dimitri cringed at how inarticulate he sounded, but his words eluded him.

"I care about you…too much," she admitted, reaching up to his hands. "I get that you dated other people, but what's going on inside me; it's like I'm feeling everything tenfold. I'm not a jealous person, I swear. But tonight I could have killed Lacey when she went to bite you. And Ilsbeth? She's just a bitch."

Dimitri laughed softly. "Yeah, that's about it. But she's a powerful bitch. So I'm trying to play nice."

"Did you ever think that maybe she isn't?"

"What do you mean?"

"Just something Lacey said."

"You can't really trust her, ya know. Tonight. Case in point."

"I know." Gillian turned around onto her knees, facing Dimitri. She pushed out of the water, her breasts dripping, and balanced herself with her hands on the side of the tub. "But maybe you shouldn't trust the witch. Maybe she had something to do with you losing your wolf."

"No, I know where I picked up this crazy bit of evil. I was there, remember."

"But Ilsbeth was too. She had reason for you to lose your wolf. Witches can be with mortals, right?"

"Yeah, but…"

"What happens when you lose your beast? You'll essentially be human. Maybe you'll continue not to age, but you'll still be vulnerable like a human. No shifting. No pack. No mate."

Dimitri's blood pumped hard as Gillian formulated the accusation that had grown from the seed Lacey had planted. He shook his head, and wiped his hands on his towel. Here he had a beautiful wet and naked woman in his room but they were discussing evil that had no bounds. He swore to himself that before the night was through, they'd be back to making love instead of talking about his exes.

"Just listen," she persisted. "If you weren't wolf, then you wouldn't need to mate. She could be with you…there'd be nothing stopping you from being with her."

"Except for the fact that I don't love her. I wasn't even close to falling in love with her, so there's no way that would happen," he argued. He laughed as he spoke, amused at how Gillian didn't know how much he liked her. "I want to be with you, Gilly. Not because you're my mate, either. I mean, sure, that's what brought us together. But you're brave. And you don't give up. I want to be with you…just you."

A smile broke across Gillian's face at his confession.

"I want to mate with you now," she declared. "I don't want to wait."

"I don't know if that's such a good idea," Dimitri found himself saying. He'd kill to mate with her, but that was exactly the problem; her tiger would die.

"Why would you say that? No, forget it, I know why. Is this about me?" Gillian splashed hot water over her chest, trying to warm herself.

"Of course it's about you," he snapped, torn about what to do. He didn't want to hurt her any more than he already had.

"Tonight I heard a howl..." She looked down into the bath, then slowly lifted her gaze, aware that she'd dropped a bomb. "I heard...I think it was my wolf."

"You what?" His voice grew louder. He shoved out of his chair, and began to pace, plowing his fingers through his hair. "This is crazy. We haven't mated yet. There's no way...we must've done something...what about your cat? I saw what you did to that guy tonight. A wolf couldn't do that by itself. And when you shifted, you were a cat. I saw your tiger with my own two eyes."

"I don't know what's happening, but I know what I heard. Before Lacey came into the bathroom I was all by myself."

"You know what this means?" he huffed, concerned about her feline.

"I'm changing. I can already feel it."

"Because I marked you, goddammit," he said, flooded with guilt.

"I let you. I wanted it as much as you did," she insisted, fingering the area where he'd bitten her. "It's done. And there's something else...something I haven't told you."

"What?" he asked, scrubbing his face. Goddess, what hadn't she told him? When she didn't answer, he approached the bath and sat down in front of her, resisting the urge to take her in his arms.

"I should have told you...I just didn't want you to want me because of it. Chaz, he knows. It's what he wants. It's why he won't give up." Her voice cracked.

"I don't know what you're about to tell me but we'll deal with it. What is it?"

"My mother told me…Jax thinks that…"

"Fucking Jax knows this secret and you haven't told me? Honesty, it's all I ask," he yelled. Dimitri could forgive many things, but lying wasn't one of them.

"Just, please let me finish. I don't even know if it's true. It's like this urban legend about our breed. But Jax thinks it's true. He knew my father, so maybe he saw it firsthand."

"What?" His patience grew thin.

"Supposedly when I mate, the person I mate with…"

"Me. I'm the person you're going to mate with, Gilly. You're mine," he asserted.

"You…you'll take on attributes of my tiger. I lose my cat, but somehow you get them…like gifts. You'll be stronger. Your teeth, your claws, they can change. You'd still be a wolf, but you'd gain her strength."

"You've got to be kidding me?" Léopold had mentioned that she might have gifts but he'd always thought whatever it was had to do with her healing abilities.

"I'm not joking. I lose my ability to shift to tiger. Well, we don't even know if that's true but I can feel her fading already. My mate, on the other hand…you, you'll be able to call on her."

No longer able to restrain himself, Dimitri took her by the arms, gently pulling her upward, until they were inches apart, face to face. "Why, Gilly? Why after all this time did you keep this a secret?"

"I'm sorry. I know I should have told you but…"

"It didn't make any sense why Chaz was after you. He's doing all of this just so he can steal your power?"

"Yes," she nodded.

"Did your father do this to your mother? Did he hurt her?"

"No, no. She loved him. She always made sure I knew how much he was loved…how much he loved me. They knew when they mated that this could happen."

"You haven't answered my question, though. Why didn't you tell me about your gifts? Did you think I'd steal from you?" He felt her shiver, and pressed her to his chest.

"No. Yes. No, it's not like that. I'm just afraid. I didn't want you to want me so you could be Alpha." She tried to pull away but he held her still.

"We need to get one thing straight, darlin'. I chose not to kill Chaz that night. I don't want to leave to be Alpha of someone else's pack. I don't want to be Alpha of my pack either. If I wanted to challenge Logan to be Alpha, I could do it any damn day of the week. But I don't. Dealin' with the weight of the pack is something that Logan took on when Marcel died and he's got a load of responsibility on those shoulders. Our pack has had enough upheaval in the past twelve months. What I did choose was my position as his beta, supporting Logan, because I love him. It's where I'm most needed in our pack." Dimitri took a deep breath. He couldn't believe she'd hidden the truth from him, thinking he'd want her gifts. His Alpha knew what he was capable of when it came to a battle of strength, but when Logan agreed to lead the pack, Dimitri had made a deliberate decision to support his friend. "Gillian, do you think so little of me that I'd be just like Chaz? That I'd take a mate just so I'd be able to sprout tiger fangs? Seriously?"

"You don't understand. I had to be sure…after what happened with Chaz. I didn't know you."

"I'm not like Chaz. And you know it."

"I just…I just wanted to be loved by someone. Not because I can give them something. Or because of who I am. I hate this mating thing…I just want to be able to choose on my own who I love. I don't want some stupid fate thing to take over my life. I want you…I want you to choose me for me," she cried. "Is it so much to ask? Don't answer because there is no other way for us."

"Gillian, I can't change our circumstances. We are who we are."

"In here." She pounded her chest with her palm. "This is what should matter. I needed to know that you liked me for me, not because I can give you something."

"Goddess, you know I care about you. Why do you think I'm worried about mating you? I don't want to hurt you. To know that I'll be the reason you'll lose your ability to shift…I just don't know if I can do that to you. It's not fair to you." He cupped her face, his thumb tracing her bottom lip.

"All I know is that I can't lose you," she responded. "If we mate, there's still a chance I can give you my gift. This thing with Ilsbeth. What if she did this to you on purpose?"

"What does any of this have to do with Ilsbeth?"

"Because maybe she has no intention of really healing you. Think about this. If she's so powerful and all knowing, why did she have to bring in someone else to help her? Maybe she's just waiting this thing out…waiting for your wolf to die. If there's no wolf, then she certainly doesn't have to worry about you finding or at this point, keeping your mate. Once your wolf is dead, there's no reason to mate with me."

"Listen, I'll be the first one to admit that Ilsbeth was pissed at me, but I don't think that she'd go that far."

"Really? What makes you think she wouldn't? She's not just a little bit upset with you. I saw the way she was looking at you…the way she touched you and no matter what you say, she still wants you. I may not know witches very well but I know when a woman is jealous."

Dimitri sighed, thinking it had been one hell of a night. As much as he loathed to admit it, Gillian's theory had merit. A pit of disgust curled in his stomach as he realized that Ilsbeth could have done this to him on purpose. The night he'd come out of hell, having saved Logan's daughter, Ilsbeth had given him a look of pity. At least that's what he'd thought at the time. Maybe it was guilt for what she'd done? Anger boiled inside him as he gave the situation new perspective.

"Even so, the sorcerer seemed legit. I've got to give his spell a try. There aren't many options left on the table."

"What if…" Gillian paused. "What if we mate tonight? My gifts…they could destroy this thing inside you…maybe forever."

"No. No way. You're grasping at straws. This thing with my wolf. You tried healing me before and it only worked temporarily. I'm not doing that to you."

"I am not grasping at straws. Am I desperate? You're damn straight I am. I'm not going to sit back and wait for the witch who did this to you to save you," she cried, pushing out of his arms. "No, just let me go. You don't believe me. You don't believe I can do this."

"Believe what? That you want to kill yourself to save me?"

"I'm doing this to save us. Us!"

Dimitri shook his head and blew out a breath.

"I healed you once," Gillian pressed. "My ability to heal is still there, maybe not as strong as before, but when we mate, my gift, it may be enough."

"No." Dimitri couldn't allow her to sacrifice herself for him.

"Please, Dimitri. Just hear me out. Maybe when it's all said and done, I'll never be able to shift as cat again, but my wolf, she's there. I just know it…she's in here." Tears streamed down her face and she swiped at them, turning her head away. "You have to let me do this for you. I need you in my life. There's not much time left. Tonight you couldn't shift. Soon there won't be a wolf to even save."

"Please don't cry, Gil," he pleaded.

"I'm losing my tiger already. You're losing your wolf. We can save each other. And I'm not crying," she said with a small smile.

"Okay, tough girl. So those aren't tears, huh?"

"No," she lied, beginning to laugh. She wasn't sure if it was out of frustration, grief or the fact that she was sitting naked in a tub arguing with her handsome beta, who looked like he was about to go feral at her suggestion.

"I don't like lying," he replied, unfolding a large black towel.

"I'm not lying," she stated with a grin.

"I think you might be. You've done many things today to get yourself in trouble. You goin' for broke?"

"Not crying. You see any tears here?" She lay back into the tub, intentionally keeping her erect nipples at the surface so he could see them. "I'm merely trying to get you to see things from my perspective."

"What are you doing, cher?"

"Nothing, what do you think I'm doing?" She gave him a seductive smile.

Dimitri wanted to argue that she was wrong, that they shouldn't mate, but he craved the woman before him. The Goddess had given him a fighter, to be sure. In the past week, she'd killed and maimed, protecting herself from the enemy. Her spirit never faltered despite the fact the war was far from over. The more he thought about it the more he thought she was right about Ilsbeth. *Could she heal him by mating?* In lieu of hard evidence one way or another, he wasn't convinced either way.

Regardless of whether or not it was true, his wolf would demand their mating sooner or later. With her naked and flirting, he was definitely leaning toward sooner. The only real way to deny their mating would be for him to leave, to physically separate himself from her. Doing so was as impossible as asking him to fly to the moon on the wings of an eagle. It just wasn't happening.

Her amber eyes flashed, bringing him back to the crux of the situation. *Mate or not to mate?* The only thing he knew for certain was that he'd make mad love to the woman in his bathtub tonight and wait until tomorrow before deciding on their mating. It would tear him to shreds if she chose not to mate with him in the morning, but he wanted to give her time to make sure that she wasn't overreacting to the earlier trauma. Her choice had to be made with a clear head and heart.

Dimitri's cock jerked as his mate turned up the heat, cupping her breasts, teasing him. He laughed, guessing that she was attempting to use her feminine wiles to get her way. *Yeah, doesn't matter. Kinda likin' it.* Dimitri kept his eyes locked on his mate, as she played with herself. The sexy lil' vixen didn't realize the fire she was starting.

Dimitri glanced over to his cell phone, attempting to check out the time. He knew Jake would be home any minute, and they didn't have much time to make love without an audience. He hesitated, wiping his hands on the towel, but as she pinched her nipples into hard points, Dimitri lost control.

Gillian sensed the exact moment that Dimitri had shifted his position on their mating. A sense of victory and relief filled her chest. She knew it was crazy to fall for someone after only knowing them for a week, but the entire concept of mating wasn't based on reason. Destiny drove two souls to merge hearts, not logic.

Love wasn't supposed to make sense, she supposed. Love just was. She smiled as the thought popped into her head. *Falling in love?* She couldn't even say what she felt was love, mostly because she never had really been in love. But what she did know was that she'd sacrifice everything for Dimitri, her wolf, her heart, her life.

She'd purposefully taunted him with her white lie, telling him that she hadn't been crying. It had hurt that he hadn't jumped at the opportunity to mate with her, but she could see the conflict in his eyes, having believed she'd never shift again. And she, too, had believed the same until earlier when she'd heard the wolf. Like an owl in the woods at night, it had sounded its unique call. The realization that she'd transform again gave her hope that she could survive mating and save Dimitri all at once.

Gillian watched intently as Dimitri silently contemplated her words. Filled with a longing for him, she touched herself, hoping she could seduce him into making love. She craved his hands on her body. Intimacy with her mate would wash away the evil of the day, refreshing all that was well with her life.

As he turned to her, she'd begun to fondle her creamy flesh, pinching her tender peaks. The hunger on his face sent a jolt of lust to her sex. She squeezed her thighs, in response to the ache that built between her legs. With her eyes pinned on his, she deliberately let her left hand slide down her stomach into the bubbly water.

Like a cobra, he struck, tearing off his shirt and jumping into the tub, still wearing his pants. She gasped as he straddled her with his legs, water sloshing onto the floor. Her hands went from her own skin to his. Dimitri raked his hands into her hair, stealing her mouth in a hard, possessive kiss. His tongue forcefully slid through her lips, exhaustively exploring every inch of her warmth. She fought for breath, surrendering to his savage kiss, his hands fisted in her hair.

"Fuck, Gilly," he groaned. "Look what you do to me."

He grabbed her wrist, setting her hand onto his steel-hard cock. She clutched at the wet denim, earning a hard groan from Dimitri. Breaking free from his lips, she sought to taste him, biting and licking at his muscular chest. Reaching his nipple, she nipped him until he cried out at the sensation.

"Oh no, kitten. I'm having none of that," he told her, tugging her head away. His eyes were wild with desire; his lips turned upward in a devious smile. "Tonight, you're submitting."

"What makes you think that?" she challenged with a giggle, her hair still held tight in his grip. At the sight of his wet slippery abs, her lips parted. She tilted her pelvis upward, grinding her mound against his erection.

"Bad kitty," he scolded playfully.

Before she could return his banter, he wrapped his hands around her waist, and stood up straight in the tub. In one smooth movement, he threw her over his shoulder with ease, her legs dangling over his chest. Water splattered all over the floor as he stepped out of the bath.

"What are you doing?" she screamed, laughing at the same time. "You're making a mess."

"My mess, my house, my woman," he responded.

"But…"

"I think it's 'bout time for that lesson in submission. What do you think, Jake?"

"What? Jake's here?" Gillian strained to see as Dimitri twisted his body, giving her a view of Jake, who was standing in the doorway. She gasped in embarrassment, but oddly, the idea of him watching made her hot with arousal. On the plane, he'd seen her suck Dimitri's cock and she'd secretly fantasized about Dimitri's earlier warning that he'd be there again.

"I was going to ask how Gillian was doing but I guess all's well that ends well. Hey, Gilly."

"Hi," she giggled, giving him a wave. "Would you please tell this caveman of a beta to put me down?"

"Wouldn't dream of it, sugar. I expect this is going to be fun. Wish I could participate, but I got a feeling you two got something going on that needs settling."

"My mate's been askin' for a lesson in submission. And during our lil' talk, she bit me. That's twice now."

"That doesn't sound very submissive to me," Jake laughed.

"And I do recall me promising her that when she submitted you'd be here to watch, so feel free to take a shower. You do want him to watch, don't you, Gilly?" he asked, smoothing his hand over her bottom. "You seemed to like it when we were flying."

"I never said that…" Gillian silently cursed, wondering how Dimitri knew she was turned on by the idea of it.

A hard slap hit her bottom and she screamed out loud. The hot sensation caused her to wiggle against him, needing to alleviate the pressure between her legs. Her pussy ached with need, and she dug her fingernails into his back, trying to get him to move to the bedroom.

"I'm thinking maybe after we mate, she may even want to play with both of us," Dimitri suggested. "Do you want Jake to touch you, Gilly? Do you want to play with the big wolves?"

"I can't talk like this," she protested. *Yes, I want to play all right.* She was falling in love with Dimitri and sought to explore her sexuality within the safe confines of their mating.

"Yes you can. No more lying." Dimitri slapped her cheek once more. "Tell me, do you want Jake to touch you?"

"Please…Dimitri." She dug her face into his back, but her smile gave away her desire.

"I'll take that as a yes, darlin'." He smiled to Jake, who in response reached to stroke Gillian's smooth globe, eliciting a small hiss from her. "See Jake, she does like that."

"Your mate is so soft."

"She is. Ah, look at how you respond, Gil. Does it feel good to have both of us touch you?"

Jake ran his fingers down the crevice of her bottom, brushing over her rosebud, his fingers lightly grazing the wetness of her core. Gillian squirmed, her hips pressing back into his touch.

"Yes, Dimitri, please…" she gasped. If he didn't make love to her within the next two minutes, she'd rip out her hair. The man was infuriating and hot, so very, very hot.

"You're suffering aren't you, my lovely mate? We'll leave Jake now. Time for our lesson."

"Shower." Jake pointed to the clear blocked-off stall. Since the bathroom was made entirely of glass, he could easily see them on the bed and they could view him.

Gillian kicked her legs as Dimitri strode into the bedroom. She laughed as she attempted to bat his ass through his wet jeans and promptly earned herself another swat on her wet bare bottom.

Dimitri bent, carefully depositing her on the bed. Gillian went to scurry across it when he latched onto her legs.

"Sweet, Gilly. I'm not joking about your submission tonight. You're going to be wolf soon."

"Yes," she breathed. As she lay belly down onto the white cotton down comforter, she relaxed into his hold.

"You're mine, do you accept this?"

"Yes."

"Do you trust me?"

"Yes."

"Put your hands to your sides. No arguing, understand?"

When she didn't respond, he swiftly spanked her twice. He cupped her reddened cheek, and slid a finger into her slick pussy.

"Ow," she cried and then moaned in pleasure as he entered her.

"Now that I have your attention, I'll ask you again. Do you understand?"

"Yes," she breathed. His low voice sent a delicious chill down her spine. At his command, she stopped trying to get away and lowered her arms.

"That's a girl. Now, I'm going to move you sideways here, because I want you to be able to see Jake watching you."

"Why would you want that?"

"I want to be able to share with you what it's like to submit, to be with other wolves. I also know that you seem to be interested in this sexually. Does it turn you on to know that someone could watch you?"

"I don't know. I guess so. It seems wrong, but I know wolves do it."

"Lots of people do it, not just wolves. And there's nothing wrong with it as long as it's consensual. Do you want Jake to watch us fuck? If you want him to leave, I'll tell him right now."

"Yes." Gillian groaned at her admission. She dug her face into the blanket, having a hard time believing the words that spilled from her mouth. Deep within her, she wanted this, to know that she was being possessed by Dimitri with Jake watching. But it was more than that; she wanted to see Jake's reaction, watch him touch himself. As if Dimitri read her mind, he probed further.

"You want to see him, too, don't you?"

"Yes."

"Look at him. Someday we can play with Jake, too. Do you want that?"

"Maybe," she hedged, still embarrassed by her own desires. "He's attractive…but he's not you."

"Whatever we do, I'll always take care of you. You come first in everything I do. We're wolves…what you feel for me, what I feel for you…we'll always have that connection. Just you and I. But playin'? If we choose to do that, it's our decision, but you'll always be mine and I'll be the same with you."

"I won't share you with another woman," she admitted.

"That's fine, because you're the only woman for me. When and if we play with Jake, we'll decide together to do it. Okay?"

"Okay," she agreed.

"Tonight I just want you to enjoy watching and being watched."

"Yes," Gillian breathed. Her pulse began to race as she glanced over to the shower, and Jake's eyes fell on hers.

"Now back to our lesson," Dimitri laughed.

"Please, I'm so hot. I can't take it…"

Dimitri tugged on her legs so that they fell over the sides of the bed, her bottom completely exposed to him. He reached over into his drawer and took out a few small items, placing them on the bed. Unscrewing a small blue bottle, he poured the cinnamon-scented oil into his palms.

Gillian slowly turned her head, the side of her face pressed into the mattress. She lifted her eyelids, taking in the sight of Jake. Stark naked, the water sluiced down the sinewy muscles of his back and over his chiseled buttocks. It was as if she was watching a movie, but she knew it was real. If she wanted, if Dimitri let her, she could walk over and touch him.

Dimitri's warm hands massaging her back diverted her attention, the spicy scent filling the room. Her body lit on fire with desire as he worked his magic fingers into her neck, slowly moving down her back, carefully working out the knots. She watched with interest as Jake washed his hair, his eyes closed, the bubbles rolling off his lithe body. He turned in her direction and she caught sight of his erection jutting outward.

Dimitri's palms reached her bottom, continuing to caress. Using his knees, he parted her legs until they were wide open to him. She looked back and saw him unbuttoning his jeans, finally shucking them off onto the floor.

"Tell me about this?" he asked, tracing a finger over her tattoo. "What's it mean?"

"Strength within. It's how I first felt when I shifted, like there was something inside me. But then I started to realize it wasn't my tiger who gave me that. I needed strength no matter what."

"You're the strongest woman I've ever met."

"Hmm? I feel like the horniest when I'm around you," she giggled.

"You're definitely the sexiest. Goddess, I love your ass. And this," Dimitri cupped her cheeks, dragging his thumbs down the crevice until he reached her puckered flesh. "I'm gonna have this, too, darlin'."

"Hmm," she replied, calmed from his massage. Gillian had never known nirvana, but expected that this was it. Relaxation and arousal swirled into one delicious reaction.

"But first we've gotta get you ready for me. We can't rush these things. I know you've had my fingers in you before, but I have something new we're going to play with tonight…besides Jake, that is." Dimitri caught Jake's eyes and reached for a small pink bulbous object. "I've got a little toy here for you, Gil."

"Toy?" Her eyes flew open in surprise.

"That's right, darlin'. Open your legs for me. A little more now." He waited as she spread herself wider, and dribbled the lube onto her bottom. He coated the soft rubber and pressed its tip into her anus. "I'm gonna go slowly."

"What? Ah…" Gillian tensed as Dimitri worked it into her.

"That's it, cher. Just relax." He continued, gently stretching her.

"I don't know if…oh my God." The foreign sensation caused her to release a small moan. Gillian had begun to gyrate against the mattress, seeking relief. His hands on her bottom stilled her movement.

"You okay?"

"I feel so…I don't know…Is it wrong that this feels so good?" she breathed.

Gillian, at a loss for words, glanced to Jake who soaped his body. Unable to do anything but enjoy the moment, she immersed herself into the delightful fullness that overtook her body as Dimitri adjusted the toy into her.

"Just imagine when I'm inside you. It's all the way in now."

Gently, he rolled her onto her back and she smiled up at him. He leaned over and pressed his lips to hers, briefly sweeping his tongue into her mouth. Gillian moaned in protest as he retreated. Her disappointment was short-lived as his hands fell to her breasts, and he circled his forefinger around her aroused tips.

"Hmm, you're so beautiful. I can't get enough of you." Dimitri smiled down at her lovingly. He abandoned her nipples, gliding his hands toward her belly.

Gillian's head rolled to the side and she caught sight of Jake watching them through the steamed glass. With his forehead resting on his arm, he stroked the lather over the length of his erection.

"Look at what you do to Jake," Dimitri said.

Gillian laughed and glanced up at Dimitri, who gave her a hungry stare.

"And this," Dimitri held her hips, trailing his thumbs over her bare mound. Working them into her slick folds, he spread her wide open. "Your pussy is…oh yeah." He flicked the pad of his thumb over her glistening nub, "so wet," then plunged his thick middle finger up into her, "tight…ah, yes."

"Dimitri," she cried, her hips pushing upward so that his finger went as far as possible into her. She went to move to reach for him but he placed a palm on her belly.

"Stay," he ordered, his voice laced with a sexy tone that surrounded her in its demand. "Play with your breasts. I want to see you touch yourself."

She shook her head no, but found herself reaching to her chest. She quivered as the pads of his fingers glided over the ridges inside her core. The sensation intensified in her bottom as her climax built.

"That's it. Goddess, you're so fucking gorgeous. This, darlin', this is the start of your submission. And it's beautiful." Dimitri added another finger, using his thumb on her clit. "Look at Jake. He's going to come with you."

Gillian threw her head back, quivering on the edge of orgasm. Dimitri began to pump into her faster, sliding into her at the same rhythm that his friend touched himself. The smell of sex teased her nostrils, and her heart pounded at the sight of her mate. His piercing eyes bore through her, emanating dominance.

"This is real between us. It's not just the mating," he assured her, curling his fingertip inside her hot channel, teasing out her orgasm. "This…is magic."

"I'm going to come," she cried, continuing to tease her breasts. Pinching herself, she surrendered to the devastating climax. As if electricity stung her body, she convulsed, her back arching off the bed. A loud grunt sounded, and she caught the sight of Jake's tightened abs crunched over as his milky essence sprayed against the glass. He looked up, catching Gillian's gaze as he turned to grab his towel to leave.

Dimitri withdrew his fingers, dragging her cream across her taut belly. Gliding his hand over her breasts, he cupped her face, his wet thumb plunging into her mouth. She tasted herself, closing her eyes.

"Up here," she heard him call.

Her eyelids fluttered open, and she focused every ounce of her attention on him. Unable to speak with her lips wrapped around his finger, she simply waited, her heart pounding in anticipation. Dimitri stroked his glistening cock, brushing its plump head over her clit. She moaned in response.

"I'm going to fuck you, kitten, so fucking hard, you'll never forget where you belong. You want this?" His strong fingers curled around his dick, tapping her clit.

"Yes," she managed, his fingers still in her lips.

"Fuck, yeah," he grunted, guiding his shaft into her.

"Ahhh," she responded. As his hand moved from her lips down her body, she cried out, his thick sex stretching her.

"Yes," he repeated.

"Fuck me, yes," she gritted out, her hands fisting the blankets.

Dimitri lifted her hips off the bed, and increased the pace. Their flesh met, sounding throughout the room, and the thought of how Jake watched them flitted through her mind, heightening her arousal. As he slammed into her, all her focus returned to the magnificent male worshipping her body with his erotic dance. Her core clamped down around him as the tingles of desire built again.

"Ah Goddess, yeah…like that," he growled.

"Harder, fuck me harder," she demanded. The urge to grab him grew but she resisted. Her hands fisted the fabric so tightly she swore it would tear.

Dimitri quickly adjusted his position, pinning her to the bed. Capturing her wrists, he held her arms above her head. The weight of him pressed down onto her, and she gasped at the intimacy. Restrained, she widened her legs, accepting his hard pounding thrusts.

Awestruck by his commanding presence, Gillian had never felt more erotic or powerful. As if she'd been caged for a thousand years, Dimitri released her from her own sexual confines. She jutted her full breasts against his sweat-covered chest, their bodies sliding together. She greedily took every inch of him inside her as he pounded himself into her pussy.

"Please, Dimitri, please," she begged. Again, she teetered on release, but only he could give her what she needed. She gladly accepted her position, certain her mate would bring her to orgasm.

"Submit, Gil," he ordered. He coiled one hand around both her wrists, freeing a hand to tend to her breast. With a primal heat, he plunged in and out of her wetness.

"Please, don't stop, please….don't stop, don't stop," she repeated as he rocked against her sensitive hooded nub. Baring her neck to him, she let him guide her into release, giving into him the only way she knew how. Heaving for breath, her body shook, the frenzy of orgasmic pulses rolling through her.

As her climax continued, her tiger roared, demanding her due. *My mate.* Giving herself over to her beast, her canines extended. In a flash, she bit deep into his flesh, breaking his skin. Blood rushed down her throat, and she succumbed to the mating.

"Holy fuck! Gilly, no," Dimitri yelled, his orgasm rupturing throughout his body.

Immediately, he registered her intent. *Mate.* Unstoppable and deliberate, his wolf surfaced, breaking through the shackles of the evil eating away at him. Although he'd never intended to complete the mating, his instinctual response was quick and unfettered as he struck her neck with his fangs. Her essence flowed into him, nourishing his craving for the only one who could save his soul.

Gillian shattered, never having experienced the blood of the lupine. *Dimitri.* Like the shards of a broken mirror clattering onto stone, every presupposition she'd had about who she was and what she'd expected from love was destroyed. She'd told herself that love was something that needed to grow over time. The lie crashed around her. Love was a commitment, devotion to each other. Embracing trust and submission to their fate was all she needed to move forward.

A tear escaped her eye as she reached for her tiger who only purred, disappearing into the darkness. Her lifelong friend perished without protest. In the distance, a triumphant howl sounded, its song comforting her. Unfamiliar, the melody of its cry revitalized her, confirming her decision to mate.

Her palms traveled over Dimitri's skin, seeking his wolf, exploring to make sure he was healed. Allowing the heat of him to penetrate her pores, she sought answers. In the silence of their reflection, she recorded the strength beneath his flesh. His wolf ran free, no longer encumbered by the parasite. Gillian supposed she should be crushed by the loss of her cat, yet joy for Dimitri resided deep in her chest. She felt vindicated by her actions; she'd rescued her great wolf.

"Gillian. Goddess, what have we done?" Dimitri cried, the stupor of climax subsiding.

"Hmm?" Gillian asked.

He rolled off her, lifting her onto his chest. Pushing himself up to lie on a pillow, he cradled her tiny form.

"You bit me…"

"It's done. You're whole," she whispered, confident that she'd done the right thing. Her body fell limp against his and she pressed her lips to his chest. "You're mine."

"No, Gilly. I shouldn't have…We should have waited." He cuddled her closer. "I'm sorry. Your cat…"

"I'm better than I've ever been in my life. You have no idea how I feel about you, do you?" she posed. "You're well now. It's all that matters."

"But…"

"I'm going to be just fine. As sure as I know you are my mate, I will shift again. Stop worrying," she told him. The warmth of her love for her beta blossomed in her heart and mind. There was no explanation that would satisfy a scientific mind for how she felt. She was done trying to plan every detail of her life. Destiny had led her to Dimitri, and she'd surrendered to fate, accepting her new life with her wolf.

Dimitri wrapped his leg around hers, creating a protective cocoon. The wolf inside of him rejoiced. The second she'd bitten him, the spell of his imprisonment had broken, releasing the evil back into wherever it had come from. He fought the emotion that rose in his chest. There was no way he'd ever be able to repay his mate's selflessness. She'd stolen the decision away from him, piercing his skin, initiating the mating. In doing so, she'd alleviated the guilt he'd forever carry if he'd done so himself.

A surge of power pumped through his body; the recognition of his century-old strength emerging once again. Dimitri blinked through suppressed tears and gazed up through the skylight to the stars. A month ago he couldn't have fantasized a more perfect existence. The loving, self-sacrificing female wrapped around him had become his world, and he prayed he'd be able to keep her safe.

The full moon beckoned. A second chance at meting out justice was upon him.

Chapter Eighteen

Dimitri stirred, the beams of the late morning sunshine warming his face. Gillian writhed against his heated skin. The slickness between her legs painted his hip, alerting him that she was awake. His eyes flew open as her soft hand wrapped around his already hardened cock. Her hand traveled up and over his abdomen.

"Gilly," he hissed.

"Shhh," she hushed. With the pad of her thumb, she swiped at the wet slit of his arousal.

"Aw fuck," he said, jutting his hips in tandem with her slow strokes. "What are you doin' to me?"

"No talking," she commanded, asserting her dominance.

In all his life he'd never been submissive, yet in the delicate balance between sleeping and waking, the desire to surrender to her demand reigned. Tendrils of her hair teased his chest as she peppered kisses on the smooth skin beneath his arm, down his side and onto his hip. Her lips continued their sensuous journey to the muscular cut V above his groin.

Dimitri heard her exhale softly, her warm breath along the sensitive ridge of his dick. Clutching his shaft with one hand, she lightly raked her nails down his abdomen. Dimitri sucked a breath as the hot moistness of her mouth surrounded him. Arching his back, he lifted his pelvis as she held him firmly by the root and swallowed his entire sex. Her head bobbed up and down, branding him with her lips. Her fingers moved to his tight sac, gently caressing. As her mouth descended, tantalizing him with her tongue, her other hand moved to his ass, where she teased the stretch of skin between his testicles and anus.

"Ah, Gilly," he growled as the dark sensation tempted him.

Her fingers traveled further, circling sensitive puckered flesh. Dimitri cried out in aching desire as the tip of her finger probed him. His balls drew tight, pressure mounting from within. Dimitri swore, realizing he was seconds away from coming in her mouth. He reached for her shoulders, dragging her up his body. She moaned in protest, but he silenced her with a deep, passionate kiss. Their heated connection broke their power exchange. Guiding her upward, he forced her to straddle his chest. He directed her legs so that her knees were on either side of his head.

"Come here," Dimitri growled, shifting her hips, yanking her closer to his lips. "Goddess, I love the smell of you. You know I like to cook, but there's nothing like having my mate for breakfast."

With a smile, he gazed between her legs. He took to her glistening pussy like a fine meal, dragging the tip of his tongue through her lips. She hovered above him, accepting each lash with pleasure. He gripped her ass, pulling her flush to his mouth. Sucking and lapping at her core, he tasted arousal and sex upon her.

With one flattened palm against the wall, she writhed against his face. As he plunged his tongue up into her core, she screamed in orgasm. Taking her swollen clit between his lips, he milked every spasm from her before releasing her hips.

"Dimitri," she panted, recovering from her climax.

"Gilly," he breathed. He slid her down his body and sheathed himself inside her ready center. "You…are…"

"I…I…" Gillian tried to speak, but her words were lost in his kiss.

"Feel how much you mean to me…can you feel it?" he asked, thrusting up into her.

"Yes," she affirmed. Leaning upward, she wrapped her fingers around his wrists, caging his head with her arms.

Passion claimed them as Dimitri allowed Gillian to sink down on him. Resisting the instinct to dominate, he celebrated the way she'd taken control. He marveled as she threw her head back, her breasts arching toward him, yet still out of the reach of his mouth.

"Fuck yes," he grunted as she rose up, slamming herself down onto him.

The threads of his restraint shattered, and he grabbed onto her hips. She ground her pelvis into his as he made short, deep strokes up into her. As the explosive orgasm rocked into him, he called out her name. She released a cry of pleasure, ecstasy flowing through her.

Dimitri fought for breath, bringing her into his embrace. He felt as if he'd run a marathon, his heart thumping in his chest. Physically and emotionally, he was overwhelmed by Gillian. *Life is incredible*, he thought. *No, my mate is incredible.* Feelings he'd never experienced surfaced. It was more than just possession; he needed her in his life, protecting and loving her. *Am I in love?* As much as he tried not to believe it was true, in the recesses of his mind, the thought spun, bringing him to a new level of happiness.

"I love this," Gillian smiled.

Realizing she'd almost told Dimitri that she loved him, Gillian wrapped her arms around his neck, burying her face in his chest. *Oh Goddess, I'm falling in love with my wolf.* No matter how insane it was to develop feelings so quickly for someone, the damage had been done. Every time they made love, exchanged a laugh, another piece of her had been destroyed, only to be reborn and renewed as his mate and lover.

DIMITRI

Dimitri clicked out of his email, his thoughts drifting to Gillian. Like an earthquake, she'd shaken his very existence. He laughed to himself, recalling how he'd mercilessly teased his Alpha when he'd found his mate. Only now did he comprehend the wonderment of mating. An incredible rush of happiness welled in his chest, the strength of her blood renewing his wolf and his soul.

He knew he should regret how they'd mated, her forcing his hand, but he couldn't summon any. Still, though, he remained amazed at Gillian's gift. Even this morning, she'd continued to give to him and appeared at peace with her decision. She'd told him that she was no longer able to feel her tiger, but that the wolf within her paced. How she'd merge with his pack was still in question. She may have been willing to submit sexually, but doing so within a group dynamic remained to be seen. Her beast had been independent and dominant, and he wasn't convinced that anything had changed.

Jake entered the kitchen, jarring him from his thoughts. He gave a wave and picked up his coffee, taking a draw of the black chicory.

"Afternoon." He glanced to catch the time on the wall; it was nearly one o'clock.

"Hey." Jake moved to the coffee pot and rummaged through the cabinet, searching for a mug. As he poured himself a cup, he looked around the kitchen. "What's up? Cooking spree over?"

"You know I only do that when I'm thinking."

"Upset is more like it."

"All is well with the world, my friend." Dimitri smiled, his eyes lighting up over the rim of his coffee. He set it down and gestured to the food on the table. "Sit. Brunch. Eggs. Bacon. Yogurt. Granola. Fruit."

"What the hell? I was hoping for flapjacks and biscuits."

"No way, bro. Eatin' healthy. I gotta maintain my girlish figure," Dimitri joked, touching his hand to his belly. "Keepin' it tight for my woman."

"Yeah, right. As if you don't work out every freakin' day anyway. What is up with you?" Confused, Jake had expected them to deal with the fallout from the drama of last night's killing in Mordez.

"I'm great. No, scratch that. I am phenomenal." Dimitri laughed and slapped his friend on the shoulder.

Jake shook his head.

"You wanna know why I'm in such a good mood?"

"This have anything to do with Gilly?"

"Close. This wolf here," Dimitri set his cup on the counter and held his arms wide open, "is officially mated and lovin' it."

"You're fucking kidding me, right?" Jake asked, astonished at his beta's declaration. "I was there for most of the, uh, show last night and you're telling me I missed this?"

"Nope. Not kidding. And yep. Ya missed it." Dimitri laughed, exhilarated with his news. "It's done."

"Don't you think that's a little quick? I mean, you just met her less than a week ago. Don't get me wrong, Gilly's great and I've heard that mating thing is hard to fight. But I thought the marking would give you some time. Do you love her?"

"Number one. Yeah, it's fast. Number two. Don't care. Too late now. Number three. I'm not an idiot. Of course I was goin' to wait to mate with her. But there were extenuating circumstances." Dimitri avoided the last question. *Do I love her? Goddess, help me.*

"Extenuating circumstances, huh?" Jake shook his head in disbelief. He reached for a piece of bacon and popped it in his mouth. "What in the fuck could cause you to go and mate her when you couldn't even shift last night? Obviously your wolf had enough in him to drop fangs, but shit, you've got issues. You should call the witch."

"Don't need her."

"Have you lost it? All that sex knock your brain around?"

"Maybe you need a demonstration." Dimitri stripped off his shorts, and made his way around to the open area of the family room.

"Not sure what demo you got going on but seeing you nekkid has been done. I'll give you last night. That was freakin' awesome, but bro, we're alone. Everything ya got there," Jake gestured to his groin, "seen it."

"I'm not talking about sex," Dimitri said. "I'm talking wolf."

Calling the power within, he allowed the seamless transformation to commence. The spectacular brown wolf barked and growled. He stalked up to his friend, who wore an expression of amazement. Jake reached out to Dimitri, running his hands through his fur as if to confirm what he was seeing was really happening.

Easily shifting back into human form, Dimitri crouched at Jake's feet. The thrill of the metamorphosis left him energized, optimistic and looking forward to the full moon.

"But last night? You couldn't…"

"Gillian," Dimitri stated, his voice serious. "She did this."

"What?"

"Her breed. It's why Chaz was…is after her. Her mate would inherit her gift. The spirit of her beast. The mating healed me. She healed me."

"I don't understand how…"

"She lost her tiger. It's gone." Dimitri raked his hands through his hair and reached for his shorts. He put them on and waited on Jake's reply.

"She can't shift anymore? No way. She was beautiful. Her cat…just no."

"This is why she always stayed away from wolves. She knew she'd find her mate. I wanted to wait, but last night…" Dimitri paused, recalling how she'd bitten him. "We'd discussed it and agreed to wait until the morning to make a decision. But then she bit me. Really bit me….hard. Not a mark. She broke skin. It's not like I had a choice. Once she drank from me, I was done for. Game over." Dimitri picked a bowl off the table and spooned in the yogurt. "I wish I could feel guilty. I know we should have waited, but my wolf wanted her so damn bad. I can't even blame it on him. It's me. She's mine. I want her in my life."

"You're in love with her," Jake laughed.

"I cannot confirm or deny those allegations," Dimitri said with a sly grin. He could hardly believe it himself that he was falling for one female. The idea of him being with one woman for the rest of his life had been a foreign concept, but this morning, he couldn't see himself with anyone else.

"So that's how it's gonna be? Okay." Jake shot him a sideways glance and picked up an apple out of a basket on the table. "You got it bad."

"Maybe I do. Again, that falls into the category of 'don't care'. She's mine and no one's taking her away from me now."

"Again…what about her shifting? What's the deal?"

"Don't know yet. She said she can feel her wolf. Heard her last night when she was at the club. Gillian seemed okay with everything this morning."

"I don't know how. Think about it. You've been an animal your entire life. And poof. It's gone."

"I hear ya. Even after she told me her theory about being able to heal me with the mating, I didn't want to do it. But what's done is done. There's nothing we can do but wait and see." Dimitri didn't mention to Jake that he might have super kitty powers. But his wolf was healthy and robust, as if nothing had ever happened.

"So is she going to try to shift? Before the run tonight?"

"I'd like to see her try. Let's give her some space, when she gets down here, okay? I want her to eat and relax before we start shifting. 'K?"

"You got it."

Dimitri nodded to the steps, alerting Jake that Gillian was coming downstairs. She may have already heard part of their conversation, but he'd been serious. Gillian needed both sustenance and rest if she was going to try to shift and run with the pack. Knowing how she'd battled the wolf in the bathroom the previous evening, he was certain she'd be ready for revenge. Taking a deep breath, he steeled himself for the conversation.

Gillian adjusted the straps on her bikini. An odd sense of calm had settled over her mind. It was as if their mating had infused a shot of happy juice into her veins. Showering, she'd thought of her tiger, still unable to feel her. But the wolf inside paced, growing stronger. There was no doubt in her mind that she could shift. She'd been tempted to transform right there in Dimitri's bathroom, but thought better of it, considering she should have the support of others as she did so.

She dragged the brush through her hair, securing it into a ponytail. As she turned to go downstairs, she smiled, seeing Dimitri's mark on her shoulder. Feeling light as a feather, she bounded out of the room. Giddy like a schoolgirl, she couldn't believe they'd mated.

Never wanting Dimitri to feel guilt for their actions, she'd taken the decision away from him. Knowing that his wolf had been fully restored, her heart was full of pride and what she knew was the seeds of love. Hearing voices coming from the kitchen, she smiled.

"Hey there," she called, her bare feet padding across the smooth wooden floor. She fell into Dimitri's embrace, giving him a quick kiss.

"You trying to get me back in bed, woman?"

"What?" she laughed

"That bathing suit is killin' me. You're gonna give me heart failure."

"You're the one who gave it to me." She shoved at his muscular arms, ones that never moved from her waist. "I need sun. I'm tired of lying in bed."

"I can give you something to do in bed if you want," he countered.

"Is that right?" She smiled. "Guess I better eat something to keep up my strength."

"Hey there." Jake waved hello and opened the refrigerator, looking for orange juice.

Gillian gave Dimitri a devious grin and broke free of his arms. Slowly approaching Jake, she glanced back to Dimitri right before she swatted Jake's bottom. He jumped, nearly banging his head on the inside of the fridge.

"Hey, now. What's that for?" he asked, smiling.

"That's for not coming to my rescue last night." She pointed a finger at him.

"What can I say? I know better than to interfere when my beta's trying to teach his mate how to submit. Although I must say, D, I don't think you trained her very well. She just spanked me."

Dimitri raised his eyebrows, shrugged and laughed.

"And this," Gillian wrapped her arms around Jake, hugging him, "is for saving me last night."

"Now this is more like it. Oh yeah." Jake returned her embrace, watching the look of amusement on his friend's face.

"And this," she stood on her tip toes and kissed his cheek gently, "is for last night. Turns out, that after you refused to help me, I got lucky…really, really lucky."

"Aw baby, I'm the one who should be thanking you and D."

She reached behind him, grabbing a bottle of water, then pulled away from his arms. Unscrewing the bottle, she gave him a flirtatious wink before taking a drink.

"She's somethin'," Jake said, still surprised. He held his fingers to his lips, and looked to Dimitri, who seemed to enjoy the way his mate had thrown his friend off kilter.

"Yes, she is." Dimitri drew Gillian into his arms. They exchanged a brief embrace, and he guided her to the table. Standing, she began to pour herself cereal.

"I've gotta make a call to Logan, let him know what happened last night," Dimitri announced.

"Last night?" Wide eyed, Gillian looked at Jake and then Dimitri.

"Not everything, cher," he assured her. "I want to let him know I'm healed, find out what dickhead told him."

"Dickhead?" she questioned.

"The wolf from last night. Logan has him held up in a cell. They're coming soon."

Gillian silently nodded in response.

"Can you two play nicely while I'm gone?" Dimitri asked.

"Hey, I'm not the one who's slapping asses this morning. Look to your girl over there." Jake grinned at Gillian.

"What? His ass was just there...waiting for me. Besides, it's true. He didn't save me. All's fair."

"Also, I forgot. Jax texted me earlier. I sent him my address, so he should be here any minute," Dimitri mentioned as he walked out of the room.

"Do you have any sunscreen?" Gillian asked.

"What?" Dimitri turned, giving her a questioning look.

"You know. Sunscreen. I want to lay out for a bit."

"You don't get sunburned. You know that, right? You're a shifter."

"Yes, but I don't want to dry out my skin." Gillian smiled, giving a side glance to Jake. "Besides, Jake, here, owes me. I think a nice back rub will suffice."

Dimitri laughed in response. "No sunscreen, but the lotion's underneath the sink. And before you make any wise cracks, wolf, I like to keep my skin soft, too, okay? No judging. I'll be back in a bit," he told her.

He thought to tell her he loved her as he left, as if he wouldn't see her for eons. The words caught in his mouth; he was aware that it was completely irrational. Yet as he walked down the hallway, looking over at his mate, her smile melted his heart and he was certain he'd fallen in love.

Chapter Nineteen

Gillian stretched her hands above her head, reveling in the sunshine. The deck provided a spectacular view of the bayou, and Gillian began to understand why this place was so special to Dimitri. The day he'd refused to kill Chaz, unwilling to take over his pack, had confused her up until now. Most wolves aspired to be Alpha, no matter the circumstance. But Dimitri showed steadfast loyalty to both his Alpha and pack.

The quiet hum of crickets serenaded her as she spread a towel on the chaise. She smiled at Jake who joined her, wearing only his shorts. Barefoot, he trod across the cedar planks. Silence settled, each unsure of what to discuss. Gillian, unable to handle the quiet contemplation, broke the reticence.

"So…about last night. I meant what I said."

"Thank you," he responded.

"For what?" she asked.

"Dimitri."

"He told you?"

"About your mating? Yeah, he told me. You okay?"

"Me? I'm fine."

"But your cat? If it were me…"

"I think I can shift… we'll see. I just can't feel my tiger. She's gone," she replied.

"Last night in the bar. When we saw you on the floor…the way you'd attacked that asshole. Dimitri's lucky to have you for a mate," Jake began, reaching for the bottle she'd set on the outdoor table, unable to look her in the eye. "Anyway, just wanted you to know I'm grateful. D is a tough son-of-a-bitch, but this thing with his wolf…he would have lost his family, our pack. You changed all that."

"He's my mate. I can't explain it more than that."

Gillian avoided Jake's question, realizing she really didn't have answers. All she had were feelings, the kind of feelings that wouldn't be shaken no matter what happened in the future. None of it made sense, except for the fact that it felt right. After years of hiding from wolves, their mating had turned her world on its side.

Crawling onto the chair, she lay on her stomach. She took a deep breath and blew it out as her muscles began to relax. She blinked, her eyes focusing through the slit of gate surrounding the deck. In the distance, small lilts of waves rolled through the water, the tide receding. Warm strong hands settled on her back.

Jake remained quiet as he caressed the balm onto her skin. Gillian recalled how, on Dimitri's instruction, she had thoroughly enjoyed watching Jake in the shower.

Although she thought him good-looking, she'd never been with two men at once and had never dared to imagine a scenario where she'd engage her fantasy. Yet Dimitri continued to push her sexual limits all the while making her feel as if she was the only woman in the world. She supposed it was the wolves, their openness that was rubbing off on her as she began to look forward to the possibilities and what Dimitri would teach her next. Closing her eyes, she fantasized, imagining her hands touching them both. As her body began to heat up in more ways than one, she smiled.

"What are you thinking about?" Jake asked, his hands moving down the back of her thighs.

"Um, just thinking about how good the sun feels," she lied. His hands were like sweet goodness all over. He moved to the soles of her feet and she released a loud moan.

"The sun, huh?" he laughed.

"Oh my God. Do. Not. Stop," she groaned.

"Hey now, what's goin' on out there?" Dimitri called from an open window, holding his cell to his chest. "No gettin' fresh with my mate, wolf. Lotion on her back. Nothing more."

"You're getting us in trouble," Jake teased.

"Hmm…it feels good, though." She laughed. Gillian gave a squeak as Jake smacked her butt, and lay next to her on a twin chaise.

"Better?" he asked, pushing on his sunglasses.

"Yes, thanks. Very nice. I was great before the rub, but now I feel awesome. I almost started purring," she said. *No I didn't. Never again will I purr.* A hint of sadness tinged her heart as she thought the words, reminded that she'd never be feline again.

The doorbell and commotion in the house caused her to lift her head. Hearing male voices, she assumed someone from Dimitri's pack had come to see him. She took a deep breath, focusing on the sounds of birds chirping.

"Hey, baby sis," Jax called from the kitchen.

Gillian startled at the sound of her brother's voice. "Jax. We're outside."

She jumped off of her chaise to greet him. Even though they'd recently established their familial connection, her heart filled with happiness as she caught sight of her brother strolling out onto the deck. His blonde hair reflected like an angel's in the sunlight. He was dressed casually, wearing a t-shirt and shorts, but there was no mistaking his commanding presence. Nick walked behind him, giving her a wave.

Jax opened his arms to Gillian and she fell into his comforting embrace. Her protector, she owed him her life.

"Jax, I'm so glad to see you. Is it weird to tell you that I missed you? I know we're just getting to know each other, but you feel like family," she admitted.

"We are family. You're not alone anymore," he assured her.

"Thanks." She kissed his cheek and broke their hug.

"What about me? Hello? Chopped liver over here?" Nick gave her a wide smile, holding out his arms.

"He just wants to hold a hot chick in a bikini," Jax commented. "Be careful with my sister."

"Hi, Nick. Sorry." Wrapping her hands around his neck, she gave him a quick hug. "Thank you for coming down. And thank you for not being my mate."

"Oh my Goddess," he exclaimed. Nick leaned in and sniffed her. "You didn't?"

"Didn't what?" she asked.

"Jax. Really? You're not going to say anything?" he asked.

"He's her mate. Always has been. Question is, what's happened that has my beta in a tizzy?" Jax gave her a scrutinizing look.

Gillian bit her lip and looked to Jake, who gave her a smile before he headed inside. She mouthed 'chicken' at him as he left. She guessed he didn't want to be around for the fallout; a serious conversation with one badass New York Alpha. She looked to the ground and wrung her hands.

"It's done," she said softly.

"What's done?"

"We, um, we completed the mating last night. Now I know that you might not understand, but," she began. Cringing slightly, she made eye contact with her brother. "He's a good man. An even better wolf. He needed me."

"Come here," Jax said. Gillian slowly padded over and was surprised when Jax brought her into his arms again.

"Tell me what happened. I know he's your mate, but why so soon? It's your gift, isn't it?"

"Yes. He's been ill. I don't know if he told you or not. That witch. She did something to him. And wolves will never stop trying to get me. I just decided he was worth saving. I need him in my life."

"Did he know about your gift?" Jax growled protectively.

"No. If he'd wanted to be Alpha, he could have done that when he had Chaz the first time. Last night, the vampire…what she said. It just made sense. The witch was never going to cure him. She wanted him," Gillian explained. "And that was just too damn bad because there was no way I was letting her kill my wolf. He's mine."

Jax laughed. "Possessive already?"

"Yeah, I am. Dimitri's wolf was dying. I told him that I thought I could heal him. But he didn't want to so I…you know, I bit him."

"You started the mating? Without his permission?"

"Well, technically if you put it that way, I guess that is what I did, but I prefer to look at it as me taking the initiative."

"You are your Alpha's sister," Nick interjected. "Dimitri's going to have fun with you."

"It's done. And it worked. But my tiger…"

"She's gone?"

"Yes, I think so. But Jax," she whispered. "There's a wolf in me. I can feel her. I heard her last night, even before we mated. I want to shift. I've just been waiting."

"What for, girl? Come on now. Show us what ya got!" Nick said excitedly as if he'd been given a new toy.

Jax kissed her forehead and she fought the urge to cry. She wasn't sure how he'd react, but he was understanding, caring; everything she needed her sibling to be. He cupped her cheek in his hand and smiled down at her.

"Congratulations, sister. I'm so happy you're a wolf. I would've never forced this on you. I want you to know that. And even though I have a pack, you're blood." He turned to Nick and nodded. "You and Nick are my family. And he's right. Let's see what you've got. I want to see you shift."

"Really?" Gillian asked. Excitement lit through her as she realized she was going to do it. She thought to wait for Dimitri but then she decided it would be a wonderful surprise for him to see that she was all right, that she could, indeed, shift.

"Yes, let's do it. You go first and we'll run with you a bit." Both Jax and Nick began to undress in preparation.

"Okay, but not too far. I want to surprise Dimitri," she told them. Stripping out of her bathing suit without a care, she bounded onto the lawn.

She smiled at Jax and Nick, letting her magic flow from inside. As if she were transforming into a cat, the mystical power took over and within seconds, she stood as a four-footed wolf. Feeling lighter, she stumbled, rolling onto her side. She whined, unable to find her balance. Determined to get comfortable in her new form, she tried again, her paws gripping the grass. She forced herself upward, thrilled when she finally stabilized her footing. Instinctively, she went to roar, but nothing emerged. Frustrated, she cringed and cowered toward the ground.

A large black wolf approached, flanking her. He barked, as if to teach her. She sniffed, recognizing him as Jax. A smaller light grey wolf howled in response and ran around them in circles. Gillian would have been comfortable to stay nuzzled against her brother, disappointed in her diminutive stature. A firm paw on her side urged her to vocalize.

Raising her head, she began a low growl, which grew louder until it resonated throughout the yard. With a final effort, a loud bark resounded and she celebrated by running around, chasing Nick. Gillian realized the strength, speed and agility of her feline hadn't faltered, yet she'd suspected her ability to leap was stilted. Nevertheless, it didn't thwart her excitement that she still could shift.

She and Nick circled the Alpha in play, taunting him with a nip. After two rounds of their antics, Jax sprang after her, forcing her to roll to the ground. With his forepaw over her belly, she cried, unable to move. Gillian didn't do submission well, she knew. The feeling of helplessness in her new form was unacceptable. Struggling to get out from underneath him, she growled and gnawed at her brother. Without hurting her, Jax held firm, attempting to teach his sister a lesson.

A loud blur from her side barreled into Jax, freeing her. She bounded to her feet as the two wolves tussled in the turf. Realizing that Dimitri had come to her, she ran to them. A sense of fear washed over her, seeing them fight, and she crouched, yipping loudly for them to stop. Both wolves slowly disengaged, turning to stare at Gillian.

Transforming back, Gillian sat naked on the lawn, her feet curled under her. Grateful that she'd been able to run as wolf, tears of joy streamed down her face. Unlike her mother, who'd lost her abilities, she retained the magic of a shifter.

Both Jax and Dimitri altered back to their human selves, giving each other a hard stare. But their interaction was short lived as Dimitri broke their gaze, setting his attention on his mate. He closed in on Gillian, falling to his knees before her. He took her face in his hands, his own emotion brimmed from his lashes. Guilt. Pride. Amazement.

"Gilly. You did it!" he cried. "Why didn't you wait for me? I could've helped you."

"I...I wanted to surprise you," she stammered.

"You're stubborn, you know that?" He took her into his arms, pressing her against his chest, kissing her hair. "I heard you, I knew it was you. When I saw Jax on top of you, I wanted to kill him."

"I'm okay, baby. Really. He was just playing."

"No, no. He wasn't playing. He was trying to teach you, but I'm afraid those Alpha genes are goin' to make it tough for you."

Gillian laughed into his kisses. His lips pressed to her forehead, onto her eyelids and cheeks, until he finally reached her mouth. She reached into his hair, pulling him to her, kissing him back. But as she heard voices surround them, she smiled. With her head against his, they gazed into each other's eyes one last second, pretending they didn't have an audience.

"Ah, to be young and in love," Nick mused, yanking on his shorts.

"He'll deny it," Jake said from the deck.

"I pity the beta. She's not one to be tamed," Jax noted with a grin, almost as if he enjoyed it.

"Hey, I may be wolf now, but this girl's tiger, through and through. Don't worry, I'll learn to get along in a pack."

"There's no challenging the Alpha, Gilly," Jax huffed. "Or your beta for that matter."

"I wasn't challenging anybody. I was simply trying to get out from underneath you big hunk of a wolf. "

"Good luck with her," Jax warned.

"There's nothing wrong with her. She's just spirited, is all," Dimitri praised her, helping her to her feet.

"He's got it bad," Nick jested.

"Oh he does," Jake agreed.

"Ya'll are jealous," Dimitri shot back.

"Don't pay those boys any mind, baby. There's only one man I'm submitting to, and it's not them." She winked.

"Seriously, folks. I just got off the phone with Logan. The guy we picked up last night said Chaz brought in half his pack, thinkin' he's going to get his due. He wouldn't say where they're holed up, but we think they're waitin' on the full moon to make their move." Dimitri hated changing the subject, but they were in for an attack this evening.

"Gillian's not going," Jax stated.

Gillian opened her mouth to protest but Dimitri interrupted before she had a chance to speak.

"Gilly, I know you want to come, but Jax might be right. I think maybe you should go with some of the younger pack members. They're goin' into Baton Rouge. There's a secure gated wildlife sanctuary up that way. It's far enough away from where we run, where they'll be safe from Chaz. Wynter's taking Ava out of the city...we've got a few of the males going, too, for extra protection just in case. The full moon's tonight and you're gonna want to shift. You'd be safer there."

"Why would you want me to go there when I can help here?" she asked. Confusion washed over her face. *No fucking way*, she thought. *I'm going to help kill that asshole who tortured me and who's trying to wreck my life.* "No, wait. Don't tell me. It doesn't matter. I'm going with you. You just saw it. I can shift. I'm not staying back."

"I know you're strong, cher. But you're new at this. Jax and Nick, they'll come with us. Chaz doesn't have a chance with all of us here. You, on the other hand, are a new wolf. You could get hurt." Dimitri tugged on his shorts, and reached to hand Gillian her bathing suit.

"No, Dimitri." Gillian grabbed her things and stormed over to the deck. "I'm the one who was captured and tortured by that maniac. Now that he can't have me or my gifts, he's going to want to punish me for killing his friends. I'm not going to sit here and let people I don't know go out there and fight for me. Not without me by their sides. No way."

"Look, you did great just now. Don't get me wrong, you're a fighter, but you've never run with a pack," Jax reminded her.

"So what? I'll stay with the pack. Of everyone talking right now, I'm the one who, as shifter, has killed the most wolves from his pack. I may not be a tiger any longer but I'm still strong."

Dimitri sighed and put his hands on his hips, shaking his head.

"I can do this. Believe in me. It's not right to let you all go out there and put your lives on the line while I'm safe. Please, Dimitri. Please, I swear I'll stay with the pack. I'll do whatever you tell me to do," she begged.

"She goes," Dimitri snapped. "I've seen this woman here, and she's tough. And she's right. She's not a damsel in distress. She's defended herself before. We just need to keep her tight in the pack."

"Okay, okay. As much as I hate to say it, she knows the adversary better than we do. The way she just fought me back there," Jax smirked, "she's going to be as good as any male out there. I don't know whether it's the tiger in her or what but she's really strong."

"Thank you," she said softly, her head hanging low.

Dimitri wrapped a strong arm around her shoulders, and she melted into him. He'd stood up for her, believed in her. And her brother, who she once hadn't trusted, now trusted her as well.

Gillian contemplated her decision, knowing she could die. Yet she refused to allow fear to blur her judgment. She was determined to get Chaz out of her life, once and for all, even if she had to kill him herself.

Chapter Twenty

"Logan and Jax are taking the lead tonight," Dimitri informed the small group who waited outside his home. The full moon rising shone brightly onto the bayou, its reflection glistening off the small waves. "Gilly, you'll stay with Nick and me. Since I'm not running with Logan, Jake's gonna be running with the pack."

"You don't need to stay with me," Gillian began.

"No, darlin', that's where you're wrong. Ya'll know I love Logan, and my place would normally be at his side. But not tonight."

"But…"

"No argument, Gilly," he growled. "Logan and I have discussed this. You have no say in this decision. You stay with your mate, tonight. I know you can hold your own, but it's my responsibility to help you learn how to run within the pack and protect you if necessary."

Gillian startled at his dominant command. She refused to lower her gaze despite her wolf cowering in her mind's eye. The last time he'd said similar words they'd been in the bedroom, submission in a different form. Yet tonight, it'd be in a pack. Gillian wished it would come naturally to her, yet acquiescing felt artificial. She recalled her conversation with Dimitri. *Submission is about trust.* No matter how independent she'd been with regards to her tiger, she trusted Dimitri.

"Okay," she managed. Gillian's heart squeezed as a small smile formed on his lips and his face softened. She saw relief in his eyes. He wanted her to be safe tonight.

Dimitri brushed the back of his knuckles against her cheek, and turned to Jake.

"You ready?"

"You bet. Hey, where's Leo?" Jake asked.

"Let's just say I've got him on standby. This is a wolf dispute. Logan's not going to want him involved unless things go south," Dimitri explained. "Wynter's taking Ava out of town. We don't want to risk them trying to attack our homes. Given the extremes this guy went to to force a mating, who knows what he'll try?"

"Ah, the putrid smell of desperation," Nick commented.

"Yeah, I think maybe he thought he'd come here just for you, but when he finds out you've already been mated, he's going to go off. Hell, he brought his pack here," Dimitri offered. "He has his jet at the airport. Some of them flew commercial. I've never seen anything like it."

"Who even does that?" Nick said.

"Someone who wants power they don't have," Jax said.

"Well, we don't always get what we want. My gift is gone." Gillian looked to Dimitri, her gaze steeled in determination. "He's going to regret coming here."

A large wolf approached, giving a commanding bark. Several dozen wolves followed.

Gillian's nerves jittered as she set her eyes on the pack. As a tiger, she'd been unaffected by any shifters she happened to pass in the middle of the night. But as wolf, the hum of their energy was palpable. Like an orchestra, they played as one, each individual wolf playing their own part for the greater good.

"Stay with me," Dimitri said, stripping off his jeans.

"I will," she promised.

"Whatever goes down, do not go it alone. Don't leave the pack. If something happens to me, stay with Nick. You sure you still want to run?"

Gillian nodded as he embraced her, kissing her in front of the entire pack. His lips destroyed any remaining wisps of trepidation. As he released her, she wished she could tell him that she loved him. Her heart overflowed with emotion and she fought to keep it at bay, knowing it was not the time to disclose her feelings.

The magic of the moment broke as Dimitri released her hand and shifted. She followed his lead, transforming and padding alongside him. They broke into an easy lope, yet the tension remained high. Amazed at how natural it felt to be in a pack as wolf, she took a deep sniff. Even this early in her journey, she was able to identify pack members by their singular recognizable scent.

After an hour of traveling through the soft brush, they stopped to drink from the bayou. She observed how the other wolves kept watch over each other, aware of the gators that lingered, waiting on their next meal. Heat lightning flashed in the distance and she glanced to the stars. The moon still shone brightly, but a dark line in the sky warned of an impending storm. Thunder cracked, and she instinctively huddled into Dimitri. She felt his muzzle underneath her own, and gave him a quick lick, letting him know she was all right.

A chorus of barking commenced and through the din, she heard the sound of shots being fired. The pack split up, groups of three to five wolves dispersing into the brush. Dimitri growled, warning her to stay against a tree. Out of the corner of her eye, she spied a human atop the hill. Sparks lit up the darkness as the bullets sprayed into the forest. Her stomach lurched as a glint of light illuminated Chaz's face.

The sickening cry of wolves being attacked trumpeted into the night. Aware that her pack mates might have been injured, her adrenaline pumped. Instinct enticed her to go on the offensive, but both Nick and her mate warned her back, keeping her nestled between them. A blood-curdling whine tore through her as bullets whizzed by their heads. Dimitri barked in command and took off toward a thicker patch of trees. With Nick behind her, she followed him.

By the time they'd reached safety, she noticed Nick had gone missing. Dimitri shifted back, holding his fingers to his lips.

"Stay here," he whispered to her. Mouthing the word, 'silver', he pointed to Jax, who lay bloodied against the dirt, having been hit in the leg. He pointed up the hill to Logan. A hundred yards away, their Alpha fought Chaz. Both had transformed to wolf, the gleam of their fangs intermittent as the clouds moved in, blocking the moonlight. A second wolf attacked, latching itself to Logan's hind quarters. Dimitri sniffed into the air, hoping to scent Nick or Jake but he couldn't locate them. With Jax injured and Nick and Jake missing, Logan was alone.

Gillian shook her head no, realizing he was going to go to his Alpha. It was his role, she knew, but she was terrified. The smell of blood hung heavy in the air, and Gillian's urge to fight back began to supersede her desire to submit to his wish to stay put.

"I'm serious. Do not follow," Dimitri told her. "Just stay here under the brush where I can see you. Logan's getting torn up over there. I fucking hate leaving you but he's in trouble. Where the hell are Nick and Jake?"

She whined in response and swiveled her head, looking for Nick, who was supposed to be behind her. Unable to see him or Jake, she scratched at Dimitri's arm, growling in distress. Something was wrong, very, very wrong.

"Right here, behind this tree. Stay put," Dimitri repeated, shifting back to his wolf.

As he took off toward Logan, a torrential downpour commenced. Gillian heard a small cry, one made from a familiar human voice. She hesitated. Dimitri would be pissed if she left her position, but with the hard rain she was no longer visible to him. An agonizing moan resonated through the patter of water drops, and she took off in search of its owner.

Sheets of rain cut through the night, and within minutes the ground was saturated. Several howling wolves called into the clatter nearly stopping her dead in her tracks. She'd never expected that as pack, she'd instinctively feel and know their pain, their fear. But it was a small gurgle that caught her attention. Turning toward the noise, she slid into the deep mud, her claws clutching at the dirt. Scenting the air was difficult due to the potent ozone, but as she stumbled forth, her heart caught.

Barely visible in the mist, she caught sight of Nick clutching at his throat. Shifting back to human, the cold driving pellets rocketed into her skin. Her vision came into focus and she stifled a scream. Stark white, he looked grey, almost as if he was glowing. His eyes bulged, a hard rattle came from his chest and she threw her hands over his. Gillian applied pressure in an attempt to stem the hemorrhage. Blood spurted through her fingers and she cried out helplessly for Jax.

"Jax, please." Her slippery hands shook as she attempted to close his wound. "No, Nick, please Goddess, no. You need to shift."

"Jax," he croaked. "Love him. Sorry."

"You tell him yourself. Please Nick. Please, I need you to fight." Gillian gently laid her body next to his, hoping that she'd be able to warm him, to heal him. Her tears mixed with the deluge falling from the sky as she tried to summon the power that had belonged to her cat. With her face on his chest, she heard his heartbeat slow, and the realization he was going to die hit her. "No, Nick. We need you. Jax needs you."

Gillian searched deep within her psyche for her healing powers. Weak, her energy flickered like a defective light bulb. Her concentration faltered upon hearing a hiss escape his lips. As Nick's final breath ceased, his limp arms fell open, his spirit ascending to the Goddess. Gillian fought the hysteria that seized her at the realization he'd stopped breathing. Sobbing, she caressed his cheek, refusing to believe he was dead. Growls in the distance reminded her of the imminent danger, but she refused to leave him behind.

A branch broke, alerting her, and she sensed the Alpha. *Jax.* When he reached Nick, he gave a mournful howl and promptly turned to his human form.

"Nick." Jax fell to his knees, raking both his hands through his wet hair.

"I'm sorry. I'm so sorry. He's gone. I tried to heal him but it was too late." Gillian backed away from Nick, placing a final kiss to his brow.

"Nick," Jax repeated. Sitting in the muddy grass, he gently cradled his friend in his arms. Burying his head into Nick's hair, he sobbed, crushed by his loss.

Gillian put her arms around her brother, and he clutched at her, seeking comfort. Five more shots rang out into the night, startling both Jax and Gillian. She searched the darkness and caught sight of Logan falling to the ground. Dimitri ran across through the woods toward Chaz, who'd begun firing again. Her beta ducked and weaved, lurching onto his enemy's back. Chaz, shifting to wolf, went feral, his eyes glowing red. The crunching of teeth against bone reverberated in the wind.

A surge of hatred coursed through Gillian, and her beast growled in response. The barrage of rain falling wasn't enough to drown out the sound of the small roar in her chest, and she rejoiced at the realization that somewhere within her the great cat lived. Tearing across the woods, Gillian let her power flow. While she was still a wolf, her claws and fangs extended further and sharper, like she'd known as a tiger. With unleashed fury, she lurched at Chaz's back and swiped her talons at him, tunneling his flank wide open.

The split second reprieve was all Dimitri needed as he lunged for the Alpha's throat. His teeth sunk deep into Chaz's fur. The beta thrashed, gnarling, until he'd ripped out his opponent's trachea, tearing at the tendons. Blood sprayed as Chaz hit the earth and Dimitri howled in victory.

Killing Chaz would have been cause for celebration if it hadn't been for the burning hole in Dimitri's gut. The grief from his mate flowed through him. He transformed, Gillian smashing into his embrace. Her tears warmed his wet skin. Taking her by her shoulders, he gently pushed her away so he could look at her. She gasped, crying and shaking her head.

"What is it?" he asked, his eyebrows drawn tight in concern.

"Nick, it's Nick," she cried.

"No."

"He was behind us. I don't know what happened."

"Fuck," Dimitri grunted. Something else ate at him. He'd seen Logan lope off, having been hit by a bullet. He scanned the woods, searching for his Alpha and Jake. "Jake. Logan. Where are they?"

"I don't know. I didn't see..."

"Logan! Jake!" Dimitri called, his voice bellowing across the bayou.

He began to run on foot, sniffing into the air. Within seconds, he'd managed to find Jake lying up against a Cyprus tree. Dimitri closed his eyes, willing himself to remain calm. A hole the size of his fist had blasted through his friend, blood painted over the large man.

"Jake, can you hear me?" Dimitri knelt, taking Jake into his arms. Unconscious, Jake didn't move. Like a ragdoll, his arms fell open, his head rolling side to side as Dimitri lifted him.

"Logan's coming." Fresh tears came as Gillian took Jake's hand in hers.

"Logan...Oh Goddess. Logan, please. He's not doing so well." Dimitri's voice wavered as he pushed the hair out of Jake's eyes.

"He's gotta shift," Logan said.

"He's been out before. Remember that time with Leo. Just tell him to shift. Command him."

"Shit, I can't believe this. Nick is dead. Now Jake," Logan lamented.

"Jake isn't fucking dead. Come on, Logan. We need to do this," Dimitri told him. The only words Dimitri wanted to hear were that Jake was going to live. It had to work.

Logan took a deep breath and exhaled, nodding in agreement. As the pack began to gather, Dimitri gingerly set Jake in Logan's arms. As he backed away, his mate came up behind him, circling his waist with her hands. She lay her cheek to his back, sniffling.

Logan whispered to Jake, and Dimitri closed his eyes, putting his hands over Gillian's. He'd been given so much in his life, blessed in many ways. He silently prayed, hoping the Goddess would spare Jake's life. But when Jake didn't regain consciousness, his heart broke, the grief pouring like a river into his chest.

Chapter Twenty-One

"I know you were close to him, D," Logan said, putting his hand on Dimitri's shoulder. "I care about him too."

"I *am* close to him. As in present tense. Jesus Christ, Logan. He's not dead yet." Dimitri pushed away from his Alpha. He carefully sat on the bed next to Jake and took his friend's hand into his own.

Recalling the evening's events, he sighed. With nearly a dozen Anzober wolves dead, including Chaz, most of the Acadian wolves had stayed to help move the bodies. Dimitri had called Léopold to assist Jax with Nick's remains. The vampire had known the New York Alpha for years. As much as Dimitri had wanted Léopold to stay, Jax was despondent and Gillian hadn't wanted him to go alone to his jet.

Dimitri had carried Jake the long trek home on foot. When they'd arrived, he'd taken him to the first available bed, which was in the downstairs guest room. In the open brush and again at the house, Logan had failed to elicit a response from Jake despite repeated commands for him to shift. The fist-sized hole in his chest no longer bled, yet the wound hadn't healed. With Jake's heartbeat irregular, they all believed it was only a matter of time before he died.

"Where the hell is Léopold?" Dimitri asked Logan.

"I'll go call him again. They probably aren't even at the airport yet," his Alpha responded.

Gillian exited the bathroom, a towel wrapped around her. Intent on cleaning Jake, she'd brought warm washcloths to his bedside. Seeing the Alpha, her eyes lowered submissively to the floor. As she padded over to Jake, Logan approached her, cupping her cheek.

"It's okay, Gilly. You'll get used to having an Alpha."

"Sorry, I just…I'm not used to being wolf." She lifted her chin, looking into his eyes.

"My mate. She wasn't always wolf either. I promise it'll get easier."

"The shifting was easy, but being with the pack. It felt…"

"Overwhelming?"

"Yeah. I'm used to being on my own. My cat," she looked to Dimitri, "she's independent. Tonight, I don't know. I can't feel her when I'm here, but when I attacked, I felt feline. I felt it in my claws. You saw what I did to Chaz."

"You're strong…stronger than most wolves." Logan wasn't sure what to say about her transformation. They'd all seen the damage she'd inflicted on the Alpha's back. The gash had been much deeper than most wolves were capable of doing with their paws alone. "We'll work it out. I'm here for you if you need help."

"Thanks." Gillian gave Logan a small smile, still unsure of how it would be to have to answer to an Alpha.

As she approached Dimitri, he turned and wrapped his arms around her waist, resting his head against her belly. She dropped the wet cloths next to him and cradled his head in her hands.

"I'm so sorry," she said, her voice quiet.

Dimitri didn't respond as anger and grief seized him. He held onto the hope that Léopold could use his ability to materialize back to his home and would agree to turn Jake. However, Dimitri knew that Léopold didn't give his gift freely. The only wolf he'd ever saved had been Wynter. Logan had told him that Wynter had lingering side effects from being given so much blood. Even if he could get Léopold to agree, he was unsure of Jake's feelings about being saved by a vampire.

A kiss to his hair brought his thoughts back to his mate. Her presence calmed him, and he held her tightly. His safe harbor, he thanked the Goddess she'd initiated their mating.

"Baby, why don't you go clean up?" Gillian gave him a squeeze. "I feel better now that I took a shower. I'll stay right here with Jake. I'm going to clean all this blood off him. You're covered too."

They'd been coated in dirt and body fluids from their battle. Dimitri had insisted Gillian go take a shower when they'd returned. Between Nick, Chaz and Jake, she'd been covered in blood. He looked at his own hands, the dried caked grit stuck to his palms.

"Go on. If there are any changes, I swear I'll come to you," she promised.

"She's right, D. You're wearing Chaz's scent," Logan informed him.

Dimitri gave him a hard stare.

"Yeah, yeah. I know. Me too." Logan rubbed at his forearms.

"I'll take the guest shower," Dimitri told her. "You sure you'll be okay alone with Jake? If there's any change at all, come get me."

"I swear it." Gillian took his place on the bed and began to gently clean Jake's face.

"Here's your phone." Logan pressed open the door and tossed him his cell. "I'm sorry D, but I've gotta check on how the wolves are making out with moving the bodies. I also have to make sure that Wynn and the others are okay. I'll come back and check on Jake in a bit, see if I can get him to rouse. His wound doesn't look as bad as it did earlier. He may just need time," Logan offered.

"I'm gonna call Léopold again," Dimitri said.

"You know, Leo might not want to…" Logan began.

"I know. I know. I'm calling him anyway." Dimitri turned his focus onto his phone, leaving the room.

Gillian watched as Dimitri slowly went into the bathroom. His sadness emanated through her. She shook her head, aggravated that she was helpless to alleviate his suffering. Alone with Jake, she focused on cleaning his skin, hoping he'd miraculously wake. Inch by inch, she worked, carefully navigating around the puncture in his chest.

When she heard the spray of the shower, she finished washing away the last bits of dirt from his body and tossed the dirty linens aside. She hadn't wanted to give Dimitri or Logan false hope, but she'd set her mind on trying to heal Jake. Prior to mating, she would have easily been able to call her powers, but in the woods with Nick, her healing ability had waned. Given that there weren't many viable options, she had to attempt it.

Peeling away her towel, she knelt onto the bed, and gently lay on Jake. She closed her eyes, trying to picture her cat, to conjure the magic. A small smile formed on her lips as the first tingle rippled over her. Her hopes were dashed when she was unable to maintain the energy she needed for healing to ensue.

"What's going on?" Gillian heard Dimitri ask. She cursed, aware that she'd been caught.

"I just...I want to..." she hesitated.

"Want to what? Wait, are you fixin' to heal him like you did with me?"

"I know it's stupid, but I had to try. When we ran tonight, I tried to save Nick. I felt a flicker of something, but it wasn't enough," she explained.

"But you felt something?" Dimitri approached her.

"Yeah, I could feel a little bit of my cat. And just now, again, just the smallest...I don't know. I know it sounds crazy. I'm just thinking maybe...if you got my gift, we could heal him together." Gillian pressed up to look at Dimitri, her forearm on the bed. "Do you feel my cat? Anything at all?"

"When we mated, you got rid of that thing inside me, but I really don't feel very cat-like. I'm still just me. You saw me tonight. I'm wolf." He paused, unconvinced it would work. "Listen, cher, I'm desperate too, but maybe we should just wait for Leo. I've seen what he can do."

"As much as I'd love your friend Léopold to show up right now, he's not here. I know you want him to help but we don't know if he will. And Jake? Would he want that? I don't know about you, but I'm not sure I'd want all that vampire blood in me anyway."

"I'm not going to let him just die on me."

"Then, please. Let's just try," she said, her voice cracking. Her heart broke for him. Although they hadn't said it out loud, they both felt responsible for what had happened.

"I don't know about this." Dimitri raked his fingers through his wet hair.

"Please." Gillian looked to Jake and back to her mate.

"Okay, okay, we'll try it. What do you want me to do?" Dimitri asked, resigned.

"Get underneath him, maybe if we're on both sides of him, it'll be enough."

"Don't get your hopes up. I'm telling ya. Since we've mated, I haven't felt special mojo, not like what you did to me."

"We've got nothing to lose. He's dying. I can hear his heartbeat slowing. Please, he needs us close. Just take my hands."

Dimitri tore off his towel with a growl. Naked, he slid into bed, lifting Jake so that his back was on his chest. Gilly reached for her mate. Their bodies tangled into one, she took a deep breath, concentrating, and began to direct them.

"Just feel me, baby. You know that special energy we have when we shift?" she asked.

"Yeah?"

"It's kind of like that, but restrain it. Don't let it go that far. Don't shift. When I healed you, I let my energy flow. You need to focus it…focus on directing it into Jake."

"But I don't think…" he began.

"Don't think. Just close your eyes. Feel me. Listen to my voice. Feel your magic. Search for my cat…look for her. You're my mate. She's in you now."

"I…" Dimitri's voice trailed off as he concentrated. As wolf, he'd never had to think about shifting. Being wolf was as natural as breathing.

"That's it. I'm going to start, but my energy is weak." Gillian began to purr, forcing the sound from her throat. It wasn't organic. As if she were a human mimicking an animal, she allowed the noise to grow louder. Slowly, the hum built, bombarding every cell in her body.

"Oh my God. I feel it," Dimitri cried out. "It feels…it feels like…electricity."

"Help me," she told him. "Find my cat."

In his mind's eye, Dimitri saw his wolf. He stood stoic, waiting. Soon the small sizzles going through him became rhythmic jolts. A loud roar sounded, the tiger coming forth. Shocked by the sight of her, Dimitri gasped for air. He'd never seen anything like it. The resplendent animal came forth, driving through pounding pulses of magic.

As if Jake's pain were his own, he sucked a deep breath, the slicing hot agony of the silver fragments dissolving into his flesh. Darkness began to close in, both animals fading into obscurity. He attempted to speak, but his throat closed, his lips moving without words.

Jake stirred above him, and he heard Gillian's voice.

"Jake, Dimitri, you okay?" she asked. Dimitri's eyes fluttered open, with a surreal awareness that told him his friend had survived.

He felt the weight of Jake lighten on his chest as he slid out from between them. Gillian's soft breasts pressed into his chest, the scent of her shampoo teasing his senses. Her silky palm glided against his cheek.

"Dimitri? Can you hear me? Please, say something," she pleaded.

"Gil, did you see it?" he asked, still shocked by what he'd seen.

"Did you see my cat, baby?"

"You're beautiful, do you know that?" Dimitri smiled as she came into focus.

Gillian released a sigh of relief, and they both laughed.

"If I'd known all it would take was getting shot to get into bed with you both, I'd have done it sooner," Jake joked, shifting up onto his side.

"Jake, oh my God. How do you feel?" Gillian exclaimed. She threw her arms around his neck and kissed his cheek, her lips lingering next to his.

"Now this is what I'm talking about," Jake teased, his eyes meeting Dimitri's.

"Jesus Christ, Jake. You scared the shit out of us. Are you for real? Let me see you," Dimitri insisted.

Gillian kissed him once more before sitting back on her heels. Both she and Dimitri watched as Jake ran his palms down his chest and patted his abs.

"Not sure what you did, but I'm good as new."

"You need to be thankin' Gillian, here. She's the one who suggested we try to…"

"My cat's inside him." Gillian diverted her eyes to her hands, which she held tight. Although she'd willingly given up her ability to shift as a feline, a sense of melancholy filled her chest. She'd been unable to heal Jake on her own.

"No fucking way. You're a cat?"

"Way." Dimitri sensed Gillian's change of mood, and brushed his knuckles under her chin.

"We got lucky. I just wish I'd been able to heal him like I'd done with you," she said softly.

"Hey, cher. You did this. We're a team now, you and I. And us, with the pack. There's no going it alone." Dimitri took her hands and brought her to him. Gillian fell into his embrace, exhausted from their night.

"Gilly, look at me," Jake said. His eyes moved from Dimitri and locked on hers. He reached for her, his fingers trailing over her shoulder, down her arm. "We're all connected. Tonight you must have felt the pack?"

She nodded, grateful for the commitment to Acadian wolves, for helping her and Dimitri kill Chaz. Without reserve, they'd accepted her during their run.

"I feel you. What you did for me. Even though I was unconscious, I knew you were there. When you were healing me, it was you and Dimitri. I felt both of you."

"But I wasn't able to do it by myself."

"Exactly."

"This may have been an unconventional mating, but it's done. We're one now." Dimitri took her hand.

"Never alone," Jake added.

"Thank you." Gillian glanced at Jake then Dimitri. "Both of you."

Their heated gaze smoldered, her eyes never leaving his. She reasoned that it may have been the mating or the run driving her heightened libido and emotions. After learning to grow comfortable within her own skin, there was no way she'd ever leave. Together, they'd taken her gift and saved Jake. Dimitri had come into her life like a hurricane, sweeping her off her feet, changing her perspective.

She parted her lips, her eyes focused on him. But before she had a chance to speak, Dimitri wrapped his fingers around the nape of her neck and captured her lips. Aware that Jake had left the bed, she thought for a second to end their embrace, but Dimitri's fingers speared into her hair, demanding her attention. As he deepened the kiss, she slid her palms up his chest, her fingertips teasing his flat nipples. He growled at the intrusion, flipping her onto her back. She squeaked as she fell back onto the bed, his legs straddling hers.

Frantically, she nipped at his lips. His energy poured into her, and the realization hit her that she was finally free, as was he. Free to love, to live, to begin their future together. A surge of passion coursed through her, her wolf seeking his. His hardened cock lay heavy on her thigh, and the touch of him sent desire to her core.

Aching for him, she strained to bow her pelvis into his, seeking the relief she needed. He wrapped a hand into her hair. Their lips forced apart as he tilted her head, exposing her neck. She bared herself to him, relaxed into her submission.

"Yes, that's it, my little wolf. Don't move," he told her, sucking her earlobe.

She gasped, her nipples grazing his chest. His warm wet tongue traced a small circle behind her ear, slowly making its way down to her chest. A clean fragrance mixed with his masculine scent, brushed by her nose as he buried his face into her cleavage. Gillian moaned as he licked, circling her areola.

"I love the smell of you, the taste of your skin." His lips claimed a rosy peak, and she gasped as the delicious pain sent quivers of desire straight to her core. Wetness dripped onto her inner thighs. Once again, she lifted her hips, attempting to get him to enter her, but it was of no use, as he held her down firmly with his torso.

"I love your breasts." His moist tongue traced a path around her areola.

As he made love to her nipple with his mouth, she cried out in pleasure. All Gillian could think about was how she yearned to have him inside her. Moreover, she wished she could tell him how she was falling in love with him, but she held back, not wanting to scare him with her feelings. Even though they were mated, it seemed too soon to say the words that would reveal her heart. A firm pinch to her taut tip, brought her out of her contemplation and her eyes flew open to meet his.

"Your arousal….it's intoxicating." Dimitri smiled. He grazed his nose in between her fleshy mounds and sniffed.

Gillian's face flushed, her nails digging into his shoulders.

"How far would you go to experiment, cher?"

"Hmm?"

"You're safe with me always."

"Yes, I know."

"The last time we played with your submission I saw the way you watched Jake."

Gillian turned her head in embarrassment, the thrill of watching Jake stroke himself still fresh in her mind.

"No hiding." He cupped her chin.

"But it's not right…everything that just happened."

"Everything that happened is exactly why we should be together. We did something special tonight. All of us."

"But how I feel...I shouldn't feel like this." Her desire for the secret fantasy blurred with shame.

"We're wolves, Gilly. That means we're sexual. Being turned on by watching or being watched is natural. I'll share you tonight, but I won't lie," Dimitri reached between her legs and clutched her mound, "this may be the only time I ever do. You're mine."

Gillian's breath hitched at his commanding tone. His thumb slid through her wet folds, teasing her swollen nub.

"You felt the pack tonight...your libido heightened. It's a full moon, time to be wild." Dimitri closed his eyes and howled.

"Jake's nice, but Dimitri, he'll never be you. No one will ever be you."

"Do you trust me?"

"Yes," she whispered, her voice quivering. Excitement rippled through her veins, the anticipation of making love to both men.

"I'll be in control tonight, not him, not you, understood?" Dimitri growled, his thumb swiping up and down her slit.

Dimitri didn't wait for her response as he kissed her, driving a long finger deep inside her hot sheath. Gillian panted into his mouth, their tongues sweeping against each other's. As he began to pump into her, she writhed underneath him, unaware that Jake had come into the room. A knock jarred their attention. She gasped as

Dimitri tore his lips from hers. His finger still deep inside her, he gave her a sexy smile before turning to Jake, who stood with a wet towel slung around his hips.

"Hey, sorry, D, but I just wanted to let you know that I'm going to go home now. You mind if I borrow some jeans? I want to take my bike home."

Gillian's heart raced; her insatiable hunger left her starving. Dimitri caught her gaze as if to warn her of his intentions.

"Come join us."

"Stay," she heard herself say. Gillian caught Dimitri's smile as she extended a hand forward.

"Are ya'll sure? I swear I'm okay. You don't need to babysit me." Jake inhaled deeply, taking notice of Gillian's flushed skin, her full breasts. His cock jerked, shifting the white terry cloth.

Gillian nodded, grunting as Dimitri plunged into her again with his hand. Her eyes locked on Jake's as he sat on the bed.

"Look how beautiful my mate is." Dimitri sat up, resting back on his heels. He backed up, so that he could part her thighs further. With her legs spread wide open, she lay exposed to them.

"Ahh." Gillian's eyes darted to Jake's, her hips moving up to accept Dimitri inside her.

"Gilly's special, all right," Jake agreed, allowing her to take his hand.

"Yes she is. She's inexperienced in our ways, but she's very aroused and all wolf."

"Please Dimitri," she cried. With their eyes upon her flesh, her desire spiked. The pad of his finger curled inside her core, causing her to quiver.

"Not yet, my sweet lil' mate." He glanced at Jake. "We're going to take care of you tonight."

"Gilly?" Jake asked, his hand slowly sliding up her arm.

"Yes," Gillian breathed, giving him permission. Her body lit on fire as Dimitri sank two fingers into her and Jake's palm glided over her silky skin. Gently he caressed her, playing with her breasts.

"She's so soft," Jake whispered. He lay next to her on his side, letting his hands roam over her.

"It feels so…" Gillian lost her words as she gyrated rhythmically to Dimitri's sensual probing.

"Touch him, cher," Dimitri directed.

With her eyes on Dimitri, she slipped her hand underneath Jake's towel, wrapping her palm around his swollen shaft. He groaned as she swiped her thumb over his weeping head. Jake tore the loin cloth away so he was bare and Gillian broke eye contact to watch her small hand stroke up and down Jake's cock.

"That's it. See how good that feels. So natural," Dimitri coaxed.

"I've never…I've never done anything like this," she began.

"It's all good. Let your wolf guide you. Remember what you told me, don't think. Just feel." Dimitri withdrew his fingers from her, and she moaned in displeasure.

"Don't stop," she demanded.

"We're just getting started," he assured her. Taking his dick into his hand, he pressed the length of him through her lips, coating himself in her cream.

"I don't think your mate has learned submission very well," Jake noted, giving her tip a hard pinch.

"Hey." The sting on her nipple sent a jolt to her pussy. She sighed heavily.

"I think you're right. Maybe she needs something to keep her busy?" Her beta suggested in warning.

Gillian's eyes widened, both excited and worried about what Dimitri had in mind.

"Suck his cock, Gil," Dimitri told her.

With her eyes on Dimitri's, she leaned toward Jake. She hesitated, waiting for approval from her mate.

"Go ahead. That's it, darlin'. I want to see you take him all the way into your mouth."

Gillian smiled, closed her eyes and then blinked them open, nodding in acceptance. Craving both men, she tugged gently on Jake, as he brought his hips nearer to her. The clean scent of Jake's shower was thick in the air as she brushed his broad head over her lips.

"Oh, Goddess," Jake groaned. His hand fell into Gillian's mane, stroking her locks as she took him inside her mouth.

"You're so fucking hot, Gilly." Dimitri continued to coat himself in her wetness, teasing her clitoris but not yet entering her.

Gillian moaned in response, jutting her hips upward. Sucking Jake hard, she gasped as Dimitri drove himself into her. Simultaneously and with her eyes on her beta, she relaxed, taking Jake far down her throat. Like a lollipop, she licked his shaft, grunting every now and then as Dimitri thrust deep inside her. She embraced her loss of control as Dimitri held her hips, slowly pumping in and out of her.

"Yes, so good," Dimitri said.

"Aw, fuck," Jake groaned.

"Yes, that's it. Take all of me." Dimitri slowed his pace, plunging into her until he was balls deep.

"Oh shit," Jake said, Gillian sucking him hard. His hand glided down her abdomen until he reached her slick mound. "Your pussy is so…"

"Fucking tight," Dimitri finished.

Gillian released Jake from her mouth, continuing to cup him with her hand. As Jake applied pressure to her clitoris, she almost flew off the bed.

"Yes, don't stop, yes," Gillian screamed.

"That's it, Gilly. Come for us."

"Ah, I…" Gillian's body lit on fire with passion. The words escaped her.

"I think she likes that. How 'bout a little harder," Gillian heard Dimitri say. With her core full and fingers on her clit, she saw stars, her climax slamming into her. She shook uncontrollably, both men giving her no quarter.

With her breath ragged, she barely had time to recover as Dimitri quickly flipped her onto her stomach. She rested her hands on Jake, who'd helped move her into place. He seated himself in front of her, waiting on Dimitri.

"Up onto your knees, cher. Relax your head there onto Jake," Dimitri guided.

She rested her head on Jake's thigh, and took his cock into her hands. She caught sight of his smile right before she slipped him into her lips. The sound of Jake's head thumping against the headboard in pleasure made her giggle, but she managed to stay on task.

A cool gel dripped onto her bottom taking her off guard, but as Dimitri's fingers warmed the slippery fluid over her back hole, she registered his intent. She moaned as his fingers pressed into her pussy, but it was his thumb probing her puckered flesh that caused her to tense.

"I'm going to fuck this sweet little ass of yours, tonight." Dimitri gently worked his way into her rosebud.

"Dimitri…it's so, ah, tight." Gillian withdrew Jake from her mouth.

"Relax, now, cher. I've got you. You're okay. Just let me ready you."

"That's it, Gil," Jake praised her as she took a deep breath, rubbing her breasts against his thigh.

Gillian could feel the flood of wetness flow between her legs as Dimitri withdrew, then guided two fingers into her ass. Instinctively, she wiggled her bottom, trying to get him to go deeper.

"We're both going to make love to you. You ready, darlin'?" Dimitri asked with a smile, amused at how much she was enjoying his touch.

"Ahhh...yes." Her body relaxed into the dark sensation. Gillian moaned in pleasure, rocking back into his hand.

"I'm going to need you to let Jake go, so I can move you up a little."

"Dimitri," she cried. Gillian's orgasm began to build, the flickers of electricity running from her chest down to her clit. She wished she didn't like the feel of his fingers inside her but the more he stretched her, the more she wanted him.

"I know you want to come, cher, but let's get you in position," he directed.

Doing as he'd asked, Gillian let Jake slip from her mouth, and pressed up onto her palms. Letting Dimitri guide her hips, she crawled up so that she straddled Jake's hips. She met Jake's gaze and her lips parted as he leaned forward to touch his lips to hers. It was a soft kiss; more than friendly, yet it didn't have the passion that she only shared with her mate. She wasn't in love with Jake, but she cared about him. His gentle caress of her cheek told her that he reciprocated, understood the nature of their sexual encounter. Neither she nor he was in control, yet they both embraced their close relationship.

The cold gel dripped onto her bottom once again, jarring her back into the moment. So close to coming, she ached between her legs. The tip of Jake's cock grazed her clit and she shivered. Gillian attempted to move her hips toward him, but Dimitri held them firmly in place.

"You ready, Gil?" Gillian heard Dimitri ask. She panted in anticipation, waiting for him to direct her.

"Yes," she breathed, just about coming undone as Jake took her breasts into his hands. "Please…I can't wait. Now…do it now."

"She is a demanding lil' thing," Jake noted with a sultry smile. He rolled her firm nipples with his forefingers and thumbs.

"You really aren't getting the concept of submitting are ya, darlin'?" Dimitri resisted the urge to spank her and instead removed his fingers.

"Please, no don't go. I need you. I can't…I'm so close." Gillian seriously thought she'd lose it. He was teasing her she knew, but her orgasm was so close. She began to claw at the sheets.

"Easy now, Gilly. I'm not goin' anywhere. I'm going to go slowly. Hold still for me." Dimitri took a deep breath and guided himself into her tight ring of muscle.

"Oh my God. Yes," she cried.

"That's a girl. Breathe and push back onto me," Dimitri instructed.

A flash of pain registered and then ceased as Dimitri pressed the head of his cock into her bottom. She gasped as he pushed in further, trying to follow his directions. Breathing deeply, she panted. Her entire body felt as if she'd combust with desire. She attempted to move, but it was useless, as Dimitri held her firmly around the hips.

Jake lovingly ran his fingers over her shoulders as she took all of Dimitri inside her.

"That's it. Relax. Don't try to force it, Gil. Just a little bit more of me." Dimitri released a loud breath, fully seated inside her. "I'm in all the way."

"Oh God, please...I need you to fuck me now," she demanded, feral with lust. She bit her lip out of frustration.

"I know, just let me go slowly." Dimitri gently slid out and back into her, getting her used to the sensation. "You're so goddamned tight. I'm not going to..."

"It feels so good...please don't stop," she pleaded.

"Now Jake's going to join us, you ready, Gil?"

Gillian nodded, her eyes on Jake's. He brushed his cock over her clitoris a few times and she groaned in ecstasy. Within seconds, she felt him separate her folds, pressing himself into her.

"Oh yeah," Jake grunted.

"You okay, darlin'?" Dimitri asked, wrapping a strong arm around her waist.

Gillian, so desperately full and aroused, nodded. Dimitri pushed her limits, bringing her to levels of ecstasy she'd thought she'd never understand. It was as if they were no longer individual people, their souls and bodies united as one. She loved him even more for allowing her to explore her fantasy, expanding her world.

She closed her eyes, utterly engrossed in the sensation of being pleasured by two men. As they began to plunge in and out of her, she gave herself over to her dark fantasy.

Her mate commanded their experience, his love for her evident in each stroke. Dimitri's hand glided upward to support her chest, claiming her as his as he bit down into her shoulder.

She cried out, allowing him to bring her torso upward slightly so that she was seated on Jake. With each strong thrust, she ached with a pulsing need. As if Dimitri had read her mind, he found her clit, squeezing it between his fingers, driving her over the edge.

Gillian's orgasm slammed into her, rocking her entire being. Screaming Dimitri's name over and over again, she panted for breath, her release rolling from her belly to her limbs. Jake's muscles tightened underneath her as he pounded up into her, coming hard. She heard Dimitri grunt, his cock thrusting into her.

"Oh Goddess, I can't hold it." Dimitri lost control as her contractions rippled through her core, stimulating his cock through the thin membrane. Spilling his seed deep inside her, he stiffened against her. "Fuck, yes."

As the last waves of her release ceased, tears of pleasure came to her eyes. She closed them, immersing herself in the surreal afterglow. Her skin continued to tingle as exhaustion claimed her. Dimitri's lips pressed to her shoulder as he carefully removed himself. She felt Jake gently slide out from underneath her and she cuddled into the comforter, barely aware of the warm washcloth between her legs. As her mate cleaned her, she moaned, satisfied and relaxed. She felt Dimitri pull the covers over her, his abdomen warming her back as he spooned her, encircling her within his strong arms. His soft lips met her hair. Within the safety of his embrace, she fell asleep.

Dimitri took another draw of her ambrosial scent into his nostrils, amazed that the Goddess had given him such a brave and sensual mate. From her reaction to watching Jake in the shower, he'd known that their time with him would be special. But now that they'd experimented, the possessiveness of his wolf growled, warning him not to share her again.

He glanced at Jake, who'd wrapped a towel around his waist and had lain back onto the bed on his side, watching them. Dimitri's heart had nearly broken, seeing his friend near death. Guilt for what had happened to Jake racked his thoughts. Like the Alpha, as beta, he was responsible for protecting those in his pack.

"You almost died tonight," Dimitri murmured over Gillian's head, catching Jake's attention. He played with her hair as she slept soundly.

"Yeah, I guess I did. This immortality talk is crap. Oh we can live a long time, but every one of us has a weakness, including those vamps," Jake mused.

"True. You headed back home?"

"Yep. Chaz is dead, I assume?"

"As a doornail." Dimitri's expression flattened, growing solemn. "So is Nick."

"Nick is dead? Goddammit." Jake shook his head and blew out a breath. "I didn't know him that well but he seemed like a good guy. Is Jax okay?"

"Don't know. Léopold went with him. Losing a beta…you know it's gonna affect his whole pack. Let's just hope Jax is strong enough to survive this, because Gilly just found her brother, and she seemed like she was growin' kind of attached to him."

Only once in his lifetime had Dimitri watched an Alpha lose his beta. He'd been a boy at the time. When the Alpha had gone missing, his mama had told him that he'd gone to find himself. But he'd known, even at that young age, that their Alpha had killed himself. Like the connection between him and Logan, the Alpha and his beta were as bonded to each other as he was to Gillian.

"You think he'll make it?"

"Don't know. I'll ask Leo tomorrow. Right now, all I wanna do is go to sleep."

"I'm goin' to go, give you guys some privacy." Jake pushed up to sit on the bed. He paused, glancing to Gillian and then to Dimitri. "Tonight…I needed this more than you did. You and Gilly, you know I love you, right? I don't mean to get mushy and shit, but I've never been so close to the other side…never in my whole life."

"We all needed this tonight. Seeing you like that…"

"Hey, I'm good now." Jake smiled. "Gilly's really special. I'm glad you found your mate."

"Someday you will too."

"Maybe. But for the record, I'm not lookin'. I guess it's in destiny's hands."

"Yeah, well, destiny handed you your ass tonight."

"Yes, she did, my friend."

"Speaking of destiny, I see food in your future." Dimitri's tone changed, reflecting his usual jovial attitude. "That's right, bro. Tomorrow, you'd better get over here and make us breakfast. I'm getting tired of cooking and I have a feeling my mate's going to be keeping me mighty busy for a while."

"Ya'll know I don't cook. Take out, okay? Beignets?"

"You bet," Dimitri replied, pulling the covers up further onto his chest. "Hey, can you do me a favor before you go?

"Sure, what do you need?"

"Can you text Leo and Logan? Make sure they know you're okay. And lock the house on your way out, 'K?"

"Done and done." Jake gave a wave on the way out the door.

Dimitri heard the sound of his footsteps patter up the stairs to his bedroom, presumably so he could borrow clothes and get dressed. Within minutes, he heard his boots pounding downstairs, ending with the creak of the door opening and shutting.

He lifted his head, elated to see the small smile on Gillian's lips. His heart crushed with an emotion that he hadn't experienced in his whole life. Not only had Gillian courageously fought with the pack, she'd given her cat to him, saving his wolf. Their sexual compatibility was icing on the cake as far as he was concerned, but the fresh memory of being inside her caused his cock to twitch. He silently laughed to himself, thinking that he might be spending the next couple of years locked in a bedroom.

As he lay his head back down, he pressed his lips into her hair, softly whispering the words that were true to his heart. "I love you, Gilly."

Chapter Twenty-Two

Gillian stirred, smiling as her eyes fluttered open. She glanced back to Dimitri, who, although lost in sleep, kept his arms firmly secured about her waist. Pressure in her lower belly had caused her to wake. As much as she loathed leaving the warmth and safety of her mate, the call of nature was greater. Carefully, she peeled Dimitri's fingers away, gently kissing his cheek before she got out of bed.

After using the bathroom, she plunged her arms into the sleeves of a spare robe that hung on the back of the door. She tied the sash, and brought the lapels to her nose, deeply inhaling Dimitri's masculine scent. With a satisfied smile, she quietly padded out of the guest room and into the kitchen.

She reached for the refrigerator door, opening it. Rummaging around, she found a pitcher of filtered water and grabbed a clean coffee mug out of the dish rack. As she went to pour, she heard a high-pitched cry. The recognizable sound of a kitten in distress pierced her chest.

Setting down the cup, she approached the sliding glass doors. She called Dimitri's name, hoping he'd hear her. Her fingertips curled over the metal pull, her thumb flicking the lock open. She called to Dimitri once again, concerned that a stray animal had been hurt. The hairs on the back of her neck stood up, her intuition warning her of danger. Whatever had attacked the young cat was still out in the yard. A loud cry sounded again, sending her into action. As she flung the glass open with the force of ten men, her protective instinct overrode self-preservation. It was as if the remaining tendrils of her cat called on her to save the young feline.

She tore out onto the deck and the screeching continued. Letting her nocturnal vision come into focus, she scanned the yard. She quietly advanced but saw nothing. Dimitri's footsteps sounded in the house, when the sharp slicing pain of claws stabbed into her neck, causing her to freeze in place. A bony hand dangled a kitten, barely twelve weeks old, in front of her face. Gillian's heart caught as it dropped to the ground, safely landing on its feet and scurrying underneath the crawlspace.

Gillian went to scream but as the talon pierced her skin, it restricted air flow to her windpipe. She gasped for breath. Her eyes widened in panic. Unable to see her attacker, her gaze darted from side to side. Heart racing, she lost her concentration; her ability to shift failed her. Terror seized her body, blood flowing from her neck. Gillian swiveled her head, which drove the slicing barbs further into her flesh. She caught sight of Lady Charlotte behind her, her fangs dripping with saliva.

"Get the hell off of my mate," Dimitri growled, barreling through the exit.

"Dimitri." Gillian's lips moved but only a gurgle of his name escaped her lips.

"Don't move, wolf," the vampiress hissed.

"You're going to die tonight," he calmly stated.

Dimitri calculated his next move, observing that the vampire had gone stark raving mad. Her usually coiffed upswept hair had mushroomed, tendrils sprouting all over like overgrown weeds. Her lips were cracked and reddened, making Dimitri wonder if she'd already killed someone. Her blood-stained shirt and pants hung loose on her scrawny frame.

"This is all your fault. You needed vampire blood…came to me for help. He killed her," she spat.

Gillian's arms gripped at Charlotte's wrists, attempting to dislodge her hold. But her iron-clad grip wouldn't budge. The more Gillian struggled, the deeper the vampire's nails curled into her throat.

"Killed who?" Dimitri asked. Deliberately, he stalked toward her.

"Lacey. Léopold did it. He killed her. And for what? Because she'd taken money from a wolf?"

"No, because she signed Gilly's death warrant. Rules are rules, vamp. You've got to either have a death wish or be fucking stupid to mess with Leo. You know it. I know it. And Lacey knew it. She gambled and lost."

"Shut up! You don't know what you're talking about!" Lady Charlotte screamed.

"Nope, I think Leo got this one right," Dimitri mused, giving her a cool smile. "I wonder how long it took for him to kill her. A minute? No, no, no. Not my boy. He strikes as fast as a cottonmouth on a hot summer day. Those fangs probably sucked her dry in seconds."

"I said, shut it, wolf." Lady Charlotte extracted a silver dagger from her back pocket and tore open Gillian's robe. "I'll gut her right now, I swear it."

"Or maybe he just cut off her head. Nah, Leo's not much for weapons, I suppose," Dimitri pondered, edging closer to her. "Ya know he told me he can make it hurt, real bad. I bet that's what he did."

Gillian tried to shift, extending her claws. Lady Charlotte swiftly responded by jabbing the knife into Gillian's abdomen.

"Nice try," she jeered. "No shifting for you."

The razor-sharp weapon lacerated Gillian's creamy skin, crimson droplets spilling down her torso. Her throat constricted; she coughed, her breathing growing ragged. As a fingernail pressed through to her trachea, a drowning sensation commenced, Gillian's lungs filling with blood. Eyes bulging, she hoped the bond she shared with Dimitri would somehow allow her to silently communicate with him. But he wasn't looking at her. She couldn't understand why his gaze was firmly pinned on the vampire.

"You know, I thought you were kind of smart when I first met ya, bein' that Leo went to you for help and all. But all I see now is a pathetic excuse of a corpse, refusing to take responsibility for her own mess." Dimitri's eyes flared at the sight of his mate's injury. He carefully strategized his attack. If he moved too quickly, he knew Lady Charlotte would flay her open like a fish. Gillian's ability to shift had faltered, she couldn't fight back.

"Lacey was my lover. Before you say anything, always know that it was me who let her fuck you. Me! I did that. I gave to her, cared for her. She was mine. And now because of this piece of shit cat here," Charlotte shook Gillian until her body went listless, her legs barely holding her upright. Acidic tears rained down Charlotte's cheeks, hate spewing from her mouth. "She's gone. Léopold showed no mercy that night in the club. He killed her, and now I'm going to kill your mate. If you'd never set foot in my club, none of this would have ever happened. An eye for an eye. I want justice."

"This isn't Gillian's fault. Ilsbeth is the one who…"

"Ilsbeth," she scoffed. "You're a fool, you know that. She's the one who set the dominos in motion. If I'd known at the time, I'd never have agreed to give you the blood."

"What are you talking about?"

"She's always wanted what she couldn't have. I should've known how far that bitch would go."

"I broke off with her months ago. Maybe she didn't like it but she's always known that I'd find my mate."

"She's clever, I'll give her that. Making it so you couldn't shift. Trying to kill off your wolf. She put on a good show. You bought it hook, line and sinker. The sorcerer...that was a nice touch."

"You're lying," he growled.

"Truth hurts, doesn't it? Had to torture it out of her. But as you can see, I have a penchant for the fine art of persuasion."

"Fuck," Dimitri cursed. Even though Gillian had tried to convince him, he'd held out hope that Ilsbeth hadn't been responsible for his affliction.

"Don't fret now. Ilsbeth got hers."

"What did you do? Where's Ilsbeth?"

"I ruined her life the way she's ruined mine. Don't worry, she's still alive. Death is too good for her," she sniffed. "Let's just put it this way, she won't be casting any more spells for a while...if ever. It will be as if she never existed."

"You'll never get away from Leo." Dimitri's eyes narrowed on her, his voice emotionless. He moved a few more feet closer, his body preparing to shift.

"I'll leave town. I'll leave the country. None of you can touch me."

Gillian's vision blurred as her spirit faltered. Their argument was but static in her ears, her mind no longer able to process their words. She reached within her mind's eye and saw her wolf struggling to appear. The soft roar of her tiger echoed in her mind yet she couldn't see her anywhere. Her eyes fluttered open and she caught

Dimitri's gaze but for a moment. Her heart broke for him, the life draining from her body. She loved him heart, body and soul. If she was going to die, she was going to tell him before she left this earth.

"Dimitri, please," she begged, her voice barely audible. Tears sprang from her eyes, her fingers too weak to hold onto the vampire's forearms. As her lips moved to say the words, no sound could be heard.

"I love you," she mouthed, her eyes rolling back into her head. A blanket of unconsciousness fell over her as she began to convulse.

Dimitri had managed to distract Lady Charlotte long enough to close the distance, yet it hadn't been enough. Gillian's confession spurred his wolf into a feral state. Dimitri lost the restrained control he'd demonstrated, determined to kill Charlotte. Transforming seamlessly, his wolf launched itself at the vampire, shoving them all down into the dewy yard.

Lady Charlotte threw Gillian aside, launching her barbed fist into his flank. Like a missile, it cleaved through him. The intense pain drove him into darkness, but the beasts inside him fought through the haze, both the wolf and the tiger coming together as one. As they merged, he felt as if he'd been hit by lightning. The sizzle of their interaction cracked a loud thunderous explosion into the night.

Calling on the tiger, he shifted fully into the great cat, his massive paws tearing up the turf. Enraged, he barely registered the slice of her knife into his hindquarters. As

Charlotte sank her fangs deep into his shoulder, he repelled her with a tremendous shake of his muscular body, smashing her into the ground. She raised the blade to slay him and he swiftly evaded her knife, his sharp claws tearing across her throat. Blood sprayed into his thick fur, and he roared in victory as Charlotte's head rolled from her body, quickly turning to ash.

As he shifted back, the unimaginable reality slammed into him that he'd somehow become feline, driven by his need to protect his mate. But the fleeting thought disappeared as he saw Gillian lying unconscious on the ground. The cicadas sang in anguish, as if they were aware that she'd been critically injured. Dimitri scooped her up into his arms, pressing the wound together with his fingers.

"Gillian, please," he cried. Spent, and uncertain if he could heal her like they'd done with Jake, he commanded her. "Listen, Gilly. You have to shift. Can you hear me? This is your mate. Gillian!"

Gillian moaned, aware of him calling her name. No longer in pain, the endorphins rushed through her body, causing her to feel as if she was floating up to the sky.

"Goddammit, Gillian. You will shift. Do you hear me?"

"No, no…I'm flying…I'm leaving," she murmured, her face pale.

"No, Gilly. Stay with me. You're a wolf. Now, shift," he demanded, his eyes brimming with tears. He could tell that she was lost in some sort of haze, unaware of her situation.

The sound of Dimitri yelling startled Gillian back into reality. She clutched at the wound in her belly. Panting, she began to beg. "Oh my God. Please stop the pain. I'm going to die. Please stop it…"

"Yes, you're in pain. That means you're fighting. You have to do as I say. You will listen. Submit to me now. Do you hear me? I am your beta. And you will obey."

"Oh God…I don't know…help me." Gillian began to scream as she flittered in and out of consciousness.

"Obey and shift," he ordered, his voice dominant. No longer could he afford to treat her with kid gloves, he had to appeal to her wolf's sense of the pack.

"Shift," she repeated.

"Shift now!" he yelled at her.

Dimitri breathed a sigh of relief as the magic that was the wolves circulated around them, and within seconds, his little black wolf was lying before him, whole and healed. He plowed his fingers into her hair, kissing her fur. He'd seen Logan command his wolves to shift a million times, but never had he done it himself. Having killed the Alpha, Dimitri was certain that his Alpha tendencies had graduated; no longer would he be able to keep them secret within his own pack. Yet the desire to remain in the bayou with his Acadian wolves would far outweigh the need to dominate Logan or to lead his own pack.

"Jesus, Gilly, you scared the shit out of me," he told her, patting her on her rear. "You need to learn submission."

She barked at him, nearly nipping his fingers and began to run circles around him. Dimitri fell back on the heels of his hands, shaking his head at her.

"You," he pointed to her as she growled and wagged her tail, "are in so much trouble it's not even funny. There's no bitin' your beta, cher. Not unless you want a punishment which I have a feelin' you're itchin' to get."

Gillian whined, pressing her paws to the ground and bowed her head. She rolled over onto her back and whimpered, then shifted back into her human form. Dimitri leaned forward, easily scooping her up into his arms, embracing his mate.

"I love you," she whispered, her lips to his chest.

"Goddess, I love you, too," he replied, kissing the top of her head. "I love you so damn much. I never thought I'd fall in…"

"Love?"

"Yeah that."

"Yeah that," she laughed. "Me either."

For a long minute, they both sat silent, contemplating their confessions. They touched and caressed each other's skin as if they hadn't seen each other in years.

Gillian paused, and looked around the yard in surprise, unaware of what had happened to Charlotte. The last thing she remembered was hitting the ground.

"What did you do with the vampire?" she asked, her eyebrows drawn in concern.

"About that. It's a funny story." Dimitri paused. He wasn't sure how to tell anyone, let alone Gillian, that he'd shifted into a tiger. He hardly believed it himself. It was as if he needed video evidence to confirm his actions. It was so entirely unbelievable, he needed a day or two to come to terms with the cat inside him.

"I'm afraid to know. No, wait. Is she gone?"

"She's gone." Dimitri pulled her closely against his chest, hiding his expression of amusement.

"Dead?'

"Yeah."

"Even better," Gillian replied, relieved that they were safe from retaliation.

"But you, my little wolf, are in trouble for trying to bite me. You know, Leo's taught me a few tricks…he loves spankings." Dimitri smiled, coiling his hands around her wrists, giving her a fair warning.

"Spankings, huh? Something tells me I'm going to enjoy it," she said with a coy grin. "Maybe I should bite you more often."

Gillian gasped as Dimitri swiftly flipped her onto her back, pinning her to the ground. His hands held hers to the sides of her head, and he let the pressure of his hips immobilize her. He may have been in love with her but she would soon learn that he wasn't joking; she'd surrender her control to him. Her wolf would demand it, regardless of what the cat had taught her, and he'd enjoy every second of the struggle.

"Now," he whispered into her ear. "This is much better."

"Hey," she giggled. Her cheek brushed the cool grass. "Don't I get a break? I was just attacked by a vampire."

"You seemed pretty healthy to me a few minutes ago. You've got some sharp fangs, cher," he growled, sucking her earlobe with his lips. Taking it between his teeth, he tugged until she moaned.

"No fair," she cried.

"This isn't about fair," he laughed. "This is about you and me. And you're about to find out why I'm the beta of this pack."

As Dimitri took her lips, he felt her body go limp, submitting to his will. Twice during the full moon, he'd almost lost someone he loved. But the exhilaration of having her back in his arms, the knowledge that she could shift, washed away any lingering concerns. When he'd entered his home with her in his arms, he'd never been happier in his entire life. Their home, their future, their love. A new life with his little wolf.

Chapter Twenty-Three

The wind whipped Gillian's raven locks around her helmet. The warmth of Dimitri heated her palms as she fingered the ridges of his abs. She laughed as he slapped her wandering hands that had traveled underneath his t-shirt. He'd insisted she keep her arms wrapped around his waist, but her caress to his bared skin had proven to be far too distracting. The soft blindfold around her eyes kept her in darkness.

After two weeks without Dimitri, Gillian was ravenous for him. Not being able to spend days and nights with her mate had been a necessary evil. She'd gone to New York City with her brother while Dimitri had traveled to San Diego. As much as Gillian had wanted Dimitri to come with her to Nick's funeral, Jake had needed his help to settle the Anzober wolves.

Initially, Jax had been reticent, but eventually he'd broken down, confiding in Gillian, accepting her comfort. She'd held him as he cried, and did her best to console him. Despite his grief, he'd continued commanding his subordinates, conducting business as usual and planning future issues of ZANE.

During the days leading up to the burial, she and Jax spent hours talking, catching up on childhoods lost. They'd pored through old photographs. For the first time in her life, she'd gotten a glimpse inside the world that had eluded her. His mother, a Nordic wolf, had been a beautiful woman. Sadly, she was killed during a territorial dispute shortly after Jax had been born, and he had few memories of her. The Alpha, their father, had been strikingly handsome, also with blonde hair, yet he looked more rugged than her brother. She could see why her mother had fallen in love with him. Not only was he good-looking, Gillian learned he had been steadfastly loyal, a great warrior in his time. He'd been an Alpha through and through. His blood ran thick in her veins and she suspected her difficulty submitting came naturally.

Gillian had chipped away at the anguish that consumed Jax. She'd felt hopeful, thankful that she had a brother. He too, had expressed his happiness that they were no longer alone. But the day of the funeral, Jax fell back into his dark depression. Since Nick had been well loved by wolves and humans alike, they'd held a public memorial service in Central Park. Afterwards, they'd traveled to the Fingers Lakes region to hold the private burial on pack lands.

Later in the evening, on a damp night during the new moon, they placed Nick into the trenched earth. Gillian and Jax had shoveled the dirt onto the deceased body. An audience of wolves stood watching, the earthy aroma fresh in the air. Sweat and tears misted their bodies, grime staining their skin. With their bare hands, they attended to his gravesite until they'd patted the mound tight.

After a long run with his pack, they'd traveled by limo in silence back to the city. It was as if a switch had gone off; Jax had withdrawn from both her and his pack. On her insistence, he'd flown with her back to Louisiana. She'd lied, telling him she'd felt uncomfortable flying alone, urging him to come with her. The reality was that she thought he could use a change of scenery.

But once they'd arrived in the city, he'd arranged for Dimitri to meet them at the airport, explaining that he planned on traveling, needing to find peace. Gillian knew that despite her concerns, Jax had to deal with his grief in his own way. Having no mate or children, her brother had spent years confiding in and caring for his beta. It was as if he'd lost a mate, and she was worried that he wouldn't recover. As he hugged her goodbye, he whispered in her ear, promising that he'd be okay.

Sadness filled her heart, watching Jax reboard his plane. But as she turned to leave and saw her mate, Gillian's libido roared to life, her emotions instantly transforming into lust. Dimitri casually leaned on his motorcycle, waiting for her arrival. She ran to him, stopping short of his embrace. The sight of her beta took her breath away. Altogether sexy and confident, his wicked smile made her want to tear off her panties and beg him to fuck her right there on the tarmac. But in his typical dominance, he'd controlled the situation, first by kissing her senseless, then promptly blindfolding her before she had a chance to speak. He straddled her on his bike, running his strong hands up her inner thighs. She gasped, her nipples hardening in response. Her vision, cloaked in blackness, heightened the sensation. Even though she was well aware they were still at the airport, it was as if they were the only two people in the world.

As they rode, Gillian had no idea of their destination. She relished the feel of his ripped torso against her palms, inhaling his distinctive scent. With her head pressed to his leather jacket, she lost track of time. She couldn't say for how long they traveled, her stiff peaks denting into the hard expanse of his back. The vibrations from the seat reverberated in a sensual tempo against her groin. By the time they'd arrived at their final destination, she'd nearly come undone. She hadn't anticipated that their traveling arrangements were only the beginning of the delicious torture her mate had planned.

As he helped her onto the ground, the salty mist hit her face. Licking her lips, she tasted the briny air. She'd never heard of a beach near New Orleans, yet she swore she heard waves.

"Where are we?" She laughed as he gently pulled the helmet off of her head. His fingertips trailed along the nape of her neck.

"It's a surprise," he promised.

Gillian could almost visualize his devious grin behind the lilt of his southern accent.

"Can I remove this..." She reached for the blindfold, and immediately received a jolting slap on her bottom. Through her jeans, it felt more like pressure as opposed to pain, but the message was received.

"No peeking. You'd think spending so much time with your Alpha brother would've taught you a few things," he whispered in her ear, his chest to her back. "You don't listen very well. I'm afraid we are going to need to have multiple lessons...ones involving just you and me."

Gillian giggled, her arousal spiked. Every cell of her body awakened to his touch.

"Not funny, cher. Feel what you did to me on this trip." He set his hands on her hips, tugging her backward. He took her hand, leading it behind her back and pressed it onto his enormous erection. "I said, no touching my skin. You almost caused me to wreck."

"It's been two weeks. It's not fair to expect me to keep my hands off you," she protested with a broad smile.

Dimitri brushed his lips to the sensitive area behind her ear. A firm palm traveled from her belly, rising slowly between her breasts and over her chest until his hand was wrapped around her neck. His other fell between her legs, cupping her denim-covered mound. "Goddess, I missed you...every square inch of you."

"I missed you too...so much." Gillian released a moan, her body falling limp against the strength of her mate. After her long visit with Jax, always being careful not to offend other wolves within his pack, she'd grown exhausted of wearing a mask of serenity. She didn't want to think, she just wanted to feel and exist within Dimitri's arms. Nothing else mattered. Letting go of her inhibitions was impossible except when in the care of her mate.

"It's very difficult being apart, our wolves, our souls needing each other," he growled, grinding his hard arousal into her bottom. "But tonight, we're alone. Just you and I…all night long."

"Please," she cried. Her palms pressed backwards, digging her nails into his muscular thighs.

"I love hearing you ask, cher. So nice." His soft lips peppered kisses along her neck.

Gillian sighed with anticipation, as his tongue danced over her skin. The rush of desire ached between her legs, her body tensing.

As quickly as his hands left her body, they returned, lifting and cradling her against him. She heard his feet moving upon the ground, but didn't ask where they were going. She didn't care. Wherever he took her, she'd follow. He'd give her what she required; the trust and love for her mate was steadfast and complete.

A door creaked open, alerting Gillian that he'd entered a room. Yet, she got the distinctive feeling she was still outside. The roar of the ocean breaking against the shore confirmed her suspicion that he'd brought her to a beach. Unable to hear another soul, she assumed they were alone but couldn't be certain. He set her on her feet, kissing her once again, leaving her breathless as he tore his lips from hers. Before she had a chance to say a word, he spoke.

"And now that we're finally alone, I need to properly prepare you," he drawled.

"Prepare me for what? Dimitri!" Gillian gasped his name, the fabric of her t-shirt rolling up over her head. With a snap of her bra, she was exposed. The instinct to cover herself was overruled by the cuff of fingers around her wrists. Unable to see, she groaned, as warm lips suckled her nipple.

"Ah, yeah, that is what I've been cravin'…sweet." Dimitri licked circles around one areola then paid attention to the other. "Delicious like warm peaches. 'Cept no sharin'. All for me."

His bare chest brushed hers as he released her. The cool sea air blowing against her wet tips caused them to further swell into tight peaks. Before she had time to speculate exactly where he'd taken her, or if anyone could see them, she heard her zipper opening. Seconds later, she stood devoid of clothing.

"You're so beautiful, Gil."

"Baby, you have no idea how much I want you."

"I think I do, because I've been needin' you just as bad. Do you know I like surprises?"

"Surprises, huh?"

"I've got a big one for you, but first," Dimitri kissed her, slipping his fingers through her glistening folds.

Gillian melted as he kissed her, moaning into his mouth as he plunged two digits deep inside her. Her core tightened around him in response. She'd been on the precipice of coming for the past hour and knew she'd fall hard and fast.

"That's it, cher," he encouraged, briefly tearing his lips from hers. His forehead pressed to hers, and he sighed. "Fuck, I love watching you come."

His thumb strummed her clit. With her body already on fire, she shook, letting the orgasm she'd held at bay roll through her.

"I…I…oh God." Gillian attempted to articulate her pleasure, but the convulsions of her climax seized her, making it impossible for her to speak. The love for her beta had taken everything she'd ever known and made it seem insignificant. Her heart felt as if it would burst.

"You okay?" he asked.

"I'm more than okay. Great. But I need you. Please don't make me wait."

Shaken, she smiled, still unable to see. Having relied on him for balance, she felt abandoned as his hands left her skin.

"Patience, little wolf. Stay there," Dimitri ordered, releasing her waist. He stepped back, admiring her gorgeous body and smiled as she brought her hands to her eyes, toying with the fabric. He inwardly laughed, knowing how difficult it was for her to take orders. Although she tried, submission was sometimes a struggle, and he expected it was something she might never fully learn, given her feline and Alpha ancestry. "Do not touch that blindfold."

Dimitri had waited weeks to tell Gillian about his ability to shift to cat. It had been extraordinarily difficult to leave his mate to go to San Diego, never disclosing how he'd killed Lady Charlotte. Before telling her, though, he had to be certain that what had happened was real. He'd reluctantly agreed that she should go with her brother to New York. After what had happened to Nick, she was Jax's only blood. Watching the interaction between them caused his chest to ache, knowing that she'd been raised in isolation by her mother, and now her brother had become compromised. She and Jax needed each other, but Dimitri knew the Alpha had a long road ahead of him.

In truth, Dimitri would never have taken her to the West Coast, not after what had happened to her there. With the trauma fresh in her mind, it was best she healed her wounds away from California. The long trip had been arduous at best. The pack had been disjointed, many families losing members, ones who'd come to Louisiana under Chaz's orders. Dimitri was grateful that Logan hadn't insisted that he take over as Alpha, instead assigning Jake to the temporary position. Neither Dimitri nor Jake wanted to move so far away from Acadian wolves. With their pack in disarray, Jake would lead them for only a few months, eventually allowing the natural order of selection to determine their new Alpha.

As Dimitri watched Gillian stand on the deck naked, a satisfied smile crossed her face. He stepped away toward the bed and stripped. He'd practiced his transformation many times, since it had happened the night of Lady

Charlotte's attack. As he reflected on that night, he recalled her chilling words. Ilsbeth hadn't been heard from or seen since, but after what she'd done to him, he hadn't gone looking. The only person he'd shown or told about the tiger had been Logan. Thankfully, his Alpha had merely laughed, finding it monumentally amusing that not only had he been mated but now he shifted to both wolf and cat.

"Gillian," he called, summoning his transformation.

"Yes, sir," she teased.

"Take off your blindfold." The magic flowed through him. Passing over his wolf, he announced his arrival with a thunderous roar.

"Oh. My. God. No way. I mean yes," Gillian stammered.

Amazed, she stared in disbelief, unable to move her feet. Her magnificent beta had taken on a feline form. She took a deep breath, slowly walking toward the bed. Tears came to her eyes as she set her palms onto his gold and black striped fur. Even though she hadn't been able to shift back to her cat yet, she, too, felt her inside and was convinced that someday soon, she'd have both animals within her reach. But the spectacular sight of Dimitri lying on the bed was surreal.

Dimitri gave a final growl, shifting back to his human form. As he did so, he rolled her onto her back.

"I wasn't sure how to tell you," he said, his lips brushing her sternum. Excitement and relief tore through him as he saw the delight on her face. He buried his head between her breasts.

"You… I've never seen a male…I mean, a male tiger…an animal like you. You were just…beautiful."

"Hmm….I like the sound of that. So I'm your first, huh?"

She laughed in response, plowing her fingers into his hair. The weight of his body against hers pressed her into the soft mattress.

"A virgin. Yep, I've got myself a virgin," he teased.

"Not exactly a virgin, but yes, you're still my first. My first in so many ways," she replied, continuing to smile.

"I love you." He stilled, his voice growing serious.

"I love you, too. I never thought I'd find anyone. And now…"

"Now, you've got yourself a tiger by the tail?"

"A little pussy cat?" she joked.

"Speaking of pussy," he laughed, pushing up onto his hands. Dimitri loved teasing her, making love with her. He wasn't sure whether it was her quick wit or her stark independence that drove him mad with hunger for her, but with her warm and ready underneath him, he didn't care. They had a lifetime and more to discover all the reasons they loved each other.

"I think I'm going to like this part." Gillian grinned, her golden eyes flickering with arousal.

"You and me both, cher." Dimitri took her lips with urgency, sucking and pressing his tongue into her mouth.

Giving her no time to rest, he guided his thick cock to her entrance, sliding into her with one strong thrust. Her tight channel fisted him, yet accommodated him as if she were a custom glove. She moaned in pleasure as he passionately kissed her. Never taking his lips off hers, he reached for her legs, wrapping them around his waist. His hand found her full breast, the hard length of him pounding into her. Rough and wild, he laughed as she nipped at his lip, nearly drawing blood. Feral, they made love, letting all inhibitions go.

"Dimitri," she screamed as he thrust into her, the bed springs creaking.

"I love you," he responded with a grunt. "Do you hear me, Gil?"

"Yes. Yes, I love you, too. Dimitri, please, oh God, yes, that's it…please," she begged. Her head thrashed from side to side as she came undone, their passion unleashed. Gillian lost herself in her release.

Dimitri dug his fingers into her bottom, guiding her hips back and forth as he slammed into her. He held his breath, as his own orgasm exploded.

The starburst of their simultaneous climax pulsated through them, leaving them in a state of delicious exhaustion. They lay motionless, immersed in the love they felt for each other.

Dimitri sighed, brushing the hair from Gillian's face. When she smiled up at him it was as if she'd reached into his chest, holding his heart in her hands. Everything he was and would be was hers. His tiny mate owned his heart, even if she didn't know it. Gillian had been the gift he'd never expected, one he'd treasure all his immortal days. He cuddled her into his chest, his lips to her forehead. Lovers and soul mates, they lay watching the sunset, looking forward to endless days and nights, together forever.

Epilogue

Jax gritted his teeth, the corrosive scotch burning over his tongue. From the circular balcony of his private VIP lounge, he watched the twenty-somethings move as a mass, undulating on the dance floor. The pounding bass and flashing lights charged the jam-packed New York City dance club.

The bar had been a regular haunt of his and Nick's. From their eagle's nest, they would observe the fine-looking women, often poaching one or two for their own entertainment. Other times, they'd simply play chess, discussing business and their plans for the weekend. *Never again.*

Seventy-two years as best friends. Twenty-seven of those as Alpha and beta. The bitter taste of grief and rage boiled inside Jax. What had gone down in New Orleans should have been nothing more than picking a flea off a dog. They'd gotten sloppy. He'd gotten sloppy. Guilt for not watching Nick and underestimating the Anzober Alpha's strategy ate at him.

He downed another shot and slammed the glass onto the stainless steel table, reflecting on his current state of affairs. He'd always known Gillian had existed, but he'd purposely left her alone. He supposed his stepmother had good reasons for leaving the pack. Between the loss of her husband and the loss of her tiger, she'd gone to great lengths to put distance between herself and New York City. He could have easily located his sister with one call, yet seeing the devastation Mirabel had suffered when his father died, knowing she'd never shift, he couldn't bring himself to inflict that kind of pain onto his own sibling. A firm believer in fate, he was of the mindset that if it was meant to be, they'd find each other.

Jax thought it ironic that as the Goddess took one loved one from his life, she gave another, Gillian. Reminiscing about his father had been solacing, never having discussed his life and death with another person, let alone a family member. Even though he and Nick had been inseparable, the topic of his father had been off limits. The only thing to have been said about him was that Jax had loved him and that he was a great warrior. The detailed memories of his father teaching him to hunt, singing to him as a boy had been lost, buried deep, until his long talks with Gillian brought them to the surface. Having never known her father, she'd laughed and cried while listening to his childhood stories.

He'd wanted to stay with Gillian in New Orleans. However, his pack needed him to act as Alpha, to guide them through their loss. Their collective mourning resonated throughout every cell of his body. He had to settle his own mind for the sake of his wolves, as his torrent of grief was crushing them all. Coming back to New York City was unavoidable. The magazine wouldn't run itself; his conglomerate was in desperate need of attention. As chief operating officer, Nick had taken care of day-to-day operations, and Jax loathed having to take action to find his replacement. That task would be easy compared to selecting a new beta, something he could not even begin to comprehend doing.

Leaving Gillian had been paramount to ensure her happiness. Newly mated, she and Dimitri required time alone, without her needy big brother in the wings. It killed him to leave her just as they were starting to connect, but as Alpha, he never questioned the validity of his decision.

Jax sighed, glancing at the beautiful women who pranced like peacocks around the bar. On any given night, he and Nick may have easily indulged, either alone or sharing a female. While they may have played the game, always honest about their status as non-mated wolves, Jax had at one time suspected his mate existed.

Kat Livingston, sister to the Lyceum wolves Alpha, had crossed his path one icy Christmas evening. She'd arrived at his private event with a mutual friend. Immediately, he'd taken notice of the mysterious striking woman, hearing her intoxicating laugh across the room. Introducing himself, he'd taken her hand in greeting. For a long moment, they'd stood silent, their eyes locked as the electric current seared their palms. The scent of her drove his wolf to howl for the one he'd thought was his mate. With haste, she'd broken the connection. She gave him a small smile and explained that she had to leave to get back home for the holidays. Nick interrupted but for a moment and when he'd turned back to see if he could get her contact information, she'd already left.

She'd gone to Philadelphia, implying to her brothers that he'd attempted to force a mating. Nothing could have been further from the truth. While he may have called Kat and her brothers, he never once sent his wolves after her. Disgusted with her antics and lies, Jax let it be, eventually making peace with Tristan.

Jax Chandler didn't chase women. Quite the opposite, women chased him. Powerful and charismatic, the Alpha had no intentions of further pursuing the cagey female he'd met that snowy eve. He chalked up his wolf's interest in her to a rare miscommunication and never gave it another thought.

As he poured his third glass, however, he wondered if maybe he'd been wrong to give up so easily. He sighed, thinking he must be losing his mind. The strain of his depression from losing Nick weighed heavily on his heart as he contemplated stepping down as Alpha. He fantasized about going off into the wilderness of Canada, becoming a lone wolf. It would be a struggle to get out of bed every morning, let alone continue to act as if everything was business as usual. By the end of the week, he'd make his decision. Above all else, he'd do what was in the best interest of the pack, even if that meant disappearing into obscurity.

As he brought the rim of his glass to his lips, he heard a scream from below. Often the elicitor of this response both in and out of the bedroom, he was attuned to the difference between sounds caused by delight, ecstasy or pain. This one was induced by terror.

Even though it wasn't his responsibility to intervene, he set down his drink, honing in on the source of the ear-piercing sound. A crowd had gathered in the center of the floor. A woman, he presumed, had fallen to the ground, not necessarily unusual for a dance club. Her black-leather bondage heels were attached to long shapely legs.

His friend and owner of the club, Finn, peeled back the layer of spectators, allowing Jax to identify the owner of the gorgeous pins. *Kat?* Heart racing, he jumped to his feet, frantically tapping at the elevator door that led from his suite down to the main area. After what seemed like centuries, it slid open and he descended.

Jax raked his fingers through his hair, second guessing what he'd thought to be true. It made no sense that Kat would return to New York City. *Why would she come here again after telling her brothers that I was trying to force a mating? If she wanted to see me, why wouldn't she follow protocol, letting me know she'd arrived?*

The heavy metal doors slid open and he yelled over to Finn, attempting to catch his attention. His commanding presence registered with nearly every soul in attendance, the crowd parting as he stalked toward the injured female.

The music ceased and the house lights shone brightly, illuminating the floor as if it were daylight. An eerie sense of calm followed, soft chatter resounding throughout the club.

Jax pulled out his phone and tapped in 911. Taking sight of Finn holding the woman in his arms, he intervened.

"What happened to this female?" Jax asked, his booming voice reverberating over the hushed whispers of the patrons.

"I don't know. She's out cold. Must've slipped."

Jax knelt, carefully cradling her head.

"Get these people out of here," Jax ordered.

Finn quickly ushered people toward the door, emptying the area.

Jax studied the female's face, recalling the contours of Kat's profile. While the woman appeared familiar, her hair was blond. Her scent registered neither human nor wolf. Although she looked similar to the woman he'd met long ago, he wasn't a hundred percent certain she was who he'd thought she was. His concern lifted as she began to awaken, her eyes fluttering open.

"Kat, sweetheart. Are you okay?" he asked softly.

His caring tone of voice surprised him, but his expression remained impassive, as he was well aware that other pack members were watching. Her blue eyes caught his, a look of confusion on her face.

"Who's Kat?" she responded. Clutching at her belly, she moaned. "Help me."

"I've got you," Jax told her. Perplexed, he shook his head. It was unusual for his first instincts to be wrong.

Whether it was due to the death of Nick or finding Gillian, Jax Chandler didn't know, but he considered that for the first time in his long life, he'd been thrown off his game. Never one to second guess his decisions, he committed as the emergency workers arrived. As they strapped the beautiful stranger to the gurney, he rose to his feet. With a nod to Finn, he proceeded to follow them.

"I'm going with her," Jax declared.

"Sorry sir, only family." The paramedic, a human and unaware of his status, attempted to hold him back with an arm.

"She's my wife." As the lie slipped from his lips, he saw Finn's jaw drop. He glared at his friend in warning not to reveal his identity. Regardless of whether or not she was Kat, his wolf urged him to go with her.

"Jax," Finn called. "You need me to go with?"

"No, I've got this," Jax said, his voice wavering.

Even though his gut told him not to go alone, he couldn't bring himself to ask for help. While he was close to Finn, it felt wrong to have him go as if he was replacing Nick. No, it was Nick's place to travel with the Alpha, to be at his side.

He paused, catching Finn's concerned gaze and stepped into the ambulance, taking a seat next to the fragile-looking woman who lay motionless on the stretcher. The doors slammed shut, the emergency vehicle's sirens blaring into the night as it sped off toward the hospital. Jax was startled as her fingers reached for his. He glanced to their joined hands, hoping he'd done the right thing.

"Don't leave me," she whispered, her eyes closed.

"I'm not going anywhere," he promised.

"No, Jax. You aren't," she responded.

As the blade sliced into his thigh, he hissed in pain. Shock and confusion played across his face. The woman on the gurney flickered in his vision like a hologram. As the poison pumped through his heart, he succumbed, wishing he'd never come back to New York City.

The Immortals of New Orleans

Kade's Dark Embrace
(Immortals of New Orleans, Book 1)

Luca's Magic Embrace
(Immortals of New Orleans, Book 2)

Tristan's Lyceum Wolves
(Immortals of New Orleans, Book 3)

Logan's Acadian Wolves
(Immortals of New Orleans, Book 4)

Léopold's Wicked Embrace
(Immortals of New Orleans, Book 5)

Dimitri
(Immortals of New Orleans, Book 6)

Jax's Story
(Immortals of New Orleans, Book 7)
Coming Spring 2015

About the Author

Kym Grosso is the award winning and bestselling author of the erotic paranormal romance series, The Immortals of New Orleans. The series currently includes *Kade's Dark Embrace* (Immortals of New Orleans, Book 1), *Luca's Magic Embrace* (Immortals of New Orleans, Book 2), *Tristan's Lyceum Wolves* (Immortals of New Orleans, Book 3), *Logan's Acadian Wolves* (Immortals of New Orleans, Book 4), *Léopold's Wicked Embrace* (Immortals of New Orleans, Book 5) and *Dimitri* (Immortals of New Orleans, Book 6).

In addition to romance, Kym has written and published several articles about autism, and is passionate about autism advocacy. She also is a contributing essay author in *Chicken Soup for the Soul: Raising Kids on the Spectrum*.

Kym lives with her husband, two children, dog and cat. Her hobbies include autism advocacy, reading, tennis, zumba, traveling and spending time with her husband and children. New Orleans, with its rich culture, history and unique cuisine, is one of her favorite places to visit. Also, she loves traveling just about anywhere that has a beach or snow-covered mountains. On any given night, when not writing her own books, Kym can be found reading her Kindle, which is filled with hundreds of romances.

• • • •

Social Media/Links:

Website: http://www.KymGrosso.com
Facebook: http://www.facebook.com/KymGrossoBooks
Twitter: https://twitter.com/KymGrosso
Pinterest: http://www.pinterest.com/kymgrosso/

Printed in Great Britain
by Amazon